PRAISE FOR *SHATTER CREEK*

'An edge-of-your-seat, fast-paced thriller with a twisting, complex plot that makes it impossible to tell who the good guys are but keeps you rooting for gutsy female protagonist, Detective Sergeant Casey Wray. Rod Reynolds has created another cracker of a series!' Andrea Carter

'I loved *Black Reed Bay*, and *Shatter Creek* is equally terrific. Casey is as compelling a character as you'll find, and I am delighted she's back!' Trevor Wood

'A welcome return to Detective Casey Wray's small town. Complex, engrossing and atmospheric. An authentic and epic thriller that completely immerses you in its world' Nadine Matheson

'Reminiscent of Dennis Lehane and early Scott Turow ... I love this author's meaty plots' *Prima*

'Unpredictable and beautifully written' Michael Wood

'Bold, taut and gritty, this sophisticated novel puts its protagonist and the reader through the wringer at every twist! *Shatter Creek* is everything a thriller should be – a masterclass' Steph Broadribb

'Starts off at breakneck speed and doesn't let up. Full of intrigue, action, twists and turns, you're never quite sure which way Rod is going to pull you. There are two things I do know: Casey Wray is fast becoming one of my favourite protagonists, and after finishing the final page, I immediately wanted more. An easy five stars!' Chris McDonald

'The plotting is excellent, nice and twisty and completely unpredictable, just the way I like it' Liz Barnsley

'Brilliant sequel to *Black Reed Bay*, I raced through this pitch-perfect crime thriller.' Espresso Coco

PRAISE FOR THE DETECTIVE CASEY WRAY SERIES

'Urgent, thrilling and richly imagined. Without doubt his best yet' Chris Whitaker

'Reynolds captures the claustrophobic feel of a small town ... a tense slice of American noir' Vaseem Khan

'If you were hooked on *Mare of Easttown*, this will be right up your street ... I read this obsessively' *Prima*

'A thrillingly complex narrative' *The Times*

'Electrifying' *Crime Monthly*

'An awesome read. A turn of the screw in every chapter' Oscar de Muriel

'If you love Harlen Coben and Lee Child, you will love this ... cinematic, epic, you will forget to breathe' Miranda Dickinson

'Compelling and stylish, with devious twists and a cleverly crafted ending. Very, very impressive' G J Minnett

'A twisty, high-stakes, high-voltage murder mystery' Tim Baker

'In Casey Wray he has created a series character with an engaging mix of guts and vulnerability, ably supported by a strong supporting cast' Shots Magazine

SHATTER CREEK

ABOUT THE AUTHOR

Rod Reynolds is the author of six novels, including *Black Reed Bay* and the Charlie Yates series. His 2015 debut, *The Dark Inside*, was longlisted for the CWA New Blood Dagger, and was followed by *Black Night Falling* (2016) and *Cold Desert Sky* (2018); the *Guardian* has called the books 'pitch-perfect American noir'. Born and raised in London, in 2020 Orenda Books published *Blood Red City*, his first novel set in his hometown, which was longlisted for the CWA Ian Fleming Steel Dagger. Then in 2021, Rod returned to US-set stories with *Black Reed Bay*, the first book in the Casey Wray series – described by *The Times* as a 'superior cop saga' and 'thrillingly complex'. *Shatter Creek* (2025) is the second book in the series.

Rod previously worked in advertising as a media buyer and holds an MA in novel writing from City University. He lives near London with his wife and daughters. Follow him on X/Twitter @Rod_WR, facebook.com/RodWR and his website: www.rodreynolds.com.

Also by Rod Reynolds
and available from Orenda Books
Blood Red City

The Detective Casey Wray Series
Black Reed Bay

SHATTER CREEK

ROD REYNOLDS

**ORENDA
BOOKS**

Orenda Books
16 Carson Road
West Dulwich
London SE21 8HU
www.orendabooks.co.uk

First published in the United Kingdom by Orenda Books, 2025

A catalogue record for this book is available from the British Library.

ISBN 978-1-916788-09-1
eISBN 978-1-916788-10-7

Typeset in Garamond by www.typesetter.org.uk
Printed and bound by Clays Ltd, Elcograf S.p.A

For sales and distribution, please contact *info@orendabooks.co.uk* or visit *www.orendabooks.co.uk*.

For Margaret Winter
1944–2023

PROLOGUE

Casey stayed low to scoop up her sidearm as she ran across the driveway. Another gunshot rang out behind her, cracking off the tarmac somewhere to her left. Everything haywire, no sense of how much it'd missed her by.

She made it to the far side and threw herself behind the patrol car, landing hard. The impact sent another wave of pain through her ribs and she clutched her side. At first she couldn't move, lying face down behind the cruiser, her lip grazing the asphalt as she tried not to cry out, waiting for the pain to ebb enough that she could push herself up onto one elbow. She turned and propped one shoulder against the cruiser's door, and snatched a breath. Looking up, she saw a clear-blue sky she would've sworn was tinged with crimson.

The quiet was brutal. A gentle breeze swept in off Black Reed Bay, just enough to carry off the sound of his footfalls if he was creeping around the cruiser. She pulled her phone out and hit redial.

The ringing tone sparked instant regret – a reminder of the missed opportunities to see through the lies, the chances she'd had to prevent this. In her failure, a sense of complicity in the coverup – blindness to its existence no excuse. And now this; a last-ditch attempt to make things right, going down in flames before it'd even started.

She set the call on speaker and reared up a few inches to peep through the cruiser's windows, but there was no sign of him. The guesthouse was to the left, the woman's scream still echoing in Casey's ears.

Billy answered, and she cut him off in a hissed whisper. 'Ten-thirteen, officer down—'

CHAPTER ONE

One week earlier

Dispatch had the location of the shooting as Eighth Street and Villanova. Billy took the wheel so Casey could work the radio while they drove, a high-speed run along the expressway to the western edge of Rockport. Almost eight-thirty on a Thursday morning – rush-hour, but they were headed against the flow that had the other side of the roadway slowed to a crawl. The first 911 call had come in six minutes earlier, a report of shots fired, the caller unclear if the shooter was still active. Casualties unknown at the time, but uniforms had since arrived on the scene and found a body.

'What else do we know?' Billy said.

A lights-and-sirens callout was a rarity for the detective bureau, and Casey noted the composure in his voice with a twitch of pride. Hot-blooded Billy Drocker, the department's mustang of a rookie, starting to sound like a pro. 'One vic confirmed. Patrol are treating the scene as active. Indications there could be more than one shooter.'

'What's the firepower?'

'Unclear.'

The lack of information cast a long shadow, where the spectre of rolling up on a mass shooting always lingered. Rockport had been spared that nightmare so far, but with every tragic headline, the possibility seemed to creep closer.

'Tactical's on alert in Harrison,' Casey said, the implication clear to both of them. If a Tactical team were needed, the response time from headquarters in the east of Hampstead

County was a minimum of eighteen minutes. The standard-issue vests Casey had thrown in the trunk would offer some protection against a handgun, but a round from something bigger would punch through them like tissue paper.

Billy blew out a breath and focused on the road again.

Casey ran through details in her head. She didn't know the area around Eighth and Villanova well. It was a nondescript part of town, not far from where Coleman Carrington Park began, separating Rockport from neighbouring Newridge. Studying a map of the block on her cell, it showed a 7-Eleven, a gym and a handful of other businesses spread around. There were no schools in the immediate vicinity – a small mercy.

Billy took the exit off the expressway and kept pushing hard along Eighth. Even as her adrenaline surged, Casey felt as if she was slotting into a groove she'd been seeking for two months. She'd worked other cases since the brass gave her back her badge, but this already had a different feel. In a crisis, none of the other bullshit mattered; suddenly she had a sense of purpose again – the one gift the job bestowed in return for all it took away.

A voice came over the radio, Dispatch cutting into her thoughts. 'Reports of further shots fired. Two further 911 calls received from civilians.'

'Description on the shooter?' Casey said.

'Negative. No reports of visual contact at this time.'

'Jesus,' she said, under her breath. 'We're going in blind.'

'Air support is already airborne, should have eyes on the area in a minute or two.'

Even as the dispatcher said it, the sound of distant rotor blades reached them. Up ahead, an empty patrol car came into view, parked across the Villanova Road intersection, its lights flashing silently. To their left, two uniforms were covering in the doorway of a redbrick Starbucks, one of them peering around the corner to look west along Eighth, the other gesturing to the people sheltering inside the store to stay down. Through the window, a pair of scared faces peeped from behind a couch.

Billy made a left and pulled up alongside the uniforms as Casey radioed 10-84 to Dispatch to confirm their arrival at the scene. The notification of non-uniformed personnel in attendance came back across all their radios in concert, followed immediately by another update. 'Unit Two-Alpha-Four headed west on Eighth continuing pursuit. Still no visual contact reported.'

Casey didn't recognise either of the Patrol officers on the corner, so she held her badge up as she called out to them. 'I'm Casey Wray, this is Drocker. What've we got?'

The cop peering around the corner turned to face them, the other one saying something into his radio. 'One victim out front of the Strongbox gym, two units along.' He pointed in the direction he'd been looking. 'Caucasian male, forty to sixty, gunshot wounds to the head and torso. Unresponsive when we got here, no vitals. We were still assessing when we heard more shots.'

'You heard more shots yourself?'

'Yeah, to the west of our position, further along Eighth.' He gestured again, waving his arm to indicate somewhere past Strongbox. 'Three, maybe four rounds. Teller and Chau had gone on ahead looking for the shooter, we were attending to the vic.'

Casey jumped out of the car and inched towards the corner to look along Eighth. Past the Starbucks was a bar called Ellie's, then Strongbox gym, the victim on the sidewalk in front of it, lying on his back. His feet were pointed towards the street, maybe a hundred yards from where she stood. The sidewalks were empty in the area around him, but far off in the distance, maybe four or five blocks away, she could see vehicles and civilians moving around.

She called over to the car. 'Billy, check the location of those last shots-fired calls. We need to get those people off the street.' Then to the uniforms: 'You get a look at the shooter?'

They shook their heads at the same time.

'How long for the medics?' Casey said.

'Three minutes was the last update. Actually...' The uniform pointed behind her, an ambulance racing towards the intersection.

Casey waved both arms to flag down the driver and he pulled up sharply. 'The vic's over there,' she said, pointing down the street. 'Unresponsive and no vitals according to my guys, but the scene is still hot. Last shots heard were to the west of here.' She glanced back to the uniforms. 'How long since you heard them?'

One of them checked his watch. 'Four or five minutes.'

The EMT driver nodded *got it*, shifting in his seat to peer along the road ahead.

'What's your response protocol for active shooters?' Casey said.

'It's my call, depending on the threat assessment at the scene.' He checked along the street again, deciding what to do, then glanced at his partner next to him in the cab, already nodding. The driver turned back to Casey. 'We'll go, so long as you can cover us.'

Billy cut in. 'Big – Dispatch has the most recent call coming from a payphone a block north of here on Villanova.'

'North?' Casey said, looking around the intersection in all four directions. 'Shit. We've got no idea where this is coming from.' To the uniforms: 'Any indication how many shooters?'

'I don't...' The first uniform held his hands up, helpless. 'Sorry, ma'am, I don't know. I didn't see anyone.'

She looked at Billy again and pointed to the radio. 'Location and status on Two-Alpha-Four?'

Billy radioed in the question and waited for the response. 'They're two blocks north of Eighth, on LaSalle, continuing the search. No visual, no further shots reported. Three more units in the area now, all reporting the same. They don't even know if they're looking for a suspect in a vehicle, on foot or what.'

That put the patrol car northwest of where they stood now, which might or might not line up with the call to 911 reporting shots from due north of their position. Casey looked around one more time, the sense that they were just as vulnerable standing on that corner as anywhere else firming up inside her. She nodded to the EMTs. 'Let's go.'

The driver pulled away almost as she said it, and Casey took off running along the sidewalk towards where the man lay, Billy right behind her. The block was a collection of low-rise commercial units, separated from each other by parking lots and access roads, leaving Casey and Billy open to an ambush from any one of a dozen angles. It was a tactic they'd been briefed on earlier that year: death-wish shooters dropping a victim in plain sight so they could pick off the first responders who caught the call. She sprinted across the parking bays along the side of Starbucks and made it as far as Ellie's, pressing herself tight against the front wall of the property. The bar was closed, the inside dark, no movement that she could make out through the window.

The EMTs pulled up adjacent to the victim on the sidewalk and Casey sprinted the final few yards to where he'd hit the ground. Coming close, she could see a wound in his head leaking blood down the left side of his face. The wound in his torso wasn't as easy to make out, the entire front of his dress shirt soaked red. Casey stepped back to give the EMTs room to work, checking both ways along the street with her sidearm drawn, watching for any sign of the shooter returning. Billy was on the far side of the vic, doing the same.

Strongbox was washed in two shades of blue, one from ground level to head height and a darker shade from there to the roof. The front of the building was windowless, giving the place the appearance of a concrete block – maybe part of the gimmick – with the gym's name stencilled across the front in six-foot-tall white lettering. The entrance was a single glass door, also tinted dark blue, offering no visibility beyond.

The door twitched as Casey was looking. She aimed right at it. 'HCPD – come out slowly, hands showing.'

The door was cracked ajar and a pair of hands appeared, followed by a man poking his head through the gap. His eyes went to Casey's gun, then straight to the body on the sidewalk. 'Oh fuck...'

Casey called out to him. 'Sir, is anyone hurt or wounded inside?'

He shook his head, tight movements. 'I don't think so.'

'Is anybody in there carrying a weapon?'

He shook his head again. 'I don't know. No, I don't think so.'

'How many people do you have in there?'

'Ten, twelve maybe? What the hell is happening?'

'Did you get a look at who did this, sir?'

He shook his head again. 'First I knew about it was when Ginny came and got me.'

'Who's Ginny? Is she there with you?'

'Yeah, she's ... Hold on.'

The door closed over and Casey kept her weapon aimed at the entrance. She checked over her shoulder and saw Billy had his weapon aimed at the same spot. 'Stay ready back there, Bill.'

'Got it.'

After a few seconds, the door twitched again.

'Come out slowly, hands first.'

The same man appeared again, nudging the door wider to reveal a woman in pink-and-black workout gear standing next to him with her hands up. 'This is Ginny.'

'Virginia,' the woman said, staring at the EMTs crouched over the body. 'Oh my god.'

Casey lowered her weapon to her side and moved quickly across the sidewalk. 'Miss, did you see who shot this man?'

Her face went white and before she could answer, she doubled over, dry heaving at first and then letting loose a line of watery spittle. Casey shot Billy a look to say *cover me* then grabbed the woman's arm, the man from the gym doing the same on the other side, and they guided her to the ground to sit with her back against the doorway wall.

'It's gonna be okay. Keep your head between your knees, take deep breaths.' Casey turned to the man. 'Can you get her some water?'

The woman was trembling. Casey crouched in front of her and put a hand on her arm. 'Miss, I know how traumatic this is and I want to give you space to process it, but we don't know anything about this shooter right now, so anything you can tell me will be crucial.' She stole a glance behind her to check Billy was still covering her, alert to possible danger from the doorway, the street – everything.

'I didn't see anything,' the woman said, keeping her eyes turned to the ground. 'Just the guy and the blood. He was already like that when I went out.' She dabbed her mouth with the back of her hand. 'The woman told me – she came in screaming.'

'Ma'am? What woman?'

'The woman with the kid. She came in off the street, she was freaking out, so I went outside to see what was going on. I don't know why, I wasn't ... I wasn't thinking, I guess. He was already lying there, like he is now. Just like that.'

'Did you see anyone running, a vehicle taking off? Anything like that?'

'No, no, just him, like how he is now.' She jutted her chin to indicate the dead man, refusing to let her eyes stray from Casey, trying to block it all out. 'I couldn't ... I couldn't understand why he was lying in the middle of the sidewalk. It didn't seem real, like he was playing around, y'know? Taking a nap? Then I saw the blood and I guess I ran inside and got Brandon, I can't even remember. I didn't know he was dead. I thought he was just ... I thought he fell or something.' She glanced up at the man from the gym, now standing next to Casey.

'You mentioned a woman with a child? Is she still inside?'

'I don't know, I didn't ... I couldn't find Brandon at first, he was in the bathroom, and I don't think I saw her after that.'

'Did anyone else enter the building after you saw the victim?'

'I didn't see anyone,' Brandon said, 'but I don't know. When I was in the bathroom, they could've ... I guess anyone could've come in.'

Casey touched the woman's shoulder gently. 'Thank you, ma'am. Just take it easy a minute.'

She stood up and backed away, seeing another ambulance coming down the street, trailed by a patrol car. The two uniforms from the corner were approaching on foot, and Casey waved them over.

'One of you stay with her, make sure she's okay and get her details. Get some backup over here too as soon as you can – there were ten or twelve people inside the building right after the shooting. I need you guys to go talk to them and see if you can get any kind of ID on this shooter. If you see a woman with a kid in there, talk to her first – she might be the first person who saw our vic. If she—'

'CASEY!'

She pulled her sidearm as she heard Billy's shout, whipping around, looking for the threat. But Billy was standing a few paces past the dead man, staring at the sidewalk like he'd dropped something.

She started to go to him, but he raised his weapon and took a step forward, then another, then jogged to the far edge of the Strongbox building, where an access road led around back.

'Billy? What is it?'

He edged his way around the corner then stopped dead for a beat, staring at something out of Casey's line of sight. Then he holstered his weapon and dropped into a crouch. 'Get the EMTs.'

Casey ran towards him, passing the victim on the sidewalk, then seeing the blood trail she realised Billy had been following. Two small drops at first, then a gap to a larger one, then a near-continuous line. She came round the corner and saw a woman slumped against the wall in a seated position, chin to her chest, her stomach spilling into her lap.

CHAPTER TWO

Twenty-four hours earlier

Casey tapped her phone screen with one finger, entering the same five starting letters she used every day, one eye on the podium at the front of the room, which stood empty, awaiting the arrival of County Executive Franklin Gates.

'What's a rise?' Billy said from the seat next to her in the back row, making no secret that he was reading her screen. 'Isn't that two words?'

'Arise. As in *come in to existence* or *happen*. One word.'

'For real? Sounds like two words to me.'

She hit enter and waited as the five letters flipped, the A and the E turning orange to signal she had two letters correct, but in the wrong places. 'See – "arise". Wordle doesn't let you guess a two-word phrase.' Casey held the phone up to his face for him to see.

Billy seemed to think for a second. 'But how would it know? It's just a game. Maybe they screwed up. What if the guy coding it didn't know it was two words?'

'The guy who coded it made millions of dollars – he's smart enough.'

'Doesn't automatically mean he can spell right.'

'It's one word, same as, say, dipshit. Quit it.'

The woman in the seat in front glanced back over her shoulder at hearing the curse, and Billy nodded to her, trying to stifle a grin like a chastened schoolkid. 'Ma'am.' Then he turned to Casey again. 'I still say it's two words.'

'Yeah? Well, I got two words for you, pal. Get—'

'*A rise.* As in, "I, Detective Billy Drocker, am trying to get a rise out of you." And I'm succeeding.'

Casey tilted her head, trying to stop herself from breaking into a smile while she shot him a look of disgust. But she couldn't help herself. 'You're an idiot.'

Billy grinned. 'You can't talk to your partner that way.'

Partner caught her off guard. A harmless joke, Billy oblivious to the effect the word still had on her.

Dave Cullen was two months in the ground, her former partner's death like a rock caught in her chest – painful, unmoving, without resolution. Grief that she couldn't rid herself of, no matter how hard she tried. Grief he didn't deserve; the revelations in the wake of his death, his lies, should've absolved her of any sense of loss, and yet here she was, the pain almost as raw as the day he'd been gunned down.

Thinking of his wife, his kids. The true victims. Three times she'd called Luisa, Dave's widow, in recent weeks, wanting to check in on her, but the calls had gone unanswered and unreturned. Casey knew – hoped – it wasn't personal. The blame Luisa attached to HCPD in the wake of his death made Casey a painful reminder of everything she'd wanted him to walk away from, and if cutting Casey out of her life made that easier, she'd respect that, no matter how much it hurt.

As far as Casey was concerned, Luisa never needed to know it was Lieutenant Ray Carletti who'd arranged Dave's murder. She wished she could live in that same ignorance.

Despite herself, she still thought of Ray on a daily basis. Their boss, friend and mentor; the man who'd destroyed them all, who'd tried to have her killed. The man who she'd never acknowledge a part of her still loved like a father.

A message made her phone buzz, and she realised it was still pointed for Billy to read.

His face changed instantly. 'I'm gonna go ahead and pretend

I didn't see that,' he said, before she had a chance to turn it away from him. She turned it round and saw a text that said: *Ready to quit yet?*

Casey swiped the message away, eyes still on the screen as she spoke to Billy. 'Good. Because I'd hate to have to take your tongue out with garden shears.'

'Uh-huh. Straight to violence – very cool.' He leaned closer. 'Look, seriously, though, if you ever wanna talk about anything – the job ... I mean, I know I'm the rookie and all that—'

'Forever and in perpetuity.'

'I'm trying to be serious, Big.'

'Say it with me. I. Am. The. Rookie. Forever...'

Billy sighed. 'Yes, I am the rookie, forever and in perpetuity...' He rolled his eyes. 'But if you ever *did* need someone to talk to, I promise, I'm a pretty good listener.'

She laid a hand on his arm, about to dismiss the offer with a crack about it sounding like one of his pickup lines – but the way he was looking at her, clumsy but earnest, killed the notion. The vibe would be all wrong, like yelling at a puppy who'd peed on the rug only because it couldn't make it outside in time. 'Sure thing. Thanks.'

She unlocked her cell, still unsure how to reply to the message. The third of its kind in a week, she'd held her silence so far – but that'd only served to increase the pressure in her head, the right response proving elusive.

Her phone's browser opened up on the *News 7* page, the press briefing the top story. A red Breaking News tag next to a chyron that read: *County Executive to outline next phase of police shakeup.* She clicked on the live video feed and straight away picked out the back of her own head in the back row. Instinctively, she turned it to one side and then the other, as if she was looking in a hairdresser's mirror, the movement feeding through to the screen in her hand a few seconds later. Her hair looked no better from behind than from her regular view, barely contained in a loose ponytail, and she swore again that she'd make an appointment at Marcy's for a cut and dye job her next day off. At least she couldn't make out all the grey hairs at that distance.

The briefing room – an over-cooled conference room on the second floor of the headquarters building – looked bigger on the screen than in person, the cameras at the back somehow stretching the room while at the same time making it appear more crowded. An array of suits lined the rear of the podium, all of them from the county executive's office, but only one she knew by name: Rita Zangetty, chief of staff to the man himself. Zangetty's mouth was barely visible, her lips were pressed so tight, and Casey saw her check her watch twice then signal to someone out of sight to the right of the stage. The body language was easy to read: her boss was already five minutes late to speak, and Rita was pissed about it.

Rumours of what might be coming had been flying for twenty-four hours since the announcement of the briefing. The investigations – state, federal – into criminal activities within the Hampstead County Police Department had so far led to the dismissal of four officers, all of whom were expected to face criminal charges, and there was talk of more coming down the pipe. Now the chatter in cop Facebook and WhatsApp groups held that today was the day they brought the hammer down.

Casey was the silent voice of doubt on that score. One of the few people still alive who knew more about the truth than the investigators, she also knew there was so much more to come out. The shape of the story as it'd been reported was that

Lieutenant Ray Carletti was the mastermind behind a small group of rogue cops who'd run shakedowns on dealers, sold stolen drugs, and run a string of girls on the side. Words like 'limited' and 'contained' kept coming up in the reporting. The name of former chief Brian Hanrahan, the real kingpin, had been kept out of it, as had the full extent of his crimes. That was despite Ray leaving a detailed posthumous confession attesting to the scope of Hanrahan's corruption.

A lifetime cop who'd played on his Irish roots to cultivate the image of a regular-Joe-made-good, Brian Hanrahan had used the department to build his own criminal empire. Prostitution, drugs, loansharking – anything that happened on the street, Hanrahan had a piece of it. Run by a network of dirty cops that included Ray Carletti, Casey had stumbled across the darkness at the heart of HCPD while investigating the disappearance of a young woman, Tina Grace, from one of the barrier islands across Black Reed Bay. The search had led to the discovery of a group of bodies in a desolate oceanfront marsh and, eventually, to Hanrahan and the revelation that he'd ordered the murders to silence the women he'd abused in the early days of building his outfit. Turned out Tina Grace was the 'lucky' one who slipped the net.

The media had avoided reporting that Hanrahan's death was by his own hand due to sensitivity protocols around suicides, so any public perception that had formed had coalesced around the idea that the shock of the HCPD revelations had brought on a heart attack. A handful of reporters and their editors knew better, but with none of them willing to risk their access by rocking the boat, that line held.

Some days Casey wondered whether that narrative had been purposely shaped. Whether it was a deliberate attempt by forces within HCPD to protect Hanrahan's reputation and, by extension, that of the department. With Hanrahan and Carletti both dead, and having been cleared of involvement herself, there was a temptation for Casey to put it all behind her and try to move on with her life. But anytime she got to thinking that way, she found herself back in that car with Tina Grace, the lone survivor, hearing her detail Hanrahan's inhumanity; the women he'd killed just to protect himself, Tina's years of living in terror at the fear of being recognised and targeted. And then Casey got mad all over again.

'Detective Wray?'

Someone tapped her on the shoulder. She swivelled in her seat to find a woman trying to get her attention – the chief's executive assistant, leaning awkwardly over the back row of chairs. Casey stood up to face her. 'Sorry, I was in my own world.'

'We need to bump you up in the diary,' the woman said. 'The acting chief wants to see you as soon as this is done.' She twirled the pen she was gripping in her fist, indicating she meant the briefing.

'Okay, sure. Is that a good thing or a bad thing?' Casey said.

But she was already moving off, eyes scouring the room for whoever was next on her list to find. 'Neither, it's just a thing.'

Casey sat down again to find Billy grinning at her. 'Oh, wow, Big, the boss wants to see you *urgently*. I guess today really is the day.'

She tugged gently at her bottom lip. Acting Chief Stephen Keirn had run the Admin Division under Hanrahan. Casey could recall a time when he'd carried the nickname Kleenex Steve, back when he was a lieutenant, on account of the stereotype of Admin officers having a role limited to wiping the noses of 'real cops'. It was a notion the brass had worked hard to stamp out, an unfair reflection of the work the different departments within the division carried out, and that push, combined with Keirn's rise through the ranks, had seen the moniker all but disappear. But she'd never met a cop who didn't think it'd suited him at the time.

Elevated to the top job by the county executive after Hanrahan's death, Keirn's appointment as acting chief was a strategic move by Gates designed to give himself options down the road. As a cop who hadn't gotten his hands dirty in years, Gates could sell Keirn to the media and the public as a clean officer, put in place to run the department while the investigations played out – but one still tainted enough by association with the old guard that any new revelations that might emerge could be hung around his neck, *if* the need should arise.

Keirn's assistant had contacted Casey the day before, summoning her to meet with him, no agenda offered. All she'd been told was to attend the briefing first, then hang around headquarters for an hour until the appointed meeting time – but the plan, apparently, had changed.

'What do I call you when they make you lieutenant?' Billy went on. 'Is it, like, Lieutenant Big, or Lieutenant Wray?' He rubbed his chin as if he was pondering the options. 'How about Big Lieutenant?'

'You can just call me Casey. After I fire your ass.'

Billy turned away smiling, the point scored. Back at the office, the expectation seemed to be that the promotion was a done deal, and the team had been ribbing her about it for days. Dana Torres had deadpanned her while explaining that she'd follow Casey's orders but never salute her. Billy had been calling her 'Loot' on the ride over to Harrison that morning. Even Jill Hart, the youngest member of the team and too timid to join in the teasing, had been quietly asking around if it would mean a new detective sergeant coming into the department to take over Casey's spot.

Casey tried not to dwell on it. She'd put her application in on a rare day when the righteous anger overcame the internal voice of doubt telling her she wasn't up to it. Surprised to find she'd made the shortlist, she'd been called to two rounds of interviews, one with Captain Sharma and two lieutenants from Harrison, and the second with Keirn himself, not even noticing that both panels were all male until Dana pointed out how ridiculous that was 'two fucking decades into the twenty-first century'.

Afterward, Casey had heard, unofficially, that she'd impressed. But anytime she allowed her mind to tiptoe towards the prospect of stepping into Ray Carletti's shoes, the excitement she felt became indistinguishable from terror. So she shut it down and pretended it wasn't happening.

A murmur rippled through the crowd, quickly overtaken by a hush as County Executive Franklin Gates crossed the stage and took the podium. Acting Chief Keirn was two paces behind him, taking up a position behind his boss and to the right – exactly the kind of deferential show of support he'd been brought in to deliver.

Tall and lean in a navy suit and red tie, Gates had managed to keep hold of the physique of the college swim team standout he'd reputedly been thirty years earlier. It was in contrast to Keirn, a head shorter and looking stiff in his dress blues.

Gates bent the microphone towards himself as he started to speak. 'Thank you for being here today as I set out the next stage of my office's response to the issues within the Hampstead County Police Department.'

Someone in the crowd muttered, 'Issues,' and scoffed, chuckles rippling outward.

'Today I can announce that the Hampstead County District Attorney will be bringing charges against the four officers dismissed from HCPD last month, and will have the full support of the county in seeking the maximum sentences applicable under the relevant guidelines.'

The last part made Casey raise her eyebrows. It was tougher language than he'd used before. She glanced at Keirn's face, but of course he'd been briefed beforehand, so he showed no reaction.

'Furthermore,' Gates continued, 'I can announce that an additional three officers have, this morning, been dismissed from duty, as a direct result of the ongoing investigations into misconduct within HCPD. The district attorney will now be pursuing charges against those individuals as well, and will again be seeking the most severe punishments permissible.

'I have come before you today to tell you that there is no room in our police department for corruption. We place our trust in the HCPD to protect and serve our communities, particularly the most vulnerable amongst us, and when that trust is abused, it is a betrayal of those fundamental values for which we expect our officers to stand – and a betrayal of every single one of the very many honest, diligent and dedicated men and women who work day in, day out, to serve our citizens.

'Therefore, beginning immediately, I have instructed Acting Chief Keirn, in concert with my office's special advisory taskforce, to begin a root-and-branch review of HCPD. Every aspect of the department will be examined, including culture, values and working practices, and where misconduct is uncovered, a zero-tolerance approach will be taken. I expect this to lead to a significant change to both the structure and operation of HCPD, and accordingly, I have asked for initial recommendations for reform to be on my desk no later than eight weeks from today.'

Billy looked at Casey with bug eyes. 'Holy shit.'

'I want to reiterate that this process is as much about creating a police department fit for the brave and hardworking men and women who make up the vast majority of our serving officers as it is about ensuring that our citizens can have complete trust in their public servants.' He looked across at Keirn, and the two men exchanged nods. 'I'll go ahead and take a couple questions.'

Hands shot up as fast as the noise level, the reporters in the front rows talking amongst themselves even as they jostled to be asked.

'Sir, what does the police union have to say about your plan?'

Gates gripped the lectern in a power stance, feet spread. 'The union wants the same thing we all do – a police department of which its members can be proud, and which empowers them to do the job they signed up for, which is to protect and serve our communities.' He pointed to another reporter.

'Sir, will the outcome of this review factor in to who's appointed as chief of police on a permanent basis?'

Keirn glanced at Gates – no more than a flick of the eyes, but Casey caught it.

Gates adjusted his hands on the lectern. 'Acting Chief Keirn retains my full confidence at this time. Next question.'

'Sir...'

Casey tuned it out, getting to her feet, Billy following suit when he realised she was about to make a break for the exit.

He caught up to her in the hallway outside. 'Hey, Big, what's he saying? Are we all getting fired?'

'No, we're not.' She stopped and turned around so they were face to face. 'I mean, probably you, but not the rest of us.' She jabbed him in the arm when he didn't react to the joke. 'I'm kidding. Listen, it's a political thing – they've got to be seen to be doing something, right?'

'Then why do you look so spooked?'

She tried to sound casual. 'Who's spooked?'

'Level with me? Please?'

She glanced at her feet, felt her phone buzzing like crazy with messages as the news got out. 'It's not the way I expected them to go, that's all. But it's just politics. They'll change things up like they always do, find a couple scapegoats to weed out, and move on.'

'Zero tolerance though? If they come after every cop who ever bent the rules, that's half the department.'

'Four-fifths would be my guess.'

'C'mon, I'm being serious.'

'Billy, you'll be fine.' She clapped him on the shoulder. 'You haven't been around long enough to screw up that badly.'

But his eyes had travelled to someone coming down the hall behind her, and she turned to see Rita Zangetty approaching.

'What's up, Rita?' Casey said. 'Your boss looked good up there just now.'

'Not hard when he's got your boss standing next to him. Keirn looked like he just had his toenails pulled out.'

Casey smiled. 'Is that how you guys convinced him to agree to tearing up his own shop and making every cop hate him in the process?'

'You all hate him already,' Zangetty said, pulling a face of mock innocence. 'Anyway, the acting chief knows how this game works. Franklin's going to make one of those words disappear from his title pretty soon, and he knows which one he'd prefer it to be.'

'Damn, we're all out of pretence today, huh?'

Zangetty shrugged. 'We don't have a lot of choice.' She glanced behind herself, checking who was in earshot, then pressed in closer. 'Keirn's got to provide cover one way or another – Franklin's taking friendly fire.'

Casey wrinkled her face. 'What do you mean?'

'Mark Harden's gearing up to run against him in the primary. The party's furious about it, but there was no deal to be made to get him to stand aside. Believe me, we tried.'

Casey looked to the side, nodding. She'd heard Harden's name mentioned on the news – one of the new generation of ambitious pols looking to build a profile. 'Blue on blue. Okay, now I get it – so Gates is trying to thread the needle between appearing tough on HCPD without sounding like he's part of the "defund the police" crowd. I should've realised that was an election speech back there.'

'You're always fighting the next election...' Zangetty said. 'Anyway, I believe you're on your way to see Keirn now, is that right?'

Casey nodded, realising, belatedly, that this wasn't a chance meeting in the hallway. 'Why do I feel like I've just swallowed a tasty worm and got a hook through my lip?'

'You make me sound so calculating. I love it.' Zangetty smiled and lowered her voice. 'Is there worse to come, Casey?'

'Worse?' Casey rubbed her throat. 'Why don't you tell me.'

'What does that mean?'

'Lotta names didn't make the nine o'clock news – somebody, somewhere is deciding who gets exposed and who doesn't.'

'You think we have that kind of sway with the FBI running the investigation?' Zangetty rolled her eyes. 'Pffft. They're keeping some parts close. That's as much as I can glean.'

'Why?'

'You think they'd tell us anything?' Zangetty scoffed. 'We wouldn't be having this conversation if I knew what the Feds were thinking.'

Casey started to see the outline of Zangetty's problem. 'It was your boy Gates who made Brian Hanrahan chief, so it doesn't hurt you guys if his name is kept out of it, huh?'

Zangetty stonewalled. 'I'm not pushing an agenda here...'

'That'd be a first.' Casey winked as she said it, but immediately worried she'd gone too far – until Zangetty laughed. Rita Z was a realist, and that was one of the reasons why Casey found her easier to tolerate than most other pols. Plenty of them had Zangetty's drive and ambition, but not many had her ability to laugh at themselves for it.

'You didn't let me finish,' Zangetty said. 'All we want to know is what's coming – forewarned is forearmed. You were on the inside, so...'

The kind of thing Casey had heard over and over. Somewhere between an appeal and an accusation.

Zangetty must've caught Casey's expression souring because she started to walk it back immediately. 'Bad choice of words,' she said. 'You were the one who exposed them, is what I meant. I just want to know if there's worse to come. Completely off the record, of course.' A glance in Billy's direction. 'We can talk some other time if you'd prefer.' She flashed him a manufactured smile, as if to say, *Nothing personal*.

Casey suddenly felt exhausted to her bones. The weight of it all was crushing, and every time she felt as if it was lifting, even a little, it pressed down again with greater force. 'There can't be any worse than what was going on – and Hanrahan was up to his neck in it. I told the Feds everything I know, and my guess would be they know a whole lot more besides. How much of it comes out...' Casey held her hands up.

Zangetty met her gaze a moment, then nodded with a rueful smile. 'I guess we're all stuck on this damn train for as long as it takes.'

'The victims deserve better.'

'I know. They always do.' Zangetty looked down, solemn, but Casey caught her steal a glance at her watch. 'Anyway, I better not keep you. Keirn will be waiting.' She looked up, all business again, eyes switching to Billy. 'And who's this?'

'No idea. He just follows me around all day.' Casey held her hand out, presenting him. 'Detective Billy Drocker, this is Rita Zangetty, chief of staff to County Executive Franklin Gates.'

'A pleasure, ma'am.'

Zangetty smiled. 'Nice to meet you, Detective. Look after this one.' She gestured to Casey. 'She's the best we've got.' She said it with a smile and wink as she moved off, leaving it open to interpretation if it was meant as a compliment – or simply a dig at how low the bar was set in HCPD.

Casey checked her cell. The message at the top of the screen stood out:

Now is it time to quit?

She put it away and looked at Billy, who was still watching Zangetty walk off down the hall. 'Will you get your jaw off the floor?'

Billy rubbed the back of his neck. 'You think you could get me her number, Big?'

They took the elevator up to the chief's office, Casey scanning through her messages again as it climbed. At least a dozen were some variation on *Holy shit, have you seen this?* and the cop message groups were already buzzing with speculation about what would happen next. The consensus was summed up in a post from one of her old Patrol sergeants: *We're fucked.*

As she skim-read, her cell lit up with an incoming call. She answered and brought it to her ear. 'This is Casey.'

'Yes, hello … Are you – is this Detective Wray?'

She didn't recognise the voice. 'Yeah. Who's this?'

'I'm … Actually I'd prefer not to say right now. I wanted to talk to you, uh, soon if possible. It's quite important. Really important.'

It felt like he was readying to pitch her life insurance. 'Uh-huh. About what?'

'It's not really a conversation to have on the phone.'

'No? Where should we have it?'

'Well, that's the reason for the call. I wanted to arrange to meet.'

The elevator binged on reaching the seventh floor and the doors slid open.

'Look, I'm kinda busy right now so why don't you come down to the department sometime and you can tell me what's on your mind. I work out of the—'

'I know where you work, Detective, that's a non-starter.'

'Excuse me?'

'It concerns Ray Carletti. And some other acquaintances we share.'

Casey stood perfectly still in the middle of the elevator,

white noise in her ears. Billy had already stepped out and was looking back at her from the corridor. He put his arm across the doors to stop them from closing prematurely, his face a question mark.

'Who is this?' Casey said. She swallowed, trying to compose herself again. She squared her shoulders and walked out of the elevator.

'I have information you might find interesting, and, well, to be honest, I want to put it to work.'

The skin on her arms prickling now. 'Then come down to the department this afternoon and we can—'

'Not there. I already said.'

'Why not?'

'Safety.'

'Safety? What does that mean? Are you in danger?'

He scoffed, a small exhale – no humour in it. 'We all are.'

Casey stopped again, Billy turning back to her, a look of concern now.

The man spoke again. 'Look, let's talk. Tomorrow at ten am, there's a bench by the East Gate at Coleman Carrington Park. I'll find you.' He was gone before Casey could say anything more.

She held her cell over her bag, hesitating before she dropped it inside as she tried to process what she'd just heard. Finally, she let go and zipped the bag shut.

'Big? You okay?' Billy said.

The worst timing ever – her certainty that there was no way she'd go to meet this crank already beginning to falter. She looked along the corridor; the chief's PA was standing in the wide doorway, expecting them. Casey adjusted her jacket, buying herself another second or two, then carried on.

'You can go right on in,' the assistant said as they reached the office. 'He's expecting you.' She rounded her desk, pointing out a leather couch across the room to Billy. 'You can have a seat here, Detective.'

Casey knocked once and opened the door to the main office, her thoughts running faster than her pulse. She tried to regain focus by drilling down on the questions that mattered.

If he made her lieutenant, could she do the job? Could she do *that* job? It wasn't like she had a real choice. If she said no, it signalled a lack of ambition that would end her career. But if she took it on, what was she inheriting? Three good but inexperienced detectives, two vacancies that might not be filled because of budget cuts, and a unit carrying a stain so deep, the brass might resolve to break it up anyway.

They were side issues, all of them, and she knew it. Bottom line: she was scared of standing in *his* shoes. Of whose baton she was accepting, of what the lieutenant's job had made Ray Carletti and what it might make her in turn.

All of it passed through her head in the second it took the acting chief to rise from his seat. There were two chairs facing his desk, one of them occupied by a woman Casey had never seen before. She had shoulder-length auburn hair and watery blue eyes that leant her face a softness the rest of her features couldn't carry off. Her expression was serious, heavy with intent, and Casey's first thought was Internal Affairs. Again.

But she was way off.

'Detective Sergeant Wray, thank you for coming,' Keirn said, accepting her salute. 'I want you to meet Helen Dunmore, your new lieutenant.'

CHAPTER THREE

Twenty-four hours later – Eighth & Villanova

The EMTs tried to stabilise the woman on the spot, but she was losing blood too fast. Within ninety seconds, the call was made to move her to the ambulance for transport to the emergency room at St Mark's.

The risks attached to moving the woman were huge, which told Casey all she needed to know about her chances.

She could see Billy further up the street, moving from person to person. There was a vacant property on the lot next to Strongbox and beyond that a sign for a 7-Eleven. Two more patrol cars had arrived, parking in the street by where the dead man had fallen, and the presence of HCPD was enough to bring some civilians out from wherever they'd been sheltering. A drip became a steady flow, and the block filled with dazed faces, becoming even more chaotic than it already was. Billy was trying his best to catch people as they emerged, assessing potential witnesses, but there were men and women crying, strangers hugging each other in shock, a mom gripping two children to her chest. One man fell to his knees on the sidewalk and began to pray.

Clusters formed around the uniformed officers, some witnesses eager to talk to the police. Casey could see the cop who she'd first spoken to on the corner surrounded by three men and two women, all talking at once as he tried to make notes. From an investigatory standpoint it was a disaster, but Casey's biggest worry was if the shooter came back – or if they were already moving through the crowd. In the confusion, they were all sitting ducks. She radioed Dispatch for an update.

'Every available car is either there already or on the way. Still no description of a suspect. We have Patrol criss-crossing the area around and to the north of your location, where the last shots were reported, but right now we're looking for suspicious vehicles or behaviour, nothing more concrete than that.'

'When was the last report of shots fired?'

'911 took a call from a payphone on Villanova, north of Eighth.'

'Yeah, I heard about that one. Nothing since?'

'Negative.'

'Copy.'

Casey radioed instructions for assembly points to be set up, one at either end of the block, and for uniforms to ID and question as many of the people there as they could. But no matter how efficiently they worked, there would inevitably be some who slipped through the net, often unaware they might possess vital information. The hope was always for a witness who'd seen the whole thing and could give them a description, a licence plate or even a suspect name – but that was almost never how it played out. Assembling a picture of a scene like this was like piecing together a jigsaw, and it only took one witness not to realise the significance of the small detail they'd seen to leave Casey with a gaping hole.

She jogged further along the street, double-checking for victims the uniforms ahead of her might have missed and looking for any clue to the shooter's direction of travel. But by the time she was a hundred yards west of Strongbox, it was the civilians who were asking the cops what had happened, the shouts of 'active shooter' having been enough to send folks running for safety without knowing what was going down.

She doubled back on herself. To her left, a man was on one knee next to an older woman who was sitting on the street. Seeing Casey's badge, he called out to her. 'Detective!' he held up his hand. 'Detective, here...'

Casey angled over to them. 'Sir, ma'am, are you okay?' She crouched down in front of the woman, who was pale and looked to be in shock.

'I'm just lightheaded. I'm fine, I'm fine.' She waved Casey away. 'It all just hit me at once and I got dizzy.'

The man was holding a water bottle in reach for her to sip from. 'Just keep taking deep breaths. We'll get someone to take a look at you.' He glanced over at Casey. 'Chris Calder. I'm off-duty out of the Fourth. Can we get an EMT over here? She collapsed right by me. I think she might've hit her head.'

Casey glanced down the street. 'We've got two vics they're working on right now, but there's backup on the way.' She turned to the woman. 'Ma'am, do you know what day it is?'

'It's Thursday. I told you, I'm fine.'

'Can you tell me the name of the president?'

'I'll tell you his name's Biden, but he's not my president.'

Casey touched her lightly on the arm. 'I think you're going to be okay, ma'am. We'll get someone to take a look at you just as soon as we can.' She turned to Calder. 'Did you see the shooter?'

He was already shaking his head. 'I had my AirPods in. First I knew something was up was when I saw people running every which way. I ducked behind the dumpsters by the 7-Eleven over there, I was trying to creep towards the street to look, but then I heard more shots and I backed off. Sorry.'

'Hey, it's okay. Are you hurt?'

He shook his head again. 'There was a pickup. It was going

some. I only saw it as I was turning around, dark red kinda colour. I just caught a glimpse. Didn't get a look at the plate.'

'Make and model?'

'Like I said, it was just a glimpse. Sorry.'

'No problem. You did good.' Casey radioed in the description of the vehicle to Dispatch, then stood up. 'I've got to get back to the scene. You have a pen and paper?'

He looked down at himself, jogging pants and a T-shirt, as if in apology. 'I was just out for a run...'

Casey handed him a pen and tore a handful of pages from her notebook. 'Here, write down everything you can remember for me. Stick around. I want to get a full witness statement, okay?'

He took the pen and nodded. 'Sure, no problem.'

Casey took off, heading east again, after a few paces spotting the first man she'd spoken to coming out of the gym, now standing in front of the 7-Eleven. He was wearing Strongbox-branded workout gear and glancing around wide-eyed.

Casey weaved around a cluster of people all talking over one another to get to him. 'Sir, have any of the officers had a chance to speak with you yet?'

He shook his head. 'Is it over? Did you get the guy?'

Casey reached for her notebook again. 'We're still searching for a suspect. Can I take your name, sir?'

'Brandon.'

'Last name?'

'Sarciniak.' He spelled it out, the pronunciation different to how it was written.

'You work at Strongbox?'

'Yeah, I'm the shift supervisor. I just got on at eight.'

'And you didn't see the shooting outside?'

'No, it's what I told you before – first I knew about it was when Ginny came running to get me.' He looked left and right along the street, as if trying to spot the woman he'd been with before, but she wasn't anywhere in sight, leaving Casey hoping she was being looked after somewhere. She made a mental note to go check on her when she had a second.

'Did you go out to the victim on the sidewalk at that point?'

'No, I was afraid of getting shot. Ginny went out, and I told her not to, but she was, like, in a trance. I saw him lying there from the doorway while I was calling after her, but I was just trying to figure out what the hell to do, so I went right to the desk to call 911. There was this woman with her kid, the one that came in, and she was screaming that, like, someone was shooting up the street. Ginny was back inside by this point, and I couldn't see anyone else out there, so I locked the door and tried to get everyone to go into the office.'

That part caught Casey's ear. Ginny – Virginia – had told her the woman coming in off the street had first alerted her to the shooting, and that she was gone by the time she'd fetched Brandon. 'Did you know the woman?'

'Never seen her before.'

'Did you get a name?'

'No, we were all just ... It was crazy in there. I wasn't thinking about her name or whatever.'

'Do you know where she is now?'

He looked around again, one direction then the other. 'I don't see her out here.'

'Where was she last time you did see her?'

'I don't ... I'm not sure. I told you she had a kid with her, right?'

Casey nodded. 'How about the victim on the sidewalk – did you recognise him?'

Sarciniak shook his head. 'I didn't want to look for too long, but I don't think so.'

The victim was wearing a business suit with a dress shirt and shoes. There was no workout bag in proximity to where they'd found him, but that didn't rule out the possibility he'd been on his way to or from the gym. 'Would you know all of your patrons by sight?'

'No, no way. I work eight to five. People come in different times of day. I know a lot of the regulars, but not all of them.'

'Okay.' Casey shifted her weight onto her other foot. 'Sir, there was a second victim found to the side of the gym. Were you aware of that?'

The change in his expression gave her the answer before he could say a word. 'Shit, what?' He looked back towards Strongbox. 'How many...?'

'We're only aware of two so far, but this is an ongoing incident.'

'So there could be more? This is like ... I mean, Jesus, you see these things on the news, shootings, but...' Sarciniak's eyes widened. 'Did the guy go inside anywhere? Like, could he have come inside the building?' He swallowed, bringing a trembling hand to his throat, realising just how close his brush with death really was.

'We don't know exactly what's gone on here today, but you did the right thing, getting inside and locking the door.' Casey was nodding as she spoke, trying to reassure. 'Do you have security cameras on the premises?'

'Yeah, but they only cover the inside. Nothing on the street.'

'Sure. We'll need to take a look at them anyway.'

'Uh, yeah, that's okay, I guess. I should probably check with my boss. In case there's, like, a privacy thing or something?'

'That won't be an issue,' Casey said, starting to move off.

'Okay, walk with me, please. I need your help to find the woman with the child.'

'Why? Is she in trouble?'

'We just need to know what she saw. You didn't hear any of the shots yourself?'

He took a slug from his water. 'The music. It's loud inside, you can't hear anything from the street.'

Approaching the gym, the sidewalk around the male victim was being taped off, the body still in place but his top half covered with a foil blanket. Sarciniak glanced at it and looked away as they passed, closing his eyes for a second.

Once inside the gym's reception area, Casey found the two uniforms she'd detailed there speaking to witnesses. Two men were standing and answering questions from the officers, another five civilians sitting on a long couch across from the desk, Virginia one of them, and Casey felt a small sense of relief at seeing she looked okay. There were two other women, but neither of them had a child with them.

Casey came up alongside the uniforms. 'Guys, have you seen a woman with a young kid anywhere in here?'

The two officers shared a look. 'This is everyone was here when we got here. We missing someone?'

Casey turned to Sarciniak. 'You said you barricaded folks in the office?'

'Yeah, it's over here.' He led her behind the counter and into a small office with two desks, one against either wall. The room was trashed, papers and bottled waters scattered across the carpet, the smell of sweat from a dozen scared people in the air, but otherwise empty.

'Is there another way out apart from the main entrance?' Casey said.

Sarciniak nodded. 'There's two fire exits lead out back. Want me to show you?'

'It's fine, in a minute.' Casey went back out to the reception area and held her hands up. 'Ladies and gentlemen, did anyone see a woman with a child leave the building?'

There was silence, the small group exchanging looks with each other before a young man raised his hand. 'She was here. I didn't see her go, though. She was right there, pretty much where you're standing. Only just remembered her when you said that.'

Some of the others nodded in agreement.

'How old was the kid?' Casey said.

'Like, two years old?' the man said.

'A year maybe,' Sarciniak said, at the same time.

'No way,' another woman said. 'She wasn't even a year yet.'

'She?' Casey said. 'So the child was definitely a girl?'

All three agreed. 'She had on one of them headbands with a pink bow on it,' the same woman said. 'The kid was screaming and crying, and the woman was holding on to her for dear life.' She mimed pressing a child to her chest, covering its head with her arm, to illustrate what she meant.

Casey thanked the group and stepped outside to look for Billy, but he was nowhere to be seen. She called his cell, and he picked up straight away.

'Big?'

'Where you at?'

'Inside the 7-Eleven. We got a couple people here were too scared to come out.'

'They see anything?'

'Doesn't sound like it. Hiding at the back of the store, as far from the windows as they could get.'

'Okay. Have you seen a woman with a little girl anywhere? Kid could be anywhere from six months to two years.'

'Uh, there were a couple women with kids on the street, but none that were that young. I didn't speak to them.'

Casey looked up and down the block for what felt like the millionth time, clusters of civilians, police, EMTs all around. There were only two kids she could see, both of them older boys. 'Shit.'

'Big? You okay?'

She blew out a breath. 'Yeah. I think we lost our best witness already.'

CHAPTER FOUR

Casey propped the conference-room door open with her foot as the rest of the team filed in. There was an urgency to the procession, Billy and Jill rushing to take a seat, but Dana Torres stopped in the doorway with a look of concern on her face.

'Heard about what happened in Harrison with the chief yesterday. They really went and put someone else in charge?'

Casey nodded, trying to look breezy. 'Guess so...'

'You okay with that?'

'Kind of a surprise is all.' She shrugged, looking at the floor so Dana wouldn't see her eyes. 'But that's the brass, right?'

Dana nodded. 'Still. They made the wrong call. It should be you.'

Casey faked a rueful smile. 'Maybe.' She let the door go and came over to the table, waiting for Dana to take her seat before she addressed them all. 'Okay, we're four hours into this and here's what we know. Spoiler alert: it ain't a whole lot.

'Victim one: Caucasian male, pronounced dead at the scene. No ID found on the body – we have no clue, as yet, as to who this man is. Approximate age, forty to sixty. Five-ten, a hundred and ninety pounds, medium build, sandy hair, wearing a business suit. Gunshot wounds to the head and torso. No wallet, no cards, no phone – nothing in his pockets except a key fob for a Mercedes Benz that we're yet to locate and – get this – one thousand dollars in cash.' Casey pointed to the map on the projector screen. 'The vic was found here, in front of the Strongbox gym on Eighth. Two of the employees present at the gym this morning got a look at the body, but neither could provide an ID, and in fact both stated they did not believe he was a member. We've contacted the rest of the Strongbox staff – we're still waiting to hear back from a couple, but none of them so far can put a name on our guy based off of the description. We've put out standard appeals for information as to his identity, but unless he got caught on one of the surveillance cameras in the area before the shooting, we don't have a picture we can share. The lack of wallet, ID etc, found on the victim might've otherwise pointed to a robbery motive, but the cash being present seems to discount that.'

'I thought we were dealing with a random shooter here?' Dana said.

'That's one scenario, but I don't want us to be blinkered in terms of motive.'

'Understood.'

'The cash – was it exactly one thousand?' Jill asked.

'Yes it was...' Casey said, drawing the word out as she

skimmed her notes to double-check. 'Hundreds. All hundreds. What's on your mind?'

'I'm just wondering about it ... such a specific amount, what was it for?'

'Drugs?' Billy said. 'Weekend coming up, stopping off to pick up some supplies, something went wrong?'

'A thousand dollars' worth?' Dana said.

Billy twirled his pen. 'Maybe he was throwing a party.'

'Then why'd the shooter leave the cash?' Dana said.

'Maybe he had more on him and they missed some,' Billy said.

'Missed a thousand bucks?'

'If they panicked...' Billy shrugged. 'I'm just putting it out there as a possibility.'

There was an edge to the exchange, Dana looking at Billy with her head tilted as if he didn't know what he was talking about. Casey held her hand up to put an end to it before it could develop any further. 'Look, we don't know anything for certain right now, so we keep all options on the table.' It wasn't the first time she'd picked up on something between the two of them – nothing more than an undercurrent, but one that hinted at some resentment between the cop who'd spent years working her way up through the ranks and a hotshot who'd been fast-tracked right out of college.

Casey turned to the next page of her notes. 'Moving on – our second victim is twenty-two-year-old Sheena Rawlins, currently in critical condition at St Mark's. Latest we've heard from the medical team is that her odds are eighty-twenty against.' Casey glanced at the presentation screen behind her, an excuse to look away for a beat. The thought of another young woman fighting for her life was triggering, the horrific murders she'd uncovered across Black Reed Bay still so raw. She reached for her water and took a sip before continuing. 'Sheena's a resident of Newridge and a regular at Strongbox gym, which we've confirmed she visited this morning immediately prior to the shooting. She was—'

The conference room door cracked open, and Casey looked up as Lieutenant Helen Dunmore took a tentative step into the room.

For a second, the silence was total.

'On your feet, lieutenant present,' Casey said, the words coming automatically.

Billy and Jill stood to salute, Dana taking her time in following suit, but Dunmore motioned for them to sit down again.

'Lieutenant ... we weren't expecting you until Monday,' Casey said.

Dunmore came a little further into the room, standing awkwardly between Casey and the door. 'That was the plan, but under the circumstances...' She gestured to the map. 'Please, don't let me interrupt.' She dragged a spare chair over from the corner and positioned it by the wall, signalling for Casey to carry on. 'I'm really just here to observe right now.'

Casey glanced at her notes again, the sudden weight of expectation making the words dance in front of her. 'Well, it's great to have you onboard.' She'd planned out what she wanted to say in the briefing, but suddenly her mind was blank. 'Let me make some introductions real quick: this is Detectives Dana Torres, Jill Hart and Billy Drocker,' she said, pointing to each in turn. 'Maybe now you guys will get some real leadership around here.' She winked at Jill as she said it but was immediately unsure why she'd done so, nerves making her act out.

Dunmore flashed a brief appreciative smile. 'I'm sure you've done a great job, Sergeant.' She nodded to the others, opening a notepad. 'It's good to meet you all, there'll be time for proper introductions later. Please, continue. Where are we up to?'

Casey felt the other three looking to her for their cue as to how to react, prompting a quiet unease in the room. Dunmore made a point of keeping her gaze directed at the screen, pretending not to notice. But for Casey, the feeling of embarrassment was like fine needles pressing into her skin. 'We were...' Casey cleared her throat. 'We were just running through what we know about the victims. Did you want me to start over?'

'Thank you, but I read the reports on the way, just pick up wherever you left off.'

'Sure, okay, no problem. So as I was saying, Sheena Rawlins was in Strongbox this morning for a workout and left the premises at approximately eight-fifteen – security-camera footage should give us an exact time. Sadly, we know what happened next.'

'We managed to get in contact with a sister, Nicole,' Billy said. 'She works in the city. She was on her way to St Mark's, last I heard.'

'What about a mom/dad/boyfriend/girlfriend?'

'The sister says she's the only family Sheena's got.'

'Damn,' Dana said. 'Poor kid's gonna need all the love she can get.'

Dunmore leaned forward in her seat. 'Can you bring me up to speed on suspects, Sergeant?'

'Right now, being frank, we don't have any. We've got plenty reports from pedestrians in the area, and we've taken statements from all the store employees, but what it boils down to is that no one we've spoken to saw the actual shooting take place.'

'Eight o'clock in the morning and no one noticed gunshots?' Dunmore said.

'No, that's not...' Casey looked up, glancing at Dana uncertainly as she did. 'What I mean is no one knew it was happening until they heard the shots, and then it was chaos.' Casey moved to the screen and pointed. 'So, Eighth is a four-lane street running east-west. The two vics were found here and here, outside Strongbox gym. Across the street here, directly opposite, the old firehouse takes up more than half the block, and that's abandoned. This lot, next to Strongbox, the premises are empty, and on the other side there's a bar, Ellie's, that doesn't open till the afternoon. So there's not a lot of foot traffic once you get past the Starbucks on the corner.'

'What about inside the gym itself?' Dunmore said. 'No witnesses?'

'The first they knew was when a passerby came in off the street in distress – a woman with a young child. We're still trying to identify her.'

'Do we find that plausible?'

Casey pressed her lips together. Out of the corner of her eye, she saw Jill look over at Dana, then at Billy, unsettled by the direct nature of the question. 'Yes, ma'am, I think so. There are no windows along the front of the building. The only sightline to the outside is through a single doorway in the reception area – all the studios and equipment are to the rear of the building. The first vic would only have been visible from a tight angle on one side of reception, not from the front desk. And the second vic was around the corner. The supervisor who was working said the music's too loud to hear anything from outside.'

Dunmore held Casey's gaze without saying anything.

'I'll run through what we do have,' Casey said, breaking off from a look that felt just a little antagonistic. 'The first 911 call came in at 8.18 this morning, one of twelve calls over the next three minutes reporting shots fired, made from cell phones in various locations along Eighth in the vicinity of Strongbox. One of the calls came from an off-duty patrolman, Christopher Calder – he's based at the Fourth precinct, one of two off-duty cops who happened to be in the area at the time. The second was Jeff Ziegler, based out of the Second; Ziegler didn't see anything. He was driving to Coleman Carrington Park when he saw the commotion and detoured to try and render assistance, but Calder lives a half-dozen blocks from the scene and was jogging on Eighth when the shooting started. He didn't see the shooting or the shooter, but he did see a truck speeding by, headed west on Eighth – dark red, something like a Chevy Silverado or similar. That's partially corroborated by one of the other 911 callers, Ephraim Hiltzer, who was going into the 7-Eleven.' She pointed to a spot on the map. 'And also a caller named Robert Pfohl, who was coming out of the Starbucks on the corner here.' She moved her finger to the intersection of Eighth and Villanova. 'Starbucks guy said he wasn't clear about where the shots were coming from or how many shots there were.' Casey grabbed her laptop. 'He said, and I quote: "There were three or four vehicles went by me when I looked, a couple, maybe three sedans, and a truck, I think." The truck was red or brown, he couldn't recall what colour the sedans were other than dark, or maybe metallic. He told us there were maybe a half-dozen people on the sidewalks, but they were all running in crazy directions when he looked up, so he couldn't tell if any of them were the shooter.'

'You're using the word shooter, singular – do we have anything to indicate whether it was one or multiple?'

'We've recovered four 9mm casings from the scene so far, and the techs say they appear to be from the same handgun – ballistics will confirm. No prints recovered. Preliminary searches of the primary scene are ongoing, but it's an area covering a half a block, and as well as whatever trash was already in the street, there was all the stuff people lost or dropped going for cover – hats, bags, and so on – and everything that was discarded in the aftermath as people came out onto the street again. No weapon has been recovered so far, though. My feeling is it's a single shooter, but you're right, I'm not ruling out multiple.'

'Okay. So what did the 7-Eleven customer see?'

'Mr Hiltzer...' Casey glanced at her notes, the sudden pressure turning all the information that she'd kept straight in her head into a jumble. 'Mr Hiltzer said he first looked over when he heard the shots. He thought he heard maybe six or seven in total, but he didn't see who fired them or where they were coming from. He was going into the store, so his back was to the street initially, but when he turned he saw a red truck go by and people running for cover. A blur.'

'So does that mean we still have nine further 911 callers to identify?'

Casey shook her head. 'No, ma'am, we've spoken to all but one. This is just the most pertinent of what we've learned.'

'Understood. And what about all these folks running for cover?' Dunmore said, studying the map. She got up and pointed to Starbucks. 'If this guy saw them from the corner, the people running must've been closer to the action.'

'We've identified three of the pedestrians on the street who confirmed hearing the shots, and we're in the same boat with all three. None of them saw the exact moment – vague descriptions of "chaos" and "people running everywhere", no one able to say they saw who fired the shots. Conflicting descriptions of what vehicles went by, but the red truck's come up a couple times, as you heard. None of the witnesses could give us any plates, even a partial. We've put out the standard appeal for cell-phone or dashcam footage from vehicle drivers in the area at the time.'

'So Starbucks guy – Mr Pfohl, did you say?'

Casey looked down, double-checked, nodded.

'Mr Pfohl said he saw maybe a half dozen people on the street and we've only found three so far?' Dunmore said.

'That's correct, ma'am. We haven't identified the rest yet,' Casey said. 'We've got appeals out for anyone who was on that section of Eighth, but you know how that goes. There's all kinds of reasons why folk might not want to speak to us.' It used to be unpaid tickets or the occasional outstanding warrant that kept potential witnesses from coming forward, but a general mistrust of cops had taken root in some communities in recent years, and more and more they were finding people wouldn't come forward out of fear.

Casey's thoughts circled back to the woman with the child the Strongbox employees had spoken about. There was a good chance she'd been the closest witness to the shootings, which would make her statement invaluable – but no one at the scene had been able to identify her. It was as if she'd walked out of Strongbox and disappeared. 'As a priority, we're working on locating the woman with the child who ran into the gym to raise the alarm, to find out what she saw. Hopefully we've got her on camera at Strongbox so we can get a visual.'

'And turning to the second victim, Sheena Rawlins,' Dunmore said, 'was she communicative when you found her?'

Billy jumped in. 'No, ma'am. I was first to reach her. She was unconscious. I checked with the EMTs afterward, but she didn't say anything in the ambulance either.'

Casey looked down at her notes, trying to anticipate what questions would come next, relieved to be out of the spotlight for a second.

Dunmore tugged at her earlobe, staring at the screen. 'I sure as hell hope she pulls through. For her sake and ours.' She looked at Casey again. 'You mentioned camera footage – what do we have?'

'Strongbox, Starbucks, 7-Eleven, but they're mostly internal. We're checking anyway, of course, but from what I've seen, only the cam at the 7-Eleven covers any external areas. There's no residential property in the immediate vicinity, so that limits the private options. We've got a few cell-phone videos that we've reviewed, but everything we've got so far was taken in the aftermath, and/or by folk sheltering inside the various buildings. We'll keep working on that, obviously.' Casey moved back to the map. '911 also took a report of shots fired from here, a payphone a block north of the Eighth and Villanova intersection. That call came in at 8.24, and the caller hung up before they could get any details from him.'

'So we don't know if the last caller was reporting the same shots, or if this was a separate set?'

'That's correct, ma'am. A crew searched the area around the payphone, but they came up empty.' Casey brought her hands together in front of her and faced Dunmore. 'So altogether, we've got shots fired across a diameter of about a half-mile, and over a period of two to three minutes.'

'Depending on how many it actually was, it might preclude a single shooter carrying it out on foot,' Dana said.

Casey nodded, already finding herself watching Dunmore for a cue to what to do next. 'Just so you know, we've put in a request for a cell-tower dump – the top-level stuff will come quickest, but that might show any unusual patterns of cell-phone activity in the area at the time.'

'Okay.' Dunmore stood up. 'Is that everything for now?'

Casey looked around the table to check no one else had anything to say before she answered. 'I think so, ma'am.'

'Thank you, everyone. Let's get back to it. Sergeant Wray, could you stay behind a moment?'

Casey was already tidying away her notes, and she looked up at hearing her name. 'Of course, sure.'

Billy led the way out of the room, shooting Casey a look like he was asking if she was okay. Jill was right behind him, eyes trained on the floor. Dana dawdled a moment gathering her pen and notebook, stealing a glance at Casey as she did so and meeting her eyes as she passed her in the doorway. Casey raised her eyebrows, briefly, trying to portray a lightness she didn't feel inside.

When Dana was gone, Dunmore closed the door.

Casey squared her shoulders and came over to face her. 'Like I said, good to have you here, Lieutenant. They're a really good crew. They're going to do great for you.'

Dunmore put her hands in her pants pockets. 'Do you mind if I call you Casey?'

She shook her head, the question catching her off guard. 'Not at all.'

'Casey, I'm a great believer in addressing issues head on. I don't know how you feel about that?'

Casey hesitated, not sure where the question was leading. 'Uh ... sure, of course. I'm all for getting things out in the open.'

'Is that how you work?'

Casey squinted. 'I'm not sure what you mean, ma'am.'

'I did my homework on this unit before I took the job, Casey, so I know a little about Ray Carletti and what he had going on here.'

Casey felt herself sag; it should've been a fresh start, but she felt like they were already back in the gutter. 'Yeah, well, if you'll pardon my speaking bluntly, Ray really fucked things up.'

One side of Dunmore's mouth curled up. 'That he did. And I think we can treat each other like adults and assume there's a whole lot more to the story that didn't make the news.'

Casey looked away – this was the last place she wanted to go right at that moment.

'Don't worry, I'm not asking you to lay it all out now. What I did want to say, though, is that I know you were close to Carletti and I know he was lining you up to take over from him.'

'No, ma'am, Ray didn't...' Casey dipped her head, flexing her hands, trying to compose herself. 'Ray Carletti never intimated that to me. It's a whole lot more complicated than that. I never for one second thought Ray was going anywhere.'

'But you interviewed for the job.'

'Well, sure. I mean, I figured I had nothing to lose. But that doesn't mean I ever assumed—'

Dunmore held a hand up and Casey fell silent. 'All I wanted to say was that, judging by the look on your face when you walked into Keirn's office yesterday morning, no one had warned you that they were bringing me in.'

Casey felt herself blush.

'Yeah, I know that feeling,' Dunmore said. 'Don't take it personally. We're women. The men think this is their job and we're supposed to just fall in line.'

'I guess it was just kind of a surprise. Like you said.'

'Right. So what I'm telling you is that if you feel like you can't work under me, I'll understand and I'll support any request you want to make for a transfer.'

Casey put her hand over her mouth to hide her shock.

'You don't have to decide now—'

'No ... Lieutenant, it's just not something I ever thought about. I have no problem working under you. I never assumed I was just going to take over.' Casey let out a nervous laugh then stifled it, worried it would undercut the sincerity in her words. 'Ask anyone who knows me – that's not how my brain works.'

Dunmore kept eye contact for a second, her face a blank slate, but with cheat notes on the other side that only she could see. 'As I said, you don't have to decide right now.' She opened the conference room door and held it for Casey. 'Thank you, Sergeant.'

CHAPTER FIVE

'But how did she say it?' Billy said, glancing across. 'Like she wants you out of your own unit?'

'It's not my unit,' Casey said. 'Watch the road.'

Billy looked ahead again. 'But she told you to put in for a transfer?'

'She said I could put in for a transfer if I wanted.' Casey yanked at her seatbelt in frustration, pulling it taut across her chest. 'I don't know. It was like a twenty-second conversation. I might've got it wrong. You saw what she's like, she's hard to read.'

'I was just trying not to say anything dumb.'

'But that's exactly it. I felt like she thought everything I said was dumb. It's the way she looks at you and goes quiet. I felt like I was back in high school.'

'You did fine, Big.'

Casey brought her cell phone to her ear, her second try at reaching the stranger who'd called the day before, asking to meet about his information on Carletti. She'd already missed the time he'd set, and now it would have to wait.

Overnight, she'd wrestled with whether or not to agree to his request, going back and forth in her head until a crappy breakfast of dry Cheerios – she'd forgotten to stop by the store to buy milk – and black coffee – ditto – pissed her off enough that she'd decided she'd just shoot him if he turned out to be a nutjob. Or, more realistically, arrest his ass for wasting her time. But like so many decisions she agonised over, it turned out to be wasted energy, the shootings on Eighth meaning she'd be working every minute until further notice. When she'd called the guy earlier to tell him that, his phone just kept ringing – and now it was doing the same.

But as she was about to hang up, the line went quiet. She thought it'd cut out, but then realised there was someone on the other end, saying nothing. Casey checked the screen, saw the call timer counting seconds, confirming it was connected. 'Hello?'

She heard a quiet click, the sound of someone's lips parting.

'Hello? This is Detective Casey Wray. You called me yesterday?'

No reply, just a gentle rushing sound, like a breeze passing over the speaker.

'Hello?'

Billy glanced across at her, trying to figure out what was going on.

She let out a sharp exhale. 'Hey, are you there?'

Still no response. Someone was on the other end, listening or waiting. In the silence, a different presence than she'd felt the day before, more brooding.

Then the line went dead. Casey took her cell from her ear and stared at the screen. 'Weird,' she muttered to herself.

'That the guy from yesterday?' Billy asked. 'What'd he say?'

Casey nodded. 'Yeah. One call and he's already ghosting me. Like every guy I ever dated.' The joke was half-hearted, the call leaving her more unsettled than she wanted to let on.

She went back to the battered department iPad in her lap and hit the icon to restart the footage she'd been trying to watch, a cell-phone video taken by one of the witnesses on Eighth Street. But she struggled to focus, something the caller had said the day before ringing around her head – his reply when she'd asked him if he was in danger.

We all are.

It was the intimacy of it that'd annoyed her at the time, the implication that she was somehow bound to this stranger through a shared threat. She didn't even know his name, for Chrissakes. But now it seemed to weigh a little heavier.

They drove in silence a few moments, Casey lost in that thought, Billy drumming one thumb on the wheel the way he did when he was chewing something over.

Eventually Casey looked over at him. 'What?'

He shrugged. 'You think maybe Dunmore could've been trying to be supportive?' he said, not sounding convinced. 'She said it's up to you, right?'

It took Casey a second to switch gears, back to the

conversation before. 'Yeah. But what she said and how she said it weren't the same.' Casey watched the video as it played on, but after a few seconds she realised she still wasn't paying attention and hit pause once more. 'Ah, crap, I don't know. It was just the way she was talking about me and Ray. Like she could have any understanding of that whole deal, you know what I mean? I don't even understand it my goddamn self, and she wants to tell me she knows all about it?'

He'd been her mentor for years. The man who'd seen qualities in her she'd never recognised in herself, the father figure who'd stood next to her at her own mother's funeral. And yet it turned out there was a side to him she'd never known existed, weak and cruel, and she had to remind herself of that fact every time she thought about the moment he'd forced her to choose between his life and her own.

'And she doesn't think I'm enough of a professional to work for someone else? Like I'm gonna go cry in the corner because I didn't get a job I never thought I'd get? Come on.'

'I mean, I don't want to sound like I'm kissing butt, but me and Jill always figured you were next in line.' He frowned, as if annoyed at himself for speaking out of turn. 'Y'know, one day,' he said, almost in mitigation.

'You and Jill? You guys having a little town hall or something?'

'What? No, just … you know. We were talking. Two noobs comparing notes.' Billy made a left at the intersection with Fourth Street, St Mark's coming into view in the distance. 'Everyone thought you were a lock to get it.'

She looked over at him and then away again. 'I appreciate that. When she walked in yesterday, I felt like I'd let you all down.'

'None of us were thinking that.'

Casey smiled inwardly. 'Don't be nice to me, Bill, I don't handle it well.'

She went back to the iPad and scrolled the video back to the start. It was one of a handful they'd collected from witnesses that morning, the footage onscreen taken by twenty-six-year-old Stephen Dupree, who'd stopped by the 7-Eleven to buy cigarettes and a lotto ticket on his way to work. The video started after the shots had been fired, Dupree running back into the 7-Eleven with a shout of 'Shooter, shooter,' from somewhere down the street just audible. Inside the store, the panicked clerk could be heard telling him to hide at the back of one of the aisles. Up to that point, there was little to take from it, the camera shot swinging around wildly as Dupree had scrambled for cover.

But once inside, Dupree had paused by the door, recording the scene outside through the window. The street was maybe thirty yards distant across the store's parking lot, but still close enough that Casey could make out the vehicles he'd captured passing by on Eighth. As she watched, a rust-red pickup accelerated hard to overtake the sedan in front of it, crossing the screen in less than a second. She rewound the footage to watch again, the pickup swerving wildly to go around the other car. She watched through to the end, counting four vehicles altogether – the pickup plus two sedans headed west, and one sedan headed east. The vehicles were in profile, meaning none of the plates were visible, but the pickup looked like a Silverado, lining up with what they'd heard from the other witnesses. The techs back at the department should be able to come up with makes and models for the other vehicles.

She watched the video through once more, the whole thing

less than twenty seconds in length. Two individuals ran down the street, separately, but too far away to make out clearly. In the background, the store clerk could be heard hollering to get away from the windows, even as Dupree himself could be heard saying, 'Holy shit' over and over, like a crisis mantra. After a few seconds more, the camera had panned to the floor and then the recording stopped.

She pulled out her cell and dialled Dana just as Billy turned into the hospital parking lot.

'Detective Torres.'

'Dana, it's me. I'm sending you a witness vid from this morning, it shows a red pickup speeding along Eighth – it looks like a Silverado, so I guess it's the one the other wits were talking about. No plate visible, so can you see if you can find any other angles on it as a priority?'

'Sure thing, I'll take care of it now.'

'Thanks.' Casey hung up and scrolled the footage back to the pickup again and paused it there. It looked like there was only one person inside, but the image of the driver was just a blurred silhouette.

'You okay?' Billy said, and Casey realised she'd been staring at the screen in silence while he'd been waiting for her to get out of the car.

'Yeah, I'm fine.' She closed the iPad cover and reached for her door but the newsreader speaking on the radio made her pause again.

'*Police are, this afternoon, seeking information on the identity of the victim of a fatal shooting this morning in Rockport, in southern Hampstead County.*

'*The victim, who police sources say was found with no identifying information on his person, is one of two people gunned down outside a gym in western Rockport in an early-day shootout this a.m., in what sources are calling an attempted mass shooting. The second victim is understood to be in critical care at a local medical facility.*

'The deceased is described as a white male, forty-five to fifty-five years old, five feet ten tall and approximately two hundred pounds, with short sandy-coloured hair. Hampstead County PD are appealing for anyone with information as to the victim's identity to contact them urgently.

'The shootings this morning are said to have shocked locals in the western part of Rockport, on Long Island's southern shore. One dismayed resident described the area as "quiet, boring – murders happen in the city, we don't get that here."

'Sources speaking on condition of anonymity told WFKA News that Hampstead County PD are at a loss to explain the shootings, and are yet to identify a suspect or suspects, with one describing the investigation as "stuck in the starting blocks."'

'What the hell?' Casey hit the button to turn off the radio. 'What *sources*?'

'Assholes. There's always someone wants to stir the pot.'

'Yeah, but why go to the press already?' She climbed out of the car. 'At least give us a chance to screw up the investigation before they go telling people about it.'

St Mark's was a state-of-the-art facility completed three years earlier. Rising to eight storeys, the whitewashed tower loomed over the rest of the neighbourhood, a visual reminder of its importance in terms of the influx of jobs and money it'd brought to Rockport. Casey recalled when the doors had first opened, the *Courier* dubbing it 'St Franklin's' after Franklin Gates, who'd won his first term as county executive in part on the strength of his campaign promise to secure Rockport as the chosen site for the facility.

For Casey, the visual prompt was more personal, one she'd prefer to leave behind. Just weeks after the opening, she'd endured six of the worst days of her life there, watching her mother's organs gradually shut down. Dosed up on morphine, Angela Wray had spoken only once in the time Casey sat with her, apologising to Casey's long-dead father that his dinner wouldn't be on the table on time. On the last morning, Casey had been woken from sleep by her mother squeezing her hand. Disorientated, not even realising that she'd dozed off, Casey at first thought she'd dreamt it. But then her mom had squeezed once more, the lightest of pressure across her knuckles. Casey studied her face for signs of intent, but Angela's eyes remained closed, her expression in sleep unchanging. She knew, in all likelihood, that it had been an involuntary movement, a twitch brought on by whatever her mom was seeing, lost deep inside of herself. But she was gone within the hour, and later Casey would convince herself that it had been Angela's way of saying goodbye.

Casey and Billy walked along a short corridor to the ER reception desk, where one of the nurses informed them that Sheena Rawlins was still undergoing emergency surgery. 'She's lost a lot of blood, Detectives. We won't be able to tell you any more until they're done. She was in bad shape when they took her in. Her sister is here, and one of your guys is watching her.' The nurse pointed over her shoulder. 'Take that corridor, you'll see him.'

They followed the corridor to a brown doorway, a uniform

Casey didn't recognise stationed outside. 'How's she doing?' Casey said when they got to the room, jutting her chin to indicate the woman behind the door.

'She didn't have much to say. I guess she's in shock. I didn't press it, my sergeant said to sit tight for you guys.'

Casey nodded and opened the door to what turned out to be a small break room for hospital personnel. Nicole Rawlins was sitting on a plastic chair in one corner, staring at her iPhone. She looked up when they came in, her eyes stitched with red.

'Ma'am, I'm Detective Casey Wray, this is Detective Billy Drocker. We're investigating the shooting that took place this morning, I'm so sorry for what's happened.'

Rawlins was wearing a light-grey business suit with a white blouse, her hair tied back, the resemblance to Sheena not immediate. She shook both their hands in turn, her lips parted, but saying nothing, an uncomprehending look on her face. It was an expression Casey recognised from countless victims and their relatives over the years, that spoke of the hollowing sense of fear and helplessness that followed in the wake of an act of violence.

'Ma'am, has someone been by to update you on your sister's condition?'

Nicole nodded, the movement stilted. 'The doctor came by. All she said is they're doing everything they can and they won't know more until they're done operating.' She was staring past Casey, her eyes out of focus. 'I'm sitting here, and I know she's close by, but I don't even know where, and she's slipping away.' She raised her phone as if in disgust that she was doing something so mundane in a moment like this. 'I want to be doing something, but ... What do I do? What am I supposed to do?'

Casey shifted slightly so she was in her eyeline. 'Ma'am, you're here, and that's everything you can do right now. There's no rulebook for a situation like this. I am truly sorry about what's happened to your sister, and I want you to know that HCPD is treating this case with maximum priority. We're going to do everything we can to find the person or people responsible.'

The words were boilerplate and most people didn't even register, but something in what Casey said sharpened the look on Nicole's face. 'Person or people?'

'Yes, ma'am. We're still gathering information about what happened this morning. That's why I have some questions I need to ask you about your sister. Are you aware of anyone who might have wanted to harm her?'

Nicole switched her gaze to Billy, then back to Casey. She shook her head. 'You think someone targeted her?'

'Being honest with you, ma'am, at this stage we don't know, so we have to remain open to all possibilities.'

Nicole shook her head again. 'I thought ... They said on the news it was a shooter, like the ones that go into schools or whatever?'

'Like I said, we're exploring all possibilities.'

'No one would want to hurt my sister. Why would they want to hurt her? She's a good person, she's not ... She doesn't go out drinking and partying, she's not into drugs or anything. She'd do anything to help anyone. I don't know one person who'd have a bad word to say about her. She works hard, she looks out for people, my god, why would anyone...?' She welled up, covering her mouth with both hands as she tried, and failed, to fight back tears.

'Ma'am, I understand. Believe me I do. When something like this happens, oftentimes it makes no sense at all, and that's why it's our job to look at everything, consider every possibility, to try and figure it out.' Casey crouched down in front of her. 'There are some more questions I need to ask you, but can I get you a coffee or a water or something first?'

Nicole shook her head and tipped it back, eyes closed. Her shoulders rose and fell with each sob, and Casey backed off until, finally, Nicole brought her head forward again and managed a full breath. 'I'm okay,' she said, voice quivering, 'I'm okay.'

'Ma'am, some of the questions I'm about to ask might seem irrelevant or redundant, but please just tell us anything you can – you never know what might be important. The first thing is, does Sheena have a boyfriend or a partner?'

Nicole rubbed her eyes with the back of her wrist. 'No.'

'Is she dating at all?'

'I don't think so right now. No one I know about anyway.'

'Would you guys normally talk about that kind of thing?'

'Yeah, absolutely, of course. We don't get to talk as regularly as we used to – I moved to the city like a year and a half ago, and I guess we don't see each other as often, but we still talk plenty. Texts, mostly, but we try to call at least once a week, something like that.' She wiped her eyes again, swallowed. 'Sheena blows hot and cold on dating. She's got this love/hate thing going on with Bumble. You know, the app?'

Casey nodded – the woman-friendly version of Tinder.

'She'll use it for a month and go on a few dates, and then she gets sick of the guys she meets and she deletes it. That's where she's at right now, I think. Then she'll get bored and download it again. Goes round and round like that.'

'Did she mention anyone she's dated recently? Anyone in particular, I mean, even if it was just a few times?'

Nicole thought for a second, drawing in another shaky

breath. 'No. Not recently. There was a guy called Adam, six months ago, or maybe a little longer. They were dating for a while but then he decided he wasn't into her. She got upset about that, but only for, like, a day or two. It wasn't a big deal. That's the last guy I remember her talking about. She does get guys hitting on her in the gym all the time though. She's a workout freak – she's got this amazing body.'

Casey scribbled down *gym – check* on her notepad as a reminder to speak to the staff at Strongbox to determine if they knew of anyone she might've rejected, or who'd been creeping on her.

'Okay, thank you. And how about her job – what does she do for work?'

'She's a beauty therapist at The Attlewood. You know it?'

Casey nodded, The Attlewood was a luxury hotel and spa outside of town she'd never had cause to visit. 'Yeah, I've heard of it. Is she happy there as far as you know?'

Nicole tugged absently at her thumb, staring at the grey linoleum on the floor. 'Sure, I guess. She says the bosses are tightwads but the clients tip well enough.' She looked up. 'Shit, you won't tell them she said that, will...' She trailed off, realising the futility of it.

Casey shook her head with a sad smile. 'No, of course not. Did she ever talk about any issues she was having at work? Problems with the clients or colleagues, anything like that?'

'No, never. I mean, she doesn't love that job, she says it's not what she wants to do forever, but she's never complained about anyone to me. I mean, sometimes she'll be like, this one said something nasty and this one's kinda stuck up, but nothing ... nothing that would explain this. Her clients are all rich old women.'

'Sure, I understand. Thank you.' Casey stood up. 'We'll take down your sister's address and a few other basic details, and that'll do it for now. Is there any other family we can contact for you?'

Nicole looked off to the side. The room was silent a moment, the sound of monitors beeping somewhere, and a trolley or bed being wheeled down the corridor. 'We've got cousins upstate and in Maryland but they wouldn't ... We're not close with any of them.'

'What about your parents, or any other siblings?'

'Mom and Dad died.' She swallowed, tears forming again. 'They died in a car wreck on I95 two years ago. Drunk driver.' Her eyes went to the floor, the wall, the floor again, universes expanding and collapsing behind them. 'It's just me and Sheena.'

Casey ran her hand over her mouth, her heart breaking all over again for the young woman. One of the things the job had taught her was that there was no justice in this life, that karma never played fair. Some families attracted tragedy as easily as others attracted money; there was no balance to any of it.

'I asked my friend Anita to come over,' Nicole said, maybe anticipating Casey's next question, or maybe just wanting to change the subject. 'She has to drop her kids at her mom's place first.' She sagged as she spoke the words, her gaze unfocused on the wall behind Casey again. Her discomfort was palpable, her expression equal parts pain and fear, and Casey saw no call to push it any further. Billy noted down Sheena's personal information and then Casey opened the door for them to leave, pausing with her hand on the handle as she did. 'Ma'am, do you or Sheena know anyone who drives a rust-red pickup truck, possibly a Silverado or similar?'

It took Nicole a second to focus on Casey again. 'I can't think of anyone. I don't know about Sheena. Why?'

'Just a lead we're following up. If you do think of anyone, give me a call? Thanks for your time.'

Outside, Casey asked the uniform to keep a close watch on Nicole, then headed down the hall with Billy. They were back at the main reception before either of them spoke.

'What do you think?' Billy said.

Casey looked out across the waiting area, a row of people seated along the wall, some bandaged or bleeding, others looking as serene as swans. 'Sheena's a pretty girl – easy to see why she'd get a lot of attention, whether she wanted it or not. Between the gym and the job, sounds like there's scope for someone to build up a thing for her in their head. But that's a big leap from where we are now.'

'My gut still says it's random.'

'Your gut's for food, not for police work, but I know what you mean. I'll feel better when we get an ID on the other vic.'

'You get the sense she was holding back in there?' Billy said.

'Who, Nicole? About the family stuff?'

'I don't know – in general?'

Casey tilted her head to one side and then the other. 'I mean, it was pretty obvious she didn't want to talk about their parents, but I get that. You pick up on something else?'

'She seemed kinda guarded to me, you know?'

'She's in shock. It might just be that.' Casey turned to head for the exit, but she stopped again when her phone started ringing. Dana.

'Tell me some good news.'

'No such thing in this business, Big, you know that – but I can tell you about a witness just called in, all apologies for skipping the scene, was late for work and worried about getting chewed out for it.'

Casey's thoughts ran to the woman with the child who'd walked out of Strongbox and vanished. 'Man or woman?'

'Man. Alfred Stackhouse, twenty-eight years old, picked up coffee in Starbucks and was headed west on the other side of Eighth when he heard the shots. He ducked for cover like everyone else, but he saw a red pickup speeding away from the scene – confirmed as a Silverado.'

'Okay, that's something. We've just finished up with Sheena Rawlins' sister, we're on our way back to—'

'Wait, that's not the headline.'

'No? Hit me.'

'Stackhouse caught a few seconds of the aftermath on his phone and we've got a partial plate. We're running it now.'

CHAPTER SIX

Casey bypassed her own desk when they got back to the department and headed straight for Dana's. Hers was the closest to the lieutenant's office, which spanned the width of the far end of the room; beyond the glass partition, Dunmore was seated behind her new desk, watching on as one of the IT crew worked on setting up her computer. The office had stood empty for months, and the sudden burst of activity was jarring.

'What have we got?' Casey said, bending down to peer over Dana's shoulder, her eyes darting back and forth to the activity in the office. Dunmore was taking a folder out of a packing box and looked over once, acknowledging Casey with a small nod.

'New girl's making herself right at home,' Dana said, catching Casey looking. 'Had the IT guy jump her right to the head of the queue.'

'Like you'd have done any different in her shoes?'

Dana shrugged. 'Sure. But they'd be better damn shoes, you can believe that.'

Casey smiled, couldn't help trying to get a look at Dunmore's feet – but they were obscured by the desk. She noticed Jill sitting opposite was smiling too, and she shot her a wink. 'You doing okay, Jilly?'

The smile disappeared, as if she thought it might get her in trouble, and she nodded. 'Yeah, I'm all good, Big.'

Dana clicked her mouse and pointed to the screen. 'The partial plate came back with a bunch of hits, but these two are registered within three miles of the scene.' She split her fingers to point out two of the listings on the monitor. 'Frederick Colossimo and DeeAnn Hillwood.'

'Either of them in the system?'

'Colossimo, but only for speeding tickets. Nothing on Hillwood. Her DOB makes her sixty-one years old, though, so...'

'So Colossimo first.' Casey took down the address and stood straight again. 'Anything else you got for me?'

Dana brought up a different window, showing a still image from a surveillance camera. 'Here's Sheena Rawlins leaving Strongbox, time stamp is 8.17am, so that's right where we thought it would be. She must've walked outside and straight into a bullet – not a lot of time to get into an argument in the street or something like that. So either someone was waiting for her, she got caught in a crossfire, or it was a random shooting.'

Casey looked at the woman in the image. Rawlins had on a grey hoodie, the straps of a vivid-pink workout top just visible underneath, a small backpack over her right shoulder. Her wet hair was tied back, her skin exhibiting the kind of glow that only exercise can bring on. It seemed impossible to match the image to the woman they'd found slumped against the building a few minutes later, her life hanging by a thread.

'Any movement on our other vic?'

'Plenty of calls, nothing that promising yet. One woman swore blind it was JFK, that "they" had been looking for him all these years and finally caught up to him.'

'Fuck's sake.'

'I know. There's a couple names we're following up on, but nothing confirmed yet – one of them we're waiting on a return call, the other, Patrol are gonna swing by the last known address.'

'Thanks, D – let me know soon as you hear, huh?' Casey glanced over at Billy, circling her finger in the air to signal they were headed right out again. Then she turned back to Dana. 'We'll go see what Mr Colossimo has to say for himself. Can you do me a favour while I'm gone?'

'Sure, what is it?'

Casey took her cell out. She scribbled down the number of the caller who'd been trying to arrange the meet with her that morning and handed it to Dana. 'This is the guy I told you about – the one who thinks he's got dirt on Ray for me.' She shook her head as she said it, still annoyed by the idea that an outsider thought they could tell her something about Ray Carletti she didn't already know. 'He's gone silent on me. Can you see if you can get an ID from the provider?'

Dana held her gaze. 'You sure you need to be doing this right now?'

'It's not a priority, whenever you get a sec…'

'That's not what I mean. I'm saying, haven't you got enough shit to deal with? Give yourself a break. We can come back to this.'

Casey tilted her head, acknowledging Dana's instinct was probably right. 'I know. But he said something about being in danger and … you know me.'

'Who's in danger? Him?'

'"We all are." That's what he said.'

'Meaning you?'

Casey shrugged, nodded, sucking her cheeks in.

'So now this jerk's got you worrying,' Dana said.

'No.' She shook her head. 'Not really. It's just … With everything that happened…'

Dana studied the slip of paper a second and nodded. 'I get it. I'll call them now.'

Casey patted her seatback and went to grab Billy, brushing her knuckles against the leather of her holster just to be sure it was there.

Frederick Colossimo's address was little more than a mile east of Eighth and Villanova, the epicentre of the investigation. The house was a redbrick cottage-style property, set back from the street by a wide manicured lawn. Billy stopped across the driveway, a maroon Civic parked in front of the garage and, behind it, a space big enough for a pickup.

Billy looked at his watch before opening his door. 'No truck. He's probably at work.'

'Yeah,' Casey said, stepping onto the kerb. 'Let's stay on our toes anyway, okay?'

Billy nodded, but Casey caught him stealing a second glance at her. It was always like that now, ever since Dave Cullen had been gunned down on what they'd thought was a routine stop to apprehend a suspect – everyone watching her to see how she'd cope. With Billy, she was pretty sure it came from a place of concern, but there were others within HCPD who still believed the ugly rumours that'd taken root in the aftermath, about the silly bitch detective who'd gotten her partner killed, and were watching to see if she'd do it again. The irony was that the truth behind what'd happened that day – that Ray Carletti had sent them both into an ambush – was the deepest betrayal imaginable of the idea of the force as a brotherhood. But almost no one knew it, outside of Casey and a handful of others, and in that vacuum, it was Casey's reputation that took the fall.

Billy knocked on the door, Casey standing a few feet back. A dog barked inside, making her flinch just as a woman opened up. 'Yes?'

'HCPD, ma'am,' Billy said. 'We're looking for Frederick Colossimo. Is he home?'

'I'm Becky, Freddy's wife. What do you...?' She scratched her arm. 'Wait, is this about the shootings this morning?'

Billy glanced back at Casey, as if he was uncertain how to play it.

'That's right,' Casey said. 'Did Mr Colossimo talk to you about them?'

'Yes, he texted me. Said some idiot was firing a gun in the middle of the street.'

'He saw the gunman?'

The woman frowned. 'I don't know. I asked him if he was alright and he said he was fine, he was in the truck and past it before it even happened. I haven't had the chance to speak to him properly yet.'

'Have you seen the news at all today, ma'am?'

'No, I just got off a twelve-hour shift at the care home. Why?'

'What kind of vehicle does your husband drive, Mrs Colossimo?'

'A Silverado.'

'Uh-huh. What colour?'

She looked wary, as if it were a trick question. 'Red. Why?'

'Where can we find Mr Colossimo now?'

She reached one hand out to lean on the doorframe, the tip of her tongue poking out of the side of her mouth, as if she was deciding whether or not to answer. 'He's on a job. Fifth and Catskill. They're fixing up a house. You can't miss it – they're practically tearing the place down and starting over.'

'He's a contractor?'

'That's right. Look, you've got me worrying now, what's this got to do with Freddy?'

'We just need to know what he saw, ma'am. We'll go talk to him now. Thanks for your help.'

❧

The drive took twenty minutes, the first route suggested by the satnav taking them right through the scene of the shootings that morning.

Turning onto Catskill, Casey spotted the red Silverado even before the jobsite. Billy drew up across the road from a neo-colonial house missing its roof and half of the top floor, the whole thing looking like it was only held together by the surrounding scaffold. Casey counted eight contractors working on or in front of the building, the sounds of hammering and sawing blasting into the car as soon as Billy opened his door.

They badged the foreman, who summoned Colossimo from somewhere round back. He took off his hard hat as he walked over, wiping the sweat from his forehead on his shirttails. He looked from Billy to Casey and decided Billy was the one he should be addressing. 'This about them shootings this morning?'

Casey let Billy answer so she could watch Colossimo while he talked.

'That's right. Can you tell us what you saw, Mr Colossimo?'

'Yeah, I was just driving to work, same as every day, then, outta nowhere, I hear gunshots and so I took myself the hell away from them. That's about all I can tell you. And, look, I know I should've probably called you guys, but I figured ... I mean, I didn't see anything, so I didn't think there was any point. There's nothing I could tell you.'

'Did you see who was firing the shots?'

'Nope. There were two or three loud bangs, and that was all I needed to hear. I put my foot down and put as much asphalt between me and the sound as I could.'

'What about the location or the direction the shots were coming from? Did you get any sense of that?'

He shook his head again. 'I looked in the mirror maybe once or twice, but I was a halfway down the block by then. I was concentrating on not hitting anyone.'

'How did you know you weren't driving towards the gunfire?' Casey said. 'If you didn't see where it was coming from, I mean?'

He held his arms out as if he was powerless. 'I just reacted to the sound, you know? Like a reflex. You telling me you'd have done it different?' He shook his head, correcting himself. 'Okay, maybe not *you,* because you're cops, but I mean someone else, Joe Public.'

'You said you heard loud bangs,' Casey said. 'You knew they were gunshots right away?'

'Of course. I know what a gun sounds like, Detective.'

'Do you own a firearm, Mr Colossimo?'

'Uh-huh. Licensed and insured.'

'What type?'

'Sig Mosquito .22.'

'Where is it now?'

'In my safe at home.'

'Have you fired it today?'

'Are you kidding me? I came to work. It hasn't left the safe in weeks.'

'Have you fired any gun at all today?'

He was holding his hard hat in front of his waist and he started tapping the brim. 'You seriously think I'm the one did the shooting? That's the best you guys can come up with?'

'Did you?'

He looked at them both, incredulous. 'I was driving to work.' He stabbed the air with his finger. 'Driving here. I've been driving the same route for six weeks, and you guys think today's the day I decided to start firing my gun out the window as I went?'

'We're just trying to get a picture of what took place out there this morning, Mr Colossimo,' Casey said, glancing at his hands again. She hooked a thumb at the Silverado on the street. 'That's your truck?'

'Yeah, you know it is. That's why you're here.'

'You happen to have a dashcam in there?'

'I wouldn't even know how to use one.'

Billy scratched his cheek. 'It's a long shot, but did you happen to catch the plates of any of the vehicles around you?'

Colossimo shifted his weight onto his other foot. 'You

coulda put the Batmobile in front of me and I wouldn't have noticed. I was just thinking about getting out of there.'

Casey looked off down the street, weighing up Colossimo's story, but one of the workers started hammering again, interrupting her train of thought. 'Would you consent to us having some swabs taken from your hands and your vehicle?'

'What for?'

'To confirm you haven't fired a weapon this morning.'

'No, I do not consent. I already told you I didn't fire any gun. Come on, this is ridiculous. I came to work same as any other day, ask any of these guys.' He waved his arm around the scene behind him.

Casey stared at him a few seconds longer, trying to decide if she made him for the shooter. There was a shine to his eyes, fear or earnestness, she couldn't tell. 'Okay. Detective Drocker here's going to take down some details.' She looked at Billy and nodded, then made her way over to the foreman.

The man saw her coming and hooked his thumb through a belt loop, jutting his chin at Colossimo as she drew close. 'What'd he do?'

'Why do you ask that?'

He shrugged. 'Cops come around, you figure someone did something.'

'What time did Mr Colossimo show up for work this morning?'

'Uh, around 8.45 I guess?'

'Is that normal?'

'Yeah, pretty much. Give or take.'

'Did he act any different this morning, anything out of the ordinary?'

'Freddy's Freddy.' He turned his mouth down, shrugging,

but saw in Casey's expression that wasn't going to cut it. 'Look, I barely seen him today. You could ask some of the other guys.' He gestured to the jobsite behind him, motioning that he had to get back to work.

Casey collared two of the men in turn, asking the same questions about Colossimo – but got the same vague answers. Finally, she gave up and circled back to Billy, who was standing by the car now.

'Anything?' he said.

Casey glanced at the blank notebook page in her hand. 'I'd get more out of their toolbelts. Colossimo say anything else to you?'

Billy shook his head. 'Some garbage about checking out a girl taking selfies with her boyfriend in a car the day before at the same place on Eighth. I think he was trying to impress me with what a player he is.'

'Gross.'

'Yeah. You like him for our shooter?'

Casey squinted. 'Not sure. Let's run his firearms licence and double-check the footage we've got to see if he stopped his truck anywhere on Eighth this morning. I'm not ready to rule him out yet.'

CHAPTER SEVEN

Casey called Dana as they drove back to the department, putting her on speaker so Billy could listen in too.

'Dana, it's me. Any update on Sheena Rawlins?'

'Nothing. I called in about fifteen minutes ago, the nurse

said she's still in surgery. She's got my cell. She promised she'd call me as soon as anything changes.'

'Goddammit,' Casey said, under her breath.

'Yeah. And you can scratch those two possible IDs for the second vic – both of them turned out to be alive and well.'

'Is it wrong to be disappointed about that?' Casey said, drawing a grim smile from Billy.

'We've got another new possible,' Dana said, 'but Switzer in Patrol is getting pissy about "sending his guys out on wild goose chases".'

'Jesus, is there any police work at all that doesn't piss that guy off? He should've been a politician, the amount he bitches.'

'It's the taskforce and this review. Everyone's on edge.'

'Yeah, I get it. What's the new possible's name?'

'Let me find it, hold on,' Dana said. 'You get anything from the Silverado guy?'

'Yeah, he's got a thing for girls taking selfies,' Billy said into the speaker.

'Huh?'

Casey took over. 'His story's that he heard the shots and took off, didn't see a thing. He refused residue swabs, but without something more concrete to link him to the shootings, I don't think we've got enough for a warrant. He admits owning a gun, but claims it's a Sig .22, so that doesn't work with the casings from the scene – can you double-check that on his licence for me?'

'Sure thing...' There was a pause, Dana saying something away from the phone. 'Okay, Jilly's on it now.'

'Cool, thanks.'

'So the new possible ID for our second vic is Landon T. Whitlock,' Dana said, picking up the thread. 'He's some kind of lawyer, got an office nearby, and his secretary says she hasn't been able to get a hold of him all day.'

'There a chance he's just been stuck in court?'

'She seemed to think not. Apparently he's not that kind of a lawyer.'

'Okay.' Casey rested her elbow on the door and googled his name. She pushed her hair back from her forehead as she waited for the results to show. 'Wait, hold on...'

She clicked on the first thumbnail to make the image bigger.

'Holy shit, I think this is him. Bill?' She turned the phone so he could see it.

'Seriously?' Dana said.

Billy squinted, then tilted the phone further in his direction. 'Yeah...' He checked the road, then looked again. 'Yeah, that's the guy. Jesus. Do we have an address for him?'

'No, but the secretary left her details.' Dana read out a cell number for Casey to take down.

'Got it, I'll call her now.'

'Wait, Case – before you go: the shift manager from the gym, the guy you spoke to?'

'Brandon somebody?'

'Sarciniak, yeah. He's got a prior for possession, the charge was pled down from intent to sell. That was Jill's catch.'

'There's them drugs...' Billy said, seemingly a swipe at Dana's earlier scepticism. 'Was he pushing through the gym?'

'It was three years ago. He was caught buying in a designated hotspot. The report reads like he was just a kid picking up for the weekend.'

'I guess he'd be the first mope to ever use that defence...' Billy said.

Dana tutted. 'Why don't you come read the report for yourself, rookie.'

'Okay, okay, we'll deal with him later,' Casey said. 'D, we gotta go. Tell Jilly good work.'

'You got it.'

Casey dialled the number for Landon Whitlock's secretary, looking at Billy out of the corner of her eye to see if he'd been baiting Dana for shits and giggles. But his gaze was locked on the road and he looked pissed off.

A woman's voice answered, thin and rushed. 'Hello?'

'Ma'am, this is Detective Casey Wray with HCPD. I'm calling about Landon Whitlock.'

'HCPD? Oh, god, is it him?'

'Ma'am, we need to speak to Mr Whitlock's next of kin urgently. Are you able to put me in contact with them, please?'

'My god, it is him. The shootings this morning—'

'Ma'am, it really is urgent we speak to his family.'

'I understand, but...' Sounds of movement came down the line, the woman hurriedly changing position and moving papers around. 'I'll get Mrs Whitlock's number. I can't believe it, this is unreal. Holy cow ... Okay, okay, here it is.' She read out a cell number and Casey scribbled it down, along with an address overlooking Black Reed Bay.

'Mrs Whitlock – is that his wife?'

'Yes. Darcy Whitlock.'

'Do you know if she's at home at the moment?'

'No clue. She wouldn't dream of telling me her schedule. Sorry. What happened to him? To Landon?'

'I can't discuss that at this time, ma'am. I'll contact Mrs Whitlock now, and then maybe she'll be able to give you some more information.'

The woman scoffed, a high-pitched laugh that died in her throat. 'Yeah, sure, maybe she'll invite me up to Shatter Creek for tea and tell me all about it. Please, I just ... I just want to know how this could happen...'

'I'm sorry, ma'am,' Casey said. 'I appreciate your help, truly.'

'Wait, Detective, what happens now?'

'Ma'am, like I said, we need to speak to Mr Whitlock's family right now, but the investigation is ongoing—'

'No, I mean what happens to me? I'm out of a job, right?'

CHAPTER EIGHT

The address was a waterfront lot shielded from the highway by a wide grove of sugar maples. The long driveway took a meandering path, weaving up to and through the trees and climbing gently through a series of switchbacks until it opened out on an expansive view of the house and Black Reed Bay behind it, the barrier islands across the water just visible on the horizon. Casey hadn't once crossed the causeways in the months since the Tina Grace investigation, and the beachfront communities that served as paradise for millions of summer vacationers existed as a permanent black spot in her peripheral vision.

A mansion in any other locale, the property seemed to sprawl across its lot; the main house took centre stage, a three-storey building showcasing a subtle mix of architectural flourishes, including Federal-style brickwork and Greek-revival columns. From one side, a double-storey annexe extended parallel to the shore, with a low-slung standalone guesthouse a short way beyond it, while a triple garage branched out from the other flank. To her left, a gentle slope ran down to a waterway named Shatter Creek, the reference Whitlock's secretary had dropped clicking into place, which separated the house from a barren expanse of saltmarsh stretching from its far bank. Close to the mouth of the channel, almost where it met the bay, a glistening powerboat was moored to a dock.

Casey pointed for Billy to pull up next to a black SUV that was parked in front of one of the garage doors.

The video doorbell lit up when Casey pressed the button, and after a few seconds a clipped voice came over the speaker. 'Yes?'

Casey held her badge up to the camera. 'I'm Detective Casey Wray with HCPD. We're here to speak to Mrs Whitlock.'

'About?'

Casey glanced at Billy, then back at the camera. 'Are you Mrs Whitlock, ma'am?'

The speaker fell silent and they waited. Just as Casey was about to try the bell again, a woman opened the door. 'I'm Darcy Whitlock, what is it you want?'

Whitlock was tall and athletic-looking, with sun-bleached hair tied in a ponytail swept forward over one shoulder. The skin on her face was flawless, either the result of good genes or even better cosmetic surgery, making it hard to put a number on her age; Casey would've believed anything from mid-thirties to mid-fifties.

'Ma'am, we're here about your husband. May we come in?'

'What about him?' Whitlock said, not moving from the doorway.

'Can I ask when was the last time you spoke to him, Mrs Whitlock?'

She glanced at her wrist, an Apple watch glowing with an array of numbers. 'When he left the house this morning. Around seven.'

'Have you had any contact with him since?'

'He's playing golf with clients at Point Loma today. And with Landon that means a round of golf and then a lunch that can end anywhere from early evening to sometime Saturday. Why?'

'It really might be better to have this conversation inside.'

'It might be better if you just tell me.'

Casey swallowed before she spoke again. 'There's no easy way to say this, ma'am, but we believe your husband was the victim of a homicide this morning. You may have heard about a shooting on the news, we've been urgently trying to identify one of—'

The door slammed shut.

Billy was looking on stunned. 'What the…?'

Before he could say any more, the door opened again, Whitlock holding an iPhone to her ear.

'Ma'am—'

Whitlock held her hand up to silence her and spoke into the cell. 'Lanny, it's me. I need you to call me back right now.' She ended the call and tapped out a message on the screen – *Call me*, judging by its short length.

Casey opened her own phone and held up the picture she'd found online. 'Is this your husband, ma'am?'

Whitlock stared a hole through the screen, her jaw rigid when she spoke. 'Yes.'

'Ma'am, I know this is an unbelievable shock. Myself and Detective Drocker were at the scene of the crime this morning and we have some certainty this man was one of the victims. Please, can we come inside to talk?'

Whitlock stood motionless when Casey put her phone away, the muscle in her jaw flexing, but otherwise showing no reaction. When she finally spoke, her voice was one of quiet fury. 'Where is he?'

'When you feel ready, we can take you to make a formal identification—'

'I said, where is he? Give me the address, I'll drive myself. Right now.'

❦

Darcy Whitlock's expression didn't change when the sheet was pulled back. The same piercing gaze she'd fixed Casey with on the doorstep took in Landon Whitlock's pale features. Even with the blood cleaned from his skin and the viewing arranged so that the shattered lefthand side of his face wasn't visible from her angle, the aura of a violent death raged in the silence of the sterile room.

'Ma'am, would you like a moment to—'

Whitlock turned and walked out.

Casey caught up to her in the corridor outside, feeling like she was chasing the eye of a hurricane, about to unleash fury on everything around it. 'Ma'am...'

Whitlock stopped and turned on her heel, standing eye to eye with Casey. 'Who did this, Detective?'

Casey's lips moved without sound at first. 'We ... This is a priority investigation for HCPD, we're pursuing every lead possible, but we don't have a culprit or culprits as yet. When you feel ready, it will help us a lot if we can ask you some questions about Mr Whitlock and see if we can—'

'What questions?' She said it forcefully enough that Casey almost took a step back.

She gestured to the corridor's bare walls. 'This isn't really the right place to—'

'What questions, Detective? Because I have a shit-ton of my own to ask, so why don't you stop wasting my time and ask?'

'Ma'am, I understand, there must be a million things you want to know—'

'We could start with who did this? My husband was killed in the street in broad daylight, and you haven't caught anyone. How is that possible?'

'As I said, we're—'

'What is a priority investigation? What does that mean?'

'It means that every resource at our disposal is being brought to bear on this—'

'Is that clown you've got playing at chief working on it?'

'Acting Chief Keirn?'

'Keirn. Is he investigating?'

'Uh ... no, he won't be investigating directly, but he's being kept appraised of—'

'What about the county executive? Is he being *kept appraised*?'

'I don't ... The county executive doesn't operate in an investigatory capacity, but I'm certain he'll be briefed.'

'Don't explain how it works to me, Detective. If they're not directly involved, then it's not a priority, is it?'

'I can assure you—'

'No you can't. Standing there with your Target suit and your empty platitudes about priorities, I promise you, you can't assure me of anything. Who's in charge of this investigation?'

'I'm the lead investigator on this case.'

Whitlock scoffed, disdain in her eyes. 'Then who's in charge of you?'

'My commanding officer is Lieutenant Helen Dunmore.'

'I don't know her.' Whitlock took her phone out and unlocked it, then seemingly changed her mind. 'My daughter will be home in a half-hour. I need to go. Christ knows how

I'm going to break this to her, but at least I can reassure her that her dad's murder is a *priority*. I'll be making some calls.'

'Ma'am, please, wait...'

Whitlock walked off down the corridor, cell phone to her ear.

❧

The sun was low in the sky by the time Casey and Billy made it back to the department, masked by a gauze of low clouds that rendered it sickly in appearance. An 'end of days' sun, Ray used to call it, Rockport caught in the pale light of a dying star.

Casey collapsed into her chair, feeling as if she'd been sandblasted. The job made it easy to fall into a kind of apocalyptic mindset – the pain and mindless violence they stood witness to every day fostering the sense of Rockport as a city on the brink. The brass had launched one of their periodic mental-health initiatives the previous year to combat the pervading negativity, bringing in mindfulness consultants who'd encouraged them all to find joy in the small things in life – a blue sky, a bird in flight – and to take time to look out for their own wellbeing and that of their colleagues. Even the brass had had the decency to look embarrassed by the crap that was served up. Casey smiled remembering how Dana wound up getting hit with a reprimand for suggesting to one of the consultants that a vending machine for Xanax was what they really needed.

Her desk was a mess of papers, files, pens and notes, the message light on her landline blinking. She went to pick up the handset just as Dana came over, a can of Sprite in one hand and a Hershey's Cookies 'n' Creme bar in the other, held out as an offering. 'Here. Dinner of champions.'

Casey put the phone down and took them with an appreciative grimace. She set the candy bar on the desk, her stomach too knotted to eat even though she'd had nothing since breakfast, and popped the soda to take a slug. 'You will not believe the beating I just took from the victim's wife. Jesus.'

'I might, because I can see it in your face. But you better save it – new girl wanted an all-hands update as soon as you got back.'

Casey puffed out her cheeks. 'What's the latest on Sheena Rawlins?'

Dana hesitated, and Casey knew what was coming even before she started shaking her head. 'She didn't make it. The surgeons tried everything.'

'Why didn't you call to tell me?'

'I only just heard.'

Casey pressed the soda can against her forehead and screwed her eyes shut, seeing Sheena bleeding out on the corner and Nicole Rawlins sobbing in an empty break room – two lives destroyed by the same bullet.

Dana squeezed Casey's shoulder.

'I can't take many more of these, D.'

'I know, it sucks. We do what we can do, right?'

'And what difference does it make?' She looked up. 'The bodies keep coming.'

Before Dana could say anything, Dunmore stepped out of her office and headed for one of the meeting rooms. 'If I could have you all join me, please?'

Jill Hart jumped to her feet, notepad and pen in hand, and Billy followed a few paces behind.

'Better go,' Dana said. 'You want me to make your excuses?'

Casey shook her head. 'I'm okay.' She took another slug of soda, held the cold metal to her temple, then stood up.

Dana didn't move, her lips pressed together.

Casey shot her a look. 'What?'

'I didn't know whether to tell you this now, but I called Verizon about that cell-phone number you gave me.'

Casey glanced in the direction of the meeting room where the rest of the team was gathering. 'Shoot.'

'It's a prepaid burner, so no name or ID attached – no surprises there. But I ran the number through the system, just to see if it came up anywhere in the records, and I got this.' Dana handed over a sheet of paper, one entry highlighted. 'This is the cell-tower dump we requested this morning – all the towers around Eighth and V. This cell phone pinged one of them less than thirty minutes after the shootings.'

Casey stared at the page, the numbers swimming in front of her eyes.

'I don't...' Casey looked away, thinking it through. 'I don't know what that means.'

Dana shrugged, indicating the same thing.

As she did, Dunmore appeared across the office, a hand on her hip. 'Casey, Dana, can you join us?'

Casey looked over, raising her hand in apology. 'Sorry, sorry, coming now.' She grabbed her things and started walking.

Dana fell in step at her shoulder. 'You think it's a coincidence?'

Casey blew out a breath, her brain fried. 'No idea.' She could see the rest of the team watching them approach through the glass of the meeting room. 'I'll call this guy again when I get a sec, figure out what he wants or tell him to get lost. Put this to bed for good.' She held up the papers. 'Thanks for this. There anything in here to help with our shooter?'

'Nothing yet. Tech are looking at it.'

They went through the doorway and Dunmore watched as Casey took her seat. 'Bring me up to speed, please?'

Casey pressed her pen against her cheek, no time to get her thoughts straight. 'Okay, so ... our second victim is confirmed as Landon Whitlock – the wife just made a positive ID and tore a layer of skin off me afterward.'

'What for?'

Casey waved it off. 'It's fine. She was in shock is all, it came out as anger. All the anger. But it means I couldn't get much out of her about our vic.'

Dana jumped in. 'Jilly's been on background.' She met Casey's eyes across the table, a look that said *take a breath*, and Casey was grateful for the assist.

Jill adjusted her glasses and picked up the pad in front of her. 'There's ... Well, there's not a huge amount of information about him online. Fifty-five years old, registered Democrat. According to his LinkedIn he was a tax lawyer for a couple of the big firms in the city, then he set up shop on his own back in 2006.' Jill looked at Dunmore and then belatedly at Casey, her cheeks reddening as if she'd been caught trying for extra credit from the new principal. 'It's listed as a financial consultancy, but he hasn't updated his profile much since then. The company doesn't have its own website, at least not that I can find, which seems kind of strange. No record, no priors – nothing about him in the system at all.'

Casey ran her finger over the tabletop. 'He told his wife he was golfing with clients this morning.'

'Is it possible he was en route?' Dunmore said.

'In a business suit with a thousand dollars in cash on him?'

Dunmore looked at her across the conference table, with what felt to Casey like reproach in her expression. 'Okay, let's come back to that. I understand we lost our other victim too. What do we have on her?'

Casey ran through what they'd learned about Sheena from Nicole Rawlins, and raised the possibility she could've picked up an unwanted admirer. 'I'll talk to the staff at the gym about it, see if they noticed anything.'

Dunmore nodded. 'What does the evidence from the scene tell us?'

It was Dana's turn to pick up her pad. 'We're still waiting on the ballistics report to confirm if all the casings came from the same gun. Nothing remarkable about the ammo, standard 9mm you can buy in Walmart or a thousand other places.' She flipped a page over. 'Confirmed that no prints were found. Initial analysis of the male victim indicates he was shot at close range, but the lab's still trying to establish how close – like, whether the assailant was definitely on the sidewalk or could've been in a vehicle. The location of the recovered casings indicates the former was most likely.'

'Chances are they were on foot,' Casey said, 'but that doesn't mean they couldn't have got right back into a vehicle and driven off.'

Dana picked up where she left off. 'Looking at the blood trail Sheena Rawlins left, it seems like she was in proximity to Mr Whitlock when she was struck, but then she managed to make it over to the side alley where Billy found her, approximately twenty feet away.'

'Presumably looking for cover,' Dunmore said, shaking her head in horror.

'We haven't turned up any links between the two victims so far,' Jilly said, taking over. 'Landon Whitlock's secretary told us she'd never heard the name Sheena Rawlins. She also stated that, to the best of her knowledge, Mr Whitlock's not a member of the Strongbox gym and has never used the place. She hadn't seen him this morning, but did say he'd told her he'd be out golfing with clients too. She couldn't offer any explanation for his movements being as they were.'

'She know anything about the money he was carrying?' Casey said. 'Or the lack of personal belongings?'

Jilly was already shaking her head. 'She said it was unusual – that he never normally carried cash. She couldn't think of any reason he'd have that much on him today.'

'What about his car?'

Jill skimmed the page on her pad. 'Always parks in his own space at the office lot but the car's not there, she already checked. He never walks anywhere, apparently.'

'Meaning it should be somewhere close to the scene,' Casey said. Then, almost to herself: 'So why can't we find it?'

'Are there any parking garages in the area, anything like that?' Dunmore said.

'No, street parking only,' Jill said.

'Okay. Keep looking.' Dunmore linked her fingers on the tabletop. 'As it stands, we're no closer to establishing whether either – or both – of the victims were targeted, or if this was a random attack.'

'Not yet,' Dana said. 'But the fact they apparently didn't know each other implies random is the more likely of the two.'

'What else do we have?'

'Patrol took statements from a total of twenty-seven people in the vicinity at the time,' Jill said, reading from her pad, 'and we've followed up with the ten in closest proximity, but none of them reported seeing the actual shooting. Units stopped three separate vehicles within a half-mile of the scene, two for running a red light, one for a broken rear window, but none of them were deemed suspicious on further scrutiny. We've got the plates on file. The helicopter was in the air for close to an hour, but didn't pick up any suspicious vehicles or traffic movements, or anything that might indicate a suspect.'

'They got there the same time as us,' Casey said quietly. 'The perp or perps were gone by then.'

'The biggest problem we've got is that no one we've spoken to was within fifty yards of where we found Mr Whitlock and Miss Rawlins,' Dana said.

Casey stared a hole through the tabletop. 'The woman with the kid was.'

Dunmore looked over. 'I understand we've made no progress locating her?'

No one said anything, an edge to the silence. Casey glanced at her watch. 'Almost ten hours. Feels like maybe she doesn't want to be found.'

'You sound like you have a theory why that is,' Dunmore said.

Casey shook her head, thinking about how Tina Grace had disappeared when her life was in danger. 'Takes a lot to just vanish, especially with a kid. In my experience, it's only fear makes women ditch out that way.'

Dunmore pushed herself back from the table and crossed her legs at the ankles. 'I'm due to update the acting chief in a half-hour. What's our best shot at moving this investigation forward, Sergeant?'

'If she's still alive, we have to find her,' Casey said, leaning over the table. 'Odds are she was the closest eye wit to the shooting.'

'We've got a visual for you,' Dana said. 'She pops up on the surveillance footage right after Sheena Rawlins exits Strongbox.'

'Okay,' Dunmore said. 'Get it out there, whatever channels you usually use, and make sure the media have it too. Let's find this woman and see what she saw.'

CHAPTER NINE

Casey stared at the grainy CCTV image on her screen, the camera inside the entrance to Strongbox capturing the woman from a high angle that obscured her features and those of the child on her hip. Dressed in blue jeans and a sweater, the woman had deep-red hair pulled back in a ponytail, a diaper bag only just clinging to one shoulder. Casey put a ballpark on her age as mid- to late-twenties, but there was no way to be certain. It was only then that she realised she hadn't once considered the child wasn't the woman's daughter; they could just as easily be looking for a nanny as a mom.

Casey's cell phone rang. A number she didn't recognise. 'Hello?'

'Yeah, Casey, hi, it's Rita Zangetty. I'm sorry to call so late.'

Casey looked around instinctively, the call from the county executive's chief of staff coming totally out of the blue. They'd shared a dozen conversations, at most, over the years, all of them in person – so this was new. The department had emptied out, Casey sending the others home a while earlier, only Dunmore still at her desk – but out of earshot behind the glass wall.

'Rita, hey. To what do I owe the pleasure?'

'Y'know, I don't think anyone ever took a call from me at 9.30pm and called it a pleasure, so thanks for that.'

'Shows just how much my evenings suck, I guess,' Casey said.

'It can't be that bad, surely. I hear about what you guys get up to at Shakey's Bar.'

'Shakey's is strictly for payday drinks, and all we actually do is complain about the brass. And the politicians.' As soon as it left her mouth, the crack felt too close to the bone, but Casey was too tired to care.

Zangetty wasn't fazed. 'Is that right? You guys need to come down to Quaglino's across the street from County Plaza – we're world champions at that.' She laughed, but it rang hollow, a hint at the real frustrations behind the joke. 'Seriously, though, I hope you don't mind me calling.'

'Sure.' What else was she supposed to say? She propped her head against her hand. 'What can I help you with?'

'The shootings this morning.' Rita paused, almost as if she expected Casey to protest. 'I don't know if you know this, but Landon Whitlock was a pretty significant donor to the party, including all of Franklin's campaigns, so this has come as a real shock.'

Hearing her victim's name spoken in the same breath as the county executive's was jarring, and Casey found herself looking in Dunmore's direction automatically. She hated herself for it, the way her first reaction anytime she encountered power and influence was to look to authority for reassurance. 'I ... No, I wasn't aware of that.'

'Yeah, Landon's been an enthusiastic supporter of Democratic causes over the years – he was generous with his time and his money, but also just a really great booster for us. This is just ... devastating news. For everyone, but particularly Franklin. I mean, even the Republicans liked Landon.' She was quiet a second, and Casey sensed her building up to an ask. 'So, in that context, maybe it won't surprise you to know that Franklin took a call from Darcy Whitlock earlier on. You met with her today, right?'

Shit. 'Yeah, we had to break the news to her. She took it pretty tough.'

'Uh-huh. She can be a fearsome woman at the best of times, so I can imagine.'

'What did she say?'

Zangetty took a breath and let it out. 'He didn't walk me through the ins and outs of the call, but the bottom line is that she's in total shock, as you'd expect, and it's doing a number on her, so she's casting around for answers and someone to blame. Do we have any idea who did this yet? Or why?'

Casey shifted position in her chair, caught off guard by the directness of the question. 'You know we can't discuss the specifics of the investigation—'

'No, of course, I'm not asking for specifics, Casey, I'm just ... I guess we're all just trying to understand what the hell happened here.'

'Well, I mean it's just too early to say. That's the truth of it.'

'Uh-huh, I get that. But what I'm asking is that as and when there are ... developments, you give us a heads-up. And to be totally clear, that's Franklin asking, not me. And when I say "asking" I mean ... you get the picture.'

Casey felt her face burning, the spotlight suddenly too bright. 'Surely he's got the acting chief briefing him?'

'Of course. But this is about speed.'

'But he can get Keirn on a call anytime he wants, day or night. Why me?'

'C'mon, you know how it works. By the time stuff works its way up the chain of command and across the divide to our house, the media already have it. Franklin wants to make sure we're doing right by Darcy Whitlock, and that she's getting the latest from us, not hearing it on the news. You're at the sharp end of this, no one's better placed.'

The pause that followed was a loaded one, all the different interpretations and implications running through Casey's head. Landon Whitlock lying to his wife about where he was going to be that morning; was this Franklin Gates setting himself up to run interference on potential dirty laundry? Or just working his way into Darcy Whitlock's good graces, to keep the campaign contributions flowing?

Or maybe he just wanted to know before Keirn, having been burned by HCPD once already. Now more than halfway through his second term as county executive, Gates had been seen as a lock to win a third – until the HCPD scandal blew up. His efforts to manage the fallout had drawn fire from all sides; the conservative talking head on WFKA branded Gates a cop-hater who'd overblown the situation for political gain – a monologue that'd subsequently gone viral – even as the *Rockport Courier*'s liberal opinion writer penned two columns, three weeks apart, accusing him of trying to sweep the affair under the carpet. It was a fine line Gates was trying to walk, selling Keirn as a new broom even as he set him up to take a fall should it become expedient – an outcome Keirn was fighting his own rearguard action against.

'I promise you,' Casey said, 'a case as high profile as this, the brass will be all over us, so you'll know as soon as we do.'

There was a sharp noise – not quite a tut, more like Zangetty calibrating what to say next. 'I work with politicians all day. I know a non-answer when I hear one. This is a chance to really build up some credit with Franklin – and I'm talking personally.

Everyone knows you've got the potential to go a long way in the department, you just need to give yourself the opportunity. Franklin can open doors for you that no one else can.'

She glanced towards Dunmore's office again, then realised Zangetty was plugged-in enough to know they'd passed Casey over the day before. 'I appreciate you saying that, but...'

'Casey, I'm gonna pick up the paper tomorrow morning and see three "departmental sources" talking off the record about this case. It's the same thing every time. All we're asking is that HCPD affords the same courtesy to the county executive as it does to some reporter from the *Courier*.'

Casey got out of her chair, the request made to sound so reasonable in those terms that she didn't know how to say no. 'Rita, look, sorry but I have to go.'

'Casey, it's not a big deal. This is how it works at the top table. I can have Franklin call Gates to make it an official order, if that's what you want, but you never struck me as someone who needed babying.'

Casey let out a nervous laugh, feeling way out of her depth. 'Yeah. Look I really have to go, sorry. I'll talk to you later, Rita.' She ended the call before Zangetty could say anything more.

She looked around the empty department, Dunmore so focused on something on her monitor screen she hadn't lifted her eyes once. Before, Casey would've marched into Ray's office and vented at him, knowing that he'd agree with every curse word she fired off about having a politician as their ultimate boss. In response, he'd have made her drink the whisky he loved, and that she hated, and told her what to do for the best. Now she stood alone, hands on her hips, missing him in spite of herself.

Goddamn you, Ray.

❧

Rockport Gables was still and quiet when Casey parked on the driveway outside her bungalow. She killed the lights and listened to the ticking sound of the engine cooling in the darkness. The temptation to slump against the window instead of immediately dragging herself into the house proved too strong, and she rested her head against the cool glass.

Her stomach kicked up in protest at the lack of sustenance, and she tried to remember what she had in the refrigerator. But the fact she couldn't think of the last time she'd been to a grocery store told her all she needed to know. She reached for her phone to check the time, but the white numbers on the screen killed her last hope: there was no point ordering pizza when she'd be asleep before it arrived.

A knock on the passenger window made her jump out of her skin. A man, standing right next to the glass so that only his arm and torso was in sight.

She grabbed her badge out of the console then leaned across to press it up against the window, cracking it open just enough so he could hear her. 'I'm police, you need to back the hell up right now.'

The man bent down, the window framing the face of Robbie McTeague. 'Good to see you too, Wray.'

Casey glared at him a second, then righted herself in the seat to throw her door open and jump out of the car. 'The hell are you doing sneaking up on me like that?'

McTeague rested his arms on the roof of the car. 'The hell are you doing sleeping on your driveway?'

'I'll sleep any damn place I want. Just because you're retired, some of us still gotta work for a living.'

The word 'retired' drew a halting smile, something she'd never seen him do in his days as Chief Hanrahan's enforcer. It was part of the contradiction that made up Robbie McTeague, one that only grew more tangled the more she got to know him. A lifetime cop, whose prominence in the department had left him so tainted that he'd had no choice but to leave the force, who nonetheless seemed happier in civilian life than she'd ever seen him with a badge. It seemed absurd now to think that it was only months before that she'd be cowed just by the sight of him.

'I'm not retired, I'm a businessman,' he said, coming around the car. 'An entrepreneur or some shit, isn't that what everyone says these days?' He held out his hand and she shook it, surprised to find that her first instinct had been to give him a hug.

'A sleazy PI is not an entrepreneur,' Casey said.

'Sleazy?'

'You're creeping around a defenceless woman's property in the middle of the night,' she said, raising her eyebrows in mock accusation.

'*Defenceless*. That's a good one.'

'There something you need, Cap, or did you just stop by to scare the hell out of me?'

He hooked his thumb at his car, that she now saw was parked down the block. 'I was waiting for you to go inside, but you were taking too long.' He dipped his head, crossing his arms. 'You didn't answer any of my messages, so I figured I'd have to stop by in person.'

The texts she'd been trying so hard to ignore, asking her if she was ready to quit; in the madness of the day, they'd gone out of her mind completely.

'Yeah, okay...' She rubbed the back of her neck. 'Were you being serious?'

He nodded, hooded eyes locked on hers.

She walked up the driveway and opened the front door, then cocked her head. 'Look, why don't you come inside.'

❦

Casey took the last two cans of Sprite from the refrigerator and found a half-full bag of chips in the cupboard, setting them all out on the countertop. 'Help yourself,' she said, nudging one of the sodas towards McTeague.

As an attempt at hospitality it was cringeworthy, and she knew it. When she looked up to meet his eyes again, she couldn't help but burst out laughing. She cupped her hands over her face, sighing. 'Like I said, I gotta work for a living.'

McTeague pressed his lips together, amusement playing in his eyes.

It was a month or more since she'd seen him last, on one of the rare days he hadn't been stuck in a room facing questions from Federal investigators. No charges had so far been brought against him in the fallout from the scandal, and she believed him when he told her he'd never known about Hanrahan's crimes. But it wasn't Casey he had to convince. Tarred by association, the truth was that even if no charges were ever brought, the cloud of suspicion would always linger over him. He knew it as well as she did.

'I owe you an apology,' he said, opening the proffered soda without taking a drink.

'What for?'

'I heard about what happened with the lieutenant's job.'

'Oh, Jesus, not you, too. I'm fine about it. I knew they'd never give it—'

'I made a promise to you. Down on the waterfront. I honestly thought I'd be able to keep it.'

She remembered the day he was referring to; the two of them looking out over Black Reed Bay, him dropping his revelation that he was quitting the force but that he'd ensure she was given command of the bureau before he left.

It was a promise he could never have kept, and she'd known it at the time – even if he hadn't.

'Forget about it.' She stuffed a chip in her mouth and crunched it, seeing real disappointment in his face. 'C'mon.'

He looked away, tongue bulging his cheek, then seemed to let it go. 'So. You think about my offer any?'

She scooped up another chip. 'Working for you? What do I know about being a sleazy PI?'

'You're being disingenuous.'

'What, you're saying I *do* know sleazy?' She raised one eyebrow in fake indignation.

'I'm saying you know that's not how it is anymore. Most everything I do is corporate work – intel, security, risk analysis. It's not glamorous, but it takes all the qualities you bring to the job – persistence, dedication, attention to detail.'

From anyone else it could've sounded like faint praise, but hearing the words come from Robbie McTeague had her floating up to the ceiling. She reached for another chip, trying to appear casual, but feeling her face flush with pride. But as she brought the chip to her mouth, the bubble that was carrying her skyward burst, as she realised she'd overlooked the obvious.

'Hey, hold on, when did you hear about them bringing in Dunmore?' She didn't wait for him to answer, snatching up her phone and scrolling back through his messages; the first one asking her to consider working for him had arrived a week earlier. 'You knew a week ago, right? Is that why you offered me the job?'

'How would I hear about it a week before it happened?'

'Right. Like cops don't talk...'

'I'm not a cop.'

'You know what I mean,' Casey said. 'You're still plugged in to everything.'

'They hated me when I *had* a badge – you think my phone's ringing off the hook now with people wanting to shoot the shit? I'm radioactive.'

Casey planted her hands on the counter. 'I am not a charity case, okay? You don't owe me anything.'

He stared at her, the same stony gaze that used to make even the most weathered beat cops straighten their backs. 'That's not what this is. The offer's a genuine one. I need someone good, someone who I can trust. You're a damn good investigator, that's the only reason I asked you.'

She held his gaze, trying to decide if he was soaping her or not. But the thick eyebrows and moustache gave him this unimpeachable look, as if every word he uttered came down from Mount Sinai on stone tablets.

'Look, you don't have to give me a yes or no now,' he said. 'I just wanted to know if you're considering it or not, because, if not, I need to cast my net wider. And I thought, with the taskforce announcement and everything, now was a good time.'

'"And everything" is doing a lot of heavy lifting right there. Why don't you just wait for them to can me then?'

He screwed his face up. 'Christ, you're hard work when you want to be. Unless you've been sticking up banks since I quit, they're not about to fire you. But by the time they gut the department and put the pen-pushers in charge, it's going to be impossible to do the job properly. Maybe something opens up for you, sure, but the workload will be crushing – ten times worse than it is now. You'll be doing your job and a lieutenant's, for people who don't care about real police work. Is that really what you want to stick around to be a part of?'

She stared at him, thinking about Dunmore's offer to support her transferring elsewhere; after their first day together, it definitely felt more like a shove than a helping hand. 'Look, I'm sorry I didn't get a chance to message you back. We caught the double shooting this morning, and you know how a day like that goes. I have to focus on that, for the time being at least, but then I'll give it some serious thought. Promise.'

He put his hands in his pockets and nodded. 'Wray, I'm not selling you rainbows and candy bars here. PI work is all the crappy parts of being a cop and none of the glory. But the money's better, the hours can be better, and there's way less chance of getting shot.'

She waited for his words to settle before she spoke again, smiling. 'You had a week to work on it and that's the best pitch you could come up with?'

He tapped the counter with his knuckles and went to move off. 'Just let me know as soon as you can. Please?'

She held her hand up to stop him. 'Hey, wait, before you go – you know anything about Helen Dunmore?'

He paused a second before shaking his head. 'The name, but not personally. She came out of NYPD, right? Got a reputation as a straight shooter.'

'"A reputation"? You hear that from all the people that don't talk to you?'

He shrugged, the hint of a smile on his face. 'I'm a sleazy PI, right? I make a living out of knowing shit I'm not supposed to know.'

※

Casey held up one arm to wave McTeague off as he pulled away. Across the street, there were lights in the window of the bungalow opposite hers, a young couple that'd moved in a month or so back. Casey didn't even know their names yet; most days she didn't get home before ten pm, not a time she could knock on someone's door and introduce herself.

There was no one on the sidewalks, no sounds around the block, and in the nighttime air, the glow from over the way felt isolating. Most of the neighbours kept their distance from her, the cop aura driving people away – at least until there was a break-in or a suspected prowler, then everyone wanted a piece of her. It was part of the weird duality of being police – someone you trust to catch a burglar, but not enough to invite to your barbecue. As if Casey was going to break out cuffs in the backyard because some dude sparked a joint after finishing his burger.

Most cops had it the same, and it was just another reason why they preferred to spend their downtime with other cops, in cop bars, trading cop stories. But standing there alone in the stillness, it felt like the bill for all those years of hanging with Ray and Dave Cullen had come due.

The sound of her cell phone ringing drew her back inside. Coming back into the kitchen, she looked at the number and grabbed the cell up off the counter, recognising it this time – the stranger trying to set up the meet with her. 'Yeah, this is Casey.'

Silence came back at her.

'Hello?'

Still nothing. She checked the call was connected and pressed her phone to her ear again. 'Hey, look, what is this? You wanna talk to me or don't you?'

There was a gentle intake of breath. Then a beeping sound. Gone.

'Fuck's sake.' She put the phone on the counter again, but just as she went to put the sodas in the trash, it vibrated. A text message:

It's late to be outside all alone. Take care.

It felt like a belt was tightened round her chest.

She ran to the window, dialling him back. She pulled the drape aside and peered out, but there was no one in sight, no one looking on from a car or anywhere else she could see. And no one was answering the phone.

She clipped her sidearm to her belt and jogged outside, walking to the end of her drive. The light across the street had gone out, the whole neighbourhood locked down for the night, content in a sense of safety she'd long since lost.

She stood there and looked both ways along the block, hearing whispers in the shadows.

CHAPTER TEN

She must've fallen asleep with her phone in her hand because when it went off at 3.47am, it was lying on the pillow next to her face and the vibration felt like an act of violence.

Casey snatched it up and answered on autopilot, the words coming from a mouth that felt as if it was stuffed with cotton wool. 'What?'

'Sergeant Wray, it's Grainger in Dispatch.'

She opened her eyes, 'Dispatch' bolting her awake. Not the caller she'd assumed. 'Shit, sorry. What is it?'

'We took a shots-fired call – Patrol are responding and they're treating it as a suspected homicide.'

'Okay,' she said, flipping her legs out of the bed, groping for the light. 'Okay. What's the address?'

'Twelfth and Topeka. Lone female victim, Caucasian, still confirming an ID. Gunshot wounds to the head and chest.'

'Twelfth and Topeka?' Her brain was already slipping into gear, planning a route and a journey time, factoring in how long it'd take her to throw on some clothes. 'I'll be there in fifteen minutes.'

There were three units waiting for her at the scene, parked fender to fender outside a narrow clapboard house set back from the street at the end of a short gravel driveway. A wide section of the sidewalk had been cordoned off with tape, holding back neighbours and onlookers, who were mismatched in overcoats, pyjama bottoms and slippers. A faint smell of fried garlic came from somewhere, last night's cooking still lingering in the air.

A uniform was doing his best to manage the scene. Casey badged him and ducked under the tape, making for the house. There was no victim in sight, the front door closed. A nineties-model Jeep Cherokee, banana yellow, was parked at the end of the driveway to the right of the property, and it was only as she came closer that she saw activity beyond it, a group of techs clustered around an open doorway to the side of the house.

Helen Dunmore was in the middle of the group.

Then Casey saw the body, slumped in a semi-upright position against the side of the doorway like a discarded rag doll. A white woman, late twenties or early thirties at a guess. A visible gunshot wound to her face, blood running down onto her faded Guns N' Roses T-shirt. Her chin was pressed into her chest, her torso listing slightly to the right on account of the doorframe propping up her left shoulder, her legs splayed in front of her. Casey was still taking it in when she felt Dunmore's gaze fall upon her.

'Lieutenant – I got the call and came right over. What've we got?'

Dunmore nodded to the tech she'd been talking to and circled around to stand next to Casey on the grass. 'Three shootings in twenty-four hours; I don't even officially start until Monday.' She was staring absently at the body. 'Welcome to Rockport.'

'It's not usually like this,' Casey said, quietly.

Dunmore glanced sidelong at her, as if she wasn't sure how to take the comment, Casey again left worrying she should've kept her mouth shut. 'Neighbours have just ID'd her as Lauren Goff.'

Casey looked around reflexively at the mention of neighbours. The properties were staggered at different distances from the sidewalk and from each other, trees dotted around haphazardly between them, giving the street a ramshackle feel. The side door where Goff lay was overlooked only by a second-storey window in the flank of the adjacent property, a light showing through the glass.

'No confirmation on her age. We've got a number for a sister, no luck raising her yet. The house is a rental; she's lived here for approximately eight months. By herself.'

Casey motioned to the lit window behind and above them. 'Anyone see the shooter?'

'That room's used as a nursery. The gunshots woke the parents up – Mr and Mrs Suter – but whoever pulled the trigger was gone by the time they looked out. They saw our vic and called it in. They said they made the call a minute or two after they heard the shots – that was at 3.13am.'

'A boyfriend?' Casey said. 'Or a booty call, maybe – given the time of night?'

'My first thought too. The Suters said they didn't know her well enough to say whether she had a boyfriend or not, but they've never noticed regular late-night visitors. The neighbours on the other side don't appear to be home – one of these guys on the street said they're upstate on vacation.'

'From her clothes, looks like she was in bed,' Casey said, 'so either someone was already in the house with her, or someone she knew came to the door. Can't imagine she'd open up for a stranger, this time of night.'

'Yeah, looks likely she was targeted. No signs of a robbery inside.'

'What about all these guys?' Casey said, scanning the onlookers behind the crime-scene tape. 'Anyone see anything?'

Dunmore was already shaking her head, resigned. 'Everyone was asleep. Five or six of them said they heard the gunshots and it woke them up, but none of them got to the windows in time to see anyone. That's what they're saying, anyway.' Dunmore pointed towards the back of the house, a dirt trail leading off into the darkness. 'You can cut between the properties that way and the trail takes you out to the next street, or there's another track branches off east that leads to the cross street at the end of the block.'

'Easy to disappear before anyone could get a look.'

'Gives us plenty of folks to canvas, I guess,' Dunmore said, pursing her lips as she looked around, a dozen or more residences within a small radius of where they stood.

The far side of the street was a wall of mismatched backyard fences, assorted heights and colours, with a shingle-covered outbuilding directly opposite Goff's house – the neighbourhood was apparently thrown together so that each row of houses backed onto the next, instead of facing each other. 'Appreciate you coming down here, Lieutenant,' Casey said, scanning the houses and seeing lit windows in most all of them. 'I'm used to taking the middle-of-the-night calls, you don't need to trouble yourself.' She glanced at Dunmore out of the corner of her eye, then focused on the victim again. 'If you don't want to, I mean.'

Dunmore looked over. 'Thank you, Sergeant. I guess they tried us both. It's not really my style to pass it on.'

Casey slipped her phone out of her pocket and checked her call log, seeing a missed call from Dispatch right before the one that had awoken her. She felt about four inches tall, keeping her head turned away so Dunmore wouldn't see her embarrassment. Then she realised she was talking again and she'd tuned out.

'...so we're most likely looking for someone known to the victim. Obviously we need to canvas the block, but I'd assume it'll be family or friends that shed light on this one. I'll need you to go ahead and wake up the troops. I'd like all hands on deck.'

'Sure, of course...'

As Casey was speaking, a car came speeding down the block and braked hard next to the police line, stopping in the middle of the street. A woman threw the driver's door open and ran towards the closest uniform, stabbing the air with her finger. 'YOU FUCKING DID THIS. SHE TOLD YOU AND YOU WOULDN'T FUCKING LISTEN.' It looked like she was going to slam into the officer, but then she swooped past him and ducked under the tape, running towards the body, the uniform chasing after her.

'Shit.' Dunmore held her arms wide and darted to intercept, but the woman blew right by her and fell to her knees, just short of the vic.

'LORI ... Oh, Jesus, Lori...' She reached out, her fingers grasping in the air by Goff's hand, as if she wanted to touch her but couldn't bring herself to bridge a gap that was only inches wide. An alarmed tech moved over to try and stop her, but the woman tipped forward until her forehead was on the grass, sobbing silently, as if dragged down by the weight of her pain.

Casey signalled for everyone to back off and came around to kneel by the woman's side. She laid a hand gently on her shoulder. 'Ma'am...'

The woman reared up again, throwing her arm out to shake Casey off. 'Get your fucking hands off me.' Her face was a mask of rage and hatred. 'Don't touch me. You did this!'

Casey held her hands up to show she was doing as the woman asked. 'I won't touch you again. I promise. Is this woman related to you?'

She pulled up a fistful of grass and threw it at Casey, then pounded the dirt. 'She's my sister. She's my sister and you fucking let her die...'

'I'm so sorry, ma'am. I'm so sorry for your loss.'

'Don't fucking tell me you're sorry. Every one of you deserved to die before her.'

Casey sensed the uniforms behind her, already spooked, reaching for their sidearms at hearing the words, and she patted down the air behind her back to signal them to stay calm. 'Do you know who did this, ma'am?'

'*He* did. And you fucking let him.'

'Who?'

'Adam, her ex. The piece of shit. You need to find him and you need to put a bullet in his fucking head. You owe her that.' She lunged at Casey, slapping her on the arm. 'You owe her.' She tried to slap her again, in the face, but Casey pulled back out of reach just in time. Two uniforms grabbed the woman to restrain her, a third calling out a warning not to resist.

'Go easy,' Casey said, getting to her feet. 'Go easy on her.'

Dunmore was at her shoulder. 'You okay?'

'Fine. I'm fine.' She ran her sleeve over her face, trying to catch her breath.

'It's all happening tonight,' one of the techs behind them said, drawing a hard look from Dunmore.

The victim's sister was face down on the grass, bucking and kicking her legs, but the uniforms had her pinned. They cuffed her hands and brought her to her feet to haul over to one of the cars. The crowd of onlookers had grown with the new commotion.

'Once she's calmed down, let's get an ID on this ex,' Dunmore said.

Casey nodded. 'I'll talk to her.'

She followed the uniforms as they led the woman across the grass. One of them guided the woman into the backseat of his cruiser, and Casey took the opportunity to pull the other one aside. 'Do me a favour and get her some water and a blanket, please? And let me have the keys to the cuffs. She's having the worst night of her life. We don't need to make it any worse.'

'You sure about that, Detective? She went for your face.'

'I'll deal with her, it's fine.' She took the proffered keys and went over to the car.

The woman was bawling with her forehead pressed against the metal grille that sectioned off the back seats. Casey opened the door and reached inside to unlock the cuffs, the woman turning her head to look at her when she realised what was happening.

'They're gonna fetch you some water,' Casey said. 'Just sit there and take a minute.'

The woman's head was at ninety degrees, still pitched forward, tears streaming sideways across the bridge of her nose and into her hair.

'What's your name, ma'am?' Casey said.

She didn't answer at first, and Casey said nothing, refusing to meet her glare so as not to inflame her any further.

'I know you,' the woman said at last. 'That cop. You found the missing girl.'

Tina Grace: the case that would forever define her. Casey's HCPD headshot had been all over the news for twenty-four hours in the aftermath of Tina's safe return, a good-news story quickly engulfed by the emerging corruption revelations. But it still made headlines from time to time; a week ago, the *Courier* had run an interview with the Grace family, Casey's picture appearing next to theirs under a splash that was headlined, 'Back from the Dead'.

'Right now I'm only interested in helping you and your sister. What's your name?'

The woman's gaze went out of focus, brown eyes staring through Casey. 'Molly.'

The uniform handed Casey a blanket and a bottle of water,

which she passed to Molly – but she tossed both onto the seat next to her.

'Adam Ryker,' she said, sitting upright with renewed fire. '443 Van Buren Drive – that's where he used to live anyway, I don't know if he's still there.'

Casey scrambled for her notebook, caught off guard. 'He's her ex-boyfriend?'

'Yeah. He told her he'd do this. He said he'd kill her if she ever left him. That's the only reason she put up with his shit for so long.'

'This man was abusive towards your sister?'

'Why don't you fucking tell me? He never hit her – that's why you guys didn't believe her.'

'So you're saying she called the police on him?'

'Yeah, a thousand times. But he could talk the fucking devil into heaven, so you assholes swallowed his horseshit every time.' She pointed to a cluster of onlookers. 'Ask them – they all heard the fights. They called 911 too and you didn't believe them either.'

Casey glanced behind herself and realised Dunmore was a few feet away, listening in. She turned back to Molly and continued scribbling. 'How long ago did the relationship end, ma'am?'

'It didn't. Lori told me she broke it off a dozen times, but I knew she was still seeing him. He made her lie about it – to me, to her friends. He knew everyone was warning her, telling her to get out of it, so he made her lie.'

'Did you ever hear him threaten to harm her yourself?'

'Don't say "harm" like it's a fucking bruise.' She slapped the seat next to her. 'He killed her. Say the goddamn word.'

'I'm sorry—'

'You're still fucking protecting him.'

'No, I didn't ... I didn't mean it that way.'

Molly took her phone from her pocket and started scrolling, wiping her eyes on the back of her wrist. On finding whatever it was she was looking for, she held it out for Casey to take. 'He'd never say it in front of people, he kept his Mr Clean bullshit going. But these are his texts. She used to send me screenshots because she knew he'd go through her cell and delete them later on when he'd calmed down.'

Casey looked at the phone, apparently a screenshot of a text thread between Adam and Lauren, in which Lauren stated that she didn't want him to come over anymore and that he should stay away from her; his reply: *Coming there now, you let me in and you hear me out. Stupid bitch, don't make me fuck you up for real this time.*

'Swipe, there's plenty more,' Molly said. 'Look at them. What else do you need?'

Casey skimmed a few more of the screenshots and then held the phone over to Dunmore so she could see them too, a string of exchanges on different dates, all containing similar threats against Lauren.

Dunmore's mouth was a thin line as her eyes moved over the words. She passed Molly her cell back and tipped her head to signal Casey should follow her, before walking a few paces along the sidewalk. She came to a stop a short distance away, where Molly was out of earshot.

'I just got a call back,' Dunmore said. 'Adam Ryker's name is in the system. Patrol have been out here three times in six months – "Parties spoken to, no further action taken".'

'Fuck's sake,' Casey said, turning her head to the sky. 'The sister said he's got a silver tongue.'

'Lauren Goff's not the only one either, his name crops up in conjunction with two other women.'

'Shit. We need to check on them, both of them.'

Dunmore nodded. 'I'll have Patrol send units now. We've got Ryker's address on file, I'm going to go over there now.'

'I'll come with you.'

Dunmore met Casey's eyes for a second, then looked over at Molly, sitting half in and half out of the cruiser, elbows on her knees and head in her hands. 'You should stay here and deal with the sister.'

'The uniforms can take her back to the precinct, if she'll go. Victim Services can look after her in the morning. Until then the best place for her is somewhere we can keep an eye on her.'

Dunmore looked down as she fished in her pocket for something, her reticence obvious.

'You can't go over there alone, Lieutenant.'

Dunmore produced her car keys, looked at Casey again, then nodded. 'Let's see what this asshole's got to say.'

CHAPTER ELEVEN

Streetlights above strobed the car as they drove, the first murky strains of dawn beginning to tell in the lightening sky on the horizon to the east.

The address was in the northwest corner of Rockport, a part of town bounded by the 110, running northwest to southeast, and the east-west expressway, which converged just outside of downtown. To locals, the area was known as The Slice –

supposedly because it looked, on the map, like a slice of pizza, but the nickname was also a nod to the crime rates, which ran consistently higher than anywhere else in Rockport. Residents talked of the area being cut off from the rest of town; whether that was a good or a bad thing depended on who you talked to – and some days sentiment seemed to change with the direction of the wind – but the feeling had only increased in recent years since tent cities had sprung up beneath the freeway overpasses, acting almost like borders.

The drive was a short sprint that took them under the expressway and past the cluster of budget hotels that huddled around the intersection with the 110 parkway, red-and-blue logos standing vivid against a backdrop of dark concrete. Casey made wakeup calls to Dana, Billy and Jill, hitting them with the news that there'd been another homicide and that any plans they hadn't already cancelled for the next few days would now need to go. She stole glances at Dunmore as she talked, the lieutenant's face set in a grave expression that gave little indication as to what was going on behind it. Casey wondered if the comment about being landed with three murders before she'd even started was telling; if Dunmore was already feeling out of her depth.

Casey looked down at her cell phone, the call from the night before still lodged at the back of her head. With time to think, she realised she'd still not been able to explain to the guy why she'd no-showed his meeting – but surely all he had to do was turn on a TV set to know why. If this was a reaction to her standing him up, it only confirmed that the guy was a nutcase. But there were two grades of nutcase: the type who stayed behind a phone or keyboard, and the type who showed up at your house. If he really was watching her, that was a whole other level of seriousness.

They turned onto Van Buren, 443 coming into view. Adam Ryker's property was a small bungalow set across the street from a deli and a beauty salon. The garage fronted directly onto the sidewalk, the rest of the house tucked behind it and the main door somewhere out of sight. A low-rise chain-link fence ran either side of the property, disappearing in the gloom beneath a line of trees at the far end of the backyard.

Dunmore drove by and parked a short way along the street. She killed the engine and looked back at the house, her gaze lingering on Casey a split second as she turned. 'Are you ready for it if he runs?'

Casey recognised the look right away, the one that told her Dunmore had heard all the rumours about Cullen's death and wasn't sure if she could trust Casey to have her back.

'I'm ready.' She opened her door and climbed out.

Dunmore took the lead, and Casey followed a half-yard behind her on the sidewalk, worried that any misstep, any sign of nerves, would only reinforce the lieutenant's preconceptions. Better to go unseen than to make things worse, the injustice of it as exhausting as having to second-guess herself all the time.

The property was arranged in an L-shape, a narrow gravel path taking them along the side of the garage block, which made up the long part of the L. There was a large window in the wall in front of them, white shutters pinned back on either side, a blue plastic bucket underneath it containing a pile of rags. They skirted the perimeter until they came to the side of the house, finding the front door facing the fence line. The door was ajar, the darkness beyond it almost total.

Dunmore rapped on the doorframe. 'HCPD, we're looking for Adam Ryker.' She waited a second, the soundwaves seeming to reverberate in the quiet even after she stopped knocking. The cloying smell of stale weed carried in the air.

'Come on out, Mr Ryker. This is HCPD, we have some questions for you.'

No response.

Dunmore peered around the corner of the house into the backyard while Casey watched for movement inside. She shone her torch along the doorframe and the lock, but couldn't see any signs of forced entry. The place had a bad energy to it, a silent vibration in the air like a tuning fork still shimmering long after being struck.

'Can't see anything back there,' Dunmore said, facing the entranceway again. She rapped on the door this time, pushing it open a little wider. 'Mr Ryker? This is HCPD.'

It opened wide enough to see a small table had been toppled in the hallway and was lying on its side on the floor. A pot that'd been holding a spider plant was smashed into pieces, the plant and a heap of dirt dashed across the floor.

'Feels like that's enough for cause,' Dunmore said. 'Let's go.' She stepped through the doorway and called out for Ryker again. 'HCPD, Mr Ryker, we're entering the property out of a concern for your wellbeing. If you're here, come out now.'

Casey drew her sidearm and followed her into a short hallway. There was a bedroom immediately to the right, the bedclothes bundled in a heap on the floor, the room sparse but otherwise tidy. The bedside table held a half-full glass of water, along with a copy of Jordan Peterson's book *12 Rules For Life*. There were no pictures or other personal touches on the walls, but a large collection of colognes and moisturisers stood atop a cabinet opposite the foot of the bed, the lingering notes of sandalwood and citrus mingling with the persistent smell of weed. Casey stood still, listening for any sounds from inside the property.

Dunmore started to move on down the hallway. A second door on the same side as the bedroom opened into a small bathroom, a single toothbrush standing upright in a cup on the basin, a towel and flannel neatly folded on a silver rail next to the shower cubicle.

She ducked out of the bathroom and continued to the end of the hallway, Casey moving slowly behind her by torchlight. On the left was a closed door that had to lead through to the garage, and on the right the hallway opened out onto a kitchen diner, dimly lit by moonlight. The kitchenette was in keeping with the rest of the place, a single plate standing on the drying rack next to the sink, a radio on the windowsill behind it, nothing else on display, save for one decorative anomaly: an array of figurines standing in a line along the ledge. Coming closer, Casey saw they were *Pokémon* toys.

A two-seater sofa faced the TV in one corner, two remotes placed next to each other on the armrest, and a light-blue blanket was neatly folded and slung over the back. A workstation had been set up in the other corner, an oversized office chair tucked under a desk that held two large monitors, a mouse and an assortment of pens. An array of cables snaked across the desktop, all hanging loose, as if they'd been connected to a laptop.

Dunmore shot Casey a look of frustration just as Casey's gaze went to a door in the hallway that had to lead to the garage. She jutted her chin.

Dunmore saw it and nodded. Casey went over. Dunmore stepped to the side and took the handle, ready to throw it open.

A mechanical grinding sound came from behind the door.

Casey jumped to the side, the noise droning for a second or two before stopping just as suddenly. Dunmore pulled her weapon. 'Adam Ryker this is HCPD. Show yourself.'

Casey's stomach bubbled, as if it was filled with tar. Neither of them moved, guns trained on the doorway.

Dunmore looked over at Casey, sinews in her neck showing. 'Ryker, we're entering the garage. Kneel down on the ground with your hands behind your head.'

She made a silent three count then nodded and Casey threw the door open.

No movement. Peering inside, the interior was dark, the dim light from the streetlamp outside just creeping under the shutter at the far end. Dunmore signalled to hold.

Casey strained her eyes against the darkness, looking for any sign of movement. Then the sound came again and stopped, followed by a beeping noise that Casey recognised.

She reached inside to flick the switch on the wall, the naked bulb overhead throwing the space into caustic relief. At the far end, a dryer was beeping and flashing to signal it had reached the end of its cycle.

Dunmore saw it and let out a short exhale, shaking her head with her tongue in the corner of her mouth.

There was no car, no sign of Ryker. Two bicycles were suspended from hooks on the wall to their left, one a mountain bike and the other a racing model, and in front of them was a line of crates holding tennis rackets and balls, two basketballs and a football, and what looked like an array of climbing equipment. The centre of the room was taken up by a weight bench, a stack of dumbbells and kettlebells lined up alongside it, with resistance bands hanging from one of its arms. Against the opposite wall, a metal shelving unit stood floor to ceiling; on display was a tool box, various paint cans, cleaning sprays, rags and other household junk, but the contents of the lower two shelves were hidden under heavy blankets. Dunmore read the alarm in Casey's expression and followed her eyeline. When she saw it too, she glanced back at Casey, uncertainty in her face.

Casey went over and dropped slowly to a crouch, taking one corner of the blanket between her fingers. She peeled it back gently, revealing the corner of a plastic packing crate. She pulled it back a little more, just far enough so that she could make out the crate's contents: dozens of neatly stacked toy figures, all in their original packaging. She pulled the blanket back further again and saw another three boxes holding more of the same – *Star Wars*, Transformers, G.I. Joe, one box for each.

'Obsessive,' Dunmore said, looking on.

Casey put the blanket back as it had been, then lifted the one covering the shelf above. More of the same. She let out a breath slowly before standing up again.

'We missed him,' Dunmore said.

Before Casey could concur, Dunmore picked her way to the far end of the garage, her shoes scraping on the bare concrete. She opened the dryer and looked inside, scooping up a handful of T-shirts to show Casey what was in there. She dropped them back inside and went as far as the shutter, then turned and looked around again, as if the change in perspective might reveal something. The unforgiving light highlighted her sharp cheekbones, the rest of her face in shadow.

'I've got a feeling this guy's not through yet,' Casey said.

Dunmore nodded and carried on scanning. But seeing nothing obviously out of place, she retraced her steps, glancing around as she went, then continued on out to the hallway. She waited for Casey to follow, then closed the door behind her. 'Wake up your friendliest judge. Let's get a warrant and pull this place apart.'

CHAPTER TWELVE

Casey made calls while they waited for Patrol to arrive, then Dunmore drove them back to the department with the dawn creeping across the sky.

'How long were you at the NYPD, Lieutenant?' Casey said as they passed under the expressway.

'Thirteen years. Felt like longer.'

Casey smiled at the joke, looking over. 'Which division?'

'I spent most of my time at the Sixth Precinct Bureau – came up out of Patrol there. At the end I was with Central Robbery – they had me working the Joint Robbery Task Force with the ATF and the FBI.'

'I know that tone – too many Feds in your life. Is that why you left?'

Dunmore shook her head. 'It was a lot of meetings and paperwork, but I actually liked it fine. All the federal agencies were good to work with, and it was great experience. Opened my eyes to some new ways of working.'

Casey scratched her neck. 'So, then, if you don't mind me asking, why'd you take this job?' Usually it was the salary bump that lured NYPD vets over to HCPD, but with all the negative press the department had endured in recent months, it felt to Casey like there had to be more to it.

'Well...' Dunmore hit the blinker to make a turn. 'It's a long story. I put my trust in the wrong people.'

Casey waited, sensing she wanted to say more, but instead the silence stretched. After a few seconds, with the conversation apparently over, she took out her cell to Google Adam Ryker, looking for his social-media feeds – but just as she did, Dunmore said, 'Why do they call you "Big"?'

Casey brought her cell down, deciding how to tell it. She used to hate explaining the nickname because it had been intended to keep her down. In recent years, under Ray, she'd outgrown its origins, to the point that it felt less like an insult and more like a badge of pride. But the last two months had thrown all of that into reverse. 'It's short for "Big Case" Wray. It's what the old hands called me when I was starting out in the bureau. It was a rib, because they only ever let me work the small-time stuff; they told me I wasn't up to working any real crimes.'

Dunmore looked over, frowning. 'Because you're a woman?'

'Maybe.' Casey shrugged, opening her hands. 'Maybe just because I was new and young and...' She was about to say 'stupid', but something stopped her from putting herself down in front of Dunmore – as if any weakness might be filed away for use against her later. 'Anyway, it just stuck after that. I used to hate it, but now ... I guess it lost its meaning over time.' The last part didn't sound so convincing anymore.

Dunmore watched the road, not saying anything at first. Then: 'They called me all kinds of things when I started out. "Dumb Whore" was the worst, but there were plenty more. They never said that one to my face, but of course it got back to me. My sergeant at the time just laughed when I went to him about it.'

'How did you win them round?'

They came to a red light, and Dunmore looked over. 'I never tried. Why would I? Who wants the respect of assholes like that?'

Casey smiled as if she was going along with the joke, but Dunmore's eyes were hard, the sentiment sincere. Then the light changed and she looked forward again silently.

Casey stared through the windshield at the murky sky, the console between them feeling as wide as an ocean.

❧

Dana and Jill were already at their desks when Casey arrived back at the office, the pair at different stages of logging into their computers.

'Billy didn't make it yet?' Casey said.

She was looking at Dana, but it was Jill who answered. 'He's on his way – he's right behind us.'

A look passed between the two women, but Casey couldn't decipher it. 'What is it?'

'Nothing,' Jill said, eyes flicking to Dana again. 'He called. He said he'll be right here.'

'Okay,' Casey said, certain now that she'd have to make time soon to iron out the friction between Billy and Dana. 'We'll get started and you can catch him up.'

She walked them through the shooting of Lauren Goff and brought them up to speed on everything they knew about Adam Ryker. 'The lieutenant's asked Patrol to station cars outside the properties of the other two women he's linked with in the system, but I want to speak to them urgently to see if they can give us a line on this guy's whereabouts. Jill, can you get me the reports he's cited in, along with the names and addresses, please, then see if there's any family or known associates listed for Ryker? I've sent you links to his socials – grab a picture of him we can use too, please.'

Jill nodded, scribbling a list on her pad.

'Dana, I need you to run point on yesterday's shootings. Start with any updates that came in overnight from the lab or the Crime Scene guys will you?'

'Sure thing, Big.'

'When Billy gets here, I need him to set up the alerts for Ryker – get his name and face up on the website and Twitter, and make sure the media have it too: "HCPD urgently seeking to speak to him in connection with ... blah blah blah." Then I need him on background on Ryker – get whatever we can from his Facebook, his Insta, all of it, and see if they give us any clue to where he might be at. Lauren Goff's sister is in the building. I'm gonna go check on her now. Thanks, you guys – let's go.'

Casey found Molly Goff in an interview room two floors down, being kept company by a friend she'd called. The two were sat on a low couch when Casey opened the door, Molly talking on her cell phone. Casey caught a fragment of the call.

'...well you find his ass, and you take care of it—' Molly stopped and looked up when she saw Casey. 'I'll call you later.'

Casey closed the door gently, taking her time while she decided what to say. A look passed between the two women, and the second one got to her feet. 'I need to go use the bathroom.'

'You don't have to leave on my account, ma'am,' Casey said, looking at her and then at Molly.

'It's okay, Tish,' Molly said, nodding, and her friend slipped out of the door.

'You didn't find him,' Molly said, when they were alone. She'd got up and was standing in the middle of the small room, one arm across her chest, gripping her shoulder.

'Ma'am, I can't imagine how you're feeling right now, and how badly you want to see someone held to account for Lauren. Your help is going to be invaluable, so it's really important we're working together on this. Do you understand what I mean?'

'What's it matter who finds him, long as he's found?'

'It doesn't, so long as it goes the right way. And that means any information you have as to Adam Ryker's whereabouts has to come to us.'

'You didn't do shit to help my sister when she was alive.'

Casey dipped her chin to her chest, searching for something to say that wouldn't juice her even further. But before she could settle on anything, Molly spoke again.

'Shit, I shouldn't be laying that on you. You tried for that other girl, at least.'

Casey moved to the table at the side of the room, poured two cups of water and handed one to Molly. 'Did you ask someone to go by Adam Ryker's house?'

Molly stared at her without answering.

Casey held her gaze, refusing to shy away from it. 'Because the only thing that could make tonight any worse for you is if somebody does something in haste that they can't take back. I don't want anyone to end up catching a charge that they don't need to.'

'He wasn't home. I'm guessing you know that already, so what's it matter anyway?'

Casey thought about the door being ajar and the toppled spider plant they'd seen in the hallway. 'Did someone enter his property?'

Molly shook her head with a dead stare.

'Do you know where he is now?'

'No.'

Casey tipped her eyes to the cell phone in Molly's hand. 'Could you maybe give me some places you might be thinking of trying?'

Molly tossed her cell onto the couch and paced across the room to press her hands against the wall. 'I don't know any. That's the goddamn problem, isn't it?'

'Who were you talking to just now?'

'My cousin. He's helping.'

There was a silence that dragged for a moment, as if neither woman knew what to say next, the contours of the exchange still being established. Then Molly pushed herself off the wall and turned around. 'Detective, if I knew where that piece of shit was, I'd shout it from the rooftops. I don't care what happens to him, or me, or anyone else.' She held her arms out. 'What the hell have I got to lose anymore?'

'It won't always feel that way,' Casey said, softly.

Molly stepped closer. 'Look, Lori and me had so many fights about that asshole, in the end I told her I didn't want to hear about it no more. Not the breaking up, not the making up, not whether they were on or off or some other place. So that was it, we didn't speak about him – that was the only way we could get along. But that means I don't have the first clue where he would take off to. Lori told me once his dad lived in Florida someplace and his mom was off in California, but he only ever moved his lips to tell lies, so who knows if any of that was true. He told her he was an only child, but that makes me think he's probably got ten brothers and ten sisters.'

'Do you have a contact number for his mom or dad? Or an address?'

She shook her head.

'What about their names?'

She shook her head again. 'Nothing. I told you, he used to check her phone, he saw all the messages I used to send to her ... Wait, did I tell you he made her sync her account to his iPad and his watch so he could see everything she was doing?'

Casey felt a tingle of panic in her throat at the idea of someone being able to snoop through her phone at will. 'You didn't.'

'Uh-huh. So he knew damn well what I thought of him and that's why he wouldn't talk to me and why he tried to stop us from talking. Lori would never agree to cut me off completely, the way he wanted, but things were never the same way between us after she got with him.'

Casey tipped her eyes at the cell on the couch again. 'Where's your cousin headed now, Molly?'

'I don't know.' She stared at Casey, every tendon in her face straining. 'Swear to god.' She perched on the edge of a chair and pressed the heels of her hands into her eyes, grinding them. 'He's just calling people and driving around, I think. He doesn't even know Adam, he's just...' She trailed off and looked up, her eyes red raw where she'd been rubbing. 'I just want someone to do something. That's all I want. Why can't someone do something, for Christ's sake?'

Casey crouched down in front of her. 'I understand. I do understand. And I promise you, we are.'

Molly took in a deep breath and slumped back in her seat, her eyes searching the ceiling for answers. Casey recognised the look of bewilderment, the freezing-water shock that came with the violent death of a loved one beginning to give way to something deeper and even more punishing.

'Mom's gonna be here in an hour. What the hell am I even supposed to say to her? I don't have the words, I don't ... What do I say?' She held her hands up, then let them fall to her thighs with a slap. 'What do I say?'

'We have specialist officers who can help support you and your family—'

'Lori and me shared a bedroom for fourteen years – there wasn't one single thing we didn't know about each other. Not one. You know what that does to you, fourteen years? It's like you're living two lives at the same time, mine and hers. Every time one of us cried, every time we smiled, every goddamn ... Whatever she felt, I felt, whether I wanted it or not. You understand? Same for her – you couldn't help it. I wanted to kill her myself half the time. God knows we tried.' That brought an incredulous laugh to her lips, as if she'd shocked herself in saying it. 'All she wanted ... Since we were, like, eight, all she talked about was this one dream. She wanted four kids, two boys and two girls, and she wanted a house near some water. She used to say she didn't care what water, and it didn't have to be right there in front of her – she just wanted to be able to see it when she looked out the window, even if it was far off somewhere. I told her the only water she was gonna see was puddles.' She shook her head, another hollow laugh. 'I was such a bitch.'

'You can't beat yourself up.'

'I ain't even started yet.'

'We're going to find Adam Ryker, and if he's responsible—'

'If? Why the hell are you saying "if"?'

'Because we don't know until we can prove it. But *if* he's responsible, we'll do everything we can to see him held accountable. And you can help us with that, Molly, but not by sending your cousin out on a vigilante trip.'

'But I have to have something to tell my mom. What am I gonna say – her daughter got killed and I sat around and did nothing about it?'

'She'll understand that it's our job to find him.'

Molly hung her head. 'Then what do you want from me?'

'Anything you've got that can help us find Adam Ryker. His friends' names, anyone who can put us in touch with his parents or his family, his place of work – anything you can think of.'

'But it's like I said, I don't know any of that stuff. I didn't like him and he didn't like me – it's not like we sat around shooting the shit over a beer.'

'Then tell me about their relationship. Can you send me the screenshots you showed me earlier?'

'Yeah...' Molly sat forward at that. 'What about the passcode for Lori's cell – you want that too?'

Casey forced down a little smile at finally catching a break. 'Absolutely.'

'You want a coffee?' Casey said to Dana, sweeping back into the office. 'Because I sure as hell do.'

'Thanks. Jilly's on it already.'

She went to the breakout room and found Jill making a fresh batch. 'You are an angel, Jilly.' She added an extra cup to the ones Jill had already set out. 'I don't care what Dana says.'

Jill gave her a *yeah, yeah* look and smiled. 'How was the sister?'

'Angry. And some cousin of theirs is out trying to get himself in trouble looking for our perp.'

'You need me to talk to Patrol?'

Casey wrinkled her face. 'I don't think they have a clue where he's at. She's given us Lauren's passcode, so let's see what her cell can tell us.' She opened a cupboard and found an open pack of Oreos. 'You want a cookie?'

'I'll pass, thanks. They're stale.'

Casey bit into one, nodded in agreement. 'Yup.' She finished it anyway and took a second. 'Everything okay with you at the moment?'

Jill rearranged the cups aimlessly, waiting for the coffee machine. 'Sure.' She half glanced back at Casey. 'Why do you ask?'

'Just checking. With the lieutenant coming in and everything. It's a big change.'

'She's...' She reached for the pot, saw it still wasn't ready. 'It's just different, I guess.'

Casey came around next to her and leaned on the counter. 'I see you looking at me sometimes, after you say something to her.' She smiled. 'You don't need to do that, don't worry. Whatever's going on between her and me, no one's expecting you to take sides.'

Jill flushed, eyes on the pot.

Casey angled towards her. 'I mean it. You're great at what you do – she needs to see that.'

Jill splayed her fingers on the counter. 'I feel ... I just feel kinda caught in the middle sometimes.'

Casey nodded along. 'I get it. But that's for me to worry about. You just keep doing your thing.'

'Dana said the same.'

'Good.' Casey smiled. 'Listening to Dana's advice will get you arrested in some states, but she's right on this one.'

Jill laughed, briefly, but then went quiet a moment. Then: 'Billy says we should be loyal to you.'

Now Casey flushed. 'That's sweet, but it's not necessary. You guys need to focus on doing the job, that's all. Let me worry about me.'

Jill nodded, looking relieved. Finally the light blinked off and she took up the pot to pour. Four mugs – one already set out for Dunmore. When she realised Casey had noticed, she hesitated.

'Jilly, stop it. This time of the morning, you damn well better be including your lieutenant in a coffee run.' Casey clasped her hands together in mock prayer. 'But if I don't get some caffeine inside of me soon, you and me are going to fall out for real. Pour, I'm begging.'

Jill laughed. 'Okay, okay, you got it.'

Casey picked up two cups. 'I'll take this one to Dana.'

She carried them back to the main office and set one down on Dana's desk, then crouched down next to her. 'Keep an eye on Jilly for me, huh? She's getting herself worried about this Dunmore stuff for no reason.'

Dana looked around. 'She talked to you?'

'You know what she's like – I had to pry it out of her. But she told me what you said. It was the right thing – thanks. Just let me know if she's still struggling.'

Dana looked at her monitor, then her keyboard. 'Sure.'

Casey waited, feeling like she was about to say something more, but Jill appeared back at her desk before she had a chance.

'I've got those photos Molly Goff shared with us, Big,' Jill said. 'You want to take a look?'

Casey stood up again and circled round the desks. Jill's screen was filled with a picture of Adam Ryker, a snap taken with Lauren Goff in what appeared to be happier times. It showed the two lovers standing side by side in a bar, Goff angled towards Ryker with her arms wrapped around his waist, him facing the camera with one arm draped across her shoulders and a glass of beer in his free hand. She was smiling broadly, her expression one of joy, but there was a hint of strain in it too, the muscles in her face taut, as if she was willing him to share her enthusiasm. His expression was harder to characterise – a slight smile on his lips, but looking as if its presence was only to mask an annoyance. He had dark hair, almost black, that he wore short, with a bushy hipster beard, olive skin and piercing green eyes. His black tee was muscle cut, the neckline dipping halfway down his chest, the sleeves cut high to show sculpted arms.

'I never got the big-beard thing,' Casey said.

Dana had come around the desk to join them. 'Preach.'

'If he's running, it'll be the first thing to go,' Jill said, and Casey nodded in agreement.

'I wouldn't call him handsome,' Dana said, leaning over Jill's shoulder to look closer at the screen, 'but he's got a look about him.'

'I've dated worse,' Casey said. 'He's got a way with words, too, according to Molly Goff.'

'Doesn't come across on his socials,' Jill said. 'They've got a heavy flavour of that "stay toxic, kings!" attitude. It's so juvenile.'

'I guess that's what counts as a bad boy these days,' Dana said. 'So many girls I know go for guys like that. They all kid themselves, think they're gonna change them. Never works out.' She was right by Jill's ear as she said it.

'It's always been like that,' Casey said, standing back and sipping her coffee. 'Used to be a leather jacket and a cocaine habit. I guess now it's an edgy Twitter feed.'

'For guys like him, we're just sex objects,' Dana said. 'They don't know how to change or grow up.' For a second it looked as if Dana was directing the comment to Jill.

The younger detective turned to face Casey – and her back on Dana in the process. 'Those reports are on your desk, by the way,' she said. 'Everything we've got on the system about Adam Ryker.'

'Appreciate it. Maranda in Tech is downloading the contents of Lauren Goff's cell as we speak – we should have a full data dump any minute.'

Casey circled around to her own desk and picked up the printouts, glancing back at the two women. Jill was already at her screen again, but her eyes were unmoving, fixed on one spot, as if her brain was still somewhere else, and Dana was standing behind her own seat, staring out across the floor. Casey knew her well enough to recognise she was pissed about something, but it was hard to imagine Jill doing something to upset her. Maybe it was still the Billy thing, whatever that was?

Casey reached for the ceiling to stretch out the kinks in her back. She felt like she'd taken a cross-country flight, the skin on her face dry and tight, her body stiff. She carried the printouts over to the window and skimmed the reports one at a time, Rockport slowly rousing itself in the grey light of morning outside. Not quite twenty-four hours since the shootings at Eighth and V, and already they had another one fighting for precedence. Nicole Rawlins and Molly Goff in her thoughts, their hell the spur to keep going in the face of an overwhelming sense of hopelessness.

The first three reports featured Ryker and Lauren Goff, the callout sheets spaced over a twelve-month period. Different attending officers each time, each one deciding that there was no need for further HCPD involvement. The fourth report was a callout to the address of a woman named Aryana Guptil, Adam Ryker recorded as the second party. Different part of town, different caller, different officer responding again. Patrol had attended following a telephone alert from a neighbour – reports of a loud argument that the caller feared was turning violent. Things had evidently calmed down by the time the uniforms reached the scene, the summary stating that both parties had been spoken to and asked to moderate their conduct, and that no further action was required.

Adam Ryker's recurring appearance in the callouts had either been missed or failed to trigger any alarm bells. It was easy to call it sloppy policing, but the volume of domestics was overwhelming, and the brass had quietly let it be known that the time spent on non-violent domestic callouts should be minimised. Casey scribbled down Guptil's name at the top of her list of people to contact that morning.

She moved on to the next report in the pile, one that was dated to four months ago; another callout to Ryker's address, a different woman present this time—

She blinked, stared at the page.

She read the woman's name again, tiredness making her doubt herself. The letters swimming in front of her eyes.

Sheila Rollins.

Just the name, no middle initial or date of birth recorded, the officer listing the woman as resident at Ryker's property.

Sheila Rollins. On its own it wasn't enough, but the similarity set Casey's brain fizzing.

She grabbed her notebook and opened it on the page of notes from her conversation with Nicole Rawlins the morning before. Right there, staring at her in the middle of it:

Sheena Rawlins dating a guy called Adam.

'No fucking way...'

Dana looked up. 'Big?'

Casey glanced at the time. Almost six am, but too important to wait. She dialled Nicole Rawlins' cell phone and retook her spot by the window, tapping the glass rapid-fire, as the dialling sound rang in her ear.

'Hello?'

'Miss Rawlins, this is Detective Casey Wray. We spoke yesterday morning at the hospital. I'm sorry to call this early—'

'I wasn't sleeping. I've been awake all night.'

'No, of course. All the same, I don't mean to disturb you, but I need to check on something you said yesterday and it's really urgent. Would that be okay?'

She heard Nicole take a ragged breath. 'I ... Sure. What is it?'

'You mentioned Sheena was dating a man a little while ago. You said his name was Adam. Do you happen to remember his surname?'

There was a shift in urgency on the other end, Nicole alert to the implication. 'Did he do this? Is it him?'

'It's too soon to say, ma'am, but there's been a development overnight and I really do need to know his last name.'

'Ryker. Adam Ryker. But I don't have his details, I don't even know where he lives—'

'Ma'am, don't trouble yourself, we have all of that.' Casey turned a half-circle on the spot, her body pulsing with adrenaline. Dana eyed her, mouthing *What?*, but Casey turned back to the window. 'I do need to let you know that there was a shooting in the early hours of this morning, and we're looking to speak to Mr Ryker in connection with it as a matter of urgency. You might see reports about it in the media, so I wanted you to be prepared.'

'I don't understand. This is crazy. Adam Ryker? And he's killed someone else?'

'We don't know that yet, ma'am. We're in the very early stages of investigating this incident and Mr Ryker's name has come up.'

'But you think he killed Sheena. That's why you're calling.'

'For right now, we just need to speak to him. It would help me to know, though, if he was ever abusive towards Sheena, or if she ever spoke of him making threats against her?'

'She ... No, she never said anything like that to me. She literally only talked about him a handful of times. I don't know what ... She told me he broke it off with her; she called me when it happened and she was kind of teary, and I messaged her the next day and she said she was still pretty upset, so I told her the best way to get over it was to get back out there. I guess she took that onboard, because the next time we talked she was telling me she'd been on, like, five dates in six nights and it'd helped her get her confidence back. She ... Wait, she didn't...' She fell silent a second, and Casey could almost feel the panic rising in Nicole's throat. 'Do you think that pissed him off or something? Is that why he killed her? Because this was months ago and ... Oh my god, is this because of what I said? I never meant ... I never knew he'd react...' She dissolved into a muffled wail before Casey could say anything to stop her.

'Ma'am, whatever happened here, this is not your fault. Or Sheena's. There's a tendency in situations like this to look for ways to blame ourselves some way, but I promise you, this is not your fault, it's all on the perpetrator.'

Nicole sobbed down the line, and time stood still for Casey. Nothing made her feel more powerless than hearing the pain of a victim's family, knowing there were no words she could speak to ease the suffering. She waited it out, saying nothing, and eventually the crying tapered off, replaced with the sound of Nicole's uneven breathing.

'Ma'am, do you have anyone who can be with you today?' Casey said.

'I just want to be alone.'

'I completely understand that, but it's probably not what I'd advise. If there is anyone you can reach out to – maybe your friend from yesterday?'

'She's got her kids – she can't ask her mom to watch them again. Please, I just need to be by myself right now.'

'Okay, sure. Well, look, I'm gonna call again later on today to check in on you and to keep you updated, and there's a chance I might need to ask you more questions. Will that be okay?'

Nicole didn't respond at first; when she did, it was in a strained whisper. 'Okay.'

'Thank you for your help this morning, ma'am.'

Casey hung up and looked at Dana.

'It's him.' She went straight over to Dunmore's office, knocking on the open glass door as she came to a stop in the doorway. 'Adam Ryker is Sheena Rawlins' ex. They're connected.'

'What?'

'The shootings are connected.'

Dana and Jill had already come to stand behind her to listen.

'The domestics involving Ryker,' Casey said, 'one of the women in the reports is named as Sheila Rollins.'

Dunmore frowned, confused. The double doors to the department creaked and Billy appeared, then came jogging across to join them. Casey could see the question appearing on his face as she continued.

'The name sounded so similar, I thought I was being crazy – but then I checked my notes, and the sister told me Sheena was dating a guy called Adam. I just spoke with her and she confirmed it was Adam Ryker.' Casey held up the printout. 'Patrol got Sheena's damn name wrong on the report, that's why it didn't come up before now.'

'Holy shit,' Dana said. 'Is this guy on a revenge tour?'

Dunmore got up from her seat, tapping a pen against her open palm. 'There were three women in the system named in connection with Ryker – Goff's one, now we know about Rawlins, who's the third?'

'Aryana Guptil. 2230 Gracie Street. It's in The Slice, not far from Ryker's place.'

'The Slice?' Dunmore said.

Casey waved it off. 'Just a nickname. Northwest Rockport.'

Dunmore pointed to the stairs. 'I told Patrol to send cars earlier, but I think we have to assume this woman is at serious risk until we catch up to Ryker. You and Billy get out there now, speak to Dispatch on the way and have them get a status update from whoever's on the scene. Make sure they're aware of the threat profile.' Dunmore went to sit down, but jumped up again suddenly. 'And ask Patrol why the hell they didn't put this together when they sent a car to look for "Sheila Rollins". Please?'

'Sure thing.'

'I want the rest of you working on Ryker's whereabouts, and

any other exes or partners we can turn up – a guy like this is bound to have plenty and we can't assume he'd be helpful enough to only go after the ones we know about. Also, I want to know what's on Sheena Rawlins' cell phone – we know he was sending nasty messages to Lauren Goff. I want to see what hers can tell us. Let's go.'

Casey tossed the car keys to Billy, still wearing his coat. 'You drive, I'll talk.'

CHAPTER THIRTEEN

Aryana Guptil answered the door with her cell phone in one hand and a can of energy drink in the other. There was a woman at her shoulder who shared the same pale-blue eyes, so light they were almost translucent, the similarity strong enough that she had to be family.

Casey introduced herself and Billy. 'Thanks for seeing us so early, Miss Guptil. It's really important we speak with you about Adam Ryker.'

Guptil stepped back, holding the door open to invite them in. 'This is my cousin, Muneera,' she said, gesturing to the second woman. 'I had her come over soon as the other police showed up.' She glanced at the window, the patrol car parked at the kerb.

'I wanted to be here,' Muneera said, almost in protest.

'Sit down anywhere. I just need a second,' Aryana said, typing something on her phone. 'I'm booking a hotel room for tonight – no way I'm staying here. Just let me get this done.'

Casey and Billy took a seat on the sofa, and Muneera eyed them with the awkward body language of a young woman who'd never encountered cops in real life before. She looked a few years younger than Aryana, her jeans tastefully ripped, in contrast to Aryana's sleek black yoga pants. 'Can I get you guys a water or something?'

'We're fine, thank you,' Casey said, waving her hand. She looked around, the living room expensively decorated and the carpet such a thick pile that her feet almost disappeared.

Aryana finished typing and with her pointer fingers delicately swept a strand of hair from each side of her face. After a second, the phone buzzed and she closed her eyes, looking visibly relieved. 'Okay, all set. You ready to go after we get done here, Mee?'

Muneera nodded and then, finally, they had Aryana's full attention. She was perched on the arm of a chair opposite.

'So Adam really killed two people?' she said.

Casey held her hands up. 'We don't know that yet, we're still trying to establish what happened.'

Ayrana arched her eyebrows. 'There's no way you send two cops to watch my place all night if you don't think he did it. I didn't think he'd go this far, but I always knew he'd go off someday.'

'You were in a relationship with Mr Ryker?'

'Yeah,' Aryana said, rolling her eyes as if she was disappointed in herself.

'*She* was,' Muneera said. '*He* wasn't.'

'Mee! You're making me sound like an idiot.'

'No, I'm not. I'm just saying...' Muneera met Casey's eyes and looked away again, as if afraid of getting in trouble.

Casey looked from one to the other. 'What do you mean, ma'am?'

Aryana took a sip from her drink through a straw marked with a ring of dark-red lipstick near the top. 'I knew it was never a serious thing, but ... I mean, okay, I didn't know he was seeing other people, not until later on anyway, because I wasn't seeing anyone else on the side, so, you know, I assumed...'

'I tried to tell you,' Muneera said.

Aryana shrugged, rolling her eyes again. 'We were together, maybe – what was it, like four or five months?' She looked at Muneera, who was nodding. 'At the end I figured out he was dogging around. He was barely even trying to hide it. I should've seen it earlier, the signs were all there, but ... you know how it is – you kinda see what you want to see in a relationship. Anyway, I was pretty cut up at the time, for a little while...' Her eyes dipped to the drink in her hand, a faraway look that hinted at a deeper attachment than she was letting on.

'I'm sorry he treated you that way, ma'am,' Casey said. 'It's really important we speak to Mr Ryker as soon as possible. Do you have any idea where we might find him? We've tried his property on Van Buren, but if you know anywhere else he might be at, or anyone he might be with...'

Aryana's phone buzzed and she checked the screen, dismissing whatever it was before looking at Casey again. 'I haven't spoken to him since we broke up. He used to work at a marketing agency downtown – Kaleidoscope—'

'Kaleidoscopic,' Muneera said. 'That's what you told me,' she added.

'Right, right. I don't know if he still does.'

'Do you happen to have his cell-phone number?'

She raised her phone again and scrolled, looking doubtful. But then her face changed. 'Oh, wow, yeah, I do – I blocked him when we split because he kept messaging me. He just couldn't let it go – there were times he'd message me seven, eight, ten times in a minute, just, y'know, telling me he'd made a mistake and asking for another chance. He was a really persuasive guy, so I figured I should just delete him, so I wouldn't, you know, get back with him or whatever. I guess I never did.' She read out the number and Billy noted it down.

'What about his family, does he have any in the area?'

'He never ... I never met his family. He didn't really talk about them, like, ever. I kinda assumed he fell out with them or something.'

'Is there anywhere he used to hang out often – a bar, a gym, anyplace like that?'

She was shaking her head. 'He'd be out all the time. I mean *all* the time – he was never at home unless I was coming over. I thought it was because of his work, all the networking he had to do and stuff. It's so obvious now – he was always chasing other girls. Stupid me.'

'You weren't stupid,' Muneera said quietly, 'it wasn't your fault.'

Aryana flashed a downtrodden smile before she carried on. 'We'd go to bars and restaurants downtown. He'd change it up all the time, but that was just the kind of guy he was – like, really on it when it came to knowing which places were new and cool, always wanting to try somewhere different, so it never seemed weird or anything. I only figured out later that part of it was he didn't want to get caught out. He was seeing at least two other women while we were together, I found out after.'

Casey had her elbows on her knees and she brought her hands together. 'Miss Guptil, this is a little sensitive, but was Adam Ryker ever abusive to you?'

'He never hit me. Never.' She took another sip through her straw. 'But he was – I guess you'd call it emotionally abusive, but I didn't really know what that was at the time. Like, he'd lie and gaslight me – oh, and he was super controlling. Not at the start, but later on he'd tell me what to wear, what to say – he'd tell me not to talk sometimes in front of friends. We'd make plans and he wouldn't show up, or there was one time he told me to come over to his place after work and he'd fix dinner, and when I got there he wasn't home. I waited an hour and he never showed up – didn't answer my texts or calls, nothing. The next time I saw him and I asked him what happened, he told me to just forget about it. No explanation, nothing.'

'Maybe he had an emergency or something,' Muneera said, almost to herself.

'Mee, come on, you know what he was like. That was totally how he was.'

The cousins looked at each other, and Casey had the sense the relationship had been litigated and relitigated between them countless times.

Casey glanced at Billy, giving him the *anything else?* look. He shook his head and Casey got to her feet. 'You've been a real help, thank you. I've got your cell number. I'll let you know if there are any further developments. We'll tell the officers outside you're heading to a hotel, but they'll stay here until you're ready to leave.' Casey went to the door, then turned back. 'When you said earlier you always knew he'd go off eventually, what did you mean?'

Aryana waved her fingers, as if it was a throwaway line. 'It was just a feeling. No one can be that tightly wound forever, right?'

Casey thanked her again and went out onto the sidewalk,

that last line nagging at her. A life based on power and control. Now that was gone, what boundaries did he have left? Three dead, why stop there?

She was standing by the kerb when Billy caught up to her. The expression on her face must've been a tell. 'Hey, are you okay?'

Casey looked past him down the street. 'Christ knows how many exes this guy's got. Feels like we're running out of time before he goes after someone else.'

Billy flared his nostrils, nodding. 'What do we do? We can't put a car on the ones we don't know about.'

'We gotta find this asshole.' She looked over at the patrol car parked down the street. 'Can you let the uniforms know they can head off soon? I'm gonna try Ryker's number.'

'Sure thing.'

Casey tapped the number into her cell as Billy walked the short way along the sidewalk to where the patrol car was parked. She listened as it rang, watching the traffic go by, feeling the blood pumping in her wrist and in her neck. Her eyes wandered along the row of cars parked across the street, all her senses attuned to the crisp dial tone in her ear—

There was a click and Casey braced for his voice – but it was an automated voicemail greeting that spoke. The recording told her to leave a message at the tone.

'This is a message for Adam Ryker: this is Detective Casey Wray of the HCPD calling. I'd like to speak to you as a matter of urgency, please, sir, so if you could call me back as soon as possible, you can get me on this number anytime. Thank you.'

She hung up, and waited a few seconds, in case he called her right back. But the phone remained silent.

She looked around, deciding on her next move. That same

row of parked cars across the way drew her eye. There were two figures in a late-model black Lexus, a man and a woman, the man looking over at her through his open window. They'd been there the whole time, and now Casey got that magnetic sense of being watched. She took a few paces in their direction, acting as if she was looking at something on her phone, until she was close enough to make out their faces better.

It wasn't Adam Ryker. It'd crossed her mind he could've been waiting for a chance to get to Aryana Guptil, the actions of a man in his situation impossible to predict, but this guy was older, with salt-and-pepper hair. He looked out from the driver's side at Casey, not shying away from making eye contact. The woman next to him was engrossed in her phone.

Casey held his gaze for a few seconds, the man returning it with a flat look that landed right between defiance and curiosity. She thought about crossing the road to ask what he was doing, but it felt like she was acting paranoid. Then she memorised the Lexus's licence plate to note down anyway.

CHAPTER FOURTEEN

A rash of phone calls on the drive back to the station got Casey nowhere.

A call to the marketing agency Kaleidoscopic revealed that Adam Ryker hadn't shown up for work that morning and hadn't contacted them to give a reason for his absence. Ryker's manager told Casey he was, up until today, regarded as a reliable employee who was good at his job as a client-services executive, and was liked well enough by his colleagues. His failure to show had raised eyebrows – 'he prides himself on being the last guy to leave the party and the first guy at his desk the next morning' – and they'd left a message on his cell phone, checking up on him, that was yet to receive a response. The man went on to confirm that Ryker had been working the day prior, but that he worked remotely Tuesdays and Thursdays, meaning he couldn't speak to his movements at the time of the shooting on Eighth and Villanova.

In addition, two separate women had contacted the HCPD appeals line to state that they were Adam Ryker's girlfriend, and their details had found their way to Casey to call back. The first, Adele Montrose, said she and Ryker had been together about a month, and that if he wasn't at work or at home, she wouldn't know where else to suggest to find him, describing him as a guy who was always out, but never went to the same place twice. She told Casey they'd never spoken about previous partners, so the names Sheena Rawlins and Lauren Goff meant nothing to her.

The second woman, Robyn Niemenen, claimed she and Ryker had been together for six weeks, and that if he'd dropped off the radar, he'd probably talked some girl into letting him hide out at her place. She went on to say that she'd known from day one that he was sleeping around, and that she was cool with it, but the knowing laugh that accompanied this wasn't totally convincing. 'He's not the only guy I was seeing, either,' she made a point to add. Casey had left her cell-phone number with both women and asked them to notify her immediately if Ryker got in touch, ending the calls with a promise that a patrol car would be sent to each of their addresses, just as a temporary measure. Montrose sounded freaked out at the prospect, but

Niemenen seemed untroubled. 'Sure, whatever. Adam will have to get in line anyway – plenty of my exes want me dead.'

The last call she made was to Ryker's dad, Emile. It was Jill who'd dug up a contact number for him in Florida and pinged it over to Casey. When she reached him, Emile Ryker told her he'd moved south after his retirement seven years previous. Early in the conversation, it became evident that he was oblivious to the appeals for his son's whereabouts – no big surprise, given he lived at the other end of the Eastern Seaboard. She sensed no attempt at deception when he said he hadn't talked to him in a week or so, and he couldn't say where he might be at. But one piece of background he provided stood out as pertinent: Saffron Ryker, Adam's mother, had passed away suddenly three months earlier, as a result of complications arising from a Covid-19 infection. Casey offered her condolences, but Emile quickly waved them aside, explaining that she'd left the family home when Adam was nine, leaving Emile to raise the boy by himself. He sounded doleful as he said it, no trace of bitterness in his voice, and Casey found herself wondering, not for the first time, at the complexity of the emotions built up over a lifetime. He went on to say that mother and son had remained in regular contact, even after she'd made a new life for herself in California, right up to the time of her death.

'That's got to have a bearing,' Billy said, when Casey finished bringing him up to speed. 'Guy's mom leaves when he's a kid so he spends his life chasing women. Some kind of abandonment issues going on, then her death sets him off.' He flicked the blinker and turned into the precinct parking lot.

'Maybe,' Casey said, thinking back to how she'd felt in the wake of her own mother's passing. Angela Wray had been her best friend, her sounding board and the person who got under her skin the most, all at the same time. They were close enough that they grated on each other without meaning to, and that those petty annoyances were forgotten just as quickly. They'd spoken every day on the phone, but if you'd asked Casey now what they talked about, she couldn't give a detailed accounting; their chats were akin to a comfort blanket – inconsequential in substance, but all the more precious for it. Angela's death had left Casey at the mercy of a barrage of emotions; after the initial gut punch subsided, she'd swung between grief, pain, emptiness and relief, like a flag torn loose in the wind. On occasion there'd been anger too – directed at god or fate or the universe, whoever had decided her mom's last months would be ones of agony and suffering – but even the rage, when it came, had been channelled inward, fuelling thoughts of self-loathing and self-doubt; it'd never led her to want to strike out at others. But loss hit everyone different, and there was no telling what it might've set off in Adam Ryker.

Dunmore intercepted them as they crossed the office, making for their desks. She was holding up a copy of that morning's *Courier*. The headline read: 'Shootings Bring Terror to Rockport Streets'.

Casey rolled her eyes. 'Well that should put folk at ease.'

Dunmore folded the paper away and tossed it in the trash. 'There's good news and bad,' she said. 'Good news is we've located Ryker's vehicle – but the bad is that it's parked on the street outside his property.'

Casey wrinkled her face. Another possible lead hitting a dead end.

'In other words, wherever he's gone, he probably went there on foot,' Dunmore said. 'Or he started out that way, at least.'

'I'll check in with Uber, Lyft and the local cab companies,' Billy said, and Dunmore nodded.

'His dad's in Florida, mom died three months back, out in California,' Casey said. 'We've got contact details for a handful of friends and a bucketful of acquaintances. We'll get onto the most promising ones this morning, but the point is his support network is local, so my sense is he won't have gone far – especially without his car.'

'There's a team searching the property now,' Dunmore said. 'They've turned up some weed and a few pills so far – MDMA, we think – but no weapon as yet. He's not a registered gun-owner, but that doesn't prove or disprove anything.' She massaged her jaw. 'Did you get anything from the neighbours?'

Casey shook her head. 'One of the properties was empty, the other didn't hear or see him last night. They were an older couple, said they barely know the man – they'd see Ryker coming and going, taking out the trash, but apart from that he kept to himself.'

'Then he goes and shoots the neighbourhood up,' Billy said quietly, suddenly glancing at Dunmore to see if he'd screwed up. But Dunmore ignored him, her eyes on Casey.

'They did say he was barely ever at home,' Casey said. 'I don't think we'll get anything else out of them.'

'What about the ex-girlfriend?'

Casey's phone started ringing in her pocket. She pulled it out far enough to check the screen, saw it was Rita Zangetty. 'I'd better take this, sorry.' She walked a few paces before she answered and put the phone to her ear, carrying on out through the double doors and into the stairwell. 'Rita, hey.'

'This guy you're looking for...' There was a pause, as if Zangetty was checking her notes. '...Ryker? That right?'

'Yeah, what about him?'

'Is he a suspect for yesterday?'

Casey looked back at the double doors, checking she was alone, feeling like any answer she gave would be the wrong one. 'There was a shooting last night—'

'Yeah, the woman in The Slice. I saw about that. Awful. So he's in the frame for that one?'

Casey glanced at the double doors again, scrambling for a way to dodge the question. 'Look, why don't you have Gates call Keirn?'

'I told you, it's about speed. Has Keirn even been briefed yet?'

'I'd, uh ... I'd have to check with my lieutenant.'

Zangetty sighed. 'This is exactly what I was talking about, Casey. I know how things are supposed to work, but Darcy Whitlock's been on to Franklin twice already this morning and that's what she wants to know right now. Franklin's desperate to be able to give her some kind of an update.'

'Rita, I can't ... I just can't say too much right now.'

'I know that, and I totally get it. Look, if Keirn hasn't been briefed, I can read between the lines. I just wanted to check so we're not passing on bad intel. ' She let out a long breath. 'I'll tell Franklin to relay that this guy's a suspect for something else—'

'Wait, don't ...' Casey pressed her lips together, feeling like the walls were closing in around her. 'Don't tell her that.'

'Casey, Franklin's got to be able to tell her something. Don't worry, your name won't be anywhere near this.'

'No, I mean ... What I mean is, Adam Ryker, the guy we're looking for ... he may be connected to Landon Whitlock's shooting too.'

'I thought you said he was up for the one in The Slice?'

'I never said that.'

'Casey, you're talking in riddles. I don't mean to put you in a difficult position here, but I think I stressed how delicate a situation this is.'

Casey covered her face with her hand. 'We need to talk to him in connection with both incidents.'

'Both?' The momentary silence was so loud, it was as if she could hear Zangetty's heartbeat. 'You want him for both?'

'Rita, I've already said more than I should right now. We're really early into this. We'll reach out to Mrs Whitlock to keep her up to speed and when the time's right—'

'Casey, all due respect, there is no right time for you – and I'm referring to HCPD, mostly – to *reach out* to Darcy Whitlock. Franklin has made it clear he wants to manage this, and he'll make sure Keirn knows it too, so you're covered.'

Casey looked up and down the empty stairwell, Zangetty's voice loud enough through the speaker to cascade off the bare concrete.

'How close are you to finding this guy?'

'It's only been a few hours,' Casey said.

There was a loaded silence from the other end, Zangetty recognising the weasel words for what they were. 'Listen, please, I need to be able to give her something, some kind of progress.'

'We've only just identified a suspect. We're putting everything we've got into finding him, but you've got to give us a chance.'

There was a pause, Zangetty deciding whether to push harder. In the end she must've decided against. 'Just call me as soon as you know anything more. Okay? Please?'

'I can't do that.'

But with the plea made, Zangetty was gone.

Casey took a moment to catch her breath, her head buzzing with it all.

When she finally went back through the doors into the main office, Billy immediately looked up from his desk, following her with his gaze as she made her way back to her seat.

'What?' Casey said as she sat down.

'I get the feeling Dunmore was pissed.'

'At me?'

He nodded.

'What for now?'

'For taking that call. She was shooting knives out of her eyes when you went into the stairwell. I started telling her about what we got from Aryana Guptil, figured I'd keep talking until you got back, but she told me to write it all up and walked off.'

Casey glanced over at Dunmore's office, the door open but her face hidden behind her computer monitor. 'Jesus, what a fucking day.' She looked at the clock on the wall, saw it read 10.05am. She was about to go over to explain when her desk phone rang, an internal call. 'Yeah?'

'Got a woman here asking to speak to you, Detective.'

Casey's mind ran straight to an image of Darcy Whitlock, waiting to bawl her out in the reception area. 'Who is it?'

'Gave her name as Brianna Monk, she said you'd know her?'

It took her a moment to place the name. Landon Whitlock's secretary.

'Detective?'

'Yeah, sorry, I'll be right down.'

Casey headed for the stairwell. As she walked by, Dana jumped out of her seat and fell in step with her. 'You okay? You look fried.'

'Caught between a rock and a hard place is all.'

'Anything I can do?'

'If you could magic up Adam Ryker for me, it would help.' Casey went through the doors into the stairwell but stopped and turned, realising she was being flippant when the offer of help was a genuine one. 'Sorry, D, I'm short on sleep and shorter on caffeine.'

'Then go sit down and I'll make you a coffee.'

'Thanks, but I can't. Landon Whitlock's secretary is waiting downstairs for me.'

'You call her in?'

'Nope, she just showed up.' Casey pushed a loose strand of hair off her forehead. 'Hey, if you have time, could you try Ryker's buddies for me, give them a call and see if we can get any kind of a line on him? There's a half-dozen or so. Billy's got a list.'

Dana had been nodding along, but her face changed when she heard Billy's name. 'Sure, I'll get on it now.'

'Hey, wait. Is there something up between you and Rookie?'

Dana hesitated a split second. 'No, it's nothing major. I'll talk to you when things calm down.'

'Dana...?'

'No, honestly, it's cool.' She put her hands on Casey's shoulders, gripping them gently and facing her head on. 'I'll get the list, you go talk to the secretary.' She faked a smile and went back into the office.

❧

Brianna Monk was a petite woman with a razor-straight bob dyed vivid red. She took a seat across the table from Casey, popped the top off a plastic bottle and drank the last of the water inside. 'It's so dry in here, how do you stand it?'

Casey opened her hands on the tabletop. 'Uh – I guess I never really noticed. Can I get you something more to drink?' She gestured to the bottle with her knuckle. 'A soda, a coffee?'

'No, I'm good, thank you. I came down here because I figured you'd want to ask me about Landon. I was surprised no one had called me since ... well, I guess since I spoke to someone yesterday. Maybe that was you?'

Casey nodded. 'Yes, that was me and we appreciate you coming in. This is a fast-moving investigation, so we haven't had a chance to speak to everyone we'd like to just yet, but—'

'Because, you know, I've been racking my brains trying to figure out why he was on that street yesterday and it...' She reached into her bag and fished out a Kleenex, dabbing under her eyes. 'God, look at me. He could be such an asshole. I know I shouldn't say it but there's times I wished him dead – I mean, not really, but, you know what I'm saying? He was a good boss most of the time, but when he was under pressure, he could be so rude. I don't think he ever meant it. It wasn't personal ... Wow, listen to me; you shouldn't speak ill of the dead, Brianna. He always brought me chocolates and an Amazon voucher on my birthday, he'd ask after my mom and my uncle Patrick – he had lung cancer, stage four – so I think he really cared.'

'Did you work for Mr Whitlock a long time?'

'Four years. His last secretary quit because she couldn't take it anymore.'

'The work?'

Monk tilted her head side to side. 'The work. Landon. Mrs Whitlock. But I always said, it's a package deal – if you're going to take the paycheck, handling those two was just another part of the job.'

'What do you mean?'

'Well, it was like, if he wants to call me at nine o'clock on a Sunday night to ... I don't know, change his diary or set up a meeting or something, I just had to accept it went with the territory. He paid well, so you had to suck it up.'

'And Mrs Whitlock?'

'You haven't met her yet?'

'I have, briefly.'

'Okay, so you know. She can singe your eyebrows with a word. But – and don't get me wrong, I opted to keep out of her way as much as I could – I always felt like it was kind of a mask. There was a lot of resentment there, I think, with Landon and the fact she was so reliant on him for money, and she takes that out on the world. I don't have a clue how she must be feeling right now. Conflicted, I guess.'

'You're saying there were problems with their marriage?'

'I don't know, more just that ... She's an intelligent woman. She was a banker of some kind back before, but she stopped working when they had Harper – that's their daughter – and then he wanted her to stay home so she ended up playing housewife. Then about three years back she tried to kick-start her career again, but she'd been out too long and she couldn't get hired. Landon never got why she wanted to work again. He kept telling her they didn't need the money, but that was him all over – I don't know what the right word is; blinkered maybe? I guess he must've left her and Harper well provided for.'

'Mr Whitlock was a financial advisor, is that correct?'

'I guess you would call it that. He started out as a tax lawyer, but these days his work was about minimising tax exposure, moving money around, that kind of thing. He used to joke that rich guys have tax advisors, but the really rich guys have the laws changed. I could never work out if he resented the men he worked for or wanted to be like them. I guess it could've been both.'

Casey scribbled down some notes, a question moving to the forefront of her thoughts. 'Did Mr Whitlock often carry large sums of cash with him?'

She curled her bottom lip. 'I mean, I don't know, but I don't think so. He was too cautious for that. He was never flash, not in that way, anyway.'

Casey noted her answer, stealing a glance at her watch. 'I really appreciate you coming in today. I'll add all of this to our case file and if there's anything else we need to know, I'll be in touch.'

Monk reached out a hand. 'But I still don't get what he was doing on that street. He told me he was golfing, and it's not like he ever needed to bother lying to me. He could've just told me to block out his diary or whatever if he didn't want to say where he was going. That's what he'd normally do, no questions asked. God knows he never felt any need to explain himself to me.'

'I understand what you're saying and, look, when a tragedy like this happens, it leaves the people impacted with so many unanswered questions. As much as I wish I could put your mind at ease, what I can say is that as the investigation stands right now, it seems unlikely that Mr Whitlock was the gunman's intended target.'

'So it was just wrong place, wrong time?' Monk's shoulders slumped.

'I know, it seems so unfair...'

'No, it's not that, it's just...' Monk pushed her hair back with both hands and leaned forward in her seat. 'Look, Landon was a nutjob in a lot of ways. Super-cautious, super-paranoid. Every day there was someone else that was trying to scam him or "making moves" – that was his favourite phrase. I think it just came from working for rich guys all his life, because they're all the same way – it's almost like, you have to have that mindset to be a part of the club. But a couple times lately, like in the last month, he said he thought someone was following him. And, honestly, I didn't put a lot of stock in it because, like I said, he was a nutjob for stuff like that, but now ... I mean, maybe he wasn't just being crazy?'

Casey brought her chair a little closer to the table. 'Did he ... did he elaborate at all on who he thought was following him?'

She shook her head. 'Not really, he just said he kept seeing the same car in different places, usually some guy in it.'

'Did he describe the guy? Or the car?'

She shook her head again. 'Sorry.'

'Did you ever see anything yourself that made you suspicious?'

'No, never. I really thought it was just Landon being Landon, so I wasn't looking out for it.'

Casey brought up a picture of Adam Ryker on her phone. 'You might've seen we've been asking for information about this man. Have you ever come across him in person?'

Monk leaned over the table to look closer. 'I mean, there's guys look like him everywhere these days. Well, not with eyes like that, but that kind of appearance. But I don't think so. He's not someone that sticks out in my memory anyway.'

'His name's Adam Ryker. Does that name mean anything in connection with Mr Whitlock?'

'I'd have to check the computer to be sure, but I don't think so. He doesn't look like Landon's usual type of a client.'

Casey leaned back in her chair, tapping her finger on her pad in silence a moment. 'Was Mrs Whitlock aware of Mr Whitlock's concerns? About being followed, I mean?'

Monk twisted the empty bottle of water in a circle on the tabletop. 'I don't know. He never said he did or didn't discuss it with her. It was never really a conversation when he'd talk about it to me, more like something he'd say in passing.'

'Sure, I understand.' Casey flipped the cover over her pad and stood up. 'Thank you again for coming in today. I'll give you a call if we need to ask any additional questions.'

Brianna Monk stood up too. 'It doesn't sit right with me that you can kill a good man just for walking down the street.' She stuffed her water bottle in her bag. 'I hope you catch that guy and throw away the key.'

CHAPTER FIFTEEN

Dana came over as soon as Casey sat back down at her desk, a stack of papers in her hand. 'I called Ryker's KAs, managed to speak to four of them and the other two I left voicemails. I can run you through what they said, if you want, but the headline is none of them know where he's at – at least that's what they're saying. One of them gave me the name of a gym where he's a member – I'll check that out – and they had a couple of bars to try. I'll do that as soon as they open.'

'You never know, maybe we luck out.' Casey pointed to the papers she was holding. 'What's this?'

'Lauren Goff's text exchanges with Adam Ryker. Maranda

and the Tech guys sent them over. Jill and I started working through it, but I knew you'd want to have a copy.'

'Thanks. Is it all pretty grim?'

'I didn't get all that far with it yet. A lot of it's everyday boyfriend/girlfriend chat, but there's parts where it's already starting to turn heated. He seems like a pretty standard manipulative-narcissist asshole, but maybe my take on it is skewed by the rest of what we know about him.'

Casey took the papers and dropped them on her desk to start poring over. The top page of messages must've been from when the relationship first started, the tone light and flirty, winking- and laughing-face emojis in almost every sentence. She looked up at Dana again. 'Anything more from the tip line?'

'Nothing worth telling. One guy wanted to give us Ryker's home address, another offering up where he worked. Old news like that.'

She was skimming the second page of the text messages as Dana spoke, seeing more of the same. 'Thanks, D. For all your hard work.'

'No sweat. I'll even get you that coffee now.'

Casey mouthed, '*Angel*,' and looked down at the papers again. As she did, she heard Dana call over to Billy, 'Hey, Rookie, go get Big a coffee, would ya?' and it made her crack into a grin.

The first few pages were all alike, the couple flirting and joking, the messages breezy all the way through. Casey flipped ahead to the last page, seeing a half dozen messages exchanged on the night Lauren was killed, time stamped 1.46am:

Adam: *I really need to see you. Things aren't right.*
          Can I come over?
Lauren: *What? The hell?*
Adam: *I know I f'd up. Truly. Please, will you just hear*
          me out?
Lauren: *R u for real rn? It's like 2am?*
Adam: *I'll be there soon, all I'm asking is you hear me*
          out. Please?
Lauren: *FFS Adam.*

Casey flipped the page over, but there was nothing further. She went back to the last batch of messages prior to the exchange, saw it was dated ten days earlier. The couple were arguing about something unspecified, but when Lauren tried to bring it to a close by saying she didn't want to see him anymore, Ryker's reply had been ominous: *You don't get to decide that.*

Casey worked her way through months of back-and-forth messages, a mix of sex talk, arguments and a handful of apparent or threatened breakups, all interspersed with mundane exchanges arranging dinner meets, drinks or other everyday stuff. She came across the messages Molly Goff had shown her, and similar threats from Ryker besides, his ability to manipulate and need to control coming through strongly. When Lauren would turn tender, he'd go cold or ignore her altogether. In several places, she'd written *I love you*, but Casey couldn't see anywhere he'd written the same back. Most times, he seemed to have given no response at all, and the gaps in communication that followed felt like a silent scream from Lauren.

She set the papers down and rubbed her eyes, wondering what'd happened to Adam Ryker in that ten-day gap between the last argument and Lauren's murder. He'd been seeing at least two other women during that time period – the two who'd contacted the tip line – with the ever-present possibility of there being still others, as yet unknown to HCPD. Maybe Aryana Guptil was right in her assessment that he'd always been a timebomb waiting to go off; there were red flags littered throughout what they'd learned about him. But still, his progression from coercive behaviour and psychological abuse straight to multiple murders, seemed an accelerated one. The statistics showed that domestic homicides were usually carried out by men with a track record of physical abuse against their partners or family members, but as bad as Ryker's behaviour was, no one had yet put him in that category. The death of his mother three months earlier lingered as possible context for a shift in his behaviour, but if something specific had happened in that ten-day period to trigger Ryker's bloodlust, it might give her an insight into where his head was at – and who, if anyone, he might target next. The most troubling possibility was that he could target his former lovers at random, making it almost impossible to predict where and when he might next strike. Casey decided a face-to-face visit with the two women who he'd most recently been dating would be her next move, to see if there was anything else they might be able to give up on him.

The desk phone rang, snapping her out of her thoughts. She picked it up and cradled the handset in her shoulder. 'Casey Wray.'

'Detective, this is Darcy Whitlock, Landon's Whitlock's wife.'

Casey felt the colour drain from her face. 'Mrs Whitlock, hello. How are you holding up, ma'am?'

Whitlock ignored the question. 'Detective, I want to speak to you in person.'

'Sure, of course, I'm based at the Third Precinct, do you know where—'

'I'd much prefer it if you would come to the house.'

'Well, sure, absolutely. Let me see if I can get out to you later this morning—'

'I'm available now, Detective.'

Casey took the handset from her shoulder and looked at the speaker in disbelief before putting it back to her ear. 'Um ... well, I'm tied up right this second, but—'

'There are some things amongst Landon's possessions you need to be aware of, and it would be beneficial for all concerned to make you aware of them in private. If I'm required to come to you, with your colleagues and superiors present, it will be harder to achieve that.'

'Ma'am, I'm not sure I know what you mean, but anything you want to speak to me about, you can do so right here – or I'll get out to you as soon as I can. I'm sure you appreciate that this is a fast-moving investigation and I can't just drop everything—'

'I'm beginning to regret showing you a courtesy, Detective. We'll discuss it here in a half-hour, or in Franklin Gates' office later today with my attorneys present. It's your choice.'

The line went dead.

CHAPTER SIXTEEN

Shafts of white sunlight beamed through the clouds as Casey followed the winding driveway up to Shatter Creek, retracing her path from the day before. When she emerged from the stand of sugar maples, the sparkling waters of the bay unfurled in front of her, backdropping a house that seemed to glow in the sunlight. The picture-perfect scene was at odds with the grief playing out behind the whitewashed walls.

It was the wrong move and she knew it. Darcy Whitlock was twenty-four hours removed from losing her husband, so her erratic behaviour was understandable to a point. But in bowing to a threat, Casey had made herself a prisoner to that behaviour – and that wasn't a place she could afford to be. She'd thought about calling Rita Zangetty to get her take on how to play it, but Whitlock had threatened to involve Franklin Gates, which suggested going to Rita was a bad move. The thought of trying to defend herself to the county executive himself terrified Casey, especially when he had Keirn beholden to him. So instead, Casey drove the last part of the driveway and drew up beside the house, blind to whatever was coming.

Whitlock opened the door as Casey was still parking up. She had on a grey pantsuit with a white top – all business – but was barefoot. She stood in the doorway with her arms folded, but as Casey walked over, she turned her back and went inside, motioning for Casey to follow with a short flick of her wrist.

Casey did as instructed and found herself in a cavernous entranceway, doorways leading off in all directions and a wide staircase right in front of her. Large windows behind her and on the landing above allowed the sunlight to flood in, the high ceiling adding to the sense of space and grandeur.

Darcy Whitlock was waiting for her with one hand resting on the banister, her lower jaw slightly jutted. 'Who killed my husband, Detective?'

Casey stopped just inside the doorway. 'I don't have an

answer to that yet, Mrs Whitlock, but we do have a suspect we're looking to talk to urgently.'

'Were you investigating him for some reason when he died?'

'Investigating him for what?'

'That's what I'm asking you. I'd rather know the truth.'

'I ... I mean, I can't speak for the whole of HCPD, or any other agencies, but I was not, no, and there are no investigations into your husband that I'm aware of. What makes you ask that?'

'Were you sleeping with him?'

Casey closed her eyes a moment, certain she must've misheard. 'I'm ... Ma'am, sorry, what?'

'I asked if you were you sleeping with Landon.'

'No,' Casey said, too stunned to make it sound more emphatic. 'No, I wasn't. I don't ... Why would you say that?'

Whitlock stared at her, as if deciding whether she believed her or not.

'Ma'am, I'd really like to know what this is about,' Casey said.

Whitlock moved away from the staircase and ghosted towards Casey, her footsteps making no sound, reaching for something in her pocket as she went. 'This was in Landon's desk drawer. Upstairs.'

A business card. Casey took it from her fingers, saw it was one of her own.

She shook her head to signify it meant nothing. 'I never gave this to him. With respect, I'd never heard of your husband before yesterday, and to my knowledge, I've never met him. But I probably hand out a couple dozen of these a month, sometimes more...'

'Turn it over.'

Casey looked down again, already knowing what she'd see.

Her personal cell-phone number, scribbled on the back in her own handwriting. She looked up as her face flushed red, the flight reflex making her heart race even though she had nothing to hide. 'I always ... Whenever I hand one out I write my number on it.' She held the card out for Whitlock to take, her arm trembling as adrenaline surged through her. 'It's just part of the job.' She wanted to protest more but made herself be quiet, knowing the more she talked, the guiltier it made her look.

Whitlock's expression was as hard as marble as she took it from Casey's fingers. She went to stuff it back into her pocket, but in her haste the card snagged, folded and fell to the floor. She dropped into a crouch to grab it up, but her fuse had reached its end and she stayed down on her haunches and slapped the tiled floor with the flat of her palm. 'You're all liars.' She slapped the floor again and stood up, turning her back on Casey. 'Goddamn you all.' She dipped her head, her shoulders hunching as if she was weeping silently.

Casey stood frozen, too stunned to react.

When she finally stepped over to Whitlock's side, she realised she wasn't crying but fighting to control her breathing, as if on the verge of a panic attack. Casey reached tentatively for her forearm. 'Mrs Whitlock, you've had the worst shock—'

Whitlock shrugged her hand away. 'Shut up, just shut up. All of you come to me and talk to me like I'm a little idiot, and I'm through with it.'

'Who, ma'am? Who're you talking about?'

'All of you. Franklin's little lapdogs.' She took hold of the banister and squared her shoulders, gasping as if she'd just come up from underwater. 'Go back to Franklin Gates or Keirn, or whoever you answer to, and tell them I'll write them a cheque for a million dollars, right now, if they can guarantee my safety and my family's. For good. You all want my money, so let's stop the pretence.'

Her eyes were angry again, the controlled fury spilling over now, and the sudden change made Casey wonder if she was on some kind of meds. In the circumstances, it would be more of a surprise if she wasn't. 'Ma'am, I don't understand. Are you saying you're in danger? I'm sure the county executive is trying to do what's right by you.'

She screwed her face up. 'No, he's not. He looks at me and tells me he's sorry for my loss, and all I see are the dollar signs in his eyes. They've milked Landon for years, and now they're scared he's dead and I'll shut off the faucet. Is that why they put you on the case?' She waved the crumpled business card. 'Explain it to me, because nothing makes sense.'

Casey held her gaze, her eyes wide, trying to appear as transparent as possible. 'My partner and I were the responding officers on duty when the call came in. No one assigned us to the case. I can't explain why your husband had my business card, but I can assure you it carries no personal significance. The investigation is ongoing, so we can't speak in certainties at this stage, but right now all the evidence points to your husband being an innocent bystander. We believe the other victim of the attack was the intended target.'

Whitlock stared a hole through her. 'That's exactly what Franklin says.'

'With respect, and I don't mean to speak for the county executive, but I think that's because it reflects the facts as we have them right now.'

She put her hands on her hips, indignant. 'Landon was the

same way with me. He thought I believed in unicorns and fairies too. I spent years looking the other way because that's how he wanted it, but I won't do it anymore. I need to know if I'm vulnerable and if my daughter is vulnerable.'

'Right now, I have no reason to think that's the case, ma'am.'

'Really.' Whitlock held her hands out, gesturing to the house around her. 'That's a million-dollar powerboat on the dock – Lanny didn't even know how to start it. This house sits on three acres of the south shore, and we have a duplex in the city that we haven't set foot in for two years. We didn't get here by him handing out stock tips and tax advice. And now he's dead.'

'Did your husband ever say anything specific to make you think he was at risk?'

'My husband was paranoid, prone to anxiety attacks and an infrequent, but enthusiastic, user of cocaine. He spent his every waking hour afraid, in one way or another, but I couldn't tell you how much of it was real.'

Mention of coke had Billy's voice telling Casey *I told you so* in her head. 'Is there a chance Mr Whitlock owed someone money for narcotics?'

Whitlock flicked her hand to dismiss the idea, turning her head away.

'Did your husband have any enemies at all that you're aware of?'

'Not that I could name, but that doesn't mean he didn't. The truth is I don't know.'

Casey thought about Landon Whitlock's secretary and her description of his paranoia. 'Brianna Monk told us Mr Whitlock believed he was being followed in recent weeks. Did he ever discuss that with you?'

'No.' She blinked twice as she said it.

It was too fast, the answer too clipped, as if she'd been expecting the question, and Casey felt as if the sands beneath her were shifting again. She hesitated a second, thrown by the reaction and trying to assess the significance. 'You're sure?'

Whitlock fixed her with a dead-eyed stare. 'I'm sure.'

Casey struggled to recalibrate. Could it have been Ryker following Landon? 'You're aware we're searching for a man named Adam Ryker in connection with the shootings?'

'Yes.'

'Does that name mean anything in relation to Mr Whitlock or yourself?' Saying it aloud brought on an idea: could Ryker have been screwing around with Darcy Whitlock? What was the likelihood? But if that was the case, then what were the chances of Landon Whitlock and Sheena Rawlins being in the same place at the same time ... unless Ryker had arranged it somehow? That lingering question of the thousand dollars in cash Landon had on him at the time of his murder – a payoff of some kind? Or drug money after all?

'I don't know the man you're looking for,' Whitlock said, killing Casey's brainstorm dead. 'I've seen his picture. I don't recognise him.' A single blink this time. 'But if Landon knew him through his work, it's unlikely I'd know about it. I barely know any of his clients. I was only ever wheeled out when he needed a pretty face on his arm.'

Casey watched for signs Whitlock was lying, but she'd shown no reaction at all to the name. She tried shifting gears. 'We haven't been able to locate Mr Whitlock's vehicle. Have you got any idea where it would be?'

'I didn't even know where he was.' Whitlock stepped away from Casey, adjusting the jacket of her pantsuit. 'Isn't it your job to figure this stuff out?'

'Of course, but part of that is asking questions. And as soon as anything comes to light, you'll be the first to know about it.'

Whitlock tilted her head. 'Bullshit. Franklin will tell me what he wants me to know, and he'll lie about the rest. And what are we meant to do in the meantime? Just sit here and hope my husband's killer doesn't come for us too?'

'I can speak to my lieutenant about having Patrol units stationed here, if that would help?'

'Detective, I could have your lieutenant stationed here if I wanted, with Keirn fixing my breakfast in the morning. We have the best security money can buy. That's not the point – I have no interest in becoming a prisoner in my own home, or looking over my shoulder for the rest of my—'

She stopped mid-sentence, her eyes shifting to something behind Casey.

'Mom?'

Whitlock swept past Casey as if she wasn't there, moving to the open doorway behind her, where a young woman now stood.

'Sweetheart, what are you doing home?' She glanced at her watch.

'I told you I didn't want to go to Grandma's. I had Ryan bring me home.' Outside, a black SUV was parked across the driveway, a driver in a tailored black suit standing on its far side.

The girl was probably thirteen or fourteen, but the heavy black eyeliner she wore and the sickly sweet smell of vape juice that accompanied her made her seem older. Her aesthetic was full nineties retro – baggy jeans and a flannel shirt over a cutoff Deftones band tee, a centre part in her long brown hair so it fell partially over her face. The look was so at odds with Darcy Whitlock's *Vanity Fair* stylings that it screamed of rebellion against her mother, but what grabbed Casey's attention most were the girl's jade-green eyes.

'Sweetheart, there are grown-up things I have to take care of today. There's a reason I asked you to be with Grandma—'

'Jesus, Mom, when are you going to talk to me like a human being? "*Grown-up things*"?'

Whitlock hesitated, her mouth ajar, trying for a different way to say it. 'I just meant there are details I have to take care of that...' She pressed her fingers into the bridge of her nose, closing her eyes. 'It's just easier if—'

'If I'm out of the way,' the girl said. 'Nothing new there, then...'

'Harper, that is not at all what I said.'

'Who's this?' Harper said, pointing at Casey.

'My name's Casey Wray, I'm a detective with HCPD.'

'Why are you here?' She glanced at Whitlock, then back at Casey, a new urgency about her movements. 'Did you find who killed my dad?'

Whitlock stepped between them. 'Detective, please, would you wait outside for me?'

'You can't hide this from me, Mom.'

'Harper, please, this isn't a conversation you need to be a part of.'

'You want me to find out from TikTok instead? There's already, like, a half-dozen posts about it, all kinds of conspiracy crap. Is that better?'

'Harper—'

'NO.' She pressed her fingers into her chest. 'This affects me too, you know? I'm not five anymore. You can't offload me to Grandma and pretend nothing's happening.'

Whitlock took Harper's hands in her own. 'Baby, please, I

am trying my best here. For all of us.' Her voice cracked as she said it, the tendons in her neck straining. 'I asked the detective to come here because I had a lot of questions, that's all. They don't know who did this yet.'

The girl shook her hands free of her mother's, her eyes darting between Casey's and the floor, the uncertainty behind them growing like weeds. 'Then what were you saying when I came in? About looking over your shoulder?'

'No, no...' Whitlock tilted her head to the ceiling then fixed her daughter with a wide-eyed look.. 'I was in the middle of ... You misunderstood what I was saying. I was asking ... I just wanted to know what we could do to help move the investigation along. I want answers. We all do.'

Harper stared at her, poised, like a dog deciding whether to run or stand and fight. Then she started shaking her head. 'You're such a bad liar.' She barrelled past her and headed up the stairs.

'Baby, wait...'

But Harper carried on without looking back, following the L-shaped staircase until she reached the landing and then disappearing into one of the rooms, shutting the door firmly behind her.

Darcy Whitlock brought her knuckle to her mouth, kneading her lip, her eyes pointed at the staircase, but unfocused and unblinking.

Casey stood there not knowing what to say, the silence heavy and smothering, like wet burlap. Then the sound of heavy metal erupted from Harper's room, guitars, drums and a screaming singer, as loud as if the speakers were in the hallway next to them.

Slowly, Casey came around to stand at Darcy Whitlock's

side. 'Ma'am, we have an excellent Victim Services unit at HCPD, I think it would be beneficial if you speak to them – I really think they could help you both. I can arrange to have them meet with you, if you'd like, at a time of your convenience. We can discuss your security arrangements too, and any temporary measures we need to put in place.'

Whitlock turned slowly. 'I told you to wait outside.' For a second, Casey thought Whitlock was going to punctuate it with a slap.

Casey held her hands up and began to retreat. 'Unless there's anything else you need, I'll be getting back to the office.'

'Do that. Go make the coffee or whatever it is you do. I don't know why I'm wasting my time with you. I don't even care if you were fucking my husband. I'm embarrassed for him if you were.'

Casey stopped and stared at her, biting her tongue so hard she thought she'd sever it. Finally, she took a backward step, nodding to herself. 'You know what? If you have any concerns about your safety, day or night, dial 911. If you want to talk to Victim Services, I can send you a contact number. And if you think of something specific to do with your husband's work or a threat against his person, feel free to call me anytime.' Casey pointed to Whitlock's pocket. 'You have my number.'

CHAPTER SEVENTEEN

Casey slipped behind the wheel of the car, feeling as if all the blood in her body was draining into her feet. The conversation had run out of control from the first minute, and by the end, she'd allowed her emotions to take over. If going there had been a mistake, every word she'd spoken had compounded it. She shut the door and started the engine, wheeling the car around in a tight circle to take off down the driveway.

She followed the road with her pulse pounding in her ears, a rush as loud as a jet engine. Only when she'd made it beyond the maple trees, putting her out of view of the house, did she pull over and press her head against the steering wheel. A heavy grey cloud had moved across the sun, casting Shatter Creek to her right in a darker tone, the waterway sleek and black, like a rat snake making its way inland.

Casey pictured Darcy Whitlock calling Franklin Gates and instructing him to have her fired. Keirn was too weak to go against Gates' wishes and fight for her, and Dunmore would hold the door open to get her out faster. She was catastrophising, she knew it, but Whitlock was direct enough, angry enough – and maybe vindictive enough – to pursue a grudge against her, and there was no telling how she might lash out next. The behaviour was nothing new – she'd seen it plenty of times before from those who'd had their lives ripped apart by a violent death, but Darcy Whitlock's money and influence set her apart from most victims.

The phone rang and Casey looked at the screen to see Dana's number. She righted herself in her seat and ran her hand over her face as she answered. 'Dana, what's up?'

'Where are you, Big?'

'Darcy Whitlock's place – I'll fill you in later.'

'Sounds like you took another beating?'

'She doesn't like me any more than before, I'm pretty sure about that. I'm on my way back now, you need something urgent?'

'Well I was calling to give you some of that good news you're always asking for...'

'They fired me? They're shutting down the department?'

'We got ourselves a weapon at Adam Ryker's property, CSU are sending it for analysis now. The dumbass buried it in his yard.'

❧

Dana was waiting for Casey in the parking lot when she pulled into the precinct. She looked her over, squinting, as she got out of the car. 'No black eyes, no contusions, looks to me like you got off easy,' she said.

Casey shut the car door. 'Yeah, kinda beating myself up worse than Darcy Whitlock did, but whatever.'

'What's she want with you?'

Casey pressed her fingers into her forehead, unsure even where to begin. 'Landon Whitlock had one of my business cards. She found it in his desk and thinks ... Shit, I don't know what she thinks. She asked me if I was sleeping with him.'

Dana raised both eyebrows.

'I know. I felt like telling her it's been so long since I got laid, I wouldn't remember what to do, but I didn't think that would help.'

'Not convincing, either. Everyone knows it's like riding a bike.'

'Yeah, thanks, D.' Casey smiled bitterly as she pushed through the doors to the precinct. 'Anyway, then she was going off on everyone: me, Franklin Gates, Keirn – the whole town. I know she's just lashing out because it's her way of coping, but ... Jesus, it's a lot.' Casey stopped and put her hands on her hips.

'Actually, that's not fair. She's afraid. She's worried someone's coming for her and her daughter, and at the same time the daughter's lashing out at her in the same way. And you know what? I get it. Her husband catches a bullet walking down the street, she's looking for a way to make sense of it, so her head's telling her someone must be targeting them. That's easier to understand than it being some random tragedy.' Casey started walking again. 'So. Anyway. Tell me about the gun.'

Dana looked at her moonfaced, as if her head was spinning trying to keep up. 'It's a Glock nine-mil. CSU found it buried under a bucket of rags in the front yard. The dirt was all tore up, the piece was practically sticking out of the ground. Obviously did it in a hurry, thought he could make it less obvious by dumping a bucket on top.'

'Or he wanted to come back for it, which makes me worry he's not finished ... We need to find this asshole.'

They turned on the landing and started up the last flight of stairs.

'The lab's analysing it now,' Dana continued. 'Should have the results in a couple hours. The serial number's registered to an address upstate, Glens Falls, reported stolen six months ago.' They came to the top of the staircase and Dana stopped speaking to catch her breath. 'I gotta get my ass to the gym.'

'How the hell does marketing guy Adam Ryker bag himself a stolen handgun? He's got no record. Wouldn't it be easier to just go buy one from the store?'

'Maybe he was worried about it being easier to trace?'

'Maybe. But then where does he find a connect to hook him up with a piece?'

'Internet. Same as everything else. Or that one shady guy that's in every group of dude bros.'

Casey bent her head to one side, weighing it up. 'I can't get a handle on this guy's mindset, though – like, there's parts to this seem like he's been planning it for a long time, and parts that seem like he woke up yesterday and decided to go on a rampage.'

Dana opened the door to the department. 'Maybe he woke up without a morning boner yesterday. When did assholes ever make sense, right?'

Casey walked across the office, shaking her head at Dana's twisted mind. As she approached her desk, she saw Dunmore look up from her screen and rise from her seat. She quick-walked across to intercept them, eyeballing Casey all the way. 'Can I speak with you a moment, Sergeant?'

Casey's skin prickled. Had to be Darcy Whitlock had made a call already. 'Sure, of course.' Casey started to go to Dunmore's office, but Dunmore held a hand up to stop her. 'Let's go to a meeting room.'

Dunmore led the way in silence, not looking back once. Casey followed her to the set of meeting rooms that were hidden away from view of the rest of the floor. She stepped inside the first one and went to take a seat, but Dunmore stood right in front of her, her eyes hard and wide.

'Does the chain of command mean anything to you, Detective?'

'Lieutenant?'

'I've just had Acting Chief Keirn tear me apart on the phone, accusing me of undermining him with the county executive.' She stabbed a finger into her own chest. 'He thought *I'd* gone around him to brief Franklin Gates on the status of the Whitlock investigation, an update that he, quite correctly, felt should be coming directly from him.'

'Lieutenant—'

'I'm not finished, Detective. The acting chief accepted my protests, given that I have never spoken a single word to Franklin Gates in my life, but it's a black mark against my name for "allowing this to happen". I haven't been in this job forty-eight hours, and I am already on the shit list, so why don't you explain to me just what the hell you thought you were doing?'

'Lieutenant, it's not my fault. Rita Zangetty called me—'

'Who?'

'Franklin Gates' chief of staff. She called me and said Gates wanted to handle the flow of information to Darcy Whitlock himself, because Landon Whitlock was some bigtime donor and the pols want to keep her sweet.'

'And you decided that was appropriate?'

'No, but she told me Gates was going to tell Keirn that's how it had to be, so we had no choice.'

'*She* told you this. Not even the county executive – his assistant.'

'She not an assistant, she's his chief of staff—'

'And you were fine with civilians taking ownership of our investigation, and didn't even feel the need to clue me in?'

Casey had to look away. 'He's Keirn's boss. I thought...'

'You thought what?'

Casey shook her head, fuming at Zangetty, at Gates, all of them. 'I told her to have Gates call the acting chief for an update, but she said there was no time. She was about to tell Darcy Whitlock the wrong thing, all I did was stop her.'

'For god's sake, stop shifting the blame.'

'I'm not – what was I supposed to do?' Casey forced herself to meet Dunmore's eyes again. 'I had no intention of telling her anything, but she got the wrong idea about Adam Ryker and was going to pass on bad info. Wouldn't that be worse? Keirn having to call her back to tell her that actually, yes, the guy we were looking for was the suspect in her husband's murder, very sorry about that?'

Dunmore was shaking her head. 'No sale. Y'know, I knew there'd be some kind of reaction, but I never expected this. I thought you'd at least come at me head on.'

'What are you talking about? Reaction to what?'

'To me. To me taking your job. And what annoys me the most is that I came to you and told you I understood if you were disappointed, and I offered you an easy way out – and you gave me the routine about just being happy to serve.' Dunmore folded her arms. 'You could've been straight with me right then, but that's expecting too much from you, isn't it?'

'Lieutenant, with respect, that's not fair...'

'Isn't it? How long did you serve under Ray Carletti?'

'Seven years, but—'

'That's a long time to sit under his learning tree and claim not to have picked up any bad habits.'

The line made Casey rear up to her full height. 'I had IA and the Feds pick over every piece of my life, and I was cleared.'

'If I look in my garbage can at the right time, I'll find it empty. That doesn't mean there's never been any garbage.'

Casey stared at her, open-mouthed. 'You don't know anything about me. How can you say that when—'

'I know more than enough. I did my homework before I took this command. You think good police were scrambling over each other to take on this tire-fire of a department? They had to beg me just to come and interview. What happened here was a disgrace; I was given assurances no deal was cut with you when it all shook out, so that tells me either you were in it with

Carletti but smart enough to cover your tracks, or he kept you around to manipulate and you were too naïve to notice. You feel like telling me which it was?'

'Neither.' Casey stabbed her finger onto the table. 'It was neither. You weren't here, you don't know what it was like.'

Dunmore stared her down, almost daring her to go further. But Casey had no words, the shock so profound.

'I tried my hardest to be civil with you and you've thrown it in my face,' Dunmore said. 'I want this investigation wrapped up yesterday, and then you're transferring someplace else. You don't say another word to Gates' office, and *everything* goes to Keirn, via me, from now on. Do you understand me, Sergeant?'

Casey felt tears brim in her eyes, and all she could do was nod once.

Dunmore marched past her and out the door, leaving Casey alone with a voice in her head, protesting over and over again that she'd done nothing wrong. But the chaser was darker, harsher: that maybe Dunmore was right about her having been too stupid to see through Carletti.

She didn't move, didn't blink, refusing to let the tears spill. She thought of her mother, of having her wrap her up in her arms and tell her that it would be okay, tomorrow was another day. She thought of Ray, but felt disgust in herself when she realised it was because she wanted his comfort in that moment. She dug her fingers into her arms, the discomfort a reminder that the Ray she thought she knew had never existed, and that the reckoning she faced now was one of his making. It made her hatred for him rise up all over again, and that sent her thoughts running to the person who'd always hated him as much as she did now.

She took her phone out of her pocket and tapped a message: *Can I see you?*

❧

Casey went first to the bathroom, to splash her face with handfuls of cold water, then straight back to her desk. She felt Dunmore's gaze follow her as she walked, but made a point of ignoring it, damned if she'd show her any more weakness than she already had. She told herself it was better to know; that as misplaced as Dunmore's accusations were, at least now she knew why she had a problem with her.

At her desk, she reached for her mouse and kept her eyes locked on her screen. Red-rimmed and puffy, they felt the size of golf balls. There was a sombre atmosphere, the room almost silent; the ticking clock on the wall behind her sounded as loud as a typewriter.

Billy poked his head around the side of his monitor. 'You okay?'

Casey nodded without making eye contact. In her peripheral vision, she saw Dana look over and start to get up, but Casey shook her head without looking at her, and that was enough to signal that she wasn't ready to talk. Dana peeled off in the direction of the break room instead.

Her thoughts were haywire. The conversation with Dunmore played in a loop in her head. She tried to block it out, turn her focus back to the investigation, but found she couldn't pick up the mental thread. There were papers and folders all over her desk, the text messages between Ryker and Lauren Goff, the domestic-dispute reports, old case files, all of it suddenly impenetrable.

She wanted to pick up the phone and chew out Rita Zangetty for putting her in this position. She wanted to yell at her for not squaring it off the way she said she would. She knew it was out of the question. That thought kept rebounding as she clicked on the Outlook search bar and entered Landon Whitlock's name, looking for when or how she might've come across him to have handed him her card. Nothing came up, so she searched her emails. His name only appeared in the messages sent back and forth amongst the team, nothing prior to that. She looked up his contact numbers from the file and entered them into her phone, but neither showed up.

The search was fruitless, and as a distraction, it proved an utter failure.

Dana's landline rang. Casey snatched up her own phone to answer the call in her absence, jumping on the opportunity to get away from her thoughts.

'HCPD.'

'Yeah, hey, this is Leo Walker, someone there called me earlier and left me a message, said they wanted to talk to me about my boy Adam?'

'Adam Ryker?'

'Yeah, me and him go a ways back.'

'You do, huh?' Casey grabbed a notepad. 'Thanks for calling back, Mr Walker. I don't know if you're aware, but we're looking to speak to Mr Ryker urgently about—'

'Yeah, I saw his face on the news. I don't know what to tell you ... I was shocked, obviously, but also, kinda, not totally, you know what I mean? AR's always been a handful with the girls, since we were kids. One after the other, two at the same time, he didn't even care.' He chuckled. 'Yeah, I'm telling you, he was relentless.'

Casey closed her eyes, her anger rising all over again at hearing the pride he evinced in Ryker's treatment of women. 'Have you seen Mr Ryker since Thursday?'

'Nah, we don't see each other more than once or twice a year these days. We still text some, but it's different lives, right? I got a family. I can't do the partying thing anymore, not the way he does.'

'He's not at home and his employer doesn't know where he's at. Is there anywhere else you can think of that he might go to?'

'Honestly, I don't know anymore. You've probably seen his Insta feed – he's always out at some bar or restaurant, but I never even heard of half of them.' The nature of the call seemed to hit home to Walker suddenly, because when he spoke again, his voice was subdued. 'I guess he wouldn't be in a bar or restaurant right now, anyway. Sorry.'

'When did you last speak to him?'

He blew out a breath. 'I couldn't say. Months ago, at least. He was talking his talk like he does. To be honest it gets kinda boring after a while – this girl, that girl, always the same thing. He was bragging about how there were these two cousins he was dating at the same time...'

Casey opened her eyes, clicked her pen. 'Two cousins?'

'Yeah. I told him he was sick.' The pride in his voice made it clear he'd meant it as a compliment.

'Do you remember their names?'

'Sure. One of them was called Aryana, because I remember joking, being like, "Woah, Ariana Grande?" and he goes, "Nope – even hotter." The other one I can't remember, some kind of an Indian name or something.'

She scribbled the name on her pad as she wrapped up the call. 'Sir, thank you for your assistance. If you think of anything else that might be relevant, call me back anytime.' She hung up and drew a circle around it.

Muneera.

CHAPTER EIGHTEEN

Aryana Guptil had checked herself and Muneera into the Marriot downtown. Casey and Billy met the cousins in the lobby, a high-ceilinged space decorated in the same muted greys and walnut panelling familiar to every corporate hotel lounge, save for the one wall that was given over to a collage of reeds and ivy that appeared to be growing from the structure itself.

Aryana stepped out of the elevator wearing an oversized hoodie, Muneera trailing her in the same ripped jeans and black top she'd had on that morning. Aryana's eyes were bloodshot, either the strain or tiredness showing, while Muneera came over with her arms wrapped tightly around herself.

'Thanks for meeting with us again on short notice,' Casey said. 'Aryana, we just wanted to go over a few more questions with you. Would it be okay to go with Detective Drocker for a moment or two?' Casey had prepped Billy to keep her talking until she signalled to him that she was through with Muneera.

'Um, sure,' Aryana said. 'Have you arrested him? Has something happened?'

'We're still looking for Mr Ryker. Detective Drocker will talk you through what we need.'

Billy guided her to the far side of the lounge, where a bank of TVs embedded in the wall were showing SportsCenter, CNN and the Weather Channel.

Casey waited until they were out of earshot, then turned to Muneera. 'You guys doing okay here?' Casey asked. 'Must be tough on you both having to ship out like this so suddenly.'

Muneera glanced over her shoulder towards the main entrance, her arms still wrapped around herself. 'It's not so bad. We ordered room service. Ary's dad's paying, so she said we might as well make the most of it. But she's pretty scared.'

Casey nodded as she spoke. 'How did you get along with Adam Ryker, ma'am?'

Muneera shifted her weight to her other foot. 'I mean, I didn't really hang out with him all that much. I felt bad about the way he treated Aryana, but...' She shrugged, shaking her head. 'I guess I don't really know what else to say about him.'

'Were you guys close at any point?'

Muneera squinted. 'Me and Adam? No, no, he was just, like, Aryana's boyfriend. He was just, um, a guy, you know? In the background.' She hooked her thumb in her back pocket, then changed her mind and let it hang loose, unsure what to do with her hands.

'Uh-huh,' Casey said, nodding again. 'Because, the thing is, we've heard he was telling friends he was dating both of you at the same time. Is there any truth to that?'

'What?' Muneera flushed, looking like a teenager who'd just been caught with her first blunt. 'Who's saying ... Who told you that?'

'That's not important. What's important is that we find him.'

'Yeah, I get that, but...' She floated from one foot to the other, edging away from Casey. 'He was Aryana's boyfriend. I have no clue where he's at.'

'Okay, look, let me lay it out for you, ma'am. The impression I have is that Mr Ryker has a hard time being truthful, so if you tell me it's just one of his lies, that's fine. But what I want you to remember is that I'm not here to judge whatever has or hasn't gone on; my only interest is in finding Adam Ryker as quickly as possible. So if you know where he might be, or if you've spoken to him at all – now's the time to tell me.'

She shook her head rapidly. 'I haven't.'

'Have you exchanged any messages with him, emails, DMs via social media, anything like that?'

She never stopped shaking her head. 'No, I haven't. I swear.'

'Do you have any idea where we might find him?'

'He's not...' She closed her eyes, biting on her top lip.

'He's not what?'

'Nothing.' She looked Casey dead in the face. 'I haven't heard a word from him.' Her eyes filmed with tears as she said it. The longing was etched into her face, and Casey imagined her frantically messaging him over the last day or more, to no response.

'When was the last time you saw Mr Ryker?'

A tear began to work its way down her cheek and she quickly wiped it away. 'I can't...' She glanced towards Aryana, Billy having smartly positioned her so she had her back to them. 'I don't know anything about this. I haven't seen him and I don't know where he is. Can I go? Please?'

Casey stared at her a moment before she answered, searching her face to decide how far to push it. 'You can go, but I want you to remember two things: if you impede our investigation by not being straight with me, you could end up catching a charge. You don't need that. And second, Adam Ryker is a potential threat, okay? And not just to Aryana. If you hear from him, in any form, or get an idea where he is, you need to tell me right away.' She handed her a business card, her eyes lingering on the print as she again thought about the one in Landon Whitlock's possession. 'It's the best thing you can do for everyone.'

Muneera nodded, dropping her gaze to the floor.

'Just think about what I've said, okay? Call me on that number, anytime.'

Casey looked past her and signalled to Billy that she was finished. Muneera had already started edging away, and when she and Aryana met in the middle of the lobby, she wrapped her up in a tight embrace, burying her face in her shoulder.

'What did she say?' Billy said, coming over to Casey.

'She denied it, but she's lying.'

'You want me to take Aryana somewhere so you can talk some more?'

Casey thought about it and shook her head. 'I don't think she knows where he is, I got the feeling she was telling the truth about that. Let it eat at her for a few hours, see if she changes her tune.'

Casey's phone rang and she pulled it out of her pocket. 'Dana, what's up?'

'The ballistics came through. Ryker's gun is confirmed as our murder weapon.'

CHAPTER NINETEEN

The bar at the Abbeymore Hotel was a new-style place, black leather seating arranged around low glass-and-chrome tables, dark walls with patches of exposed brickwork and uncovered lightbulbs that hung down on extra-long cables to complete the look. The Miller Lite Casey had ordered ran to nine dollars, so she'd limited herself to two sips in the ten minutes she'd been waiting, using the time to watch a video recording of a Zoom call Adam Ryker had participated in the day before, just hours after the shootings. Ryker's boss at Kaleidoscopic had sent it over earlier in the afternoon, but she hadn't had the time to look at it properly amidst the scramble to run down leads on Ryker's whereabouts – a race against time given his trail was cold, and getting colder. It was a scramble that'd taken her back to The Slice to talk to the two women who'd claimed to be his current girlfriend, to his neighbourhood again to check with more of the residents along his block, and to the courthouse to get a warrant for his bank records, with pit stops at the office in between.

A day's work that'd left her exhausted, and no closer to finding him.

In the recording playing on her cell-phone screen, Ryker appeared in a box in the bottom-right corner, one of four participants in an internal meeting discussing a marketing campaign for a client who apparently wanted to make potato waffles 'relevant' again. Dressed in a black tee and wearing a slim microphone headset, Ryker spent most of the time looking at a second screen off to the side, occasionally nodding along with whatever was being said. He'd blurred his background, making it impossible to tell where he'd been during the call, but the double-monitor setup was consistent with the one they'd seen at his property, save for the fact the computer was missing when they'd been there, Ryker presumably taking it with him wherever he'd run to.

Casey watched fitfully, fast-forwarding through chunks of the playback. Then towards the end of the video, something one of the other participants was saying must've caught Ryker's attention, causing him to look over sharply at the main screen. 'Wrap it up, Esteban, we've been over this.'

'Adam, if we don't have a social strategy, we don't have anything.'

'We have a social strategy, Esteban, it's just not your one.'

'Adam—'

'I said wrap it up.'

'Okay, sure, but I'll leave it to you to tell Hugo why his campaign failed before it started.'

'Sure, no problem, I'll do your dirty work for you. But everyone knows you're scared of the guy, so why don't you just say that?'

Esteban screwed up his face and shook his head, but it wasn't convincing, and Casey could tell he really was nervous about speaking to this Hugo guy.

'Seriously, why don't you go tell him that?' Ryker said, leaning closer to the camera as if zeroing in on him. 'He might go easier on you.' He laughed at his own joke and switched his gaze back to the second screen.

'Adam, if you could engage with this more fully, we might—'

'I've engaged with it all I need to. At this point you're just wasting our time. Move on.'

There was an awkward silence, until, finally, one of the other participants, a blonde woman with a nose piercing, started talking about taglines.

Casey wound it back to the moment when Ryker was looking right into the camera. The meeting had taken place mid-morning, and Casey tried to picture the man she was looking at gunning down two people on the sidewalk just hours earlier – and making plans to murder his ex-girlfriend in the early hours of the next day. Ryker came off as distracted in the moment and arrogant in general, but nothing outwardly suggested a killer in the middle of a rampage. Then again, she knew that the impressions she formed from snippets of a work call were worth jack shit.

She looked up and spotted McTeague walking towards her, hands in his pockets and eyes scanning the room.

'Not your average cop bar,' Casey said as he drew up next to her.

'I'm not real popular in cop joints anymore,' he said. 'You mind if we sit at the bar?' He dipped his head in the direction of the empty seat next to hers that barely rose to his shins. 'Those things are a long way down.'

'Sure,' Casey said, standing up and snagging her beer, then following behind him. 'I hate to tell you, but you were never popular in cop bars. Ever.'

'I know,' he said over his shoulder, weaving between tables, 'but let me lie to myself, Wray, huh?' He made it to the bar and pulled out a stool for her, then ordered himself a drink with just a raised finger and a look.

'You're a regular in here?' Casey said, her surprise genuine.

'I bring potential clients by. Give them the impression I'm a real successful businessman, not the ex-cop they read about in the *Courier*.'

'Surely the clothes are enough to convince them of that,' Casey said, looking him up and down in fake admiration, the oversized suit and faded blue dress shirt variations on the same outfit he always wore. Only the greatcoat was missing from the mental picture of him she carried in her head, McTeague discarding it now the mercury was regularly topping sixty.

The bartender delivered a Bud and McTeague nodded his thanks before tipping it towards Casey's to clink. 'You bring me down here just to hand out fashion advice?'

'Yeah, no. I got told I dress like my clothes are from Target yesterday, so...'

He tilted his head slightly, as if appraising her outfit. 'I'd have guessed Walmart.'

She laughed, the burn catching her off guard when his expression was still so serious. 'This is Sears' premium range, goddammit.'

'Sears, huh? I'm impressed. When I started, there were guys working second jobs who still had to shop at the Goodwill.'

'Well it's good that you decided to keep the tradition up.'

He raised his eyebrows, a faux telling-off. 'So, why are we here?'

Casey cradled her bottle in her lap, picking at the corner of the label. 'The new lieutenant tore me apart today. She ... I guess she thinks I'm out to screw her over with the brass – I'm not, but she won't believe that now. She's kicking me out of the department.'

He listened with his head bowed, showing no reaction.

'Anyway, I just wanted to...' She took a sip of her beer, frustrated at her inability to voice her thoughts. 'I just needed to talk to someone.'

He looked at her sidelong, then took a pull from his beer.

When he set it down again, he said, 'And I'm the best option you've got? You're in worse shape than I thought.'

She laughed, cringing at the truth it brought front of mind: she'd lost everyone she would've normally turned to. 'Yeah, well, beggars can't be choosers, I guess.'

'You want to know what I think?'

'Uh-huh.'

'Sounds like you need a new job.'

She rolled her eyes. 'Is that the only medicine you've got, Doctor?'

'I'm serious. I told you now was the time to get out of there. Make a deal with the brass and come work with me.'

She looked along the rows of liquor bottles behind the bar, so many names she'd never heard of. 'It's not that simple.'

'It can be. If you want it to be.'

'You wouldn't have left. Not by choice.'

He nodded, conceding the point. 'But now I've hopped that fence and I'm telling you it's not all that bad.' He pointed at her with his bottle. 'What did you do, anyway?'

Casey talked him through the details of the frantic phone calls with Rita Zangetty, the promise Franklin Gates would square it with Keirn, ending with Dunmore's accusation that it was a deliberate effort to undermine her.

'Damn,' he said, when she was finished, making a whistling sound. 'So Rita Z screwed you over, huh? Or Gates did.'

'Why though?'

He shrugged. 'Unlikely it was intentional. Maybe Rita over-promised to you, or Gates just never got around to it. The county exec people don't care about cops, we're just another prop for them come election season.' He raised his beer but then lowered it again. 'I see why your lieutenant's pissed, though.'

'Do you think I did the wrong thing?'

He took a swig of his beer and ran his free hand over the back of his head, ruffling his hair. 'Don't do that.'

Casey swayed back in her seat, miming surprise at the comeback. 'Do what?'

He swivelled on his stool to face her. 'Don't give people that power over you.'

She parted her lips but wasn't sure what to say, suddenly aware that she might've misjudged their relationship. She'd started thinking of him as a confidant, maybe even a friend, but their shared history was brief and fraught.

'Look, did you set out to go around her – Dunmore?' He counted off one finger, as if it was the first point of several.

'No, of course not.'

He counted off the second. 'Are you a stooge for the county executive? No.' He counted a third. 'Were you trying to do what you thought was right? Yes.' Then a fourth. 'Are you a good person? Yes.' He opened his hands. 'You didn't need me to tell you any of those things, so you don't need anyone else to either.'

Casey tore the rest of the label off her bottle, unsure whether she'd just been told off or complimented. 'I was just looking for some advice.'

'You didn't ask for advice, you asked if you did something wrong.'

'It's the same thing.'

'No it isn't,' he said. 'Ray Carletti's gone. You don't need a replacement.'

Casey went rigid, staring at him wide-eyed. 'He's got nothing to do with this.'

'He's got everything to do with this. What I'm telling you is that you don't need a comfort blanket anymore. If you go around looking for approval, you give others power over you.'

'So you never second-guessed yourself?'

'You know I did, but that's what I'm saying.' He looked at her, an intensity in his eyes she'd never seen before. 'I trusted Hanrahan the way you did Carletti, and he used that. It cost me everything.'

'So you're telling me you're no different, that's why I shouldn't trust you?'

He closed his eyes, frustrated. 'You want guidance on an investigation, or how to play a DA, come talk to me. You ask for my advice, I'll give it to you. What I'm telling you is to stop letting other people decide your self-worth. Not just me, anyone.'

She put her elbows on the bar top and ran her hands through her hair, scraping it back until it cascaded through her fingers. McTeague sat upright on his stool and took a pull from his beer. There was music playing quietly in the background, twinkly ambient electronica that seemed to have no start or end.

'I didn't mean that to come off like a lecture,' McTeague said, softer now.

Casey gave a bleak laugh. 'Bad job by you, then.'

He sank the rest of his beer and looked over. 'I have a million regrets, is all. Ten million.' He looked past her, curling his bottom lip over his teeth. 'I so badly want to make it right, to help people so they don't make the same mistakes as me, but there's no one else wants to hear it from a bitter ex-cop, so you get a full semester's worth of tuition for the price of a beer.' He smiled, goofing on himself, and it was as if he'd fully shed the skin he'd worn for all the years she'd feared him from a distance. The man sitting next to her was nothing like the hulking captain who'd loomed over everything at HCPD for all the time she'd carried a badge, his vulnerability almost appealing.

Casey pointed at his empty bottle. 'I'll buy you another, but only if you promise class is out.'

He met her eyes again and she felt a slight flutter in her stomach; the sensation of something unsaid passing between them, the air around them becoming charged with potential. The foundations of their relationship creaking and shifting again.

He didn't answer at first, twisting his bottle by the neck as if he was thinking it over, until finally he glanced at his watch. 'I should get going. Rain check?'

Casey nodded and smiled, too eager in her effort to hide her disappointment. 'Sure. I could only get you a water anyway, the prices they charge in here.'

He got up and stood over his stool, nudging it under the bar with his foot. 'You wanna earn more money? I know a job that pays okay…'

Casey looked down, nodding. 'I'll think about it. Promise.'

He held up one hand as a goodbye as he walked off through the lounge to the exit.

Casey stared at her beer, fragments of the label still stuck to the bottle, the rest of it crumpled up on the counter. The wrong place/out of her depth/out of her mind; it all passed through her head, and she felt a little foolish, but it receded just as quickly, one-drink tiredness smothering everything else. She left a tip under her bottle and slipped off the stool.

As she turned to make for the way out, she noticed a woman across the lounge sitting by herself reading a copy of *Daisy Jones and the Six*, and a sense of recognition came over her right away. Caucasian, late twenties or early thirties, with light-brown hair and an oval face – almost the definition of unremarkable, which was what made Casey so sure she had to have seen her somewhere before to be noticing her now. She let her gaze linger a second longer, then started to move off again, still grappling with placing her. She glanced back once more as she went, but the woman didn't look up, didn't seem aware of her at all.

⁂

Driving home, Casey found herself checking the rearview every couple of minutes. Traffic was heavy heading out of town, plenty of cover if someone was trying to tail her, but the vehicles behind were different every time she looked. She kept trying to place the woman in the lounge, but couldn't make her face fit anywhere. She thought she saw a white Tesla bob in and out of her mirrors a few times, but it was too busy to tell if it was the same one.

Crossing into Rockport Gables, traffic thinned out and the streets were darker. One pair of headlights became a fixture in the rearview. They were too far back to make out the car or driver, but there was no question now they were keeping pace with her, at a distance. The glare in the mirror was like a flashlight shone in her face.

After a mile or so, Casey rolled up to a stop sign and waited, letting the other vehicle catch up. As it drew closer, she could make out the shape of a white Tesla, the driver just a silhouette from her vantage point.

Nothing moved at the intersection. The Tesla came to a stop two car lengths back. Casey sat with her hand gripping the door, trying to get a look at the other driver, deciding whether to get out or not. With the darkness and the headlights, there was no way to make out a face from where she was.

She yanked the handle and opened the door. As she did, the Tesla slipped into reverse and paused. Casey got out and started walking towards it – but the driver pulled a tight one-eighty and sped off into the night.

Casey took down the plate and saved it in her phone, but the barcode in the window was the telltale that it was a rental.

She got behind the wheel again and drove the last three blocks home. When she made it to her bungalow, she carried on by it and started a loop of the block, checking for the white Tesla or anything that looked out of place.

Coming back around again, nothing raised the alarm. She stopped short of her place and parked by the kerb, waiting and watching with the lights and engine off. The thought bouncing around her head: the Tesla tail could've been an amateur who got spooked when Casey got out – or it could've been a distraction. But still nothing moved.

At last she pulled onto her own driveway and parked, but even then she held for a few minutes in the darkness, to see if anyone would emerge from the shadows. But the block was quiet.

She walked to her front door with one hand on her holster. The door was locked just as she left it. She went inside and locked it again behind her, then drew her sidearm to check she was alone. She went through every room in darkness, only turning the lights on when she was finally convinced.

Only then did she drop onto the sofa and slump back, feeling her shirt stuck to her back with cold sweat.

CHAPTER TWENTY

Casey arrived at the office before seven the next morning, expecting to be the first one there. But on her desk, someone had left a copy of that day's *Courier*, open on the continuation of the front-page story, summarising the latest on the investigation into the shootings.

She looked around, but there was no one else on the floor, Dunmore's office open but unoccupied. Casey picked up the paper and skimmed the article, the newspaper playing catchup with the speed of developments since yesterday's edition. But halfway down the second column was a passage that stuck out:

'The second victim of the early-day slayings, named as fifty-three-year-old Landon T. Whitlock, of Rockport, NY, appears unconnected to the other two victims, leaving family and friends baffled as to the motivation behind his murder. Now, police sources, speaking on condition of anonymity, have told the *Courier* that they believe the victim may have died trying to shield Miss Rawlins from her assailant, citing ballistics and other evidence from the scene.'

Casey looked up, glancing around for someone to say *What the fuck?* to. She skimmed the rest of the article, but the passage was the only part with information new to her, so she dropped it on the desk again. She looked over at Dunmore's office once more, thinking it had to be her who'd left it for Casey to find.

She went to the break room to look for her, but the lights were off and there was no one there, so she skirted by the meeting rooms as well – all empty. She went back to the main floor and picked her way towards Dunmore's office, finally pausing in the open doorway. She couldn't see if the computer screen was on, so she took two cautious steps inside, feeling like a thief, and craned her neck to peer around the monitor. It was open on Dunmore's inbox. She started to back up but turned around in time to see Dunmore come through the double doors at the other end of the office and stop.

Casey froze. She was half in and half out of the office, and she quickly moved to step the rest of the way out as calmly as she could manage. 'I was looking for you, Lieutenant.'

'You thought I might be hiding under the desk?'

Casey blushed. 'No, I could see you weren't there. I just wanted to check if your computer was on. Someone left the *Courier* on my desk. I was trying to figure out if it was you.'

She nodded. 'Is it you talking to them?'

Casey wrinkled her face. 'No.'

'Is this semantics? Are your friends at the county executive's office leaking it for you?'

'*No.*' Casey pushed her hair from her forehead and held it on top of her head. 'I can't even tell you how crazy it is that you think I have sway with the county exec's office. And why would I, anyway?'

'That's what I wanted to know.' Dunmore started moving again and came to a stop a short distance from Casey. 'But someone's talking to the media out of turn.'

'Lieutenant, you've got me all wrong. I explained what happened with Gates and his people. They were supposed to square it all off with Keirn. I have no idea why they didn't. I don't talk to the media, I never have.'

'Who else would be in a position to speak about the investigation?'

'But it's not true. What they're saying, about him trying to shield her. That's not been discussed at all. Someone's come up with it as a theory and passed it on. We haven't made any determination to that effect.'

Dunmore leaned against Billy's desk, arms folded. 'Then why would someone tell the *Courier* that?'

Casey opened her hands. 'I don't know. At a guess, someone wants to make Landon Whitlock look like a hero.'

Dunmore stared at her a second, then shook her head and went to go around her.

Casey heard McTeague's voice, urging her to believe in herself, and she stepped in front of her. 'Lieutenant, with respect, I'm not the person you think I am. I'm loyal, and I'm absolutely willing to work for you. I don't know how we got off on the wrong foot, but I just need you to give me a chance to show you what I'm about.'

Dunmore shut her eyes and sighed. Then she looked at Casey. 'This job ... You have no idea how much is at stake for me, taking this command. I've already got Keirn coming down on me like a hammer, and every time I blink, something else happens that makes me look inept to him.'

'I understand. Believe me. But I'm not the enemy, I swear.'

'Then why does it keep coming back to you?'

'With respect, it doesn't.'

Dunmore fixed her with a gaze. She swallowed and snatched a breath, the slightest hint that she was questioning her own judgement.

Casey stepped closer. 'What do I have to do to convince you?'

'Is ... everything okay?' The uncertain voice came from the far end of the room, and they turned in unison. Jill Hart was standing just inside the double doors, still wearing her jacket and with her bag slung over her shoulder. Dunmore turned back first, sidestepping Casey to go into her office and shut the door.

Jill hesitated, staying rooted to the spot.

'It's nothing, Jilly. Come sit down.'

Casey dropped into her seat with her head spinning, every interaction with Dunmore like a test she wasn't allowed to pass. She ran the plate on the white Tesla from the night before and hit the dead end she was expecting – registered to Hertz, no driver information available. As weird an encounter as it'd been, it wasn't nearly enough to subpoena the rental company for a customer ID.

Her phone rang and she brought it to her ear. 'Casey Wray.'

'Big, this is Crick.' Devon Critchlow, one of the Patrol sergeants from the Fourth Precinct she'd known for years. 'Sorry to get you guys out of bed, but we got a body over here.'

CHAPTER TWENTY-ONE

The woodland area was the start of the patchwork of pine forests that reared up on the northwestern edge of Rockport and ran all the way to the Pine Barrens in central Long Island. From the highway, Casey and Billy followed a dirt access road for more than a mile until they spotted Critchlow and one of his men waiting for them alongside their cruiser, backdropped by a wall of pitch pines and white and scarlet oaks.

Casey climbed out with heavy legs, the sense that what was coming was all bad.

'Long time, Big, how's it going?' Critchlow said.

'Ah, you know, another day in paradise,' she said, scanning the dense treeline and beyond before turning to Critchlow again. It was only then that she recognised the second man – the off-duty uniform she'd seen helping the old woman in the aftermath of the Eighth and Villanova shooting. 'Hey, how's it going?'

He nodded, recognition showing. 'Good to see you again, Detective.'

'Yeah, don't talk to him right now,' Critchlow said. 'He's still trying to keep hold of his lunch.'

'Hey, piss off, Crick,' Calder said, looking away with an embarrassed half-smile.

'Nearly barfed when he took a look at the body.' Critchlow rubbed him on the head playfully, like a child. 'Still working up to being real police, aren't ya?'

Calder shoved his hand away, looking sick of having to put up with Critchlow's shit all day long.

Casey pointed at Billy. 'This is Billy Drocker. Bill, this is Devon Critchlow, also known as the Bullshit King of the Fourth...' Crick held his hand up, grinning proud. 'And this is – it's Calder, right?'

'Yeah.' He reached over and shook Billy's hand. 'Good to meet you.'

'You might wanna wash that thing before you use it again,' Critchlow said, nodding at Billy's right hand. 'I think you just shook the one he used to push his guts back down his throat.' He laughed at his own joke, slapping Calder on the shoulder, seemingly oblivious to the fact he was the only one having a good time. 'I'm just shitting ya.' He turned back to Casey. 'This is as close as you can drive to the scene, so we gotta hike a little way. But the body's not far. C'mon.' He started to move off through the trees, Calder going second.

As Billy went to follow after, Casey put a hand on his shoulder. 'Suddenly being stuck with me all day doesn't seem so bad, huh?'

'Is he always like that?'

'All the time.'

Billy held his arm out. 'You first.'

Casey flared her nostrils and started walking.

Critchlow led them in single file along a trail overgrown with scrub oak and huckleberry bushes. 'Who called it in?' Casey said.

'Couple hikers,' Critchlow called back over his shoulder. 'They were on the Flannery Trail headed for the Barrens. One of them stopped to take a drink of water and realised she was stood right over a corpse.'

'Nasty shock,' Billy said quietly.

'Yeah. It's the bugs that get me,' Critchlow said. 'See them crawl out of an eye socket or some shit; goddamn grubs in the mouth. They'll eat a body right up out here, strip it down for parts in no time. Saying that, this one's not the worst I've seen, so my guess is it can't have been there all that long. CSU are on their way – they'll know better.'

'Any indication how it got here?' Billy said.

'If there's walking tracks, I can't see them. Couple footprints here and there, apart from the ones me and Calder made this morning, but you can see what it's like,' Critchlow said, gesturing to the thick vegetation underfoot and all around. 'Not much to sustain an impression – but we'll flag the ones we found to CSU. There's plenty tire tracks along the access road, but I don't know what you'll be able to get from that, they criss-cross all over each other. No vehicle found in the immediate area.'

Critchlow came to a stop by a pine scorched black by a past wildfire, the two jagged stumps nearby evidence that not all the trees had been as resilient. He pointed to the base of a grey birch across the small clearing. 'See what I mean? Practically have to trip over it to see it.'

Even when he pointed, Casey couldn't make out the body at first. A stuttering bird call rang out, a siren alerting the forest to the presence of outsiders. She picked her way across the clearing, stepping over a long-fallen trunk and coming within five feet before she could make out a human form.

She crouched down and peeled back a fern branch, bringing herself face to face with the lifeless eyes of Adam Ryker.

CHAPTER TWENTY-TWO

Casey looked on as Billy took photographs on his phone. CSU would do their own comprehensive shoot to capture the scene, but in Casey's experience, it never hurt to have their own pictures on hand and easily accessible as a memory aide.

She leaned against the rough pine bark and rubbed her neck. The tension there was sprouting into a nagging headache, a sure sign that the post-investigation comedown had begun. Ryker had a single gunshot wound to the temple, a revolver gripped in his hand. He was on his back but angled to one side, his legs in a heap and one arm draped across his stomach. There was dirt caked to the side of his face, stuck to the blood that had leaked from his wound, and more staining the front of his grey T-shirt. The medical examiner's report would set out the details of Ryker's death, but just by looking at the pattern of bloodstains on his clothing, the dirt on his fingers and beneath his nails, and the scrabble marks around his lower half, Casey was pretty sure of one conclusion: the gunshot wound hadn't killed him immediately. She'd seen it before with suicides and attempted suicides – nerves, hesitation or just bad luck meant the bullet didn't do sufficient damage and the victim was left bleeding out. Sometimes it took seconds, sometimes minutes; there were even those rare cases who survived, like the Giants outfielder ESPN had run a feature on, who'd spent twenty hours alone in his apartment after shooting himself in the head. He was so disorientated when he realised he was still alive, his first reaction had been to brush his teeth, trying to get rid of the taste of blood in his mouth.

As a kid, Casey had always heard suicide referred to as the coward's way out, and as much as she understood why that was, she'd never agreed with it. Having pointed a gun at another human and taken his life with it, she could only imagine the iron will it took to turn one on yourself. What was unimaginable to her was the desperation experienced by those who did summon the will to pull the trigger, only to find they were alive long enough to regret doing so.

She pushed herself off the tree and looked at Ryker's face again, remembering the horror he'd inflicted, how many lives he'd destroyed, and the pain that would linger for years. Seeing him through that lens, a part of her hoped he'd had plenty of time to think about that before his light went out for good.

She looked across when she saw Critchlow heading for where Calder was standing, near the head of the trail they'd followed from the cars. Critchlow started to say something to him, gripping his shoulder as if it was a pep talk being offered, but then laughed and jabbed him in the ribs, to the younger man's obvious annoyance. Calder made a half-hearted effort to waft his hand away, but Critchlow brushed it off, shadow boxing and yukking it up.

'That's a win for you, huh, Big?' he said, dropping his fists and turning to Casey as she approached.

'You figure?'

He hooked his thumb towards the clearing. 'Saves you searching all over the county for his ass.'

'Is it fair, though?'

'Fair for who?'

She looked at him, incredulous. 'Who d'you think, Crick?'

Critchlow laughed as if she was joking, tapering off when he realised she wasn't. 'You think the vics or their families would prefer him in a cell over this? C'mon...'

When Casey didn't answer in the affirmative, Critchlow turned to Calder, nudging him with his elbow in an attempt to drum up some support, but the younger man shrugged and shot him a helpless look.

Critchlow looked from him to Casey in amazement. 'You guys should be social workers or something, not cops,' he said, and turned to go. He waved his arm as he walked off, as if they were both crazy.

Casey came over to stand next to Calder. 'You okay?'

'Yeah, I'm good,' he said, staring straight ahead. 'I'm good.'

'First body you caught?'

'Yeah,' he nodded, then corrected himself. 'I mean no, we've been out to natural causes and stuff, old lady in her apartment that'd been there for days, a wreck on the expressway that brought on a heart attack, that kinda thing. But this is the first time I ever saw ... y'know. This.'

Casey nodded, looking out through the forest. In the quiet, she felt as if she could still hear the last reverberations of the gunshot. 'If it helps, it never gets easier.'

He snapped his head around to look at her, surprised.

'Gets easier to mask it, easier to set it aside, but there's no magic trick. You wouldn't be human if you could look at that and not be affected.'

'Crick seems okay with it.'

'Yeah, well, he might not be human. Jury's still out.'

Calder smiled, shaking his head at the same time, as if telling himself he shouldn't be laughing.

'Making jokes and being a pain in the ass is just his way of dealing with it,' Casey said. 'It's how he tries to minimise the impact on himself. But you can't unsee what we have to see, that's what regular people don't understand. You can get inured to it, sure, but it's still there in your head, and it rewires your circuits over time without you even realising.'

Calder moistened his lips, looking at his feet. 'I think I preferred Crick's pep talk.'

Now Casey grinned. 'You'll figure it out.' She glanced back towards the clearing, saw Billy finishing up. 'Pretty intense few days for you, huh?'

'Yeah. It feels ... I don't know, strange. Being there at the start, and now this.' He pulled a face, as if accepting the randomness of fate. 'I checked in on that old lady who smacked her head. She was fine, no concussion. So that was something, I guess.'

Casey glanced at him, his voice detached and his words distant, and wondered if he was suffering the lingering effects of shock. 'Did you get yourself checked out at all?'

'Me? No. What for?'

'You get yourself caught up in something like that, sometimes it takes a bit of time to process it. Talking to someone can help.'

'Like a shrink?'

'It's not like it sounds. The department offers support for stuff like that now. Professionals – just someone you can unload on.'

'Is that what you did?'

Casey screwed up one side of her face. 'I wasn't in the middle of it the way you were. But I have in the past, sure.'

Calder put his hands in his pockets, toeing a tree branch on the ground in front of him, a loaded silence stretching. Then: 'I wasn't in the middle of it. I'm good. Anyway, the perp's dead now, so that's the end of it.'

'Totally. Hey, look, I didn't mean to overstep. Just friendly advice.'

'Yeah, no, I get it. Thanks.' He turned. 'I better go see if Crick needs me.'

'Sure. Take it easy, huh?'

He nodded and walked off, but after a few paces, he stopped and came back towards her a little way. 'Detective? You think what Crick was saying is right? About the families liking it better this way?'

Casey thought about Molly Goff and the fire in her eyes the night she'd turned up at her sister's house, ready to fight the world. About Nicole Rawlins – a different kind of strength in the face of tragedy. And Darcy Whitlock, her grief finding its expression through untamed fury. Would any of them, alone with their thoughts in the depths of night, say they would've preferred to see Ryker in cuffs? Would a perp walk and a trial, ushering in months or years of legal wrangling and emotional tumult, have given them any greater satisfaction than the knowledge he'd died alone in the dirt?

'It's not for me to say.'

In truth, she couldn't be sure either way. Death was always spoken about as a finality, but the more times she brushed up against it, the more she came to realise it left only questions in its wake, and rarely answers.

CHAPTER TWENTY-THREE

The press conference was timed to be fresh for the evening news, Acting Chief Keirn slated to take the podium in person. Casey made it to headquarters twenty minutes before the start time, feeling braindead from an afternoon of paperwork – first, writing up the discovery of Ryker's body, then updating the overall case file with everything she'd not had time to add in over the last twenty-four hours.

Adam Ryker's boss from Kaleidoscopic had agreed to make a formal identification of the body, and once that was complete, Casey was set to call Emile Ryker to inform him of his son's death, along with Nicole Rawlins, Molly Goff and Darcy Whitlock. But Dunmore had nixed the idea, electing to make the calls herself. Her motivation wasn't clear; whether it was her way of putting herself front and centre now that the case was coming together, or whether she was already cutting Casey out of the department. Whatever it was, Casey had accepted without protest, the fight sucked out of her now that Ryker was off the board.

CSU had finished their work at the scene a couple hours earlier and the Medical Examiner's office had taken custody of the body, with an autopsy due to take place imminently. The latest information she had was that they were estimating Ryker had been dead for twenty-four to thirty-six hours, which would place his time of death in the hours sometime after that of Lauren Goff. No suicide note had been discovered on or about his person, and the only belongings found on the body were the contents of his pockets: a set of house keys and a wallet containing thirty dollars in cash, his licence, gym membership, bank card and credit card, along with assorted receipts and business cards from various restaurants and bars. The one surprise had been a strip of pictures taken in a photo booth; Casey had asked the CSU tech who'd recovered it if she could sneak a look after they were bagged and when she did so, she saw four shots of Adam Ryker and Lauren Goff mugging for the camera in different poses – one smiling, one frowning, one where they were face to face as if trying not to laugh, and the last one where they were sharing a kiss. There was no indication as to when they'd been taken, but whether they were months or days old, it was heart-breaking to see Lauren Goff looking so happy next to a man who would abuse her trust in the cruellest way.

One item that didn't show up was a cell phone. Searches of the immediate area of woodland around the body had come up empty, as had further searches of his vehicle and property. There'd been no sign of his laptop either.

A cache of cell-tower data had come through from Verizon, showing the last time his phone had pinged a tower was approximately ten minutes before Lauren Goff's murder, registering on a cell site located a block from her address. Before that, there was a six-hour period when his phone had gone dark, not pinging any towers at all during that time, whereas in the hours before that, it had registered hits from various locations across Rockport – some in The Slice, a couple closer to downtown, and one on the western edge of town. The picture painted by the data was a messy one, particularly given that all the pings prior to midday on Thursday came from the tower closest to Ryker's property – suggesting his cell phone had been at or near his home at the time of Sheena Rawlins' and Landon Whitlock's murders. If he'd left it there to act as an alibi of sorts, it suggested at least some level of premeditation in the shootings, whereas if he'd simply forgotten to take it with him, it could indicate a decision to kill taken on impulse. The wide gap between the two possibilities underscored how clueless they still were as to Ryker's motivations. They'd gone back to Verizon for detailed records of his calls and messages for the seven days through Friday, and Casey was hopeful of them providing some clarity – but they were yet to arrive.

Other loose ends nagged at her. One was how Ryker had travelled to the woods. His car had remained on the street outside his house, no vehicle was found in the vicinity of the scene and there were no car keys found on his person. There were various indicators of animal activity at and around the corpse, but the idea that a squirrel or mouse had taken off with his keys and phone stretched credibility.

She knew the mindsets of suicidal individuals varied wildly – some chose to end their life in the familiar surroundings of home, or in a place of some personal significance, while others wanted to get as far away from their usual surrounds as they could, either because the emotional attachment made it harder to go through with the act, or to spare their families the horror of coming home to discover a body awaiting them. So there were plenty of good reasons why Ryker might've ended up there – but the *how* was eluding her. So far, there was nothing to indicate his death was anything other than what it appeared to be, but Casey's mind kept straying to that phone call she'd overheard Molly Goff making, urging her cousin to find Ryker and take care of him. And he might not have been the only one looking for vigilante justice.

The .22 Smith & Wesson he'd used to kill himself stuck with her as well. They'd recovered the murder weapon from his property, so why take one with him and not the other? Why two guns at all? Everything about this guy's thinking seemed impenetrable. An initial examination of Ryker's corpse had found no bruising or other markings that might indicate a struggle, while the only fingerprints recovered from the gun found in his hand were his own. That didn't preclude the possibility that he'd been compelled to take his own life, or been murdered and had the gun placed in his hand by an unknown party after the fact. DNA analysis of the hairs, fibres, and other material bagged at the scene would take longer to come through, and a partial set of footprints discovered near the body were being evaluated against those of the walkers who had stumbled across it. But the fact remained that none of the evidence recovered so far indicated the involvement of an unknown party or parties.

All of it bubbled in Casey's head as she made her way through the headquarters building in Harrison. She took the stairs up to the second floor and found the media room, where they were setting up for the briefing. Opening the door just wide enough to stick her head inside, she saw contained chaos: TV crews from all the local stations, reporters milling around talking to HCPD suits, a podium set up for Keirn atop a small stage.

It wasn't where she wanted to be. She'd planned to take the case file as far as she could for now, then head home for a hot bath, a cold beer and HBO on her iPad. Instead, the order had come via Dunmore that Keirn wanted her stationed behind him on the dais while he was speaking. What she couldn't figure out was why. The best explanation she'd come up with was that he wanted some of the shine she'd garnered in the wake of the Tina Grace story to reflect on him while he delivered what was, in the eyes of Joe Public, a swift and satisfying conclusion to a high-profile investigation; public support was one way to shore up his position. But there was also the chance that the objective was to somehow humiliate her, revenge for her perceived disloyalty in going around him to Gates.

She backed out of the media room and went to hunt for a coffee – but found herself five feet across the corridor from Rita Zangetty and Darcy Whitlock. The floor beneath her feet seemed to tilt, Casey unsure whether Whitlock would have told Rita Z about having summoned Casey to her house, or the ensuing conversation.

Zangetty's clipped 'Detective,' by way of a greeting gave her some indication though.

Casey nodded to them both. 'Mrs Whitlock, how are you, ma'am?'

'Is it true he shot himself? Or did someone on HCPD get trigger happy when you found him?'

Zangetty turned her head away, eyes bulging at the total disregard for tact.

'The autopsy's due to take place anytime now,' Casey said.

'We'll know more after that, but HCPD wasn't involved in the suspect's death, no.'

'Right.' She tilted her head to the other side. 'Landon would've wanted it that way. He was a believer in an eye for an eye. Personally, I'd have preferred to hear what he had to say for himself.' There was a glassy look in her eyes and she sounded detached, Casey sure she was medicated this time.

Zangetty leaned in. 'Darcy, I can assure you, HCPD would've preferred it that way too. The autopsy will show this was suicide, my understanding is we can be sure about that. Right, Detective?'

Whitlock held her hand up. 'Save it. I just want to get this over with.' She slipped past Casey and through the door into a side room.

Zangetty craned her neck as if she was torn between following after and staying put. She stepped closer to Casey. 'I heard about your trip to Shatter Creek. You want to tell me what the hell that was about? I thought I was clear—'

'She called me up and told me to jump, Rita, what was I supposed to do?'

'Call me.' She came around to face Casey head on. 'You call me. And then I can manage the situation, or escalate it to Franklin.'

'Landon Whitlock had a business card of mine in his possession. She put two and two together and came up with a million – she asked me if I was sleeping with him.'

Rita jerked and swallowed a laugh, slapping her hand over her mouth. She glanced sideways at the meeting room where Darcy Whitlock was waiting, the door closed, then looked at Casey again, eyes twinkling. 'And? Were you?'

Casey shot her a look of disbelief. 'Jesus Christ, Rita...'

'Sorry, sorry. It's just so absurd.' She tucked her chin into her chest, taming another laugh, then came up for air. 'My god, the bullshit we have to deal with.'

'We?'

Zangetty opened her hands. 'You know what I mean.' She laid her hand lightly on Casey's forearm. 'Look, sorry for coming off a bitch, it's just been … It's been a week from hell. Darcy dropped a hint she might support Mark Harden's campaign in the primary. She's probably just saying that to scare us because she's pissed that we'd even think about passing the begging bowl at a time like this – I tried to warn Franklin, but he never listens to me – and our data says Harden's first poll numbers are set to be strong, so Franklin's talking like he's a dead man walking. Now he's got Keirn taking a victory lap on the TV for this whole thing, and … well, you get it.'

'Yeah, I get it, and I'm just glad to be out of it.'

'Look, I know you'll tell me to wait for the autopsy, but off the record, this was what it looks like, right? Is there a chance Ryker, y'know … that someone else did this to him?'

'There are some questions I'd still like answered.'

Zangetty looked at her through her eyebrows. 'Casey, you're like a goddamn statue. I knew you'd keep all the inside stuff for yourself.' She took a second glance towards the room where Darcy Whitlock was waiting. 'I'd better go. Do me a solid – if anything else comes out that Darcy needs to know, let us have a heads-up this time, okay?'

'Rita…'

'I mean it, we need this.' She dipped her head, bringing her eyes level with Casey's. '*Franklin* needs this. The primary is going to be brutal, Harden's a great candidate and Franklin's looking scared. He's going to need every cent he can find, and

Darcy Whitlock brings a lot more than that to the table. It's an off-year election, turnout's going to be low, so we're having to work at the margins to move every vote. I can't have anything left to chance.'

'Rita, honestly, I can't. I already got chewed out—'

'How's it working out with that new lieutenant, by the way?' Rita dropped her voice to a whisper, looking Casey right in the eye. 'I hear she's a hard-ass?'

Casey held her stare. 'You "hear" that?'

'Yeah. You know, on the wind. I heard she's got Keirn's ear, too, and maybe some kind of an agenda?'

'What is this?'

'Just friends gossiping. Friends who can steer Keirn away from any rash decisions, as long as they know that friendship is reciprocated.' Still smiling, she fluttered her fingers and walked off.

One of HCPD's media relations people grabbed Casey and led her to a spot at the back of the podium, the room already stuffy and hot under the TV lights. A few moments later, Helen Dunmore appeared from the other side of the stage and took a place next to her. She glanced at her sidelong. 'Sergeant.' Then she set her eyes on the back of the room.

Waiting in silence for Keirn to take the podium, Casey felt the tension between them creep up her body like a python, coiling around her chest and throat until it became suffocating, all the while under the glare of a hundred pairs of eyeballs. Sweat started beading her hairline and her back, so it was a relief when Keirn came out, drawing all the attention to himself.

'Thank you for being here today. I'll keep this brief.' He had his head dipped, reading from his notes. 'This morning, officers from HCPD responded to the discovery of a body in the Pitchwoods area of Greater Rockport. The deceased has since been identified as thirty-three-year-old Adam A. Ryker, of 443 Van Buren Drive, Rockport. Mr Ryker had been sought as a suspect in the three shootings that occurred earlier this week, the tragic details of which I'm sure you're familiar with.

'The cause of Mr Ryker's death is still being investigated, with the Office of the Hampstead County Medical Examiner due to carry out an autopsy as we speak. Investigations into Mr Ryker's movements in the hours leading up to his death are ongoing, as are those into the shootings for which he was sought as a suspect. However, at this time, HCPD is not pursuing any additional suspects for the shootings that took place, and no suspects are being sought in relation to Mr Ryker's death.'

He said it all in something close to a monotone, lifting his head to look around the packed room only twice. He lacked charisma and gravitas, and Casey decided the only chance he had of making his post permanent was if the lack of those two qualities was seen as a way to mark a clean break from Brian Hanrahan. Or, if Gates or his successor wanted a weak chief of police they could control. She didn't like his chances either way, and while she'd lose no sleep over Stephen Keirn's future career, it made her angry that the most important job in the department would be awarded not on merit, or fitness to serve the people who paid the exorbitant salary, but on who best met the needs of the politicians and their public relations advisors.

Most of all it made her weary. As Keirn took questions, she stole another glance at Dunmore and it made her thoughts turn, again, to McTeague and his job offer. It felt like the weariness was in her bones now, an exhaustion that went deeper than any single case. This was a feeling built up over months; in the past, before Ray, she'd used adversity as fuel to make her work harder and prove everyone wrong, but this time around it felt like too big of an obstacle. Starting over again in a new department held no appeal whatsoever.

At the same time, the thought of life without a badge scared her – she couldn't remember what it was like to be a civilian. For years, her mind had been clear of doubt about her future: for all its frustrations and shortcomings, she'd loved the department, loved her work, loved serving under Ray. But all of that was gone now, and it felt like she'd spent years speeding ahead without thinking to look behind her – and now she had, she realised she was lost. At some point, she had to accept the truth: that most everything she'd loved about her life had been a lie.

Suddenly Keirn was finished and gathering his notes, and she snapped back into the moment, straightening her posture and pinning her gaze to the back wall. But as he turned to walk off, he stepped into her eyeline and shot her a look of disdain – just long enough to make it clear he'd brought her there only to look down on in his moment of triumph.

CHAPTER TWENTY-FOUR

Casey was late arriving at the office the next morning. The two coffees she gulped down on the drive over had produced the opposite of the desired effect, turning up her anxiety and leaving her nerves stretched like piano wire.

She'd been prepared for the comedown that marked the end of every major case, as the adrenaline that carried her through the intensity and the sleep deprivation cut out and she was hurled back into normal life, but the crash this time was harder and more profound than usual, the weight of the choices she had to make pressing down on her like a tombstone.

She acknowledged Billy and Dana with a nod and dropped herself into her seat. Her notepad was open where she'd left it, the licence plate of the white Tesla the last thing she'd scrawled. She'd kept an eye out for the car in the days since but seen nothing. Part of her had wondered if it was the guy who'd called wanting to meet with her then gone weird. She'd tried calling him again the night before, but it wouldn't even connect, as if the cell phone was out of signal range or powered off.

She rubbed her eyes and glanced over at Dunmore's office. The glass door was closed, the lieutenant standing in the corner of the room making a call on her cell. Casey slumped lower in her chair and glanced at the clock, already looking for a reason to get away from her desk. She resolved to check in on Nicole Rawlins and Molly Goff in person, knowing that the end of an investigation could be just as much of a body blow for the victim's families, the moment when the police, the media and everyone else moved on and all that was left was to try and come to terms with the hole that had been blown in their lives. She thought about Darcy Whitlock, having to face the same emotional reckoning. Her money and influence would bring her more attention in the aftermath than the likes of Nicole or Molly, but little of it would focus on her wellbeing. It made Casey want to reach out and check on her and her daughter – but the risk of blowback stopped her.

Casey looked up, belatedly realising the subdued mood in

the office extended beyond her own head. It was the quiet that had caught her attention; Jill wasn't at her desk, Dana had her eyes locked on her computer screen and Billy the same, and neither had said anything to her or each other in the time she'd been there. She watched on from behind her monitor for a few seconds, Dana's face curdled with annoyance, Billy straining not to let his gaze wander, no sign of his usual exuberance. She couldn't get a read on the situation.

'Guys, where's Jill at?' she said.

Dana's eyes flicked to Billy, just for a second, then over to Casey. 'She called in sick.'

Casey glanced at her cell, surprised not to have got the call direct. Jill had never taken a sick day since joining the team. 'She okay? What's up?'

'Some kinda bug,' Dana said, still frowning. Billy hadn't moved a muscle.

Casey stood up, looking from one to the other. 'Is there something I need to know about here?'

Dana looked at Billy again, raising her eyebrows in a gesture that seemed to be imploring him to speak.

Casey rested one hand on the top of her monitor. 'Bill?'

Still his eyes didn't move, but he took a deep breath, working up to something.

Before he could speak, Casey's desk phone rang. She reached for it, hesitated, shot one last look to each of them, then decided they could wait. 'Casey Wray.'

'Oh, hi, Detective, it's Brianna. Landon Whitlock's secretary?'

'Ma'am, hello. How are you?'

'Me? I'm not great, I got a headache feels like someone's drilling into my skull. It's a stress thing, I used to get them all the time – it's been better since I started taking magnesium supplements, but this whole thing with Landon, and with my job up in the air and all of that...'

Casey looked over when Billy got out of his seat and swiped his jacket off the back of his chair. Dana called out to him as he fast-walked through the office, but he disappeared through the doors to the staircase without a glance back.

Casey mouthed *'What the hell?'* to Dana, and her lips parted as if she wanted to say something, but then she opened and closed her hands as if she couldn't grasp the words she needed. She waved her arm and looked away.

'...anyway, sorry. I told myself, Brianna, the detective doesn't want to hear about your problems, you just need to get to the point.'

Casey switched the handset to her other ear. 'That's okay, ma'am, what is it I can help you with?'

'That man, Adam. I saw the police chief on the news yesterday talking about him. It reminded me that you asked about him when I saw you, so I looked through my emails but his name doesn't come up anywhere.'

'That's okay, ma'am, thank you for checking. You don't need to trouble yourself—'

'But it still doesn't make sense to me.'

'Well, I understand that feeling, but like I said when we talked, it appears Mr Whitlock wasn't the intended target of the shootings.'

'No, I get that. What I mean is that it still doesn't make sense to me what he was doing that morning. Why he was there in the first place? You never found his car, right?'

'Uh, no, not as yet. We don't always have all the answers.'

Monk sighed. 'I know. I mean, if I didn't know what he was doing, how are you guys supposed to have a clue, right?'

There was no sarcasm to her tone and Casey almost laughed at the unintended insult.

'I keep going back over the things he said. I wish I'd taken him more seriously about the guy following him,' Monk said.

Casey thought about the white Tesla again, wondered if she was becoming as paranoid as Landon Whitlock. But it also reminded her of Darcy Whitlock's weird reaction when she'd asked if he'd ever spoken about being followed. Something else she couldn't quite square off. 'Ma'am, for what it's worth, I don't think it would've made any difference. What happened that morning is not your fault.'

Monk seemed not to hear. 'He called him The Photographer once, did I tell you that? No, I didn't, did I, because I remembered it after I left last time, and I got mad at myself for not telling you. It was about two weeks ago. He came into the office and he said, "I saw the f-ing photographer again this morning. Every time I turn around he's there." Except he said the actual f-word, if you get what I mean.'

'The Photographer?' It was a detail that sparked something, but Casey couldn't place it. 'I'll make a note of that, thank you, ma'am. If there's anything else comes to light about that morning that I can share with you, I promise I'll be in touch. But please don't beat yourself up about it anymore.'

'I'll try, Detective, but it's easier said than done.' Her voice became thick with emotion. 'I miss him. I never thought I'd say that out loud, but I really miss him.' As the words tumbled out, they confirmed Casey's suspicion: Monk had been holding a candle for Landon Whitlock – perhaps undeclared or unrequited. She felt a new sympathy for the woman, her persistence borne of more than just morbid curiosity.

But the chance to offer any further words of reassurance had passed – Monk was already gone.

Casey ran her hand over her face, pulling the skin taut over her cheekbones. Then she got out of her chair and went straight to Dana's desk. 'You wanna tell me what's going on here, D? Where's Billy gone?'

Dana closed her eyes and shook her head. 'I don't know where he's gone, but you need to talk to him. I can't...' She looked up, blowing her breath out of the side of her mouth like it was a release valve. 'It's not my place to tell you, Big, I'm sorry.'

'Tell me what? I'm missing half my team, it feels like this is something I need to know.'

'I know, I know, I wish I could...' She eyed Dunmore, who was looking on now from her office, still talking on her cell. 'Honestly, you're right. Just go talk to him, he needs to man up.'

Casey studied Dana's face, the uncertainty in her expression totally alien. She pushed herself off the desk and walked to the way out, calling Billy's cell-phone number.

She caught up with Billy in the parking lot, a Nets cap pulled low over his eyes. He was taking a hit off a lurid green vape.

Casey pointed at it. 'This a new thing or are you just reliving your childhood?'

Billy looked at the vape as if seeing it for the first time and slipped it into his pocket.

Casey came over to lean next to him, her back against the wall. The view of the strip mall across the street from the precinct wasn't much to look at. 'You want to tell me what's going on here?'

Billy dipped his head and stared at the ground, kicking the wall gently with his heel.

Casey linked her hands in front of her. 'I can beat it out of you, if you prefer? I know ways...'

Billy snorted, a rueful laugh.

'Look,' Casey said, 'it's not so long ago you said to me if I ever needed someone to talk to, you were a great listener. Remember?'

Billy glanced at her then looked away, eyes shielded by the brim of his hat again.

'Now, you see, me – I'm a terrible listener,' Casey said. 'I'll interrupt you, I'll tell everyone your secrets, and I'll most likely use your shit to make fun of you somewhere down the line, so you probably want to find someone else to hear you out.' She turned towards him and clapped him on the shoulder. 'But you're okay, Billy Drocker, so I'm willing to break the habit of a lifetime for you. So, spill.'

Billy took another hit on his vape and pushed up his cap by the brim until it sat loose on his head. 'I screwed up.' He rubbed his forehead with his fist. 'I really screwed up.'

'Personally? Professionally? Sexually?'

Billy didn't answer.

'Oh, wow – all three?'

Billy shook like he was laughing silently, but Casey saw that in reality his face was wrinkled in pain.

She rolled away on her shoulder and pressed her back to the wall again, so Billy wouldn't feel like she was crowding him. They stood in silence as a pair of uniforms climbed out of a cruiser and passed by them on their way into the department, Casey nodding at both as they did.

When they were gone, Billy jammed the back of his head

against the wall, softly, then again. 'I never meant for it to go this way. I never ... Jesus...'

'Okay, you're starting to scare me now, Rookie. Please tell me you didn't kill anyone.'

'No, no, it's ... No, of course not.'

'Good.' Casey clapped her hands together gently. 'Okay, good, so that's a start. How about you tell me where Jill fits into all of this?'

He snapped his head around to look at her. 'How...?'

She opened her hands, a visual *duh*.

'Detective?'

The new voice came from behind her, and now it was Casey's turn to whip her head around. Muneera Kouri was standing by the precinct's main entrance, as if she'd been about to go into the building when she spotted Casey. She hesitated, then took a few steps towards where they were standing.

Casey shot Billy a look with wide eyes – *to be continued* – and went towards her. 'Ma'am? Is everything okay?'

Muneera was tugging on her forearm with her other hand, her steps awkward and stilted. 'I was wondering if I ... if I could maybe talk to you?'

Casey glanced back towards Billy, but he'd already taken off towards the street.

'I'm sorry,' Muneera said, holding up a hand in apology, 'I didn't mean to interrupt, I can come back...'

'No, no, it's fine. You want to come inside?'

'Uh ... actually, could we maybe talk someplace else? Not inside?'

Casey nodded. 'Sure. Follow me.'

Casey set the coffees on the table and took the seat opposite Muneera in the booth at the back of the Starbucks.

Muneera had her elbows on the table, absently running a strand of her hair through her fingers, one hand then the other, over and over. 'Thanks.'

'Did you guys get out of the hotel okay?'

She nodded. 'I think Aryana kinda liked it in the end, like a vacation.'

Casey spread her hands on the table. 'So what was it you wanted to talk to me about?'

'Did you ... Uh, did you see him? Adam? After ... y'know.'

Casey nodded. 'I did.'

'How did he look?' She cast her eyes down, then at the wall, then finally back to Casey.

'It's difficult to say.'

'I mean, did he look ... um ... Did he look scared?'

Casey shifted backward in her seat a little. 'Why do you ask?'

'He ... I mean, they said on the news that you weren't looking for anyone else in connection to what happened, so ... that means he killed himself, right?'

'There was an autopsy carried out yesterday, we're still waiting for the final report and the investigation is ongoing, so I can't really discuss it.'

'He wouldn't do it,' she said, almost a whisper.

'Do what?'

'He wouldn't do it. He was ... He's not what you're all saying he is.'

Casey stared at Muneera, taking in the red eyes that spoke of tiredness or grief or both, and a face drawn with a sense of loss. She carefully slid her coffee aside to lean closer. 'Ma'am, is there something you came here to get off your chest?'

'What you said to me, about being charged ... Is that for real?'

'It's a possibility, but it depends on a lot of things. But the truth is always the best option.'

'I couldn't.'

Casey stayed silent, leaving her the space to continue, but Muneera bowed her head, hiding her face.

'Ma'am? Couldn't what?'

'I couldn't say it. I didn't ... I thought there was no point, because you'd find him and he'd be able to explain everything, but now...'

Casey bent down, trying to make her meet her eyes. 'Why don't you tell me from the start?'

Muneera brought her thumb to her lip. 'It wasn't Adam.'

Casey waited, not moving, not blinking, the muscles in her throat twitching.

But Muneera didn't speak, didn't even look up, finally making Casey prompt her. 'Ma'am?'

She raised her face at last, the knuckle of her thumb pressed to her mouth as if she was fighting to keep a world of emotions inside her. 'If I ... if I tell you something, is there a way nobody else can know about it?'

'I can't make that promise, I'm sorry. What you just said—'

'Aryana. Does she have to know? She'll never talk to me again.'

'If you were having a relationship with Adam Ryker, it's not our place to discuss that with her. But she'd want you to tell the truth, right? The last thing she wants is for you to get yourself in trouble.'

She pushed her hair behind her ears with trembling hands. 'It was more than a relationship.' She tilted her head to one side and then the other, working the kinks out of her neck. 'I loved him, and he loved me. We didn't plan for it to be like that – neither of us wanted to hurt her, it's just how it worked out. You can't help falling in love, right?' She shook her head, trying to wish away reality. 'He didn't kill those people. He could never kill those people.'

Casey made sure to give no reaction, even though, inside, her stomach was doing flips. 'The evidence is telling a different story right now. How can you be sure of that?'

'I was with him.' She met Casey's eyes and it looked as if the weight of guilt came tumbling off her shoulders. 'I was with him at his place on Thursday morning.'

❧

With the initial admission off her chest, it all flowed. Muneera laid out how mutual attraction between her and Ryker during the early stages of his relationship with Aryana had led to weeks of light-hearted flirting – something she'd never expected to lead anywhere. Then, one night, on an evening out with a group of friends, Aryana had left the bar early on account of feeling unwell, insisting Ryker and Muneera stay behind to carry on the party without her. With mojitos flowing, the chat turned 'real', and Adam admitted to having feelings for her – feelings that she told him were reciprocated. The relationship had turned physical that night, and within a week of their first sexual encounter, Muneera considered him to be her boyfriend in all but name.

Throughout the telling, Muneera took pains to stress she'd done just as much of the running as Ryker, and that he'd never manipulated or coerced her – showing a determination to protect his reputation at every turn. She went on to explain that he'd broken up with Aryana a few weeks later, never revealing the real reason, and that he and Muneera had agreed to keep their relationship a secret even after the breakup, in order to protect Aryana's feelings.

That was the part where Casey's patience ran short. She never allowed her cynicism to show, but it was clear from the way Muneera told it that she'd had no idea Ryker was seeing at least two other women, besides her, at the time of his death – and god only knew what she made of him trying to convince Aryana to take him back not long after breaking up with her. Protecting Aryana's feelings – or Muneera's – was the last thing on his mind. 'Ma'am, I need to know about Thursday morning,' she said.

Muneera gripped the edge of the table, as if she were trying to pull it towards her as a shield. 'I stayed over the night before. I was at his place until around ten that morning. Neither of us went anywhere. He logged onto his computer at, like, 8.30am, so his boss would see, and then we went back to bed.'

Casey turned her head to the wall and scratched the side of her face, trying to get a handle on the enormity of what she was hearing. Finally, she turned to Muneera again. 'Ma'am, can you offer any proof for what you're telling me? Because the implications of what you're saying...'

Muneera took out her cell and unlocked it, jabbing and swiping the screen until she found what she was looking for. Then she turned it around and set it down in front of Casey for her to see. It was a picture of her sitting up in bed wearing an oversized T-shirt, reclining against Ryker, whose head was propped on her shoulder. They were both smiling for the selfie. 'I took this that morning, and a bunch of others.' She swiped and swiped again, showing two further similar pictures.

Casey took the phone and went back to the first picture again. It showed a white wall behind the smiling couple, matching the vacant décor she'd seen in Ryker's bedroom, but nothing else to distinguish the location. She swiped through the other pictures, but they all offered the same backdrop. She swiped up to look at the date and timestamp. 'Our guys can see if these have been altered, you know that, right?'

'Altered? What does that mean? What for?'

'What you're claiming has serious implications.'

'I know. I'm not lying. Why would I lie?'

'I'm just saying, if for whatever reason you're trying to protect him or his reputation...'

'This is the last time I saw him alive. I wouldn't lie about that.'

Casey let herself fall back against the booth, feeling like her head was coming apart. Everything pointed to Ryker, but Muneera's story would prove his innocence – if it was true. Already, the way the evidence had lined up so neatly against him set every light in her mind's eye flashing red..

'You said you left around ten that morning. Did you speak to him again after that?'

'Just a couple messages.' She took back her cell and scrolled through it, but Casey got the feeling she had every text memorised. 'Just, y'know ... boyfriend and girlfriend talk.'

'When was the last time you heard from him?'

Her eyes flicked to the cell. '1.28 in the afternoon.' She turned it around to show Casey again. A row of heart-eyed emojis stretched across the screen.

Casey laid her hands flat on the table, shaking her head. 'Why didn't you tell me this sooner? You could've provided him with an alibi.'

'I wanted to, I swear I wanted to, but...' She cradled her head in her hands. 'Aryana. I didn't want to hurt her. She didn't let on how cut up she was when Adam broke up with her, but I know she was devastated. If she found out it was because he was with me ... I swear to you, I never wanted to hurt anyone. Neither of us did.'

Casey slid out of the booth and stood up, leaning over the table on her fists. 'We spent thirty-six hours looking for a suspect who you knew was innocent. You let us put a target on his back for every vigilante asshole with a TV set. And at the same time, we've got an unknown killer on the loose that no one's even looking for. The only way you can even start to make this right is total cooperation from here on out. Do we understand each other?'

Muneera was looking up at her, eyes wide in shock.

'Come with me.'

CHAPTER TWENTY-FIVE

Casey pushed through the double doors and went straight to find Dunmore. 'Adam Ryker's not our perp.'

The lieutenant was already out of her seat by the time Casey said it, staring at her like she'd lost her mind.

'Adam Ryker has an alibi for the Eighth and Villanova shootings,' Casey said, standing in her doorway. 'He's not our killer.'

'What?'

She gave her a bullet-point overview of Muneera's story. 'She's downstairs and she's willing to let us authenticate the pictures on her cell phone, but it's going to check out. He was at home when they were killed.'

'What about Lauren Goff?'

'Unknown.'

Dana was standing behind Casey, her hand over her mouth.

'The murder weapon,' Dunmore said, shaking her head in disbelief. 'It was found at his property. The motive, the texts...'

Casey put her hands on her hips. 'Yeah.'

Dunmore had a look on her face like the ground was opening up beneath her. 'The autopsy report came back. The ME is ruling Ryker's death a suicide.'

'What the hell is going on here?' Dana said.

Casey looked over at her. 'Tell Billy to get his ass back here right now. We're at square one again and we're playing catchup.'

❧

They set up in one of the meeting rooms, Casey spreading copies of the case file on the table in front of them. At first it was only her and Dana, then Billy showed up shortly after, looking at Casey sheepishly, like he was wondering if Dana had filled her in on whatever was going on with him.

'Put that look away, Bill. I don't know what happened, and I don't care right now.' She pointed to the desk. 'We review everything. Let's go.'

Dunmore joined them a few seconds later, the ashen expression she'd worn in her office now graver. 'Keirn's on his way here now. No information leaves this room until we've figured out what the hell is going on here – that's an explicit order from the acting chief. Wray – get the girl up here now. We put her in a room and she doesn't talk to anyone else in this building.'

Billy and Dana looked up at Casey in unison, both of them with a silent *Oh shit* expression that mirrored exactly how she felt inside at the idea of Keirn getting involved personally. It took all the control she could muster not to reflect it. She picked up the phone and called downstairs to ask them to bring Muneera up to the bureau, feeling every eye in the room on her, each for a different reason.

The order given, she retook her spot at the table and focused on the papers spread in front of her. 'What did we miss, what did we ignore, what didn't add up?'

There was a momentary silence as all four of them started reading.

Billy was the first to break it. 'The murder weapon was at his house. It was used in all three shootings. What if he had someone else pull the trigger on the first two, then took care of Lauren Goff himself?'

Dana lowered the sheet of paper she'd been reading. 'What about one of his girlfriends?'

'Like a jealousy thing?' Billy said, sounding doubtful.

'He was a control freak,' Dana said, shooting him a look, then glancing in Dunmore's direction, as if reminding herself of the need to keep her temper in check. 'Christ knows what he might've said to them. He was a manipulator. If he whipped up one of these girls enough to go do it for him...'

Casey turned to Dunmore, trying to get a sense of where her head was at, but she was watching proceedings with a detached look, as if Keirn had blasted her so hard, her soul had left her body. In that moment, Casey felt sympathy for her; maybe the shared feeling that they were freefalling, with the ground hurtling up towards them.

She turned pages in the file, skimming, thinking, trying to

keep it all straight in her head. She came across the thick wad of text messages between Ryker and Lauren Goff, quickly turning to the end. She reread the last page and a half and looked up.

'Where's Ryker's cell phone?'

Dana looked at Casey with a blank stare.

'It wasn't on his person,' Casey said, 'and it didn't show up at his house or in his car.'

'Maybe he tossed it so he couldn't be tracked,' Billy said.

Casey riffled through the pages until she found the cell-tower data that gave a glimpse into Ryker's movements. 'It was at his property on Thursday morning, at the time of the shootings on Eighth and V, then it bounced around Rockport for a couple hours before going dark for six hours, into the night. When it pops up again, it pings a tower a block from Lauren Goff's house, when he messaged her to say he was coming over. Just after that, it goes dark again, and has been ever since.'

'He had to switch it on to tell Lauren he was coming.'

'Had to?' Casey said. 'Why not just knock on the door?'

'Make sure she was ready when he pulled up,' Billy said. 'Causes less of a disturbance, less chance of the neighbours seeing him.'

Dana was bent over the table, scouring the final text exchange. 'These messages came from Lauren Goff's phone, and they showed up under Ryker's name, so we know they came from his cell, but...' She hesitated, looking at Casey and then tilting her head, as if she couldn't quite believe where her own thoughts were leading her.

'Say it.'

'It doesn't mean he wrote them.'

A hush came over the room, the implications settling like a silent rain of ash.

It was Dunmore who spoke first. 'But everything lines up.'

'There were no prints found on the murder weapon,' Casey said.

'So he wore gloves.'

'What about the .22 he killed himself with?' Casey said. 'Why two guns?'

'He got hold of another piece after he ditched the one at his house?' Billy said.

'No, because...' Casey flicked through the file until she came to the report on the revolver. 'Here. It's registered to the same address in Glens Falls as the nine used in the shootings. Both guns stolen from the same property at the same time, so he almost certainly had them both all along. So again: why did Ryker need two guns?' Casey looked up, not waiting for an answer. 'No one was arrested for the robbery. I'll call Glens Falls PD and see if they had anyone they liked for it, see if we can establish a chain of possession.'

'Hold on,' Dunmore said. 'The .22 carried only Ryker's prints, and no prints were recovered from the nine. One was found in his hand and the other in his yard. Are you seriously saying someone else was using those guns and his cell phone?'

'Lieutenant, none of us wants to be wrong here, but if the alibi is solid, then this stinks.'

'But then we're left without a motive,' Dunmore said, her voice tailing off at the end, her certainty slipping away. 'Who else would've wanted his exes dead? Every piece of evidence we have points to Adam Ryker's guilt, except a claim made by one of his besotted girlfriends, who's – how old is she?'

'Twenty-one.'

'We're going to throw our whole case out on the strength of what a twenty-one-year-old girl is telling us?' She stabbed the table to make her point, but there was no conviction in it, Dunmore protesting against the reality that was dawning on all of them.

'She's got the pictures taken on the morning,' Casey said.

'What time? What time exactly?'

'Eleven minutes after the shooting on Eighth.'

'Eleven minutes? Is that enough time for him to have made it home?'

'It's a fifteen-minute drive without traffic to Ryker's property. There's almost no way.'

'Then what are the other possibilities? What if...' Dunmore pushed herself upright and paced to one side of the room. 'Surely the pictures are fake, right? Photoshop, AI, a picture of a picture, something like that? Or, what about – what do the pictures actually show? Do we know for sure they were taken at his place? What if they had somewhere nearby all set up to provide this convenient alibi?'

'Then, respectfully, why wait until he was dead to use it?'

'I don't have the answers here, Detective. Maybe it was his idea and she was reluctant. Who knows?'

Casey looked around the table. She'd considered the idea the pictures were fakes, but when she looked Muneera Kouri in the eye, she'd come away convinced that she was telling the truth. Still, Casey had to consider that, if they really were genuine, a whole new explanation for the murders was required, and none she could come up with came close to fitting the facts as they stood. Nothing about the killings made sense anymore. Worse still: there now existed the possibility that someone had been setting up Adam Ryker from the start. 'Let's see what Tech can get from her cell.'

Just as she said it, a uniform appeared at the entrance to the department, Muneera in tow. He led her across the floor, both of them looking around uncertainly when at first it appeared to be deserted. Casey went out to call them over, thanking the uniform and dismissing him.

'We're going to need to ask you some more questions,' Casey said, when the other officer was gone.

'When can I have my cell phone back?'

'I don't know that yet. Our Tech team are still working on it.'

'I'm not lying, I swear. Everything I told you is true. Adam was a good guy, he couldn't kill anybody. This is crazy – we were happy together. He didn't care about those other girls, it was all in the past.'

Casey wondered if she could truly be so blinkered as to Ryker's true nature. A man capable of cheating on his girlfriend with her own cousin; was it naivety that allowed her to believe she was the one he'd finally be true to, or was she just lying to herself?

But before Casey could say anything more, Dunmore appeared at her side. 'Miss Kouri, I'm Lieutenant Helen Dunmore. I'm in charge of the detective bureau here. You and I need to have a conversation.'

Muneera looked at Casey, almost as if asking for permission, and Casey nodded.

'Follow me, please,' Dunmore said.

Casey let Muneera go first, then started to fall in line behind her, but Dunmore looked back. 'Thank you, Sergeant, that's all. I've asked Detective Torres to sit in with us, for a fresh perspective on the situation.'

Casey stopped in her tracks and watched as Dunmore led Muneera around the corner and out of sight. Dana appeared from the bathrooms and hurried after them, looking over at Casey with big eyes that seemed to offer an apology.

Casey gave her a weak thumbs-up and went back to the conference room.

CHAPTER TWENTY-SIX

Casey sat at the opposite end of the table from Billy and the two of them read in silence, Casey speeding through the file and making notes on a pad at her side. Mostly it was questions that cropped up as she was reading, but there was a list of evidence to chase as well: Muneera's cell-tower data, to help corroborate her story. Adam Ryker's cell-phone records – see who he was speaking to and what he was saying. Eyewitness reports – what happened to the woman with the kid who'd first told the staff inside Strongbox about the shooting? The appeal for information on her identity had generated a half-dozen possible names, none of which they'd had time to follow up on. Casey bumped that task to the top of her list.

She came to the section that described the personal possessions found on Landon Whitlock at the scene – the key fob for his missing Mercedes Benz and the thousand dollars in cash. Two anomalies they'd never managed to explain; did they carry more significance in this new scenario? His car was still out there somewhere, location unknown. Jill had been coordinating with Patrol to have them check every street in a half-mile radius of Eighth and V – and still no sign. Expensive model like that, the chances were it'd been stolen and was already inside of a shipping container on its way overseas. And the money? What – or who – was it for?

She thought about Landon Whitlock's paranoia, Darcy Whitlock's fear that they were being targeted, her own crazy theory of Ryker and Darcy being lovers. Darcy had shot that down quickly, but seeing Harper Whitlock's distinctive green eyes, a similar colour to Ryker's, had left embers of doubt in Casey's mind. At the same time, it was proof of nothing – especially if it turned out Adam Ryker really was innocent.

Casey flipped to the plan of the scene of the shootings on Eighth that CSU had drawn up as part of their protocol: Whitlock on the sidewalk outside Strongbox, Sheena Rawlins struck a short distance from him, but managing to stagger to the side of the building in a vain attempt to get away. The two bullets that had torn through her stomach were found lodged in the gym's front wall, the subsequent ballistics analysis suggesting she'd been fired at by an assailant across the sidewalk from her, positioned near the kerb.

Casey turned to a fresh page in her notepad and sketched her own rough diagram, dashed lines to show the angle of fire. The likely paths the bullets had followed showed Rawlins had only just exited the gym and turned to walk east along Eighth when she was hit. That put Whitlock closer to the shooter's position, leaving open the question of how he'd found himself in the line of fire. There was nothing to indicate he'd played hero and tried to get in front of the bullets – it played well in the press, but in reality, if the shooter had come out of nowhere and surprised them both, as seemed to be the case, Whitlock would've had no time to react. Maybe the shooter was inexperienced with firearms and ended up spraying bullets everywhere, with Whitlock straying in front of him. Or maybe they just didn't care, firing indiscriminately. But the relative positions of the two victims would normally suggest Whitlock had been the target. In light of Ryker's alibi, Casey started to let the possibility play out in her head.

She looked up when she realised Billy was eyeing her from the other end of the table. 'Big, about earlier—'

'Save it, Bill. Unless you're about to confess to shooting Rawlins, Goff and Whitlock, now's not the time. I need your head in the game, so put the rest of it aside.'

He looked disappointed, but then his eyes shifted, landing on something over Casey's shoulder. The speed with which he shot out of his seat told her what it was. She turned around and saw Acting Chief Keirn walking towards the meeting room, in conversation with the assistant walking in stride with him. Casey stood up and saluted when he came through the door, Billy doing the same.

He accepted the salutes and looked at Billy. 'Can we have the room, please, Detective?'

Billy stuffed the pages splayed in front of him into the file and carried it back to his desk. Keirn's assistant shut the door behind herself as she followed him out.

Casey didn't know where to put her eyes. From the second he'd eyeballed her leaving the stage at the press briefing, she'd known this was coming. The room suddenly felt airless.

Keirn stood with one hand planted on the table, fingers braced, looking out at the near-deserted office on the other side of the glass. 'Where's Lieutenant Dunmore?'

'She's speaking to Ryker's alibi, sir.'

He surveyed the office outside again, frowning. 'And the rest of the bureau?'

'Detective Torres is with the lieutenant, Detective Hart is sick.'

He nodded, his expression unchanged, as if the explanation was unsatisfactory. Then he looked right at Casey. 'Do you believe the girl's story?'

She nodded. 'Yes, sir, I do.'

'She has photographs to back it up, I understand?'

'Yes, sir. Our Tech guys are checking them out now, but from speaking to her, I'm pretty certain they're genuine.'

He swallowed, his nostrils flaring. 'Why didn't this come to light sooner?'

'Sir, she's the cousin of one of Ryker's former partners. We had a tip she'd been in a relationship with him herself but she denied it initially. We had no indication she could alibi him.'

'But she was happy to let him carry the can for three murders she claims he did not commit?'

'She was afraid it would mean her cousin finding out she'd been cheating with her boyfriend, sir. She was waiting on Ryker to come forward and clear himself, but then he turned up dead and she felt like she had to speak up for him.'

'Those are some messed up priorities, wouldn't you say?' He made a fist with the hand he'd been resting on the table and tapped his wedding ring against the wood. 'If Ryker isn't our killer, who is, Detective?'

Casey swept a hand over the copy of the case file, still open by her seat. 'We've started reviewing everything, sir. We'll rework the investigation from the ground up. There are leads we hadn't had a chance to follow up, we'll pick them up again right away.'

'That's a lot of words to say "we don't know".'

Casey felt her stomach contract to the size of a prune. 'Sir, we're on it.'

The tapping stopped, and he fell silent. 'Are your friends in the county executive's office aware of this development?'

'Sir? No, I'm not—' She stopped herself saying anything more than was needed, unsure what story Dunmore had spun him. 'No, sir, not from me.'

'What the hell were you doing talking to them, Casey?'

'Sir, I didn't ... I never meant to give them anything. Rita Zangetty told me to go straight to them and that Franklin Gates would square it with you. I never did, but then she called again and was going to pass on bad intel, so I corrected her. That was all.'

He looked at her a long minute. She braced for him to bawl her out, but all he said was, 'Goddamn politicians,' under his breath. 'They were using you.'

Casey recoiled. 'Sir?'

He let go of a long breath and seemed to wilt with it, the fire in his eyes dwindling. 'To embarrass me.' He drifted along the side of the table towards her, dragging his knuckle along the surface, his eyes strafing back and forth along the wall as he thought about it. He came to a stop a few paces from where she stood. 'They want to make it look like I don't know what's going on in my own shop. And now an alibi turns up. Have Gates' people been speaking to this woman?'

'Sir? No, not that I'm aware of.'

'Uh-huh. I bet they dangled her an immunity deal to keep quiet until now. Can't be a coincidence this woman appeared right after I held the press conference. I hate those goddamn things. I didn't even want to do it. Now they want to make me look an idiot.'

'Sir?'

'Come on, you know what they're doing as well as I do. Gates knows he looks weak on crime and soft on corruption. What's the quick fix for that? Same as always: bring in a new chief. The more incompetent they make me look, the easier to pin every last thing that ever went wrong in this place to my corpse before they toss me in the grave.'

Casey fixed her eyes on the tabletop, stunned into silence. The stuff about Muneera sounded paranoid, but the rest of it was on the money.

He stared sidelong out the window a moment, then rose up again, squaring his shoulders. 'Well fuck that. Because if it transpires I'm required to walk back what I said, then I'll turn on the firehose and make sure all of them get sprayed with shit too.' He met her eyes. 'Casey, if you speak to that friend of yours again, you make sure she knows they're not the only ones holding cards at this table.'

Casey started to say, 'She's not my friend...' but then stopped and nodded, rooted to the spot by his gaze.

'Thank you, Sergeant.' He turned to go.

'Sir ... about the investigation. I really think the alibi is legit. How do you want us to play it?'

He opened the conference-room door, his assistant right there waiting for him on the other side. 'I need to speak to Lieutenant Dunmore. Await my orders.'

CHAPTER TWENTY-SEVEN

Casey worked in the conference room, the sky darkening outside. She finished reading the case file then made another pass, skimming for anything she might've missed, trying to view it through a new prism: Landon Whitlock as the target. If that turned out to be the case, the implications were almost too big to comprehend: Sheena Rawlins caught in the crossfire, Adam Ryker framed for her murder, Lauren Goff killed ... to complete the setup? Ray used to say that a shitty motive didn't make them more dead – his ham-fisted way of trying to get her not to dwell on how senseless most killings were. But that scenario made bile rise up in her throat.

She made calls as she worked through the file, chasing up Verizon for a response to the warrant for Ryker's detailed cell-phone records – one way to confirm Muneera's story – and following up on possible IDs for the woman with the child in Strongbox. The last call she made was to Glens Falls PD, querying if they'd had anyone in the frame for the stolen guns later found in Adam Ryker's possession. After two call reroutes, she reached the detective who'd worked the burglary, who told her the only suspect they'd identified, a local kid with a sheet a mile long, was later established to have been in hospital at the time of the robbery with a busted jaw, sustained in a drug-related beating.

She kept waiting for Dunmore to surface and tell her what was going on, but neither the lieutenant nor Keirn reappeared, and even Dana was nowhere to be seen. With Keirn's departure, Billy had retaken his spot at the far end of the table and was trying to follow Casey's lead of raking through the file, but he was restless and unfocused, making two trips to the break room for coffee, and trips to the bathroom every twenty minutes as a result. When he stood up and carried the paperwork over to the window, under the pretence of continuing to read, Casey finally snapped.

'Billy, sit down or take your ass home. I don't care which, but you're driving me crazy.'

He looked at her with surprise on his face, as if he hadn't realised he'd been up and down like a frog on cocaine. 'Sorry, I didn't mean...' He held a hand up in apology and went to pull out his chair to sit down.

'Hold up.' Casey stood up and went around the table, coming to perch next to him. 'Okay, look, whatever's going on, now's your five minutes to get it off your chest – if you want to. And if not, that's okay too, but either way, you go home, clear your head, and you come back tomorrow, *focused*. You hear me?'

He looked up at her out of the corner of his eye, his tongue bulging his cheek, as if weighing up which he wanted more. The silence stretched, but just as Casey was making to slip off the table, he broke it.

'It's Jill.'

'Uh-huh. You say something to upset her?'

'Yeah, I guess. There's something you need to know.'

And just as he said it, out of nowhere Casey knew what was coming. 'Wait, you two are...?'

Billy looked at his hands in his lap and nodded once.

'You guys?' She remembered Dave Cullen floating the idea of Jill having a thing for Billy and her dismissing it out of hand – the pair of them about as mismatched as two human beings could be. 'No fucking way.'

'It just...' His voice cracked and he reached for his coffee cup, but it was empty. 'It just happened. Wasn't planned, wasn't, y'know, a big deal, and then ... it kinda was.'

'But she's got a boyfriend?'

'Yeah. They broke up.'

'When?'

'A month ago, maybe. I told her not to do anything because of me, but she said it'd been coming, it was what she wanted.'

'So you guys are together?'

He looked up at her again but didn't answer.

'Billy?'

'She saw something on my cell. Hers was out of power so I told her to use mine to order an Uber, and a message popped up she wasn't supposed to see.'

Casey closed her eyes, seeing it. 'Another woman?'

'We never talked about it.' He put his hands on the table, splaying his fingers. 'Everybody knows how I roll, and we never spoke about anything else, so ... How was I supposed to know?'

'Oh, Jesus, Billy.'

'I never chased her, Big, I swear. I never told her to break up with Austin, I never made her any promises, we just ... fell into something.' He held his hands up as if he couldn't explain it, then dug his fingers into the side of his face in frustration. 'She knew I wasn't looking for anything serious.' He hung his head, spoke more quietly. 'I thought she knew.'

Casey slipped off the table and came to stand behind him, her gaze on the window. 'This is a mess.'

'Yeah.'

'And Dana knew about all this?'

'Jill told her some stuff. I think she's known for a few weeks. Then I guess she spoke to her this morning, when it happened.'

'Uh-huh.'

'She hates me.'

'She's protective.' Casey slowly drew in a breath. 'Go home. I'll talk to Jill tomorrow.'

'Will they transfer me?'

She let it out just as slow. 'Let's just get through the day, huh? One thing at a time.'

❧

Casey leaned closer to her monitor, studying the image onscreen while the dialling tone rang in her ear. The young woman with the child on her hip, the name *Strongbox* written across the floor in the now-familiar military-style typeface.

She clicked on the next image, a still captured a few frames later from the same surveillance footage, but the camera's placement above the main entrance meant the woman was facing away from its lens as she'd entered the building, the child obscured behind her torso. The best shot they had was one of the woman's face in profile as she'd turned her head before walking out of the camera's field of vision, but even that gave Casey little to work with. The woman's vibrant hair was the best identifying feature they had to go on, but the rest of her face was unclear, and Casey felt the lack of clarity torque her frustration again.

Still the phone rang in her ear. It was the fourth call she'd made that evening chasing up an ID on the woman, none of the previous ones panning out. Not that the other tips had been malicious; the good citizens of Rockport had responded in earnest to appeals for help identifying her, but one thing Casey had learned over the years was that a certain type of person was prone to responding to these appeals, who would swear blind it was their sister, or their cousin, or a woman from their nail bar, even though they bore little resemblance to the person being sought. Casey had never understood why; whether it was some deep-seated impulse to help that overrode logic, or an unconscious need for drama. However well meant, bad IDs clogged up the wheels of any investigation.

Dana had been all through the tape, but there was no footage of the woman exiting the building. The shift manager, Brandon, had confirmed there were fire exits at the rear of the property, but no cameras covered that area. The way the woman had slipped out unnoticed only added to the feeling she'd disappeared into thin air.

'Hello?'

Casey sat up, thrown by the sudden sound of a woman's voice in her ear, expecting to hit another voicemail. 'Yeah, hi, this is Detective Casey Wray with HCPD, am I speaking with Laura Knox?'

'Yeah, this is Laura. You're calling about Maddy?'

'Yes, ma'am. You called our tip line with a possible ID?'

'Yeah, it's her. The woman in the picture, it's Maddy.'

'You're sure of that?'

'Yeah, of course.' She laughed, disbelief in her voice that there could be any doubt. 'One hundred percent.'

'Okay, can I ask how you know Maddy?'

'She's my friend. That's why I called again. I'm worried about her.'

Casey sat up straighter in her chair. 'Sorry, did you say you called before?'

'Yeah, I never heard back. I thought you guys must've found her, but she's still not picking up and she's not texting back, so I was worried and I thought I should call again.'

Casey scanned through the log from the tip line but couldn't find mention of a prior call. 'Okay, I'm not sure what's happened there, ma'am, but you did the right thing calling again. Can I get Maddy's last name?'

'Rushton.' She spelled it out. 'It's not like her to just go quiet – she's never ghosted me before. We text all the time.'

Casey felt the hairs on the back of her neck stand. 'When's the last time you heard from her, ma'am?'

'Like, the day before. I was worried sick when I saw she was caught up in that shooting, and now nothing. But I saw the victims on the TV – none of them was her, so I don't get it.'

'Okay, I understand. Let me take her address and her details, and I'm going to take a look into this right now.'

Maple Ridge Apartments was a residential complex on the western edge of Rockport, made up of seven low-rise apartment buildings arranged around a pair of small communal squares. Passing through a gateway from the parking lot that led to the interior of the complex, Casey found herself in a garden lit only by the residual glow from the lights inside the apartments, the pathways between them mostly in darkness. Surrounded by buildings on all sides, Casey felt suddenly vulnerable, checking over her shoulder as she walked deeper into the complex.

Maddy Rushton's apartment was on the far side of the square, one of two doors arranged next to each other under a peeling Roman-style portico that felt like a tacked-on attempt to add a little class. A lamp came on above her head as she approached, and somewhere across the way a dog started barking. Casey rang the bell, but it made no sound, as if it was out of order, so she knocked instead.

There were no lights showing behind the small windows in the door.

Casey knocked again, but already knew it was futile. She'd called Rushton's cell phone twice before leaving the office, getting no response, and left a voicemail. Laura Knox told her Rushton had moved to Rockport two years prior, arriving from 'somewhere down south, Atlanta or someplace around there', and the two had become friends when they were both employed as dancers at a downtown club named Lubino's. She'd called it a classy place – 'dances only, no extras'. Casey had never heard of it, which either meant it was a new joint, had cautious owners, or was the only strip club in Rockport that was on the level.

She stepped five feet to her left to knock on the neighbouring door, but it swung open before she had a chance.

A woman in a Mets jersey stood in the doorway. 'She's not home. Hasn't been around for a couple days.'

Casey was still in the action of raising her badge. 'Is this Maddy Rushton's apartment?'

'I guess. I always call her Madeline – that's how she introduced herself to me.'

'Do you have any idea where she might've went?'

The woman wrinkled her nose, shook her head. 'Never said a word to me about going anywhere, but I don't know her real well, so...' She shrugged, indicating anything was possible. 'She okay?'

Casey took a glance over her shoulder, the darkness of the complex feeling ever more forbidding. 'That's what I'm looking to establish. Is it unusual for her to take off like that?'

'Never known her to do it before, but I've only been renting here two months. She's got the kid, though. Can't be easy to just up sticks when you've got a little chipmunk to think about.'

Casey glanced to her left, the next pair of doorways maybe thirty feet distant. 'Is she friendly with any of the other neighbours, do you know?'

The woman poked her head out to look in the same direction as Casey. 'There's a crazy smell of weed comes from those two apartments – don't know which one it is so I avoid them both. They only go out at night, anyhow – never seen them talking to Madeline, she's an early bird. You should talk to Willy, he's the super. I see them talking all the time. He's got a soft spot for her. I know he does repairs for her off the clock, stuff like that. Probably thinks he can talk his way into her bed, but like my dad says, there's no fool like an old fool.'

❧

Casey climbed back into the car and drove to Casita, the neighbourhood restaurant where Laura Knox had told her Rushton was now working. Knox told Casey she'd already stopped by and been told Maddy was off sick, so her expectations were low, but it was still a box she had to check.

According to Knox, Rushton had given up her dancing gigs around eighteen months ago, soon after finding out she was pregnant. The child's name was Lana, apparently for the singer Lana Del Rey, but her friend had never spoken about the child's father, save for saying he wasn't a part of her life – and probably never would be. The name 'Adam Ryker' flashed through Casey's mind at hearing that part; Laura said she'd never heard of him before seeing his face all over the news, but that didn't rule him in or out of contention. For Casey, it wasn't even as much as a hunch, just a formless sense that he was the thread that somehow linked the fates of everyone involved in the case, victims and witnesses alike, even if he wasn't the perpetrator. But then she realised it was the second time she'd made that leap, just as with Darcy and Harper Whitlock, and it made her think again of Ray, holding court in his office and rolling out one of his favourite sayings as a reprimand to Cullen or one of the others: *Assumption is the mother of all fuckups.* He'd smile and wink at her whenever he said it, Casey at the time happy to bask in the warm glow of his approval, but now all she could see was a sloppy drunk, waving his tumbler and spilling whisky on the desk, dispensing bumper-sticker slogans like they were wisdom.

Since becoming a mom, Rushton had switched to waitressing, picking up work at a string of different eateries, with Casita the latest. It sounded a transient life that was exhausting to Casey just to hear about, and she couldn't figure how the woman had juggled finding work, earning enough money to pay rent and put food on the table, and still managing to look after her daughter – especially with no family to call on for childcare. Laura said she'd looked after the little girl on plenty of occasions, with Rushton resorting to taking Lana to work with her other times, leaving the child in her stroller in the back, reliant on the goodwill of the other wait staff to get her through her shift. But goodwill was an exhaustible pool, and the reason why she'd had to move on so frequently.

Casita proved to be a dead end. The chef-owner said she'd failed to turn up for her shift that day, and the day before, and hadn't returned his calls. He mentioned her 'blonde friend' stopping by to ask after her whereabouts, but he hadn't seen HCPD's appeals for her identity, so it hadn't set off any alarm bells at the time. He said he'd assumed her absence was on account of Lana being sick – something that'd happened more than once before. There was a note of genuine concern in his voice when he learned that she'd seemingly disappeared, and he told Casey to let Rushton know that he'd keep her position open for her if she could get back to work in the next few days.

From what little she'd gleaned of the woman's life, it seemed doubtful she was the type who could easily skip out on a paycheck. There was the possibility she'd headed south, returning home to family or friends, but the forces that propelled a person to move thousands of miles across the country, with limited prospects and resources, usually negated the chance of a simple return journey. In truth, Madeline Rushton's was a profile that had Casey scared for mother and child alike; women like her disappeared from sight every day, slipping through the cracks of a system that wasn't designed with their welfare at heart. Some later turned up as victims of crime, a few as perpetrators, but the majority were never heard from again, spiralling through addiction, abuse or neglect into a void that society somehow chose to overlook.

Casey checked her cell, looking for a reply from Dana. She'd messaged her before leaving Maple Ridge Apartments, asking what'd happened in Dunmore's interview with Muneera Kouri, but received no response. It wasn't like Dana not to text back, and the collective silence around the situation was starting to drive Casey nuts.

She pulled up the number Maddy Rushton's neighbour had given her for Willy, the super at Maple Ridge. A man answered almost immediately.

'Yeah?'

'This is Detective Casey Wray, am I speaking to Willy?'

'What'd I do?'

Casey almost laughed, his directness unexpected. 'Nothing, sir, I'm looking for information on the whereabouts of Madeline Rushton, she lives at Maple Ridge Apartments?'

'Maddy? What happened to her?'

'That's what I'm trying to figure out. One of the residents told me she hasn't been home the past couple days and she's not answering her cell phone. I was told you're friendly with her?'

'No. Who told you that?'

'Sir, she's not in any trouble. We need to speak to her about an incident she may have witnessed, and her not returning to her home is a cause for concern.'

'It's nothing to do with me. I don't know where she's at.'

'This isn't an accusation, sir. I'm just looking for any information on her whereabouts.'

'Look, I see her around, I say hello, same as anyone else. I fixed her faucet one time – it was leaking, it was no big deal. That's enough to put me on your radar?'

Casey sagged in her seat, another lead running into a dead end of indifference and suspicion.

'What about her kid?' he said, blurting it out before Casey could switch tack.

'I have no information on her whereabouts either. I'm hopeful she's with her mother.'

'Aw, hell.' He sniffed away from the speaker, a raw edge to

his voice when he spoke again. 'She works her ass off for that little girl. I see her come home sometimes, and she's about dead on her feet, but soon as that girl puts a smile on her, you can see her just light up like a Christmas tree.'

'Sir, do you have any idea where she might go?'

'I swear to god, I say hello, I smile at the kid, I make dumb jokes about the Falcons, that's the whole of it. Look me up – I got no record, I've never been inside—'

'The more you talk, the more you're making me wonder, Willy.'

'Come on, officer, give me a break here. There's two hundred people in them apartments, I talk to half of them the same, the other half only speak to me when they need something. How come you never showed an interest when I called about them dopeheads living in the next apartment to hers? Or when I told you there's some creep hanging around the building taking pictures?'

The words set off a rattle in the back of Casey's mind, like an echo. 'Say that last part again.'

'What?' He sounded hesitant, backing away from it.

'About someone hanging around,' Casey said.

'I mean ... Well, okay, I didn't call you guys myself. I told building management about it, they were supposed to follow up. Security's not my job, y'know? I been telling them they need to pay a security company for years. I'm not about to pull up on a guy with a wrench in my hand and risk getting my ass shot for fifteen bucks an hour—'

'Willy, when was this?'

He took a breath and let it out, thinking. 'Couple weeks ago, three maybe.'

'Can you describe him for me?' she said, Adam Ryker's name once again on the tip of her tongue.

'Yeah, skinny, looked like he hadn't eaten right in a while. Serious-looking, just sitting there. Once or twice it looked like he was taking photos with his cell. Sometimes there was two of them, him and a girl. She was younger – couldn't figure out if she was his girlfriend or what, but he looked old enough to be her dad. Didn't look much like him to be his daughter, though.'

'Girl? As in a woman?'

'Yeah, maybe twenties or thereabouts. Too young for him, but what do I know?'

'Did they ever show an interest in Maddy Rushton?'

'I couldn't tell you if they did or didn't. I'd just see them parked across the street when I was going in and out. One morning he – or they – would be there, then they'd be gone. Couple days later, the car's back again. Must've been four or five times I saw him, maybe three times with the girl.'

Casey whipped out her pen and pad. 'Tell me again about the man.'

'What else you want me to say?'

'Give me something more. Hair colour? Short hair, long hair...?'

'Nah, short. Short hair – I mean, not a buzzcut or anything, like a normal length. Neat, side-part. I don't know how to describe the colour, kinda grey-brown.'

'Salt and pepper, you mean?'

'Yeah, that kinda thing.'

Casey felt a jolt go up her spine, remembering the man and woman she'd seen sitting outside Aryana Guptil's place that first morning she'd gone to speak with her. She licked her thumb and riffled back through her notebook to where she'd scribbled down the details – a late model black Lexus – along with its licence plate. 'You remember what type of a car they were in?'

'Yeah, it was a Lexus. Black, new – pretty sleek.'

'Did you take down the plate?'

'Yeah, but I don't remember it now. Management will have it. I gave it to Barney in the office.'

'Willy, I want you to get it for me and call me back on this number, okay?'

'Office is closed till tomorrow.'

'Do it first thing in the morning. Please?'

'Yeah, sure, okay—'

'I mean it, first thing.' There were sparks flying inside her head, a new energy that made her feel like she could run all the way back to the office.

'You telling me you think they wanted something with Maddy?'

'I don't know yet.' She thanked him and hung up, then gunned the engine.

CHAPTER TWENTY-EIGHT

The department was almost deserted when Casey got back, a lone cleaner emptying trash cans the only person on the floor.

She dashed to her desk, drawing a bemused look, and opened her computer to run the licence plate of the Lexus she'd noted down. It came back registered to an address in Locust Point, New York, a tiny neighbourhood in the Bronx. There were no flags or warrants against the vehicle, not even a traffic violation, although the owner had only registered it six months prior. She put his name through the system, but it came back clean. Switching to Google Maps, she checked the drive time from Rockport to Locust Point and it came back as fifty minutes via the Throgs Neck Bridge.

Almost eleven pm. There was a landline number listed on the record, and she felt her calves twitching as she weighed it up.

Skinny, salt-and-pepper hair. Black Lexus. Sometimes accompanied by a younger woman. Taking pictures on his phone.

She opened the case file on her screen and ran a search for the word 'photo'. It came back with dozens of hits, most of them relating to evidence photos, but one of the listings was the one she wanted: Brianna Monk, Landon Whitlock's secretary, telling her Whitlock had complained about being followed by 'The Photographer' again shortly before his death.

She was already out of her seat when an earlier hit in the list of results caught her eye. An entry by Billy Drocker, recording a conversation they'd had with Frederick Colossimo, right at the start of the investigation, after he'd been seen speeding away from the scene in his red Silverado. A detail so seemingly insignificant, she'd disregarded it:

A man and a woman parked across the street from Strongbox almost exactly twenty-four hours before the shootings – Colossimo stuck in traffic next to them, creeping on the woman in the black Lexus as she took pictures with her boyfriend.

Selfies. Colossimo had told Billy it was a man and a woman taking selfies. But now it looked like he was dead wrong.

Alone at her desk, staring out at a starless night, her head overflowing with pieces that didn't fit yet – but might. 'The Photographer' watching Landon Whitlock before his death, watching the scene of the shootings the day before, watching Maddy Rushton in the runup and Aryana Guptil in the aftermath – *if* the guy in the Lexus was one and the same. That flat stare he'd landed Casey with the one time they'd crossed paths – knowing, alert, but unafraid of being noticed.

A jump: Casey asking Darcy Whitlock about Landon's claims of being followed, and her shutting it down immediately. A denial that he'd mentioned anything about it to her before his death, one that hadn't convinced at the time, and now felt significant. Her thoughts ran to unexplored territory – was it possible Darcy had someone following Landon? 'The Photographer' as some kind of a PI or … a contract shooter, even? Brianna Monk had alluded to Darcy's dissatisfaction with her marriage, and to Landon leaving Darcy and Harper well provided for; people got killed for lesser motives than that. Still, it was a huge leap.

She was used to this process, her mind working through theories, testing and rejecting, seeking an explanation that brought everything together – but right now it still felt out of reach. She got out of her seat and walked to the window, Rockport enveloped by the night. Even the lights from the strip mall opposite looked lost in the darkness, the white lettering of the discount liquor store giving it a bleak and desolate air.

Indecision had her stalled. Would a run to Locust Point, way out of her jurisdiction, bring her any closer to finding Maddy Rushton? The first twenty-four hours of a disappearance were the most crucial, and they were well past that already. And what if Maddy Rushton really had decided to go home of her own accord, and Casey was chasing a woman who was safe and didn't want to be found?

She couldn't convince herself on that last one.

She stared at the name of the Lexus driver in the search box: Michael Stringer. Whether witness or suspect, this guy had touchpoints all over the case. That had to make him a priority. She went back to her desk and picked up her phone, dialling the number listed for the address in Locust Point. It rang for almost a minute, then cut out, no voicemail service. She typed the name into Google. The results that came back included a guitarist in a heavy-metal band, a professor and a bunch of random Facebook profiles – but none of the images were the guy she'd seen. Whoever he was, he'd left no digital footprint.

She typed a note into the case file, listing him as a person of interest, then added his name, description and licence plate to the distribution lists for Patrol with the instruction: *Urgent/notify Detective Sergeant Wray immediately if sighted.* Then she shut the laptop and grabbed her car keys.

⁂

The Throgs Neck Bridge carried her over the East River where it met the Long Island Sound. The reflection from the lights strung across the bridge's suspension cables danced on the black water below, while Manhattan shimmered in the distance to the west.

She crossed the peninsula, Fort Schuyler standing dark and imposing to her right, the stone walls illuminated by amber uplighters. But just as quickly she was over water again, and then Locust Point came into view up ahead, a scatter of lights in a dark landmass reaching out towards her.

The address was a small redbrick house that stood in the shadow of the bridge's off-ramp, two blocks back from the water. She parked out front and looked around for the Lexus, but couldn't see it amongst the vehicles along the sidewalk. The house had no driveway of its own. She climbed out and paused by the kerb, scanning both ways. Somewhere out of sight, a mournful bell rang softly, the sound coming from the gentle swaying of the boats moored in the marina.

The houses along the street were narrow and arranged close together, a mishmash of redbrick, clapboard and ranch-style homes, the only common design feature that they were all long and thin. Behind them, the bridge rose up into the distance, the red lights atop its towers blinking silently in the night.

There were no security lights or cameras on the front of the house. She crossed the narrow front yard and stepped onto the small porch, knocked quietly and waited. A cold wind cut across her, blowing in off the water and being funnelled down the street.

No answer.

She knocked again, a little louder, then took out her cell to dial the landline number she'd cribbed from the system. She could hear it ringing inside the house, but there was no other sound to indicate that anyone was home. She killed the call.

There was a single window to the side of the porch, but a roller blind had been lowered over it, cutting off any view of the inside. A narrow passage to her left led along the side of the property; she glanced up and down the street again, aware of the risk of a neighbour calling the police at the sight of what looked like an intruder, and the shitstorm that it would set off if it looked like she was acting out of her jurisdiction. But the street was silent, no sign of movement anywhere. Feeling reassured, she stepped off the porch and picked her way lightly down the passage.

The flank of the house was windowless, a wooden fence and

less than ten feet separating it from the grey clapboards of the adjacent property. The passage opened out onto a small, cracked-concrete yard, two windows at ground level. One was covered by another blind, but the second was halfway uncovered. She stepped closer to peer inside.

There was a scraping sound behind her. She spun around, reaching for her sidearm, just in time to see a ginger cat scrabbling up the fence at the rear of the property. It paused long enough to glance at her, a look she would've sworn was accusatory, then disappeared down the other side.

She stood perfectly still, her heart beating so hard she could feel it in her wrists and ears. Nothing moved. The distant sound of traffic crossing the bridge carried on the damp night air. After waiting what felt like an hour, she took her hand off her weapon and turned back to the window. She leaned close, cupping her hands around her eyes, but taking care not to touch the glass as she squinted into the gloom.

It took a few seconds for her vision to adjust. She found herself looking into a compact living room, a couch and one armchair arranged in an L-shape, a small coffee table within reach. There was nothing on the table, nothing on the walls. No TV that she could see, no books or magazines, the room so bare it could've been a show home. She wondered if this Stringer guy had registered the vehicle to a fake address, opening up the possibility that the name wasn't real either—

Something moved inside, making Casey's heart jerk again. She couldn't make it out at first, then it moved once more, bringing into view a tiny blue light, blinking slowly. She realised what it was just as her eyes adjusted and the dark shape took form: a Ring surveillance camera. It'd swivelled on its mount to point in her direction.

Controlled remotely.

Someone knew she was there. And now they were looking right at her.

She rolled away from the window and stood with her back pressed to the wall of the house, gulping silent breaths as she tried to control the rising panic in her chest.

She listened for movement. Whoever was watching could be anywhere – in a different room inside the house, or a hundred miles away. She was an idiot to come here alone, and now she was exposed.

No sounds came to her, and finally she started edging her way along the wall of the house, checking the passage was empty before rounding the corner, keeping to the shadows as she inched along it.

The street was in sight, and as she came to the other end of the passage, her car came into view too.

She stopped dead. Her windshield wipers had been lifted, left standing to attention as if the car was in the process of being detailed.

Still pressing herself into the wall, she looked both ways along the block, but the sidewalks were empty. She waited a minute, two, but no one showed. Then a shadow flitted to her right and she froze again, watching, her hand on her weapon. A few seconds later, the same ginger cat darted between two cars and disappeared.

Casey stood perfectly still, just breathing. Across the street, a lone Stars and Stripes extended from above the front door of one of the houses, fluttering intermittently in the breeze.

CHAPTER TWENTY-NINE

Dunmore called an all-hands meeting for seven am the next day, Casey arriving with heavy eyelids. She'd made it home from Locust Point after midnight with her adrenaline still running hard, meaning even though she'd flopped into bed right away, it was past three when sleep had finally found her.

She tore into a breakfast burrito as she crossed the precinct parking lot, white cotton-candy clouds hanging motionless in the morning sky. Willy, the super from Maddy Rushton's apartment complex, had proved good to his word, calling Casey's cell just before she got out of the car to relay the plate on the Lexus he'd seen – now confirmed as the same one registered to Michael Stringer in Locust Point. She'd get Billy to check back with Frederick Colossimo, the Silverado driver, to see if he could provide any detail that would mean a similar confirmation on the pair he saw, but she was ninety-nine-percent sure they were one and the same. Now all she had to do was find them.

Stepping inside, she found Jill Hart waiting for her in the stairwell.

'Hey.'

Casey came to a stop in front of her. 'You doing okay?'

Jill nodded. 'Billy spoke to you?'

'He sure did. How are you feeling today?'

'Like crap.' She took off her glasses and rubbed her eyes. 'I'm really sorry for not showing up yesterday. I couldn't...' She shook her head. 'I know I screwed up.'

'You should've come and talked to me.'

Jill looked at her, a sour look on her face as if she had doubts about that.

'What?'

'It's just ... I know how tight you and Billy are.'

Casey flicked her finger back and forth between them. 'He's my partner but that doesn't mean I'm not here for you too, right? We're all on the same team.'

'Sure. I guess. But not like ... Anyway. Sorry.'

'We don't play favourites here. You got a problem, you can come talk to me anytime.'

Jill nodded, gripping her arm across her stomach. 'Does the lieutenant know?'

'Not from me. But I gotta tell you, you can't just duck out like that.'

'But I felt humiliated. So humiliated. I couldn't face seeing him.'

Casey bent down to meet her eyes. 'I get it. And you've got all my sympathy for what happened, Jill. But this isn't the academy – the job is too important.'

'I know, I just needed some time. To get my head straight.'

Casey put her hand on Jill's shoulder, but Jill turned her head briefly to look at it, as if it made her uncomfortable, making Casey withdraw. 'This job's gonna smack you in the mouth over and over again. You've got to be able to roll with the punches and still keep your focus. Our shit is life and death – you've got to be able to compartmentalise.'

Jill's face had gone white and Casey started to worry she'd gone too hard. She realised then she was paraphrasing something Ray had said to her once, back when she was starting out in the bureau, stress and tiredness making her regurgitate the ingrained bullshit she'd been told down the years without thinking. Her instinct was to put an arm around Jill's shoulder to try and make it right, but that was clearly out.

'Look, it's going to be okay. If you want to talk to Personnel on a formal basis, we can set that up, or you can talk to me informally whenever you like. What I need to know from you and Billy is if you can make this work on a professional level from here on out, because if not, then we need to figure out a different route.'

Jill nodded, but it was shaky.

Casey glanced at her watch. 'For right now, we need to get going.' She started to climb the stairs but paused to look back when Jill remained where she was. 'Jilly, come on. We can figure this out.'

Jill looked away, chewing on her top lip, then reluctantly took the handrail to follow after.

Dunmore stood at the head of the conference table, her eyes dulled by what Casey assumed was lack of sleep. There was still a hardness there, but without the laser focus that stood out on that first morning in Keirn's office.

Casey took the last seat at the table, next to Billy, with Dana opposite and Jill alongside her. Billy was slumped down low in his chair, facing Dunmore and with his pad placed in his lap – giving him somewhere to look so he could avoid Dana's glare. Jill had her eyes fixed on the screen at the front of the room, and the air above the table between her and Billy seemed to throb, the awkwardness radiating. Casey glanced at Dana and flashed a sad smile, trying to find one functional relationship in the room, but Dana switched right back to staring daggers at Billy.

Casey rubbed the back of her neck. The atmosphere sucked,

the dynamic broken, and she wondered how the hell the camaraderie they'd built up had fractured so rapidly. For all the doubts that plagued her when it came to her ability and command presence, she'd taken pride in creating a sense of team spirit – but now even that was faltering. She glanced at Billy again and put herself in Jill's shoes. She'd treated him like a kid who made a silly mistake, but there were loose parallels between his behaviour and that of Adam Ryker when it came to how they treated women. Not the same, not as serious, but it raised questions about Billy's judgement that she'd not acknowledged at first. And maybe her own judgement too; he was a grown man, not the younger brother she'd never had.

'Good morning,' Dunmore said. 'Let's get right to it. Yesterday I grilled Muneera Kouri about her claims to being able to alibi Adam Ryker for the shootings on Eighth and Villanova. Subsequent to that, I had a lengthy update with Acting Chief Keirn, and the outcome is that Miss Kouri's cell phone is being sent for further analysis by the Technical team in Harrison. It is very much the acting chief's view that, given the overwhelming evidence against Adam Ryker, he remains the prime suspect in this matter at this time.'

'Wait, what about the new lines of investigation we've established?' Casey said, holding up her phone as a reference to the late-night text she'd sent Dunmore to update her on what she'd discovered.

Dunmore nodded once, picking up a new sheet of paper with her notes on. 'To bring you all up to speed: Sergeant Wray believes she has identified our missing eyewitness, the woman with the child seen briefly inside Strongbox – now named as Madeline Rushton. Miss Rushton's whereabouts are currently unknown. What do we have to go on, Sergeant?'

Casey picked up her pad. 'She's from the Atlanta area, only arrived in Rockport a couple years ago. Five-four, one hundred ten pounds, last seen with her daughter, Lana, who's aged under one year. She was identified by a friend and former co-worker. I've called her multiple times, to no response. Hasn't been seen at her apartment for two days, and missed two waitressing shifts in that time. She hasn't posted to her Instagram account in more than a month, but it looks like she's a sporadic user anyway, so that's not out of the ordinary, and that seems to be her only social-media account – at least in her own name. Currently unknown if the child is with her, but there's reportedly no father on the scene and seemingly not much of a support network locally. So the picture's not a promising one.'

Dana had her eyes closed and was shaking her head. 'How can a mom and kid that young slip out of sight and no one gives a crap?'

'I've lodged a request for cell-tower data with her provider, let's see what that brings. As a priority this morning, I'd like our appeals updated with her name and a better headshot – there are images on Insta we can use – and while you're there, see if we can identify any obvious anonymous accounts she's using that might have been updated in recent days.' She was looking at Jill, who made notes without lifting her eyes from her pad once. 'Billy, check the Uber and Lyft portals. As far as we know, she doesn't have a vehicle of her own, so maybe we get lucky and pick up a trail there. Also, let's check all the usual avenues – women's shelters, jails, hospitals. And while we're talking to the latter, see if we can find any birth records – we know the child is named Lana, last name possibly Rushton, but we don't have that confirmed. She's less than a year old so let's see if there are any health workers who've been in recent contact with them who might be able to give us a line on family or any other background detail.'

Dunmore brought her knuckles to her chin. 'Before we go any further, I need to state that the acting chief is adamant there be limited noise around any further lines of investigation, pending the results from Harrison. His concern is that, if there is substance to Miss Kouri's claims, we will need a media strategy in place before we proceed.'

Dana rolled her eyes.

'What about the victims' families though?' Casey said. 'They were told we had our perp. They need to know that's not solid anymore.'

Dunmore stiffened. The calls she'd made to the families would have to be walked back. 'Again, we wait. Acting chief's directive.'

'The longer we leave it, the worse it looks.' Casey opened her hands on the table, making an appeal. 'And it's just the right thing to do.'

Dunmore looked trapped, and Casey got it then – she'd told Keirn the same and been overruled. 'It's out of my hands.'

Casey drew a line across her pad with a slash.

'Last thing,' Dunmore said. 'Sergeant Wray has identified a further person of interest. Sergeant?'

Casey stood up and ran through what she'd learned about Michael Stringer and his unidentified sometime accomplice, leaving out the part where she'd made a crazy late-night dash to snoop his address. 'I'll put a call in to NYPD this morning to ask them to check by his property, but the frequency with which he's been sighted in Rockport makes me think there's a chance he's got a temporary base somewhere local.'

'You think this guy could be our shooter?' Billy said.

'I'm not making any assumptions,' Casey said, catching herself as she used Ray's word again, 'but he's cropped up at different places all over this case, so we need to find him as a priority. The licence plate for his Lexus has gone out on all bulletins to Patrol.'

'If he had something to do with the shootings or Maddy Rushton going AWOL, what's the chances this guy's still in the area?' Billy said.

'He was at Aryana Guptil's place the morning after the shootings. Seeing as he didn't split right away, it makes me think he's still got business here.'

'If he was watching Guptil, does that make him a threat to Ryker's other exes?' Dana said.

'Maybe,' Casey said. 'But he was watching Landon Whitlock too. I think we need to be open to the possibility that Landon Whitlock was the target here all along.'

'Let's look again for any links between Whitlock and Ryker,' Dunmore said, rising from her seat. 'Sergeant, stay behind a moment please. The rest of you, let's get to it.'

Casey reclined her chair a little, watching the others file out in silence. Through the glass, she saw Jill head straight for the bathrooms, Dana alive to it and following after. When everyone else was gone, Casey swivelled to face the front, linked her fingers in her lap and waited.

'You're no longer working this investigation.'

Casey snapped her chair upright. 'What?'

'Keirn has tasked me with taking charge of this personally. The others will continue to work it under my direct supervision. You're being assigned to clear the mountain of internal requests we've had to backburner the last couple days.'

'I'm on the shit-work pile? Why?'

'You know why, Sergeant.'

Casey stared at her. 'You're hanging me out to dry.'

She shook her head. 'It's not that simple. I never said this, but if Ryker's not our killer, someone has to eat turkey for the department.'

'And that's me?'

'I've already advised the acting chief that you'll be moving on when we clear this case. His feeling is that if you take one for the team on the way out the door, he'll see to it that you find a soft landing.'

Casey jumped to her feet, stabbing her finger at Dunmore. 'This is bullshit. All of it. You know Muneera's telling the truth, don't you?'

'As I already said, Keirn's not convinced—'

'I'm not talking about him, I'm talking about you. He's stalling while he leaks some bullshit about *individual failings*, but you know our shooter's still out there. How does making me ride a desk bring us closer to a clearance?'

Dunmore stared at her with eyes like deep pools, thoughts swimming behind them. She took in a breath as if she was about to say something, but let it out again and looked away.

'Look, you and Keirn can play your games however you want, but at least let me work on tracking down Maddy Rushton. She's vulnerable as hell – but we don't have to lose her to this. Please.'

Dunmore didn't say anything at first, the unspoken question hovering between them: what were the chances she was still alive?

After a long second, she faced Casey again. 'The child's not even a year?'

Casey nodded. 'Correct.'

Her gaze went out of focus, considering it.

'They're stretched out there and you know it,' Casey said, gesturing to the desks outside. 'If something happens to that kid and her mom, and it turns out we could've prevented it, can you live with that? Because I can't.' She stepped closer. 'You want my badge, you can have it when this is over, and you guys can shit on my reputation as much as you like. But let me do this first.'

Now Dunmore took a step closer. 'No one else is to know about this. You bring what you find to me alone. If word gets back to Keirn, I'll deny any knowledge of your actions, and if you screw me with your friends at County Plaza, you won't have functioning arms left to hand me your badge.'

Casey nodded. 'Understood.'

'Find them, Wray. Do not make me regret this.'

Hustling out of the meeting room, Casey only made it as far as her desk before Dana collared her. 'You got a second?' She turned and headed for the break room, not even waiting for Casey's weary 'Not really...' in reply.

When she followed her inside, Dana was waiting to close the door behind her.

'What's up?'

'Casey, this is hard because you know I trust your judgement, but don't you think you were kind of tough on Jill this morning?'

'What? What's she said?'

'She came to talk to me, she's pretty upset. She feels like you're taking Billy's side.'

Casey sagged, rolling her head. 'Jesus, I told her that's not it. I told her I felt bad for what happened.'

'Sure. But Billy walked out and disappeared for, what, almost two hours? And later on you told him he could go home and get his head straight if he wanted to. Then you're telling her she's supposed to compartmentalise and get on with it?'

'Dana, she called in sick because a guy cheated on her. Is that what you'd have done?'

'I mean, it was usually me doing the cheating, but that's not the point. She's not me, and she's not you either. And he's not just any guy. She needs an arm around the shoulders.'

'She can have it, but she needs to recognise the job comes first.'

'She knows that, Casey. You see the hours she puts in. Has she ever not come through for us?'

'It was about the mildest reprimand a person could ask for, Dana. This is out of proportion. You remember what it was like back in the day if you took sick leave as a woman?' Casey said it knowing they'd both been on the receiving end of the kind of sexist mindset that used to dominate the department; a female officer missing a shift was assumed to be on her period or pregnant – either of which would be chalked up as proof that women could never be real cops.

'You know I do, but that's not the department Jill knows, Case.'

'If me telling her she's gotta grow a thicker skin is too much, then how the hell is she going to survive in this place?'

'She knows that – that's not the issue. She thinks you're giving Billy a pass here, and I gotta be honest, I kind of agree with her. I know you're fond of him—'

'Fond? What does that mean? I don't treat any of you any different.'

'I'm not saying you do, but this kind of bullshit speaks to a serious lack of judgement on his part.'

Casey held her hands up. 'I told him he's an asshole, he knows it, but how he chooses to live his life is not my business. And it's not yours either.' She heard herself say it but realised she was defending a position she'd already started to change her mind on.

'It is when it screws with the rest of the team.'

Casey let out a deep breath, bracing herself on the counter. 'Is this why you didn't text me back yesterday?'

'What?' She looked at her, as if waiting for her to retract it. 'Seriously, Casey?'

'I'm just saying, you never replied and that's not like you.'

'You really think I'd be so childish?'

'Then why ignore me?'

Dana put her hands on her hips. 'Dunmore told me not to contact you after the interview.' She blinked, shrugged. 'Direct order. What was I supposed to do?'

'Okay.' Casey dipped her head. 'Okay, yeah, that figures.'

'I mean, there was nothing new to tell you anyway, you already heard everything Kouri had to say, and at the end, Dunmore took off running to Keirn. But she's got her mind made up about you.'

'Yeah, tell me about it.'

'Look, I know you got it tough right now. I didn't mean to come on strong.'

Casey took a breath and let it out through pursed lips. 'Me neither.' She looked up again, meeting Dana's eyes. 'What would you do?'

'About Billy? I'd tell him he's free to do whatever the hell he wants with whatever consenting adult or adults he chooses to do it with, but this is the last time he lets it impact on the job. Otherwise he gets hooked.'

'I can't say that. There's nothing in the regs against same-rank relationships. You know that.'

'Fuck the regs. He needs to know. If it had to happen, there's always a way.'

'And Jill?'

'She's got the message about toughening up and she'll work on it. Soon as she sees Billy's not getting an easier ride, she'll be fine. Just talk to her, let her know you're not mad.'

'You think she can work with Billy again?'

'I wouldn't make them partners anytime soon, but sure. She's a pro.'

Casey stood a moment, taking it onboard. Then she swept an imaginary crumb off the counter and headed for the door. 'Let me think about it.'

CHAPTER THIRTY

Casey spent the rest of the day feeling like she was digging a tunnel that led nowhere.

Maddy Rushton's cell-tower data revealed that the last ping from her phone came at 8.36am on Thursday, from a site a half mile from Strongbox. That put it approximately fifteen minutes after the last known sighting of her on the gym's surveillance footage. Casey wasn't sure what to take from that. There was a chance her cell had run out of power and not been charged since; more troubling was the possibility that something had happened to her and her phone been intentionally put out of action.

As the day wore on, the renewed appeals for information on Rushton's whereabouts started producing new leads – but none that panned out. A woman in eastern Rockport swore she'd seen her working in a grocery store, but Casey drove to the store in question and quickly spotted a young woman with red hair and nothing more than a passing resemblance. A Starbucks employee called in saying that the day before she'd served a woman called Maddy who fit the description – but a review of the store's surveillance footage again established it wasn't her.

It went on like that, hope giving way to false hope giving way to reality, as the hours slipped away. The stats said the chances of her showing up safe after that amount of time were vanishingly small, and with each minute that passed it was like she faded a little further from existence.

By six that evening, Casey was back at her desk, frazzled and no closer to finding her. The office was empty, the rest of the team on the street – even Dunmore. Casey sat alone, working her way through the updated list of reported sightings and leads, looking for the most promising one to target next.

Her cell phone rang and she snatched it up. 'Casey Wray.'

'Sergeant Wray, this is Grainger in Dispatch. Unit Three-Alpha-Three calling in with a visual on the licence plate you're looking for – a black Lexus.'

Casey jumped up. 'Patch me through, please?'

'Affirmative.'

There was a pause, then a new voice on the line. 'Big, this is Pete B. I'm travelling west on Twelfth, near the intersection with Lombard, got your Lexus two cars in front of me. You want me to pull him over?'

Casey grabbed up her keys, already heading for the stairs. Dunmore would crucify her – but she had nothing left to lose anyway. 'Does he know you're on him?'

'Negative. I was cruising and he popped up right in front of me.'

'There a passenger in there with him?'

'Yeah, looks like an IC1 female. I'll need to get closer to get a better look.'

'Negative. Stay with him. Only pull him over if it looks like he's trying to shake you. I'm on my way now. I'll be on the radio in two seconds and I'll catch you up. Do not lose him.'

'You got it.'

❧

It was one exit on the expressway, Casey touching ninety as she weaved across the lanes, lights and sirens blaring, like an extension of how she felt inside. She had the radio in her lap, regular updates coming through from Pete B as to his location, the Lexus still travelling west on Twelfth.

She took the exit and blitzed through a crowded intersection, then made the turn onto Twelfth and grabbed up the radio. 'Dispatch, I'm westbound on Twelfth, just past the expressway interchange. How far ahead of me is Three-Alpha-Three?'

She kept pushing the car faster, waiting for the response, her eyes glued to the road ahead.

'Unit Three-Alpha-Three approximately two miles west of your location, Sergeant.'

'Copy.'

Twelfth was a two-lane stretch of road that skirted

downtown then made its way west through the suburbs. Traffic was heavy but flowing, enough that Casey could get in and around to overtake, her chin almost touching the steering wheel as she leaned forward to concentrate.

'Dispatch, give me a running count. I need to know when I'm a half-mile out so I can cut the sirens. Pete, you hearing me? I do not want this guy spooked.'

Pete B answered before Dispatch. 'Got it, Big.'

'Copy. One point seven-five and closing, Sergeant.'

The road ahead of her was a blur of red taillights and grey metal, the heavy clouds that had carpeted the sky all afternoon bringing evening down early, a fine rain only adding to the gloom.

'One point five miles, Sergeant.'

She pulled around a pickup and almost ran into the back of a black Accord she hadn't seen, jamming her horn to get it to move aside. Picking up speed again, she cut a swathe through cross traffic while running a red at the Steinbrook intersection, then grabbed up the radio with her free hand. 'Talk to me.'

'One point two-five, Sergeant.'

'Big, it's Pete – we just turned north on Haverbrook. Traffic's a little lighter here. I'm gonna let him run out the leash a little.'

'Copy that.'

Casey pressed the accelerator as hard as she dared, steering with one hand, the radio in her other.

'Big, wait, we just made another right, now eastbound on Thirteenth.'

That put them a block north of where she was, headed back in her direction. With an intersection right ahead, she dropped the radio and wrenched the wheel with both hands, turning the car north on Preston and speeding to intercept. As

Thirteenth Street came into view ahead of her, she cut the lights and sirens. 'Pete, what's your ten-twenty?'

'Continuing eastbound. We just passed the intersection with Preston.'

'That's right ahead of me. I'll be behind you in twenty seconds.' She made a right onto Thirteenth Street and cut her speed when she saw the patrol car come into view up ahead. She cruised up so she was behind and to the right, catching her first glimpse of the black Lexus two cars ahead.

'Got you on visual, Big. You want me to pull him over now?'

'Negative. Let me get in front of him in case he runs.'

'Copy.'

Casey overtook the cruiser and drew up behind and to the right of the Lexus, waiting for the car ahead of her to speed up or move out of the way. She could see two shapes in the Lex, driver's side and passenger. If he was aware of the patrol car on his tail, he showed no concerns about it.

Casey pushed on again, looking across as she came level with the Lex, catching a glimpse of the passenger. It was the same woman she'd seen him with before, and the sight of her brought the rest crashing back: the bar of the Abbeymore Hotel, the woman reading a book by herself on the night Casey had met McTeague there. The night that Tesla had seemed to follow her home.

Streetlights overhead streaked white on the Lex's paintwork. What the fuck was this? Was she watching Casey? For who, and why? McTeague's proximity to the encounter only added more questions. PIs were his business. Was there a chance they were on his timeclock?

Pete B came over the radio: 'Big, you good? What're you waiting for?'

Casey locked her eyes on the road and sped up again. 'All good. Hit your lights as soon as I get him sandwiched.' She went by the Lexus and manoeuvred across in front of it, and as she took her position, Pete flicked his lights on, a red wash signalling for the driver to pull over to the kerb.

Casey's eyes bounced between the rearview and the road in front, poised to jam her foot down if he tried to run. She could just make out the driver behind the wheel now, final confirmation it was the same guy she'd seen outside of Aryana Guptil's place – now named as Michael Stringer. His face was thin, a prominent brow and cheekbones putting his eyes in shadow from her vantage point. In the seat next to him, the same young woman she'd seen him with before.

Seconds passed. Casey's palms were damp on the wheel. She braked gently, trying to force Stringer to slow, but the Lexus crept closer to her fender, so she accelerated again a little, creating enough of a gap to avoid him ramming her. But just as she was braced for him to make a move, the Lexus's blinker came on and Stringer guided it across the roadway to the kerb. Casey slowed and came to a stop a short distance ahead of it, Pete B a car length behind.

Casey brought the radio to her lips. 'Pete, I'll talk to them. I want you to cover me from the vehicle's rear.'

'Got it. They likely to be carrying?'

'Unknown. Assume yes.'

Casey climbed out and unstrapped her sidearm. She walked slowly towards the Lexus, seeing Stringer lower his window, then place both hands on the steering wheel. Rain was still falling, beading white as it caught in the headlamp glare.

Casey came to a stop five feet from the driver's door and held up her badge. 'How you doing? My name's Detective Sergeant

Wray with HCPD, that's Officer Bradley behind you. With one hand, slowly, turn your interior light on, please, sir.'

Stringer glanced at her, then slowly reached up for the dome light. Casey kept one hand on her holster.

In the dim light his face looked gaunt, but in a sculpted way, like that of a distance runner rather than through malnourishment. The woman in the passenger seat had on a V-neck tee and dark jeans, and was staring straight ahead, her expression neutral, but there was something forced about it, as if it was practised.

'Let me see your licence, registration and insurance card, please.'

'I'll need to go into my trouser pocket,' Stringer said. He spoke in a low voice, but his accent took her by surprise – British, like the ones she heard on those BBC America shows, with edges hard enough to cut glass.

'Go ahead. Keep it slow.'

He reached into his pocket and pulled out his wallet, shooting her a look when he had it in his fingers and raising his eyebrows as a way of asking if he could take his other hand off the wheel. Casey nodded. He pulled out his cards and handed them over.

Casey signalled for Pete B to come take them and run them through the system.

'Either of you have a firearm in the vehicle, Mr Stringer?'

'No.'

'You're a Brit?'

He kept his eyes fixed on a point somewhere off in the distance. 'I'm an American citizen. I have dual nationality.'

Casey squatted a little to see the woman in the passenger seat. 'May I see your ID, ma'am?'

She had her hands on the dashboard, a small clutch on her lap. 'It's in there, that okay?'

'Another Brit?' Casey said. 'Got ourselves a regular invasion here. Go ahead.'

The woman reached into her bag and produced her ID card. Casey took it and read. 'Lydia Wright. You a dual national too?'

Stringer turned to face her, the collar of his white dress shirt catching on his chin. 'What's this about, Sergeant?'

Casey handed the second ID to Pete B and turned back to the car. 'That's a great question. In fact, it's the exact question I was going to ask you.'

'I don't think I understand.'

'You feel like taking a trip to the precinct with me to help me out with a case?'

'I'll pass.'

'Yeah, I figured you'd say that. Why were you outside Aryana Guptil's residence a couple days ago? Let's start there.'

'I don't know anyone by that name.'

'No? How about Landon Whitlock?'

He pursed his lips, staring straight ahead, eyes hooded. She waited, but he said nothing.

'How about Maddy Rushton?'

He kept looking forward, tilted his chin back and took a breath. 'How did you like my place, Detective? It's not much to look at, but it's nice to be near the water.'

Casey pulled a wide grin. 'We're a long way from Locust Point. What's your business in Rockport, sir?'

'I'm here for work.'

'And what do you do for work, Mr Stringer?'

'Corporate intelligence.'

'What does that entail?'

'What it sounds like.'

'It sounds like bullshit.'

'Most days I'd agree with you.'

That brought a thin smile from Lydia Wright in the passenger seat.

'How about we stop playing games here?' Casey said. 'I've got four people dead and you and your girl keep popping up all over my investigation. Where were you on Wednesday morning, between seven-thirty and eight-thirty?' The time she could place him across from Strongbox, taking photos twenty-four hours before the shooting.

'If you're asking me, it's because you know where I was.'

'Cute. So let me change the question: what were you doing there?'

He picked at the seam on the steering wheel with his fingernail. 'In my business, information has a price – you never give it away. Your problem is that you've got nothing to trade.'

'Trade?' Casey looked off along the street, red taillights clustering in the middle distance. 'Is that how you think this works?'

'If you had a warrant or cause, I'd be in cuffs already.'

'I just told you I've got four people dead and you didn't even blink. I don't think I'm gonna have to dig real deep.'

Wright leaned forward. 'It said on the news you'd already found the guy.' The confected innocence in her tone carried a hint of a taunt.

'The case is still open,' Casey said, distracted by the sight of Pete B returning from his cruiser in her peripheral vision. Caution told her not to take her eyes off the Lexus as he walked up.

'Everything checks out,' Pete said to Casey, handing back the cards. 'All clean.' He stepped back again, answering a call on his radio.

Stringer showed no reaction, as if there'd been no doubt that would be the case. 'Still open? Who screwed up the setup?'

Casey squinted. 'Say that again?'

'Just saying. Seemed like you lot settled on a fall guy pretty bloody quick.'

From the passenger seat, softly: 'Mike...'

Pete finished talking on his radio and called over. 'Hey, Big, there's a ten-thirty three blocks away. I need to roll.'

Casey flashed him a *two seconds* sign and came a half-step closer to the Lexus. 'If you feel like giving me a suspect, I'm all ears. Because right now, I'm looking at you.'

Stringer shook his head. 'If you *feel like* framing me next, give it your best shot. We play in the big leagues – you're amateurs.'

'Is that right? Here's what I think: I think you talk too much for someone with nothing to say, so I think you're dying to tell me something. That's why you're out here driving loops, waiting to be spotted.'

That brought a grudging smile to his lips. One that was still dancing in the creases around his eyes when he turned to her. 'Maybe I just wanted to draw you out. Save you another trip to Locust Point.'

Wright looked over at Stringer. 'Stop dicking around, Mike. Let's wrap this up.'

He hadn't taken his eyes off Casey.

'Why were you sitting outside Maddy Rushton's apartment?' Casey said. 'Give me that.'

'What do you want with her?'

'Most of all, I want to know she's safe.'

'Sure. Not because she's a witness?' He lingered on the last word in a way that made it sound like a threat.

'And what if she is?' Casey drew her sidearm and held it by her thigh, the pulse in her arm pounding. 'You lay a finger on her and I swear you'll regret it. Don't doubt it.'

For the first time, he looked thrown. 'I'm not a threat to her.'

'No? Then tell me why you were watching her.'

The muscles in his jaw tightened and his nostrils flared. Then he set his eyes on a point in the distance again.

Casey switched tack. 'How did you know what was going to go down outside Strongbox on Thursday morning?'

'Can we go?'

One last roll of the dice: 'Why were you following Landon Whitlock?'

He opened his hands on the wheel, flexing his fingers, then looked as if he gave himself a silent reprimand. 'You almost had me there for a second.'

'What?'

He shook his head, disappointed in himself. 'That's what this all boils down to, isn't it? Protecting your own.'

'*Your own*? Whitlock's a murder victim. He's nothing to do with me.'

'Is that a fact?' Stringer gripped the wheel again, arrogant son of a bitch setting himself to go. But then he turned his head to look up at her. 'Then why were you calling him on the day he was killed?'

CHAPTER THIRTY-ONE

Casey sat in the car with her phone gripped in front of her, white noise in her head. She'd sent Stringer and Wright on their way, Pete B already back in his cruiser by that time, calling out to her through the window to ask if she was okay but already edging his car in the direction of the robbery-in-progress he'd been called to. She'd raised an arm in silent salute to wave him off, all she could manage through her daze.

Now she raced through her call log, scrolling back to the day of the shootings.

It was a lie. A lie that'd worked because he'd rocked her and he knew it.

It had to be a lie.

She'd never spoken to Landon Whitlock in her life. She'd checked her phone before for his number, checked her emails, and found no trace of him.

She reached the day of the shootings and stopped scrolling. Two outgoing calls to—

Holy shit...

An unknown number. The stranger trying to arrange the meet. She scrolled through the call log a little further, to the day before. An incoming call from the same number.

The conversation played out in her mind in perfect clarity: 'It concerns Ray Carletti. And some other acquaintances we share.'

The stranger wanting to meet with her at the east gate of Coleman Carrington Park at ten am the next day. A rendezvous point less than a dozen blocks from where Whitlock was murdered: 'I have information you might find interesting and, well, to be honest, I want to put it to work.'

She scrolled back to the outgoings – two rushed calls she'd made on the day of the shootings, when she'd been trying to say she wouldn't be able to make the meet. The first one unanswered. Couldn't be answered, because Whitlock was dead.

But then the second one. Someone picked up, saying nothing. And someone on that number had called her again that night, right after McTeague had left her place, but said nothing when she answered. She opened up the follow-up text that'd arrived in its wake: *It's late to be outside all alone. Take care.*

Odds on: someone else had Whitlock's phone. Someone named Michael Stringer?

Holy fucking shit...

She'd checked all of Landon Whitlock's known numbers on the day Darcy Whitlock fronted her with the business card and found no trace of them on her own cell or computer, so this had to have been a burner phone. And within twenty-four hours of contacting her on it, he'd been gunned down in broad daylight.

Coincidence was for suckers; there was no way...

Rawlins, Goff, Ryker. Making them look the other way.

But then why was Stringer outside Aryana Guptil's? She couldn't make it add up.

She sat in the car with the rain swirling around her, so light it barely spritzed the windshield. It made some sense of Landon Whitlock having her phone number amongst his possessions, but the *why* was still missing. One question answered, a thousand more running through her head. What the fuck did he know? And why did it get him killed?

Information about Carletti was worthless now. Enough dirt

had come out on him to fill his grave ten times over. No one was killing – or dying – to protect Ray Carletti.

'And some other acquaintances we share'. That part haunted her. Whitlock was plugged in at the highest levels. What did he have and who did he have it on? Enough to make him dangerous to someone?

Enough for Michael Stringer to kill him?

Another name came into her head unbidden. Robbie McTeague. Hanrahan's right-hand man. He'd sworn blind to her, from day one, that he'd been oblivious to Chief Hanrahan's crimes, and she'd believed him. But she went back to how he'd described his work when he was pitching her a job: 'Most everything I do is corporate work – intel, security, risk analysis.' That sounded a lot like Stringer's 'corporate intelligence' – and Lydia Wright had been right there in the bar at the Abbeymore the night she'd met McTeague.

Coincidence was for suckers.

She held her face in her hands, rubbing her eyes, realising she was convicting him on the flimsiest circumstantial evidence. Sitting by the kerb on a nothing street, seeing monsters in every shadow.

She knew, now, why Whitlock had been in the area that morning – he'd been readying to meet her. It also went some way to explaining why he'd lied to his wife and secretary about where he was going – no informant wants to make a lot of noise about meeting with the cops, no matter how trusted the audience.

But that still left her with a headful of questions. And as she tried to bring any kind of order to her thoughts, a new one arrived and tipped the bucket right over again: was Landon Whitlock bringing a thousand dollars in cash to the meet with Casey? And if so, what was he expecting to get for it?

As Casey burst through the stairwell doors, Dunmore looked up from her screen, her face drawn and eyes dark, and for a moment it was a standoff – Casey crossing the floor cautiously, expecting to be summoned, Dunmore looking out but not speaking.

Then she got up slowly and came to stand in her office doorway, holding her phone in one hand, a sheaf of papers in the other. 'Cell records came through. Adam Ryker was messaging friends and work colleagues throughout Thursday morning, all of it workaday stuff – one of the threads was him trying to arrange drinks for the following night. Muneera Kouri's phone was bouncing off the tower nearest his house until after ten am. And Tech came back on the photos – they're genuine.' It looked like it'd broken her to have to say it.

'You already knew that,' Casey said.

'It doesn't suit you to gloat.'

'I'm not gloating. I'm saying *you* already knew. I could tell, after you talked to her.'

She looked to the side, her nose wrinkling once, as if the truth was uncomfortable to hear. 'Where are you at with Maddy Rushton?'

'No further. But I just tracked down Michael Stringer and I think he's looking for her too.'

'What?'

Casey talked her through the car stop and what she'd got from Stringer, but took a risk with it: no mention of the calls from Whitlock's burner phone, afraid Dunmore would turn them against her. She finished on the way mention of Maddy Rushton's name had seemed to tweak the Brit.

'I'm starting to like this guy for our shooter,' Dunmore said.

Casey tilted her head, thinking. 'Yeah. But he wanted us to find him tonight. He was out there driving loops.'

'He wouldn't be the first perp who wanted to rub our faces in it.'

'I know. But something about it is off. Why not split town? Why was he outside Aryana Guptil's residence?'

'It's a start,' Dunmore said. 'Can we connect him to Sheena Rawlins or Lauren Goff in any way?'

'Not so far, but that's something we should dive into. I can contact the families and ask—'

'We'll handle it. You stick to Maddy, that was our deal.'

'But I think he's trying to find her. It's all connected.'

'Because he knows she can ID him?'

'Maybe,' Casey said, nodding, a possibility she'd considered herself. 'But then there's this: we can place him at her apartment in the weeks before the shootings – so it'd take a hell of a coincidence to have her show up right as he was shooting two other people dead.'

'Maybe she was supposed to be the third,' Dunmore said, then blew out a breath through her nose, the same frustration Casey felt.

'Does Keirn know the photos are genuine?' Casey said.

Dunmore nodded, closing her eyes. 'I think he always knew.'

'So what happens now?'

'He hasn't said yet.'

Casey circled around Dana's desk and rested one hand on the back of Jill's seat. 'Why was he so keen to shut this down with Ryker?'

'He can't afford to look incompetent.'

'Is that all it is?' Casey felt a nervous tingle in her fingertips as she said it. How long had Keirn served under Hanrahan?

'What do you mean?'

Casey weighed it up. She wasn't blind to the irony of her predicament: Dunmore the outsider, maybe the one person she could trust in the department. And, at the same time, the person who wanted her gone the most. She should tell her about the call from Landon Whitlock, and after, but she couldn't prove what had been said between them; would Dunmore ever believe it was innocent – at least on Casey's part? 'Lieutenant, is there any way we could start over, you and me? I feel like you came here with some ideas about who I am, but maybe if you just give me some time, you'll see what I'm really about.'

Dunmore put her cell phone in her pocket and dug her thumb and forefinger into her eyes, rubbing them with a weariness that told the story of a long day and longer ones to come, the job already taking its toll. 'That's not going to work.'

'Why can't it?'

She came a step closer, stacking her hair on top of her head as she pushed it to one side. 'I was on track to go the distance at NYPD. I put in the hours, I put myself forward for every extra duty going, worked with the Feds, all of it. I did that because I had ambition, and I believed I could get to the top if I worked hard and I worked smart. You asked me why I took this job? I never wanted to leave, but I got screwed over. I put my trust in the wrong person, and somehow, as far as the bosses were concerned, their failings became mine, and that was all it took. All the years, all the effort, all the sacrifices...' She clicked her fingers, her ambitions disappearing in a puff of smoke. 'So now I'm starting over, and there's no way I'll take that risk again. I can forgive a lot of sins, but I won't work with someone I don't trust. Period.'

'So now you're passing it on. Someone else's failings become mine.'

'They're your failings, Wray. Maybe if you owned them, you'd find a way to move forward.'

'I never knew about Ray.' She tipped her head back, eyes to the ceiling in frustration. 'What was I supposed to do when I never knew?'

Dunmore pointed at her. 'Even if that's true, how could you work shoulder to shoulder with them and not recognise what was happening? The biggest scandal in the history of the department, and you missed it. That's the failing.'

Casey threw her hands out in protest, reaching for a comeback that wouldn't form.

Dunmore didn't give her the chance. 'Save it. Look, the truth of it is it's in Keirn's hands now anyway. There's nothing more needs to be said.'

'This is my life,' Casey said, pressing her fingers into her chest. 'Everything you just described goes for me too, except I did it because I loved it, not for—' She cut herself off just in time.

'Not for what?' Dunmore said.

Casey told herself not to finish the thought, but before she knew what she was doing, it'd already left her lips. 'Not for a promotion.'

Dunmore stared at her, the tip of her tongue just poking out between her teeth, as if Casey's words had struck a nerve. Then she shook her head, a bitter smile turning the corners of her mouth down. 'That doesn't make you better than me, Wray. It just makes you naïve.'

CHAPTER THIRTY-TWO

She found McTeague's office next to a twenty-four-hour pharmacy, at the end of a short commercial strip located three blocks from the Abbeymore. The lights were on, the glow just catching the outline of the solitary Impala parked out front.

Casey went through the door and saw McTeague at a desk near the back of the room, studying something on his computer screen, a set of headphones over his ears. He looked up as she came in, slipping his headphones down so they hung around his neck. 'Wray?'

'Sorry to barge in. I figured you'd be working late.' Casey could see his screen by now, crystal-clear surveillance footage of a man getting into a black SUV.

He glanced at his watch. 'I didn't start until noon, so this isn't late.'

'There's me thinking you just didn't have anything better to do.'

He shrugged, getting out of his seat. 'Two things can be true at the same time.' He opened his hands as if showcasing the small office – a second desk a few feet away facing his own, bare except for a few scattered pens and a loose cable, a water cooler situated next to it, two filing cabinets, hard-wearing grey carpet tiles – a glimpse into what her future could look like. 'You want the grand tour?'

Casey faked a smile. 'Came to pick your brains and ask for a favour.'

'So that's two favours then.'

'You should've been an accountant, you know that?'

'I should've been a lot of things.'

Casey brought her hands together in front of her, nervous. 'You ever hear the names Michael Stringer and Lydia Wright?'

He looked at the wall off to the side as she said it, taking in a breath. Her stomach dropped. He was working up to a lie. But then he looked right at her again and said, 'Yeah, some kind of shakedown crew is what I heard. New on the scene, so not a lot more I can tell you. Why?'

She searched his face, trying to discern if he was holding back, but it was like trying to get a read from a boulder. 'You ever work with them?'

'You didn't hear what I just said? They're a shakedown crew, the hell would I be doing working with them?' The old gruffness back, the denial ringing true.

'The other night, in the Abbeymore lobby bar – Lydia Wright was sat right across from us.'

He tilted his head. 'How come?'

'Beats me. That's why I thought I should ask.'

'I don't get it.' He shook his head, eyes wide, looking at her for a clue – but then the penny dropped. 'Wait, you thought it was something to do with me?'

'No ... no, not really. I'm just trying to figure out who these guys are. Why'd you look so goosed when I said their names?'

'Because you're the third person to ask me about them in a month.'

Casey felt the skin on her forearms prickle. 'Who else is asking about them?'

He stared her down, disapproving, as if she should know better.

'What?' Casey said. 'It's important or I wouldn't be asking.'

McTeague took the headphones from around his neck and

tossed them on the desk. 'One was a PI over in Harrison, guy I know from way back. Another was a client of mine. That's the only reason I ever heard of them. I asked around and that's all I got back. Now you give.'

She picked at the skin around her thumbnail. 'They keep cropping up in relation to the shootings I'm working.'

'I thought you closed the case? I saw Kleenex Steve on the TV.'

'There might be more to it.'

He looked at her as if he knew she was selling a line of bullshit, but decided to let it go. 'So where do these guys fit in? As suspects?'

'Starting to look that way. Possibly.'

'Did you check they're not staying at the Abbeymore?'

'C'mon, of course I did. No one registered under those names, no one that fits their descriptions according to the staff, and no one's seen the car parked there.'

'So they're tracking the investigation by tracking you?'

'What do you mean?'

'In the bar at the Abbeymore. What else are they doing there?'

'Huh.' Casey set her jaw, an angle she hadn't considered. It even explained the white Tesla following her home that night. 'Maybe.'

McTeague crossed to the water cooler. 'What, you still think I put her there? Seriously?' He took a paper cup from the tube and filled it, passing it to her, then filled one for himself.

She took a long drink from the cup, a way to hide the embarrassment spreading across her face. 'Sorry.'

He went back to his desk and sat down. 'What's the other favour you wanted to ask?' He was slumped in the chair with his head tilted back as if affronted by the accusation, but she recognised the olive branch for what it was.

'I got a missing mom and daughter, possible witness to the shootings. The kid's not even a year old, the mom's early twenties. Neither of them seen since right after it happened.'

'Maddy something? I saw the appeals.'

Casey nodded. 'I've tried all the usual avenues and I'm nowhere. Cell phone hasn't pinged for days.'

'Not good.'

'Yeah. You think you could put some feelers out for me?'

'After you hurt my feelings that way?'

She clapped him on the shoulder. 'You're an entrepreneur, you can take it.'

He snorted. 'You're a piece of work, you know that?'

She clasped her hands together and mouthed *thank you*. 'So is that everything you heard on Stringer and Wright?'

He scratched his cheek, stubble crackling. 'Shakedowns, yeah. Executive stuff, big-ticket guys. Not a lot of intel out there on them. That's what my sources are telling me, I mean. I don't know anything about them first hand.'

'Who was the client asking about them?'

He titled his head and looked at her, a schoolteacher impression. 'There's limits, Wray. C'mon.'

'Darcy Whitlock?'

'Landon's widow?' He screwed his face up. 'Mrs Whitlock is not currently a client of the firm. But now you've got my interest.'

'Just a hunch.'

'Uh-huh. And I'm an entrepreneur.'

Casey smiled and held a hand up as she turned to go. 'You'll let me know if you find anything on Maddy?'

'I'll put the word out. But I wouldn't get your hopes up too high.'

Casey stopped by the door. 'Hope? What the hell is that?'

CHAPTER THIRTY-THREE

Pushing ten pm, but no desire to go home. Casey swung by Maple Ridge Apartments and Casita, on the slim chance that Maddy Rushton had made contact, but there'd been no sign of her at either. She hit downtown, the bus station on Second, and showed her headshot to the Hampstead County Transport guys on the concourse and a couple drivers waiting to set out, but got head shakes all round.

From there, she drove to the tent city underneath the north-south expressway, another circuit with Rushton's photo. Moving from pitch to pitch, the cross-section of people who called the place home was staggering. One man was dressed in little more than rags, his busted shoes wrapped in plastic grocery bags to keep them from falling apart. His hut was a cardboard lean-to, held up with duct tape. He told her he was a veteran of the first Iraq War who'd lost his family when he couldn't adjust back to civilian life and been on the street pretty much ever since. Casey had slipped him a twenty and thanked him for his service before she moved on. But the man in the next-door tent must've overheard, because the first thing he told her when she walked up was that his neighbour was an addict who couldn't tell the truth from reality.

Just as shocking were the young people, and even couples,

living in purpose-bought tents. iPhones, neat haircuts, clean clothes – half of them looked like they'd never spent a night outdoors in their lives, and more than one made a point of telling Casey they had paying jobs, but just couldn't afford to keep a solid roof over their heads. It made her think, again, how easy it was for people like Maddy Rushton to slip through the cracks.

No one Casey spoke to recognised her.

She stopped to pick up a burrito – only remembering after she'd started eating it that it was her second of the day – and made the short drive across The Slice to the encampment beneath the east-west expressway. Smaller and somehow darker than the first, she made the same dash from tent to tent, but got nothing close to a hit. After showing Maddy's photograph to twenty or so of the poor bastards living there, the despair got too hard to take.

Almost midnight. Her body saying *sleep* but her head running like a treadmill, no chance at rest, no point in going home. She drove to the office knowing it would be deserted. Somewhere she could think.

At her desk, she read through the latest updates on the case. A five-person surveillance detail was being drafted in from Harrison to supplement the units already deployed to tail Stringer and Wright, while headshots of the pair had already been shown to Calder and Ziegler, the off-duty uniforms caught up in the shootings on Eighth and Villanova. The report went on to say that neither recalled seeing them at the scene that morning, so the next step was to expand the pool to the civilian eyewitnesses they'd grilled, to see if any of them could step up to the plate. At the same time, dashcam, cell-phone and surveillance footage was to be reanalysed, looking for a sighting of the suspects or the black Lexus on the morning in question, while a request had been lodged with the Feds for any pertinent information they might hold on the pair. Taken together, it all added up to one thing: Dunmore was shifting the emphasis firmly onto the shakedown crew.

Casey took a blank piece of paper and sketched a rough timeline: three weeks before the shootings, the superintendent at Maddy Rushton's apartment complex spots them watching the place from the street; two weeks before, Landon Whitlock complains to Brianna Monk that 'The Photographer' is following him again; twenty-four hours prior, Frederick Colossimo spots the pair right across from Strongbox; twenty-four hours after, Casey sees them outside Aryana Guptil's – and twelve hours after that, Lydia Wright is in the bar of the Abbeymore as Casey is talking to McTeague.

She drew a line, separating the sightings before and after the shootings, McTeague's words ringing in her ears now: 'Tracking the investigation by tracking you.' Prior to the shootings, they were on Whitlock and Maddy Rushton; after, the common thread was … Casey herself.

Meaning what?

Take it back a step. Why were they tracking Whitlock and Rushton? That earlier hunch kicked in again – that despite her denials, Darcy Whitlock knew Landon was complaining of being followed, maybe even was having him followed. Tweak that, in light of what she knew now about Stringer and Wright being shakedown artists: was Darcy, or some other party, paying to set him up? Maybe using Rushton as bait?

Call the first two a strong maybe, Casey again remembering Darcy's hinky reaction when she'd asked her if Landon had talked about being trailed. Maddy Rushton's involvement felt less solid. But then what happened on the street that morning? Some kind of setup, a shakedown that went wrong? And both Landon and Sheena Rawlins wound up dead? There was no physical resemblance between her and Rushton, pretty much ruling out a case of mistaken identity – especially if Stringer or Wright were the shooters, and had to have known what Maddy looked like.

Then there was the gaping flaw in that theory: why would they kill Whitlock? His value to them was as a live target – they couldn't blackmail a dead man.

She sat back in her seat and pushed her hand through her hair, holding her head as if it might topple from her shoulders, the weight of all the unknowns building.

Her thoughts came back to Landon Whitlock. From the start, their focus had never really been on him, someone going to great lengths to push them towards Adam Ryker as their perp: the murder weapon being found at his house, the lone ping from his cell phone next to Lauren Goff's property the night she was murdered. It was all so ruthless.

Casey's fingers tightened, hovering above the keyboard. Something about that thought made her look over, checking she really was alone in the empty office. The quiet hum of the building struck a more sinister note all of a sudden, the sense that they'd been looking the wrong way the whole time as the darkness crept up on them.

She typed Landon Whitlock's name into Google, got the same threadbare results they'd turned up at the start of the case. An out-of-date LinkedIn profile, a link to an old corporate profile from when he'd worked for Ernst & Young, pre-2006, and a handful of links to newspaper articles where his name had been mentioned – charity donations, political fundraisers, society events. She clicked on the first few, and all of them turned out to relate to picture captions, Whitlock amongst the people shown in the various images. There was Whitlock in the background behind Franklin Gates at the opening ceremony for St Mark's; Landon in black tie, arm in arm with Darcy, on the steps of the old city hall for the Hampstead County gala dinner; Landon gladhanding a state senate candidate in 2014.

She scrolled on, more of the same, the words blurring into a soup. No mention of his firm, no mention of his work, no PR profiles, no personal information. A prominent Hampstead County businessman, connected at the highest levels, who'd stayed under the radar for almost two decades.

She clicked through two more pages of results, skimming them but not really reading them, before the relevant hits started to peter out. She rubbed her eyes and stretched to work the knots out of her back – but then the link at the bottom of the screen made her stop dead.

Casey clicked on it to open the page, reading the text twice to make sure she wasn't seeing it wrong. An announcement in the *Courier*'s society page, dated 2010. Proud grandparents congratulating their son and daughter-in-law, Landon and Darcy Whitlock, on the birth of their first child. A simple two-line message, celebrating a family milestone:

The birth of Lana Harper Whitlock.

Casey sat perfectly still, staring at the screen. The same forename as Maddy Rushton's daughter.

It felt as if the darkness was alive around her.

What was the significance? She jumped to her feet and

walked across the office, heading nowhere, lost in the thoughts crashing around her brain. It could mean nothing. But with Stringer and Wright's involvement, it felt like something. The two people they were watching before the shootings. She went back to her desk and grabbed the phone.

It rang as she held it to her ear, Casey eyeing the time on her computer clock and thinking it might be too late to reach—

'Yes?' That accent again, knowing and assured.

'This is Detective Sergeant Wray, Mr Stringer.'

'I know.'

'Uh-huh, and I bet you know why I'm calling too.'

'I know you're barking up the wrong tree. Your surveillance bods need better training. Tell them they might as well be wearing high-vis jackets.'

'We don't tend to take that much trouble over a couple shakedown artists.'

'Shakedown? Now I really am offended.'

'You'll get over it. The real question is whether you're good for murder.'

'Here we go. I told you, if you want to try and frame me next, it won't work.'

'What I know is that you're in the crosshairs right now. My guess is pretty soon you'll start to panic, and that's when it always unravels.'

He laboured over a breath, as if sitting up or getting out of a chair as he took it. 'Shakedown is an ugly word, but it's not entirely inaccurate. So if you know that much, tell me what my motive is for killing anyone?'

'I can think of a dozen.'

'Then I'm telling you you're wrong. Your shooter's out there right now, walking around laughing at you.'

'Then come down to the precinct and make a full statement.'

'I can't do that.'

She tossed up a kite to see if it would fly. 'Who hired you to blackmail Landon Whitlock?'

Near silence on the line, the faintest background sounds.

'Landon Whitlock and Maddy Rushton,' Casey said. 'What's the connection?'

He coughed, clearing his throat. 'Where is she?'

'Not a chance in hell.'

'So you don't know.'

'What would you do if I told you?'

'Nothing. So long as I know she's safe.'

'From you? Or did you use her and put her in danger?'

He hesitated, the sound of him forcing out an exhale. 'Not intentionally.'

'The hell does that mean? What's the connection, put it together for me.'

'Rich older bloke and a beautiful younger woman?' He scoffed. 'You really need me to tell you?'

'Landon was having an affair with her.'

He didn't answer.

'And did you tell Darcy Whitlock about it?'

Absolute silence now. A silence loud enough to drown out a thousand screams. And Darcy Whitlock with a red-hot motive.

Casey jumped to her feet and grabbed her notebook, already scanning for Laura Knox's number, the friend of Maddy Rushton who'd first provided an identification for their missing witness. 'That's all I needed to know.'

'Wait, listen—'

Casey cut the call and redialled, checking her watch and

praying she'd get an answer and not have to wait till morning. Stringer telling Darcy Whitlock her husband had been cheating on her put a whole new light on who else might've been searching for Maddy – and on a lead Casey had missed.

'Hello?'

'Miss Knox, this is Casey Wray with HCPD, we spoke before about Maddy Rushton?'

'Oh, yeah, hey. It's kinda late. Did you find her?'

'No, sorry, I wish I had better news, but I have to ask you something that relates to her disappearance. This is going to sound strange, but what colour is your hair, ma'am?'

'My hair?'

'Yeah, I know it's a weird question, but I just needed to check.'

'Brunette, why?'

'Have you changed it at all recently, like in the last few days?'

'Um ... no. Why?'

Casey tilted her head to the ceiling, a hunch confirmed. 'That's all I needed, sorry to disturb you, ma'am.'

The chef-owner at Casita had described a blonde-haired friend asking after Maddy. Casey hung up and grabbed her cell phone, searching up a picture of Darcy Whitlock, then ran to her car and drove to the restaurant. It was closed when she got there, but the lights were still on, the staff setting up for the next day's service. The same man she'd spoken to before came to the door when Casey knocked, looking surprised to see her show up for a second time that night.

'Sir, I'm sorry to bother you again, I just need thirty seconds of your time.' She raised her phone to show the picture of Darcy Whitlock she had on the screen. 'You mentioned Maddy Rushton's "blonde-haired" friend came by asking after her. Was it this woman?'

He peered at the screen, came closer, then nodded. 'Yeah, that's her. What about it?'

Casey stepped back, an involuntary movement, the implications pounding her like hailstones.

'You okay, Detective?'

Casey closed her eyes and stretched her neck, then nodded. 'Can you tell me exactly when this woman came by?'

His face creased, thinking about it. 'Uh ... this would be Thursday night. Sometime between eight and ten – couldn't tell you exactly.' The same day as the shootings.

'And can you tell me what she said? As accurately as you can?'

He brought one hand up to pull at his ear. 'It was in the middle of a service, so I don't ... I mean I was in a rush. But I guess she just asked if Maddy was here, and when I said no, she was asking if she'd been by that night, if I knew where to find her, that kind of thing. I told her everything I knew, which was nothing, and she left. Another girl came by the next day, another friend of Maddy's. I didn't speak to her but Larissa did.' He hooked his thumb in the direction of a woman placing glasses on a shelf behind the counter, who looked over at hearing her name. 'Did I tell you about that? I didn't hear about it till later. Maybe I didn't.'

That had to be the visit by Laura Knox, Casey wrongly assuming her to be the blonde-haired friend. 'Not at first, but that's fine, sir, thank you.'

The man looked baffled. 'Sure, no problem.'

Casey drifted across the sidewalk to the car. She hesitated with her hand on the doorhandle as she tried to get it all straight in her head. Hours after she'd identified her own husband's body, Darcy Whitlock was at Casita trying to track down Maddy Rushton, a key witness in her husband's murder – and seemingly his mistress. Explanations ran through her head, pummelling, overwhelming, none of them good.

And only one way to get to the truth.

CHAPTER THIRTY-FOUR

A clear night sky that showcased a carpet of stars. Shatter Creek caught the moonlight, a haunting white glow stitched through the black landscape, the saltmarsh beyond it as dark and empty as a dead woman's eyes.

Casey pushed the car up the long driveway, the sugar maples blotting out the starlight as she passed through. On clearing the trees, a single window on the second floor of the main house was illuminated, a dull glow concealed behind a curtain or blind.

Casey tried to focus on her breathing, slow the pulsing she felt in her chest, in her arms, the feeling that she was on a precipice and could end up throwing herself off it. The carrot dangled by Rita Zangetty the last time they'd spoken, about steering Keirn away from 'rash decisions', had lingered in the back of her mind all evening, ever since Dunmore made it clear the acting chief was about to make Casey his scapegoat – with her wholehearted encouragement. Bracing Darcy Whitlock now without speaking to Zangetty first – without any warning at all – was to sever that final lifeline. But what choice did she have? Anything else was a betrayal of the most basic tenets she'd sworn to uphold. Giving Darcy the chance to lawyer up would be to ensure the truth would disappear behind a wall of grey suits and dollar signs. The victims deserved better. More than that; if Maddy Rushton and her daughter were still alive, there was still a chance it wasn't too late to keep them that way.

Casey parked in front of the garage block. She called Darcy's cell phone and waited, her own phone pressed tight to her ear.

Just as Casey was about to try again, she answered.

'Who is this?'

'Mrs Whitlock, this is Casey Wray from HCPD. I need to talk to you urgently, ma'am; I'm parked outside your house and I'd appreciate it if you'd come to the door. I'm mindful of not causing your daughter distress, which is why I didn't want to ring your doorbell at this hour, but it really is important.'

'Have you lost your mind?'

'No, ma'am. I really would appreciate a few minutes of your time.'

'You have thirty seconds to get off my property, or I'm calling your bosses.'

'Mrs Whitlock, why were you searching for Madeline Rushton?'

The line went quiet, the breeze coming off of Black Reed Bay gently sweeping over the car.

'Ma'am?'

Irritated now. 'She was a witness to my husband's murder. Why wouldn't I be looking for her? If I left it to you and your colleagues, she'd never be found.'

'We hadn't identified her at the time you went to her place of work.'

The line fell silent again, and Casey felt as if she was teetering, the sense anything could happen next.

Finally, Darcy said, 'I'll open the door.'

Casey stepped out of the car and clipped her holster on, its bulk against her hip both reassuring and ominous. She stood a few paces from the front door and off to the side, ready to draw if Darcy appeared with a weapon. Her instincts told her Whitlock was more calculating than that, but she'd been wrong before.

But when the door opened, Darcy stood empty-handed and pale, still zipping an oversized hoodie over her pjs. 'Come inside.'

She led Casey through the dark hallway and into the kitchen, then shut the door behind them, sealing them in together. Casey scoped out the room, bigger than the whole footprint of her bungalow. The island at its centre drew her eye first, a knife block at one end displaying a menacing array of steel handles. On the far side from where she stood was another doorway, closed, where it led to unknown. Casey chalked up another mistaken assumption – that the two of them were alone in the kitchen. To her left was a farmhouse-style wooden table, and she took up a spot on its far side, putting an obstacle between her and Whitlock and keeping both doorways in her eyeline.

'What is it you want, exactly, Detective?' Whitlock said, stationing herself behind the island unit. Casey watched her hands in case they dipped out of sight, but Whitlock stood at the opposite end from the knife block and leaned over to rest her elbows on the marble, linking her fingers together in front of her.

'I want to find Maddy Rushton and I want to know who killed your husband and the others.'

'You people told me my husband's murder was solved.'

'It may not be as straightforward as it looked. How about

you tell me how you learned of Maddy Rushton's identity before HCPD did?'

Whitlock stared her down, something ticking behind her eyes – but then she shook her head.

'Then let's try this: what was the relationship between your husband and Miss Rushton?'

She still had her eyes locked on Casey's, but after a second or two they slipped out of focus, and her jaw went rigid. 'Landon was a weak man. The worst kind.'

Casey set her fingers lightly on the back of the dining chair in front of her, feeling them tingle. 'He was having an affair with her.'

'That's too expansive a word for it. Lanny used people, that's all.'

'In what way?'

Darcy shifted her gaze slightly, finding an indistinct point on the floor between them. 'It doesn't matter now.'

'I think it does.'

She shook her head, deep regret drilled into her expression. 'Even now he's gone, his shit just keeps pouring down.'

'Did you hire Michael Stringer and Lydia Wright, Mrs Whitlock?'

She nodded, or seemed to at least, the movement almost imperceptible.

'Were they responsible for Landon's murder?' Casey said.

'You have no understanding of this situation.'

'Because you haven't been straight with me.'

'I did what I thought was right.'

'Come to the precinct with me, then. Tell me the whole story.'

She brought her thumb to her mouth, pressing it against teeth. Finally, she said, 'No. It's better this way.'

'Did you find Maddy Rushton, Mrs Whitlock?'

'I won't answer that.'

Casey could taste her own saliva, hot and slick as it pooled in her mouth. 'Did you find her?'

Whitlock rose up slowly to her full height, meeting Casey's eyes again. 'I won't answer.'

'If she's alive, it's not too late.'

'Alive?'

'If no harm has come to her or her child, there's a chance the situation could still be salvaged, but you have to tell me what you know.'

'You don't have the first clue.'

Casey stabbed the table. 'Then explain it to me.'

'Or what?'

'Or I come back here with a warrant, take you away in cuffs in front of your daughter and have a search team tear your house apart.'

'We both know I'll never allow that to happen.'

'Try me.'

Whitlock bowed her head and spread her arms on the marble surface. The knife block was still out of reach, but her left hand rested closer to it now. 'I despise what my husband turned me into. This, this ... entire fucking situation. He was a scared and selfish man who never cared how his actions hurt the people around him. And even now he's dead, I have to stand here in my own house, in the middle of the night, listening to you demand answers to questions you don't understand.'

It felt for all the world like a justification. 'Are you saying he deserved what happened to him, ma'am?'

'No. But I'm not sorry either. I'm only sorry it's me that's left to pick up the pieces. Like always.'

As she said it, a noise from outside made Casey look around sharply. Faint, like a scuffed footfall. 'What was that?'

Whitlock had looked to the door leading from the hallway at the same time, and now she glanced at Casey, her face white. 'Go home, Detective.'

'Who's out there?' A swallow to tamp down the tremor in her voice.

Before she could answer, there was another sound – the front door opening, then quietly closing again a second later.

Casey stole a glance around her, looking for somewhere to take cover, but there was nothing. Whitlock was between her and the other doorway, but it could lead to a pantry or washroom for all she knew, no guarantee of escape. Casey stepped back from the table, reaching for her sidearm.

'No, wait—' Whitlock threw her hand out, fingers splayed. 'Put it away.' She ran over to block the hallway door they'd entered through.

Casey drew her weapon and called out to whoever was on the other side. 'This is HCPD. I am armed, and have a weapon trained on the doorway.'

Whitlock spread herself in front of the door just as it cracked open, calling out over her shoulder, 'STOP.'

Casey took a step back, pressing her back against the wall. 'Enter slowly, showing your hands, or I will open fire.'

Whitlock: 'No, no, no—'

Then a sound that cut the night: a child crying.

Whitlock stared at Casey in horror, as still as an image in a photograph.

A voice came from behind the door, straining to whisper and still be heard over the baby's cries. 'Darcy, please...'

Casey started to move towards the sound of tears. 'Step away from the door, Mrs Whitlock.'

Whitlock closed her eyes and seemed to fold in on herself, wrapping her arms across her stomach, and the door slowly opened behind her, inching her aside. Then Maddy Rushton stepped into the room, cradling a child to her chest.

CHAPTER THIRTY-FIVE

Rushton paced up and down parallel to the dining table, gently rocking the child, trying to soothe her back to sleep. At the other end of the kitchen, Darcy Whitlock poured herself a small measure of clear liquor from a bottle stashed in a low cupboard next to the stove. She brought it over to the table and took a seat across from Casey, setting the drink down. Then she reached into the pocket of her hoodie and produced a small baby monitor. She looked at Casey, then at Rushton, as she placed it in front of her. 'I only told you to listen.'

'That's what I was doing,' Rushton said, looking over at her with watery eyes, a weariness about her that reminded Casey of on-the-run fugitives who'd do something to get themselves caught on purpose, just to be free of the stress. 'You've done enough.'

Casey was standing over the table, gripping the back of one of the chairs, her eyes darting from one woman to the other. 'I think I need to understand what's going on here.'

The child's cries grew in intensity and Rushton started

swaying as she paced, fussing with the blanket the kid was wrapped in.

'Is she hungry?' Darcy said.

Rushton shook her head. 'I was feeding her while you were talking. She's just out of sorts, she needs to sleep.'

'Take her back to the guesthouse, you don't need to be here.'

'We can't go on this way,' Rushton said. 'I was listening. It's not fair on you.'

'That's not your decision to make.'

Rushton looked away, scolded. Whitlock raised the tumbler to her lips and took a sip, then cupped it with both hands.

'We've been looking for you, Miss Rushton. Were you aware of that?' Casey said.

She nodded, glancing at Casey over the child's head, pressed tight to her cheek.

'Why didn't you come speak to us?'

She looked to Whitlock, eyes wide, but Darcy said nothing, instead dipping her forehead and bringing it to rest in the palm of her hand.

Casey turned to Rushton again. The child had stopped crying now and she decided to force the matter by going right to its heart. 'Ma'am, did you see the shooter outside Strongbox on Thursday morning?'

Rushton was still looking to Whitlock, her lips ajar, uncertain what to say, but Casey couldn't tell if she was looking for permission or for help.

Whitlock waved them both away without looking up. 'She can't tell you anything.'

Casey kept her gaze on the younger woman.

'I saw...' Rushton turned away from both of them, kissing

the child on the head. 'I don't know what I saw. It was so fast. I was looking at Landon.'

Whitlock murmured something at hearing her husband's name – or maybe at hearing it from his mistress's lips.

'But you saw who fired the shots?' Casey said, gripping the chair tighter.

'I saw a man, but I didn't really see what he looked like. It was … half a second, the whole thing was, like, half a second, this crazy blur. He had a hood up, and he came … It was like he came out of nowhere. I was watching Landon, I was nervous, I didn't know what he was going to say to me, then … Next thing I knew he was on the ground. I didn't even know what was happening, then I realised this guy was there, between us, and then he was gone again.'

'Did you see if he was white or black or…?'

'White. He was a white guy.'

'Can you describe what he was wearing?'

Whitlock stood up, jerking her chair back. 'Are we really doing this, Detective? Right now?'

'We've lost so much time already…' Casey said.

'But she doesn't know anything. Don't you think I've asked?'

'Ma'am, with respect—'

'You're traumatising her.' Darcy stared at the glass on the table and reached for it as if she was headed for a refill, but then looked off to the side, rooted to the spot. 'Everything. This whole thing. Such a goddamn mess.'

'Look, there's going to be a whole heap of questions we're going to need to go through with you both, but for right now, all I want to know is who killed those people, so I can stop anyone else from getting hurt. Can you work with me on that?'

But as she said it, the baby began to wail again, louder this time, and Rushton started bobbing and swaying even more frantically, the veins in her neck throbbing.

Whitlock reached her hand out, batting her palm at Casey. 'No more. Let the poor girl get her child to sleep, for god's sake.' She went over to Rushton and stroked Lana's cheek gently with her finger. In a quiet voice, she said, 'Take her back to the guesthouse, get her settled.'

Rushton looked to Casey, as if throwing the casting vote to her.

Casey nodded reluctantly. 'I'd really like to speak to you as soon as possible, though, ma'am.'

Rushton nodded and slipped out through the door, and once again Casey was alone with Darcy Whitlock.

'You can stop looking at me that way. You'd have done exactly the same in my place,' she said, her back still to Casey.

'And what exactly did you do, ma'am?'

'She came to me. She begged me for help.' She turned now, faced Casey across the room. 'I owed her. What was I supposed to do?'

CHAPTER THIRTY-SIX

'Put your cell phone on the table,' Whitlock said.

'What for?'

'So I know you're not recording me.'

Casey set both her phones in front of her, side by side.

With Maddy Rushton gone, Whitlock had made hot tea for herself and even offered Casey one, before asking her to take a seat at the table again. Now, sitting across from her and eyeing the clock on the wall to her left, she seemed like a woman reduced – her skin grey, her eyes cast downward.

'Yes, she slept with Landon. Yes, the child is his. You can judge me for accepting that if you want, but it's him you should be judging.'

Casey said nothing, sensing she was working up to some kind of offloading and didn't need any further prompting.

Whitlock took a sip of her tea and started again, a faraway look in her eyes. 'I decided to divorce Landon a long time ago. I don't even know when, exactly – maybe it's been in my mind for years – but I really set on it about six months ago. Don't ask me why I held on for as long as I did. Maybe for Harper's sake.'

She shook her head, her mouth twisting as if she'd bitten a slice of lemon.

'The truth of it is I couldn't figure out how to leave him and still keep what I was owed. I told you he's always kept me at arm's length from his work, so I knew, without a shadow of a doubt, he'd fight me every inch of the way and I'd never get half of what he's really worth. And believe me, I earned it. I let him take my career from me, my confidence, raised our child alone, all of it, in exchange for a big house and a credit card. He thought of me as ungrateful – he could never understand why that wasn't enough.'

She stared at Casey then, as if trying to gauge whether there was a point of connection there, something Casey could relate to.

When Casey gave no response, not wanting to interrupt the flow, Whitlock said, 'Maybe you have better instincts than me when it comes to men. Anyway, that's when I went looking for a private detective. The man I hired came on a personal recommendation, a contact of a friend of mine, and he was very good. It took him no time at all to figure out Landon was being unfaithful, although I already knew that, but then he came and told me about Madeline and Lana. Later on I found out Landon had cut things off with her months earlier, before Lana was born, but the investigator found out about it somehow – like I said, he was thorough.

'Of course I was mad when I found out. More than mad – out of my mind, beyond furious. But it wasn't just about him being unfaithful.' She reached her hand out towards Casey, grasping the air. 'You have to understand, I'd begged Landon to have another child. For years. It was all I wanted, all Harper talked about, what I thought would complete our family – and he said no. You know what he told me? "I should've never had *one*." Can you fucking believe that? What kind of a man says that about his own daughter?' She stared at Casey, pleading eyes. 'Harper's actual first name is Lana. Landon chose it. He wanted a boy, of course, so he'd be Landon Whitlock II, but Lana was as close as he could get when she came out a girl. But she always preferred Harper, from when she was barely old enough to speak, so that's what she went by. He hated it, hated the thought he couldn't control her.' She smiled bitterly, shaking her head. 'How small of a man do you have to be to give your second child the same name as your first, just to try and make yourself feel important?'

She swept her hair over one shoulder, absently, then over the other, staring a hole in the wall. 'Anyway, over the years I proposed adopting, everything, but he wouldn't even entertain it. So eventually, I thought about trying for a baby in secret. I lied about birth control and managed to get pregnant. And when I finally worked up the courage to tell him – and I spent weeks worrying about it – the son of a bitch made me have an abortion. He made all these disgusting threats about leaving me and about taking Harper and making sure I'd never see her again if I didn't. I knew he wasn't bluffing, and with his money and his goddamn "connections"' – she made air quotes – 'I wouldn't have lasted two minutes. So, I did what I was told and learned to hate him even more than I already did. But what else could I do? What choice did I have?'

She looked off to the side, her eyes filming with tears, and Casey could tell Whitlock was taking up an old argument with herself.

'Then after all of that, all these years later, I find out he's had another child with ... with ... some girl. Practically a child herself.' She held her hands up in disbelief. 'I mean, it destroyed me. Almost literally.

'So I sat on it for a while, but I'm not the kind of person can just take things lying down. I can't do it. So I went to find her. And don't get me wrong, I went there ready to rip the little bitch's head off for sleeping with my husband. But after I got there, I realised I was wrong to be mad at her. She was living in this tiny apartment, behind on the rent, working shitty jobs – all just to look after his child. He'd washed his hands of her by then, of course, and I realised she was in pretty much the same situation to what I'd been in, but without any of the advantages I had. Honestly, it broke my heart. My rat-bastard husband upending another life – two lives – and walking away.

'So I stayed in touch. I helped her out with money a little bit – not that she ever asked, I want you to understand that – but then I got mad at myself for picking up after Landon, again. And then I realised, the best way to get back at him was to help her get what she was owed. I asked my detective to help me, but he said it wasn't the kind of work he did. In all truth, I think he was afraid to go up against Landon. But a few days later, he gave me the names of Michael Stringer and Lydia Wright.

'I don't think I understood, at first, who they were – who they really were – I thought they were just another couple of private detectives. But when we sat down together and talked through what I wanted and what they could do, that was when I understood. They said they'd done similar work over in the UK and that they were sure they could "compromise" Landon – that was their word – in a way that would get the outcomes I wanted.

'I didn't tell Madeline what I was planning at first. I thought she'd think I was crazy, and by then I'd started to see the possibility of giving Harper a fragment of the sister she'd wanted all along. A half-sister, at least. Not how I'd ever imagined it, not how I would've wanted it, but something. So I wanted to keep Madeline close, and only told her right before everything was ready to go. By then I knew she'd trust me, that I wouldn't scare her off. She was reluctant, a bit, but only because she was nervous.

'Anyway, that's why Madeline was on the street that morning – she was due to meet Landon. It took weeks, but with their help, we'd persuaded him to give her a sum of cash. I'm saying we, but I was in the background. He didn't know that I was helping orchestrate it, obviously – Michael and Lydia were the ones talking to him. They suggested to me to start small – that a thousand dollars would open the door to larger amounts down the line. The thin end of the wedge. But then ... well, you know what happened.'

'Wait, you're saying Madeline was there to collect? So who shot Landon? Michael Stringer?'

'No.' A tear spilled now, Darcy wiping it away violently with her knuckle. 'I don't know who shot him. I wanted to hurt him, but not like that. Money, that's what he cared about. I wanted to take that from him.' She shook her head, eyes closed. 'I didn't want him to die.'

Casey stared at her, evaluating. 'But were Stringer and Wright there with her?'

She shook her head again. 'They were close by, waiting to pick her up after. It was their suggestion to do it on the street, somewhere public they thought would be safer for Madeline. How's that for goddamn irony?

'When she saw Landon had been shot, Madeline panicked, same as anyone would. She ran into the gym because it was right there, but then she started panicking even more when she got the idea that him getting shot was somehow because of our plan. So she took off from the gym and ran. She told me all this later. She took a bus to the city, trying to disappear. It sounds crazy now, but she said she didn't even know what she was doing until she stepped off the damn thing, she just ran. But she had no money, no clothes for her or Lana, no family or friends there, nothing, so the next morning she decided to come here. I'd already been out searching for her by then, Michael and Lydia too, so when she turned up on my doorstep, it was ... honestly, all I felt was relief.

'She was terrified, utterly terrified. She still is. She's convinced that what we did got Landon killed somehow, even though I've sworn to her that was never part of it. But then when you announced it was that man, Ryker, who'd killed them all, it made no sense – she was sure it wasn't him she'd seen that day. I didn't see how she could be so certain when she barely got a glimpse of the guy who did it, but it was the beard that convinced her – the man she saw had no beard. So by the time Ryker turned up dead, she was absolutely sure she was going to wind up in jail, that she'd lose Lana, all the worst-case scenarios you can imagine, and at the same time, she was convinced there was a killer out there looking for her, who knows she's the best eyewitness the police have got. And I feel an incredible guilt for putting her in that position, so we've sat here for days going round in circles, trying to figure out if we're in danger and what the hell to do.'

She met Casey's eyes again, and for the first time, it felt like she was seeing the woman behind the mask. The question she most wanted to ask was lodged at the top of her throat: *What was Landon going to tell me at the meet that morning?* But the only other person who knew about the call to set it up was Michael Stringer, and if he'd revealed it to Darcy, she would've said something by now. As she hadn't, there was no point opening that can of worms if it wouldn't lead to answers.

Casey got up out of her seat and walked slowly along the edge of the room, trying to process it all. The enormity of it was shocking, but if Darcy was telling the truth that it wasn't Maddy Rushton or one of the shakedown crew that'd pulled the trigger, that still left her without a killer. 'If it wasn't Stringer or Wright who killed Landon, why didn't you tell them Maddy was safe with you? They've been looking for her too.'

'I couldn't. You have to understand, she was going out of her mind. I trust them, but the only person she trusts is me. She wants to shut the world out.'

Casey blew out a breath, a knot in her head so tangled she could barely unpick it. 'You should've been straight from the start.'

'That's an easy thing to say from where you're standing. But what happens to Harper if I do that? To Madeline and Lana?'

'I can't answer that.'

Whitlock nodded, running her finger over a small dent in the table's wooden surface. 'I'm only telling you all this for their sake. And now I want your help.'

Casey took a step back on reflex, just a few inches. 'Excuse me?'

'Help me find a way to explain all this, a way that protects them.'

Casey tipped sideways, coming to rest with her shoulder against the wall. 'I'm going to go ahead and pretend you didn't say that.' She rubbed her face, the weight of all the unknowns bearing down on her again. 'I'll be back here in the morning with officers from our Victim Services Unit. They can get Maddy and Lana the support they need. I'll do whatever I can to help them get straight, but I don't know what happens next.' She shook her head, despondent. 'I honestly don't know.'

CHAPTER THIRTY-SEVEN

Casey called Dunmore from the car, a wakeup that sent the lieutenant from groggy to wired in five seconds flat when she heard the revelations Casey had to tell her.

'You should've called me sooner,' was her signoff line, Casey tossing her cell on the passenger seat when she realised Dunmore had cut the call.

She drove straight to the precinct, working on exhausted but too keyed up to sleep. Nagging at her on the way: a grave doubt that any of the people blackmailing Landon Whitlock were his killer.

If Darcy and Maddy were telling the truth.

Back to what they knew for sure: Madeline Rushton was on the street that morning, in close proximity to Landon Whitlock when he was shot. She had a motive: revenge against the baby daddy who ditched out on them. Darcy Whitlock had just as big a grudge, had admitted she was seeking revenge on her husband – financial, so she claimed – but surveillance footage from her home security had confirmed she hadn't left the house that morning before the time of the shootings. That still left Stringer and Wright, who Darcy had admitted to hiring and confirmed were in the area at the time of Landon's death. She'd been adamant neither of them had killed him, but their movements that morning were still unclear. And it looked like Michael Stringer had taken possession of Landon Whitlock's burner phone.

As compelling as that sounded, for all four of them, it came down to money: as a lifeline, as vengeance, as a paycheck. The thousand dollars Landon had been carrying appeared to back that up – but what if they were lying and it'd been part of the setup, a pretext to get him there so they could kill him?

Casey made a right turn and cruised along the dead streets. That scenario didn't add up either. If the plan had been to kill him all along, why lure him to a suburban street in bright daylight to do it? Meeting in public like that was more consistent with a concern for Maddy Rushton's safety, just like Darcy Whitlock had said – somewhere Landon was less likely to act out. And then there was the child's presence; the surveillance footage showed Rushton in Strongbox holding

Lana right after the shots were fired – surely that had to rule her out as the killer?

Which took Casey back to the starting point, bouncing her head off a brick wall. If it wasn't one of them who'd pulled the trigger, who else knew about the meet that morning? If Landon was the target – which seemed the most likely explanation now – then anyone with knowledge of the meeting time and location was a possible suspect. So who did they tell – if anyone?

Casey's head throbbed, too many questions crashing around her brain. Through it all, thoughts of Sheena Rawlins and Lauren Goff, two senseless deaths that were looking even more so now.

She parked right by the precinct entrance and took the stairs two at a time.

☙

She spent two hours getting it all down, working right through the early hours.

She typed a full recounting of her night, starting with the breadcrumb trail that led to her discovery of the link between Landon Whitlock and Maddy Rushton, all the way up to Darcy's disclosure session. She kept a legal pad next to the keyboard, using it to scribble notes and questions as they came to her, next steps to take in the investigation.

The double doors at the far end of the office cracked open, making Casey jump. She yanked her top drawer open and laid a hand on her holster. 'Hello?'

The sky outside was still dark, occasional bursts of sheet lightning silently cracking through the black clouds.

'I didn't expect to find you here, Wray.'

Dunmore's voice, the lieutenant coming into view now.

'I wanted to get it all down while it's fresh in my head.'

She came to a stop a short way from Casey's seat. 'I've detailed a Patrol unit to keep watch at the end of the Whitlocks' driveway, make sure Maddy Rushton can't disappear again before we get a team out there to talk to her.'

'She won't run, she's got nowhere to go.'

'She can go anywhere she wants if Darcy Whitlock's paying.'

'Whitlock wants her close.' Casey tapped her screen. 'It's all in here. My report's ready for you to read.'

'Thank you, Sergeant.'

Casey stood up. 'I'll let you go through it yourself, but I think we need to focus on Landon Whitlock now. My feeling is that he was a target, not a bystander.'

'Okay.' Dunmore folded her arms. 'I'll assess investigative priorities once I've had a chance to read it. For now, I'd like you to take the rest of the day off.'

Casey tilted her head. 'Lieutenant, wait—'

'Just until you found Rushton. That was our deal.'

'Yeah, but that was before we knew about her connection to Landon. At least read the report first and then—'

'Go home, Sergeant. If I need any clarifications, I know how to reach you.'

Casey stared at her, searching for any sign of doubt she could play off – but Dunmore didn't flinch.

With no cards left to play, Casey gathered her things and made for the exit. A short walk she'd made a thousand times, this time feeling like it was the last.

CHAPTER THIRTY-EIGHT

Casey dumped her bag on the couch and went out to the backyard, carrying with her the pick-me-ups she'd stopped to buy on the way home: a dozen glazed donuts and a takeaway coffee big enough to fill a kiddie pool. She sat down on the step and placed her goodies next to her, the sugar and caffeine purchased in the depths of a *fuck it all* mood that'd seeped into her every pore, like cigarette smoke. But now even that was ebbing, the anger that gave the feeling its keen edge dulled by uncertainty and fear, her future suddenly a giant blank. She sipped her coffee and watched the azalea buds sway in the breeze, her appetite gone to nothing and the donuts untouched.

She sat that way for close to an hour, a jagged sun peeking between the trees in the distance and sparkling off the dew on the grass. She wanted to call someone; not for advice, not for a pep talk, just to unload, start trying to process it. A few years ago, she would've had her mom on the phone before she even left the precinct. Casey could hear the conversation playing out in her mind: dropping the bombshell that she'd been canned from the department, Angela Wray probably glossing over it in a rush to tell her about something the neighbour's cat had done. She smiled, despite herself, almost getting mad at her mom at the thought.

She could call Dana, but they hadn't spoken since the day before when she'd called her out for taking Billy's side over the Jill situation. So much had happened overnight, to Casey it felt like weeks ago – but Dana might still be simmering. She could call McTeague, but she wasn't ready for the inevitable hard sell he'd pitch at her. Beyond that, she was out of ideas who else to phone – a sad indictment of her life.

She stood to stretch her legs, filled with an unfamiliar loneliness. 'Alone, but not lonely.' She couldn't remember which movie the line came from, but it summed up how she'd always thought of herself. But the job had taken up so much of her; in the watery morning sunlight, she could see the hole that would be left in its wake, and its scale was terrifying.

She tried to block it out by thinking about ways to stay busy, be productive. A trip to the grocery store and the gym, catch up on laundry, watch all those Netflix shows.

Just listing out the options made her feel worse. It was years since she'd taken more than three consecutive days' vacation, free time an alien concept.

In the end she settled on running a bath, sinking down into the tub until only her head and hands were above the bubbles, enabling her to scroll absently through Facebook, her brain too scrambled to take any of it in. When it felt like she'd read the whole damn site, she switched to Instagram instead, but the fake, shallow lives on display pissed her off too much, so she brought up the *Courier* website.

The update on the shootings was buried way down on the homepage, someone in the department's comms team pulling a favour for Keirn. It quoted parts of a statement released by the acting chief, in which he admitted that Adam Ryker's culpability in relation to the three homicides was no longer certain, and that the department was actively following additional lines of investigation.

The hit piece was right in the middle of the article, a direct quote:

'"While Mr Ryker remains a person of interest at the heart of this case, his initial status as the priority suspect was determined largely by the officer in charge of the investigation at the time," Acting Chief Stephen Keirn said. "It now appears there were failings made on the part of the individual concerned, who has since been moved to other duties. Lieutenant Helen Dunmore, a decorated veteran of the NYPD who recently joined HCPD, is now personally directing our investigative efforts, and I have full confidence in her ability to secure justice for the victims in this case," Keirn continued.

Police sources, speaking on condition of anonymity, have told the *Courier* that Detective Sergeant Casey Wray, herself recently in the news for her involvement in the investigation into the high-profile disappearance of Rockport resident Tina Grace, had previously been in charge of the ongoing homicide investigation. Detective Sergeant Wray's current status was unknown at the time of going to print.'

'Police sources'. Fuck them all the way to hell and back.

She put her cell down on the edge of the bath and let herself sink under the water, holding her breath. This was what she was in mourning for? A bunch of rats in a sack, all trying to eat each other. A job that made her feel terrible even on the best days; a job that'd left her with no friends, no life, no future.

She stayed submerged until her lungs caught fire, a discomfort that felt good, like a cleansing. She saw stars burst on the back of her eyelids, felt her heart screaming for more oxygen to pump. Then came a voice inside – her own – telling her that the job wasn't the problem, it never had been. The choices you made got you here, for better or worse. Now you fucking deal with it.

She stayed under the water, determined to silence the voice, but it only grew more insistent, until it merged with the screaming pain in her lungs, and started consuming her, filling her, her whole world a darkness she couldn't shake off—

Casey burst through the water lightheaded, gasping for air.

❧

She was watching a *Simpsons* rerun when the email arrived, a stale, half-eaten donut on a plate next to her.

She'd told herself she wasn't going to check her work cell, but after turning it off that morning, she'd lasted forty minutes before switching it on again to see what she'd missed. After a second attempt that saw it powered off for less than twenty minutes, she'd given up and left it charging on the table next to her.

This time she picked up the phone as soon as the email notification sounded, resolved to the fact that breaking the habit would take longer than a day. The message was from the composite artist who'd been assigned to work with Maddy Rushton, circulating the suspect reconstruction the computer had churned out, based on Rushton's description. Casey opened the attachment and studied the image.

It showed the face of a clean-shaven man, his hair and ears covered by a hood. The eyes were deep-set and dark, face oval-shaped and taut, but that aside, it was lacking in detail, an explanatory note in the body of the email stating that Rushton had described the shooter appearing in front of her 'as if he dropped out of the sky' and running towards Landon. After opening fire, he'd briefly turned his head as if to look back in her direction, and that was the only time she'd caught sight of his face. It went on to say that the Victim Services officers present seemed to settle on the idea that he'd run across Eighth Street at an angle, coming from behind Rushton and overtaking her.

Casey looked again at the face, but it was generic enough that it could've been anyone and no one. The email went on to suggest that a new piece of AI-powered software be used to produce an enhanced reconstruction, but Casey couldn't see how that would help; wasn't that just asking a machine to make up the missing parts?

At the bottom of the email was the full description Maddy Rushton had provided and Casey started reading through. White male, approximately six feet tall and 175 pounds, medium build, medium complexion, unsure on hair colour, unsure on eye colour, unsure on scars or distinguishing features. Wearing a navy/dark-blue hoodie, grey joggers, white sneakers—

She sat bolt upright, knocking her plate off the arm of the chair.

She read it a second time, then scrolled up again and looked at the picture once more, seeing now that the scant details matched the real-life face.

She knew who the shooter was. And now the shooter knew where Maddy Rushton was.

CHAPTER THIRTY-NINE

Casey called the department from the car. Pushing eighty on the street leading up to the expressway, jamming the horn as she barrelled through traffic, her civilian ride getting no allowances from other drivers.

Dana wasn't picking up. She tried her phone, driving one-handed as she dialled again, but it went straight to voicemail. She clamped her own cell between her thighs, using both hands to steer as she sped around the freeway on ramp, then took it up again to redial the department. She did the math in her head as it rang; even without lights and sirens, she figured she was ten minutes closer to the Whitlock residence than anyone coming from the precinct.

If she wasn't too late already. Praying she wasn't too late already.

'Detective Bureau, Detective Drocker—'

'Billy, it's me.'

'Big? I thought you were—'

'Billy, listen, who's still at Shatter Creek?'

'Right now?'

'Right now.'

'Uh ... I'll have to check on that for you. Who're you looking for?'

'Where's Dunmore?'

'She's not there. She said she was going to Harrison earlier, said it was urgent.'

'What about Dana?'

'She took her with her.'

'Shit.'

'Big? What's wrong?'

'Billy, get on to Dispatch. I need to know exactly who's at the Whitlock residence now.'

'You mean from our guys?'

'Yeah. Everyone from HCPD, and who's in charge. Then find out who Patrol detailed to sentry the driveway.'

'You want me to call you back?'

'No, I'll stay on the line.'

'Where are you?'

'Driving. I'm on my way there now.'

'What? What for?'

'Billy, do it now. If I'm right, the shooter's a cop.'

It took Billy close on four minutes to come back on the line, Black Reed Bay just coming into view in the distance when he spoke to her again.

'There's no one there, Case. Victim Services left a half-hour ago. There's just the guy at the end of the driveway.'

'Name?'

'Mendoza, he's out of the Fourth. Dispatch is trying to raise him. Case, are you sure about this? Who's the suspect?'

'What do you mean trying to raise him?'

'I don't have his status as yet.'

'Fuck, fuck—'

'Casey, are you sure about this? This sounds crazy.'

'I know. Fuck. Who else is there with you? Where's Jill?'

'I don't know, she left earlier.' He sounded embarrassed. 'She wouldn't talk to me.'

'Jesus Christ.' Casey punched the door. 'Okay, listen, stay

put, I need you there. Stay off your cell phone until you hear from me. I'll be on scene in five minutes.'

She hung up and dialled Darcy Whitlock's number, pressing the phone to her ear. It kept ringing, then finally went to voicemail. Casey blurted out a message. 'Mrs Whitlock, this is Casey Wray, if you pick up this message please contact me immediately on this number. It's really urgent. Thank you.'

She hung up and dialled again, but still no answer.

She turned off the expressway and raced down the highway, only slowing when she approached the turnoff for the Whitlock residence. There was no sign of a patrol car.

She made a right and took the driveway's curves as fast as she dared, the house finally coming into view when she burst through the sugar maples.

A patrol car was sitting out front.

Casey pulled up behind it on the driveway and jumped out, drawing her sidearm.

She went to the front door and rang the bell, looking all around her for a few seconds before ringing again. No sound came from inside.

She followed the house's perimeter, peeping through two large windows in the side of the building as she went, seeing a spacious living room with no one in it. Coming around to the back of the house, foldaway doors stretched across the length of the living room, giving a panoramic view over the bay, but they were locked shut. She kept going, coming to another window that looked in on a study, then a second and a third, all the same room. No one in sight. It was only when she rounded the corner to reach the other flank of the house, facing Shatter Creek, that she found a back door. It was standing ajar.

She toed it open wider with her foot, her sidearm raised.

'HCPD, Mrs Whitlock, are you there?' She stepped closer. 'This is Casey Wray, Mrs Whitlock. If you're there can you make yourself known please?'

She tried to orient herself from what she knew of the house and realised she must be close to the kitchen. She inched inside, finding herself in a laundry room the size of a small apartment. A doorway to the right was closed, and she worked out it must be the one she'd seen leading off of the kitchen. She cracked it open and called out again, then waited, the silence buzzing around her like a faulty power line. When she opened the door further, she found herself in a short passageway with pantry shelves on either side of her, filled with dried spices, packets of pasta and an assortment of other foods. A door at the other end was ajar, and she opened it slowly, calling out a third time.

No answer.

It opened out onto the kitchen, the gleaming surfaces unfamiliar in the daylight. There was a mug on the long farmhouse table, the seat at its head pushed back, but no one in the room. Casey called out again and picked her way across the kitchen, then silently opened the other door. She peered through, but the hallway was empty too. She stood motionless, feeling the sweat running down her back, listening for sounds from upstairs. The whole house was silent.

Then a sound from outside. A car. Distant but drawing closer, someone coming up the driveway. She went back the way she'd come and slipped out the side door, then moved slowly toward the front of the house, staying pressed to the wall.

A department car came into view. A little closer, and she made out Dunmore at the wheel.

Casey let go of a breath and lowered her weapon, signalling to her and then stepping out into the open when Dunmore pulled up. She started jogging over towards the car, but Dunmore jumped out and aimed her gun right at her.

'Drop your weapon, Wray.'

Casey froze.

'Drop it.'

'Lieutenant?'

'We know what you did. Put your weapon down. Now.'

The call?

Casey couldn't move, everything upside down. 'The shooter's a cop, he's here.' She gestured to the patrol car. 'Christopher Calder, the off-duty who was at the scene that morning.'

Dunmore looked like she was fighting to show no reaction. 'We can't open a dialogue until you put the weapon down.'

Casey squatted down slowly, placing her sidearm on the ground, never taking her eyes off Dunmore's. 'Are you hearing me? He's here. He's come for Maddy Rushton—'

'You changed the report. Sheena Rawlins, Sheila Rollins. It wasn't a mistake – you changed the name. We found the records.'

Casey's mouth fell open. 'What are you talking about?'

'It was your login. The system keeps a record of every edit. You changed the name on the file to tank the investigation.'

'What? No I didn't...' Casey shook her head, trembling head to toe. 'I don't know what you're talking about. I swear to you—'

'Enough. I don't want to hear any more of your bullshit.'

'Lieutenant, please, we have to stop this.'

'Detectives? Everything okay?'

Dunmore turned at the same time Casey did, seeing Christopher Calder emerge from the far side of the guesthouse.

His service weapon was in its holster, his face calm. She looked at his eyes, deep-set but clear, an innocence about his face, but seeing him again, she was more sure than ever he was the man Maddy Rushton had tried to describe.

Dunmore still had her gun trained on Casey. 'Officer, go recover Sergeant Wray's weapon for me.'

Calder looked at Casey as if he couldn't believe what he was being asked to do. Then he started slowly towards her.

Casey called out to him. 'What are you doing here, Calder?'

He hesitated, looking to Dunmore for direction. 'Ma'am?'

'Ignore the sergeant – secure her weapon.'

'Lieutenant, just make him answer the question,' Casey said. She glanced at Calder again. 'Answer me, goddammit. Why're you here?'

The muscles in his jaw bulged, then he started towards her again. He walked over slowly, but just as he was about to bend down to pick up her gun, Casey spotted the anomaly.

'Where are your handcuffs?' She looked right at the empty holder on his belt. 'Lieutenant...'

He stopped, staring at Casey with tunnel vision, a rabbit-in-the-headlights look.

Casey turned to Dunmore. 'Lieutenant, ask him—'

The gunshot came out of nowhere, Casey throwing her hands to her face on reflex. Dunmore fell to the ground, disappearing from sight behind her car. Before Casey even knew what was happening, Calder had turned his weapon on her.

'What did you do?' she screamed. 'You son of a bitch, what—'

'Shut up. Right now.' Calder took a step closer, his gun pointed right in her face.

She called over to Dunmore without taking her eyes off

Calder. 'Lieutenant?' She couldn't move, couldn't even blink. 'Lieutenant?'

'I said shut up. On your knees, hands behind your head.'

Casey lowered herself onto one knee, then two, her arms shaking so hard she could barely link her fingers together. 'What the fuck is going on?'

'Stop talking.'

'Whatever happened, there's always a way out. It doesn't have to go like this.'

'The fuck would you know about it?'

'It's the truth.' Her jaw almost locked as she tried to get the words out.

'Ray fucking tell you that, did he?'

'Ray? Ray Carletti?'

'Yeah, Uncle Ray. You got no idea how much I wish I was the one put a bullet in him.'

'I don't understand. I don't understand what you're saying.'

'I don't need you to.' She felt his gun touch the back of her skull. 'Just tell me where she is.'

'Who?'

'Quit fucking around. Maddy Rushton.'

'She's gone.'

'Gone where?'

'I don't know. Where's Darcy Whitlock?'

He pushed her head forward, the gun barrel digging into her scalp. 'You get to live longer if you tell me where. You got five seconds.'

'I don't know. I swear to god I don't—'

A woman's scream cut her off, freezing everything. Maddy Rushton had appeared on the far side of the guesthouse, her face twisted in shock at the scene in front of her.

Casey reacted first, unlinking her fingers and grabbing for Calder's gun in one motion, whipping her head to the side. 'RUN...'

Calder kicked her in the back, but he was off balance, his boot glancing off her. Still on her knees and twisting to grip the gun, she somehow got her other hand up, enough that she was able to keep it pointed away from her, the barrel hovering just inches from her face.

But Calder was standing, his feet planted now, and he had all the leverage. He pushed down harder and Casey toppled to her side, clinging to the gun for everything she was worth, but no longer in control. Calder kicked her again, in the side this time, sending a stabbing pain up under her ribs and making her lose her grip on the weapon.

Calder trained it on her—

'RUN!'

A gunshot rang out. Casey screwed her eyes shut. She felt no impact and for an instant she thought she was already dead. But then she opened her eyes and realised it wasn't Calder who'd fired; he was looking up, trying to figure out where the shot had come from.

On instinct, she reached back behind her and grabbed for her own gun, her fingers grazing the metal but nudging it out of reach. The sudden movement brought Calder's attention back to Casey, and he aimed at her again, then circled around her to kick her gun away, sending it skidding across the tarmac.

Then another gunshot rang out, Calder flinching and dropping into a half-crouch, the sound coming from behind Dunmore's SUV. He waited a few seconds, then started backing away slowly, keeping his gun aimed at Casey, until he had an angle to peer around the far side of the car. A third shot broke the silence, and this time Calder pulled back to cover behind the trunk – Casey realising it was Dunmore who was firing.

She rolled to the side and stumbled to her feet, running in a crouch to scoop up her sidearm, her ribs throbbing with every step. Another shot rang out, cracking off the tarmac next to her, but all she could do was keep running until she reached the patrol car, throwing herself to the ground behind it. The impact sent another spike of pain through her ribcage, snatching the breath from her lungs. She levered herself onto her elbow and propped her back against the cruiser. Breathing hard, she glanced up at the sky and pulled her phone out of her pocket, then dialled Billy's cell, putting it on speaker.

She rose a few inches and twisted to peer through the cruiser's windows across the driveway, her ribs screaming at the movement. There was no sign of Calder. Maddy Rushton was gone too, but she hadn't seen where she went. She realised now that Rushton hadn't been holding Lana, Casey terrified of what that might mean.

Billy answered and Casey cut him off, speaking in a rushed whisper. 'Ten-thirteen, officer down. The shooter is Officer Christopher Calder out of the Fourth, active now, he's on the Whitlock property but exact location unknown.'

'Jesus Christ, Casey are you—'

'Dunmore. He shot Dunmore, send backup and medics now. Between one and four civilians present, he's a threat to all of them.'

Casey rose again, looking through the cruiser's windows. Still no sight of him, she called out, 'It's over, Calder. There's backup coming. Don't do this.'

No response.

She grabbed up her cell. 'I'm going after him. Keep the line open.' She silenced the call and stuffed it into her pocket, still connected.

Slowly, she peered over the cruiser's hood, inching along its side and watching for movement behind Dunmore's car.

Nothing.

'Hang in there, Lieutenant, there's an ambo coming.' Shouting it into the breeze coming off the bay, it felt like she was the only person on Earth.

She glanced at the guesthouse, two windows at ground level, two above, but there was no sign of movement in either. She inched out a little further, testing if he was waiting for her to break cover, but still nothing moved. She got her feet under herself, made the sign of the cross, then took off in a sprint across the driveway towards where Dunmore had gone down.

All the way expecting a bullet.

She made it to the nearside of Dunmore's car and dropped to the ground again, pressing herself against the door. 'Lieutenant?'

A quiet sound came back to her, Dunmore wincing in pain.

Casey inched toward the sound, coming around the trunk, Dunmore's murmurs becoming more desperate...

She saw and pulled back out of sight. Dunmore was on her back, blood pouring from her shoulder, her face screwed up in agony. But the murmurs weren't pain – they were supposed to be a warning. Calder was kneeling behind her, his gun touching her forehead.

He called out to Casey. 'Put your weapon on the ground and slide it to me, then toss me your keys.'

'Don't do this. It won't work.'

'I won't ask again.'

'You don't want to pull that trigger.'

Dunmore made a sound, a moan that built to a crescendo, as if a wave of pain was passing over her. Then she let out a stunted breath, two words escaping with it. 'Shoot him.'

'Half the department is on its way, Calder. You still have options here, but not if you pull that trigger.'

'I don't want to hear it. Fuck your *options*. The department fucked me. I'll take all you motherfuckers with me.'

'How? How did it fuck you?'

'I'm not here to talk. Gun and keys, NOW.'

'No one knows about it better than me. You know what I had to do for the badge. Try me.'

'You think I wanted this? I had no choice. They made me kill him.'

'Who? Landon Whitlock?'

He didn't answer, Casey taking his silence as confirmation. 'Who's "they," Calder? Who made you?'

'All I ever did was listen to Ray. Everything he told me to do. My old man's fucking cousin, what else was I meant to do? Then it all goes to shit, he winds up dead, and these new ones are telling me I'm going to jail unless I do what I'm told. "Ex-cop, you won't last a week. Go kill this scumbag."' There was a thud, and Casey flinched, but it was bone on metal, Calder punching the car. 'I DID WHAT I WAS FUCKING TOLD. I always did, and they told me I was going to jail for it. Do this, do that, fuck you ... FUCK...' The last word came out as a yell, a guttural release from the depths of his chest.

'You were part of it?' Casey pressed herself against the car, shaking, trying to come to grips with it. 'Hanrahan and Carletti?'

'I wasn't part of anything. I just did what I was told. I never knew it any different.'

'What happened on the street that morning? Why Rawlins?'

He didn't answer, and Casey felt such a welling of rage inside, it was like the air around her was vibrating. 'You goddamn piece of shit.'

'She was an accident. I never saw her, never meant ... She just stepped out and got caught. I never ... I swear to god.'

'Then you killed Lauren Goff, to frame Adam Ryker.'

'I fucked up. I knew I fucked up. Rawlins was never meant to die, if I could take it back, if I could swap with her...' He trailed off into a whimper. 'The second they had her ID, they found all the domestic shit with Ryker, and he was just sitting there, the perfect scapegoat. His record, any cop's going to make him for the shooter. So they told me I had to kill Goff to make it right.'

'Make it right?' The words came out like vomit.

'They'd have killed me if I didn't.'

'You should've let them.'

His breath ran ragged.

'How the fuck does killing another innocent woman make it right?' Casey slammed her fist into the fender, barely recognising her own voice. 'How? How, you fuck?'

'I did what I was told.' His voice cracked. 'I just did what I was told.'

Then the sound of the first distant siren came, muffled by the breeze.

Casey took in a breath as deep as the pain in her ribs would allow. She swallowed down her disgust to try one more time. 'They're here, Calder. If you explain it, if you cooperate ... Who told you to kill them?'

He made a keening sound, like a wounded animal. 'I can't. You have no idea what they'll do. My sister, my family...'

'Who? Who's doing this to you?'

The keening grew, rising in intensity with the siren. The sound of another joined it, then more, the first lights appearing on the highway below.

'Give them up,' Casey said. 'They screwed you over. Why protect them? Get a lawyer and cut a deal for yourself. Just put the gun down.'

'Jesus Christ, I never wanted this...' He sounded on the verge of tears, his voice buckling.

'Who are they? Give me a name.'

The sirens were screaming now, a stream of lights advancing towards them.

'I never wanted this...'

'Calder, give them up.'

'I can't.'

'Calder—'

A gunshot drowned her out.

'NO!'

Casey leaned around the hood, ready to shoot...

But Calder was lying on the ground, blood pouring from the wound in his temple he'd inflicted upon himself.

CHAPTER FORTY

Casey stayed with Dunmore until the first EMTs approached, running to the top of the driveway to wave them over, then leading them to where she lay. Dunmore was dipping in and out of consciousness, Casey stepping back to let the EMTs go to work, then taking off to run around to the front of the guesthouse.

Expecting the worst, she hammered on the wooden door. 'This is Casey Wray from HCPD, if you can hear me, please open up. It's safe to come out.'

She moved to the window next to it, cupping her hands around her eyes to peer through the glass, seeing an empty living room in a state of disarray, cushions tossed to the floor, a chair upturned. She rapped on the glass. 'Maddy, are you in there?'

Just as she was about to try the front door again, a face appeared in a doorway on the far side of the room. Maddy Rushton. Casey held her hands up, trying not to spook her. 'Ma'am, it's over. Please, can you open the door?'

Rushton stared at her, motionless, like a deer sensing a hunter in the woods. Finally, she slipped across the room and went through another doorway, then the front door cracked open, a safety chain strung across it.

'Where is he?'

'He's dead. You're safe now.'

Rushton looked shell-shocked. 'He was ... Why was she pointing a gun at you?'

'I can explain, but I promise you it's over. Look out the window, there's an army out there.'

'It was him. He's the one I saw.'

'I know. He came here for you, but it's over. Take your time, you don't have to come out, but I need to know if anyone's hurt in there. Is Lana with you?'

She nodded.

'Is she okay?'

She nodded again, eyes unblinking.

Casey felt a weight rise off her, a little smile breaking out across her face. 'Good. That's good.'

'But Darcy...'

Casey stiffened. 'What? Where is she?'

The door closed, and Casey felt her stomach drop. She was about to bang on the wood again, but then it opened once more, no safety chain this time.

'Please, help her.'

She found Darcy Whitlock handcuffed to a heated towel rack in the bathroom, a strip of duct tape lying on the tiled floor next to her. She seemed calm, almost detached as Casey freed her wrists, her gaze fixed in a thousand-yard stare. But as soon as Casey got the cuffs unlocked, Whitlock leapt to her feet and threw her arms around Rushton, holding her in a tight embrace for a few seconds, then letting go to do the same to Casey, almost sending her tumbling. 'I'm sorry. For all of it.' Then she took a step back, pushed her hair out of her face and tried to compose herself, panted breaths betraying the tremors still rocking her.

Casey reached out a hand. 'Ma'am...'

'Where is he now?'

'He's dead.'

She dipped her eyes to the floor, wrapping her hand around her wrist. 'Good.'

Lana Rushton was hidden in a closet in the master bedroom. Scared, disorientated but otherwise unharmed, Maddy brought her to her chest with tears streaming from her eyes, holding her as if she'd never put her down again. She kept whispering, 'Sorry,' into the baby's ear, only stopping when she saw Casey look over. 'I had to hide her,' she said, kissing her cheek then looking at Casey. 'In case he got inside again.'

Their story came out in a rush. Darcy was eager to talk, determined to prove how unaffected she was by her ordeal, but the uncharacteristic way her words tumbled over one another was more revealing of what was going on inside.

She explained how Maddy had settled Lana down for a nap, then asked Darcy to watch her for a half-hour, just long enough to take a walk along the shore for some fresh air. Darcy had agreed, saying it was easier for her to come to the guesthouse than to disturb the baby by moving her. 'Just after you went,' Darcy said, glancing at Maddy, 'I heard him pull up and I went out to see what he wanted. They'd just left, the others, so I assumed they'd sent him back for something they'd forgotten. He said he was supposed to ask a couple extra questions, so I told him to come in here with me, so I could stay with Lana. I shut the door, and when I turned around...' Her eyes went hard and she started to raise her hand to her face, but then brought it down again, still determined to keep her emotions in check. 'When I turned around, he was holding a gun.' She reached for the bedstead, resting just a finger on it to steady herself. 'He kept saying, "Where's the other one? When's she back?" All I could think about was Lana, what I'd do if he went upstairs.'

'Ma'am, where's Harper?' Casey said.

'She's safe. Her driver took her out of school and straight to her grandmother's. Maddy helped me make the call when she found me in the bathroom.'

Casey nodded, feeling genuine relief – two women and two

children who could've had their lives wrecked in any number of ways, all of them unharmed.

'Why?' Darcy said. 'Why did he do this?'

People talked about half-truths, but Angela Wray had always said to her that it was better to think of it the other way round and call it a half-lie. It was a mom thing, meant to discourage a younger version of Casey from any type of dishonesty, but it'd stuck with her into adulthood, never having its intended effect, only making her feel guilty every time she hid behind one. 'I don't know.'

CHAPTER FORTY-ONE

The real lies came right away.

There was rolling coverage on every news channel, a roadblock set up at the end of the Whitlocks' driveway that was meant to keep reporters out only resulting in them mobilising choppers so they'd have footage to show while the talking heads babbled. Casey watched the drone shots of the house, sweeping panoramas taken from above Black Reed Bay, thinking how you could still mistake it for a picture of the American Dream.

At first, the department threw the shutters down and tried to shelter behind claims of being unable to comment while an investigation was ongoing. That held for all of two hours, before word of a cop-on-cop shooting leaked, and the feeding frenzy started.

Again they stalled, the *Courier*'s cop-friendly beat reporter tweeting that unnamed HCPD sources had told him they appeared to be dealing with a tragic case of friendly fire.

Casey sat on the edge of a chair in a private room, waiting for the doctor to clear her, one floor above where Helen Dunmore was being treated. The union rep had told her that Dunmore had sustained a gunshot wound to the shoulder, the bullet entering her upper arm before deflecting off her clavicle and exiting, missing her neck – and therefore her carotid artery – likely by an inch or less. She'd been transferred to the emergency room at St Mark's, where she'd been given blood, but was said to be stable and expected to make a full recovery. The customary all-hands vigil at the hospital was prohibited on Keirn's orders, touted as inappropriate given ongoing investigations, with only selected senior officers permitted in attendance. Reading between the lines was devastating: *we have no idea how deep this goes*.

The routine was almost familiar to Casey now, the third time in a year she'd had a union rep urging her not to say anything until she'd spoken to the lawyer, the blood tests for drugs and alcohol, her clothes bagged and taken away. It only added to the feeling that it was all part of the same nightmare, as if she'd only fooled herself into thinking she'd ever woken up.

A counsellor came to talk to her, but Casey sent him away, his intentions good but misplaced. She wasn't grieving or hurting, the way she'd been after Cullen or Ray; all she had were questions this man couldn't answer.

Two suits from Internal Affairs were stationed outside her room, waiting to pounce, and Casey overheard one of them make a crack about her earning frequent-flyer miles, the number of times they'd had to talk to her. She wanted to go out and smack him in the mouth. Instead, she sat on the chair, waiting for the lawyer to show up, dreading the process – hours of telling her version of events over and over, every question a loaded one.

In the end, it took four hours from start to finish, Casey feeling wrung out by the time it was over. As the lawyer departed, Casey braced for IA to swoop in, but when the door opened again, it was a different face standing there.

Casey started to get up to salute Acting Chief Keirn, but he held his palm out. 'Keep your seat. Please.'

Casey hovered for a second, then sat down again.

'How are you, Sergeant?'

'I'm fine, sir.'

'Good.' A flat tone, no emotion. He took a few steps, finally coming to stand at the foot of the untouched bed next to Casey's chair. 'You'll forgive me if I skip the niceties. This is my understanding: Christoper Calder murdered Landon Whitlock, accidentally shooting and killing Sheena Rawlins in the process. Whoever's orders he was acting on then told him to murder Lauren Goff too, to make it appear as if Adam Ryker was the culprit. Around the same point in time, he – or an accomplice – murdered Ryker too, trying to present it as a suicide. Correct?'

No mention of the records being changed on the system – trying to give her the opportunity to talk herself into trouble; a skilful operator would've set the trap more subtly. Casey nodded and said nothing.

'Okay. So that leaves me with two burning questions, and a thousand lesser ones. First, why did he kill Whitlock?'

She stared at the floor. 'All he said is he was told to. He didn't specify by who, or why, but the implication was it was someone linked to the Hanrahan/Carletti crew.'

'Did you believe him?'

'Yes. He told me his dad was related to Ray.'

'And the motive?'

'He didn't say.'

Keirn gripped the rail at the end of the bed, leaning over it. 'I'm asking your view.'

'I guess Whitlock was tied up with them somehow.' She braced, waiting for him to say he knew Landon Whitlock had been in contact with her.

Instead he just stared down at her.

Casey looked at him stony-faced. 'And the second question? Sir?' Already knowing what was coming.

'The second question is why did you change the case report? Sheena Rawlins to Sheila Rollins—'

'I didn't.'

'I mean, obviously it was to stall the investigation.'

'I didn't change it. I was the one who pointed it out.'

'Of course. But not until Ryker was dead.'

She got up out of her seat. 'Then why would I change it in the first place? I found the problem and called it out.' She pressed her finger into her chest. 'We never would've had Ryker's name if I didn't put it together.'

Keirn straightened. 'Calder or whoever was helping him needed time to track down Ryker, kill him and kill his ex – he can't do that if Ryker's already in custody. So you changed the name to make sure no connection was made until everything was ready. Only when Ryker couldn't deny his involvement did you "notice" the mistake – knowing we'd jump on his ass as a suspect as soon as you did.'

Wrong as he was, the logic was solid. Casey turned on the spot, searching for help that wasn't coming. 'This is garbage. Someone's setting me up.'

'If it wasn't you, then who was it?'

'Sir, come on, why would I do this? You know what I went through with Ray.'

'I know your version of the story.'

She almost laughed in disbelief. 'You sound like Dunmore.'

He dipped his head to the side. 'The lieutenant provides a useful outsider's perspective on the matter.'

Casey screwed her eyes shut, rubbing her face. 'Goddammit, I did nothing wrong. What do I have to do to get this stink off of me?'

'Tell me who wanted Whitlock dead.'

Casey took a step towards him. 'I don't know. But trust me, I'm going to find out. Maybe that's what you're really worried about.'

His eyes tightened. 'What's that supposed to mean?'

'You were the one pushing to close the case with Ryker.'

He stepped around the bed to stand right in front of her. 'Do not for one second try to turn this around on me. The evidence was overwhelming.'

'And I was the only one looking past it.'

Keirn looked like he wanted to hit her. Instead, he turned slowly and walked to the door, opening it then looking back at her. 'You're on administrative leave, pending a full investigation.' He pointed at her, a vein in his forehead as thick as a worm. 'This thing keeps coming back to you, and I'm going to make sure you get everything that's coming your way.'

CHAPTER FORTY-TWO

The *Courier* broke the 'official' version of events the next morning. Five pages dedicated to nothing but HCPD and Christopher Calder, 'perpetrator of the acts of violence that have shocked Rockport over the past week, and whose chilling actions leave HCPD and County Executive Franklin Gates with questions to answer of the most urgent nature'.

It read like bad fiction. The article stated that while it was too early for the investigation to reach any official conclusions, police sources had told the *Courier* that Patrolman Calder's name had been included on an updated list of officers due to face sanction for their involvement in disgraced former HCPD lieutenant Ray Carletti's corruption racket. It went on to note that Calder was a second cousin of Carletti's, their fathers paternal cousins.

Facing dismissal from the force, and likely criminal charges, Calder had attempted to rob Landon Whitlock, a prominent local businessman, likely driven by a desire to quickly raise funds that would allow him to flee the state. In the event, the robbery had gone wrong somehow, with both Whitlock and Sheena Rawlins, an innocent bystander who had exited the adjacent gym and been caught by stray bullets, winding up dead. From there, Calder had discovered Miss Rawlins had been involved in a tumultuous relationship with Adam Ryker, and had murdered or suborned the murders of both Mr Ryker and another former partner of his, Lauren Goff, in an attempt to frame Mr Ryker for all three killings. The report went on to note that police sources were urgently investigating the possibility of Calder having had an accomplice who had assisted him in his crimes.

That last part felt like a message directly from Keirn to Casey.

For his part, Franklin Gates was already trying to turn the crisis to his advantage, his statement to the *Courier* in response to their report noting that it reaffirmed the essential and urgent nature of the review into HCPD that was already being conducted by his taskforce, and that he had instructed them to ensure no stone was left unturned. His closing line was another thinly disguised election pitch, reassuring citizens he wouldn't rest until corruption in HCPD had been stamped out for good.

Casey put her iPad down and felt like she was going to barf. She hadn't slept a minute, the weight of the allegations levelled against her beyond anything she could've imagined before.

Someone was setting her up. Her computer password lived on a slip of paper in her top drawer, each new iteration listed below the last. She knew it was stupid, she knew it was against the regs to do so, but it was too late for regret. She'd made it easy for someone to put a target on her back, and that thought contributed to the sense of nausea that had eaten her up from the inside all night and into the morning.

But the burning question was who? Duty logs confirmed Chris Calder was on the street at the time the records were falsified, meaning someone else had been a part of it. Somone on the inside – but how close?

The darkness was still there. Any thought that it'd ended with Hanrahan and Carletti was proven to be wishful thinking. And now it was going to claim her too.

A knock at the door made her startle. She walked over and checked the spyhole, seeing Rita Zangetty waiting on the porch.

Casey opened the door slowly. 'Rita?'

Zangetty looked her up and down. 'Casey, don't take this the wrong way, but you look terrible.'

Casey stared at her. 'What's the right way to take that, Rita?'

Zangetty held her hands up. 'Sorry, sorry. I've had way too much coffee already today. I heard they benched you. You doing okay?'

'Not even close.' Casey opened the door a little wider. 'And don't take this the wrong way, but what the fuck do you want?'

'Are you mad at me for something?'

Casey started to say she was still mad for the way she'd fucked her over with Keirn and Dunmore, but she couldn't work up the fire. 'No. I'm just worried sick.'

'That's why I'm here. Can I come inside a second?'

Casey held her arm out limply, inviting her in.

Rita stepped inside, spotting the iPad on the couch, the *Courier* article still showing. 'Nasty piece of writing, huh?'

'It's mostly bullshit.'

'Of course. Everyone's jockeying to get ahead of this thing. What did you think of Franklin's statement?'

'Self-serving and about the only thing he could say.'

Zangetty laughed. 'I wrote it. That's pretty much what I was going for, so that's good.'

Casey closed the iPad case and flopped onto the sofa. 'Look, uh, you might not want to be seen with me right now. You know Keirn's coming for me, right?'

Zangetty nodded. 'That's why I'm here. Keirn knows he can't survive this, so he's looking for any ammunition he can lay his hands on. Sounds like you gave him a layup.'

'I didn't do it.'

Zangetty wrinkled her face. 'I was pretty sure of that anyway, but then I had a call from Darcy Whitlock this morning. She told me the full story of what really happened out there and what you did. You know how she is, so when she started bawling while she was talking to me ... I mean, I nearly fell out of my seat.'

'What did she say?'

'I won't bore you with the details, but let's just say you've made a friend over there. And when she heard about your, let's say, troubles, she said she wanted to pay for you to get a proper legal defence. Not the shmoes the union will set you up with, someone real. Top dollar.'

'What?'

'Yeah, she wants to fund the whole thing. I mean I was pissed as all hell, obviously – that's money that might've made its way to our campaign otherwise, but...' Zangetty shrugged, smiling.

'I can't ... I can't accept that.'

'You *like* the idea of going to jail or something?' Zangetty reslung her bang over her shoulder and stepped to the door. 'She's a good ally to have, Casey. Don't let yourself get taken down because of pride.'

With that, she was gone.

Casey perched on the edge of the couch, staring at her hands. They were trembling. But for the first time that day she didn't feel sick.

She was still sitting that way when there was a knock at the door again, and Casey got up to see what Zangetty wanted now.

But when she opened up, it wasn't Zangetty on the other side.

Two faces, so unexpected that for a flash she wasn't sure it was real.

Michael Stringer and Lydia Wright.

Casey checked both ways along the street, half expecting to see IA waiting with cameras. 'What do you want?'

Wright held up a bag of Krispy Kremes. 'Peace offering.'

'Are you fucking kidding me?'

Stringer shook his head. 'You saved Maddy Rushton's life. I'm grateful.'

'Grateful?'

'Mike's got a saviour complex when it comes to vulnerable women like her,' Wright said.

'Piss off.' He half smiled and turned to Casey again. 'I read you wrong. I thought you were the same as all the other cops round here.'

'The fuck is that supposed to mean?'

'Whatever you think of me, I'm not in the business of letting someone like her get hurt. She's an adult, she knew what she was getting into, but it's not me to just walk away. I had to know she was safe. She disappeared that morning, when everything went crazy. Soon as we realised what was going on, we tried to find her to get her out of there, but she'd already vanished. I knew she must've seen the shooter, so you'd all be looking for her. With what we knew about Landon, we figured it had to be a cop or ex-cop who pulled the trigger, so there was no way to know who to trust.'

Casey looked on in disbelief. 'You don't know a goddamn thing about me.'

'Look at it from our perspective – he calls you on a burner phone and within twenty-four hours he's dead. It looked for all the world like you were involved. You would've made the same assumption.'

She stared him down, one hand ready to shut the door. *Don't play their games, don't play...* 'Why did you figure it had to be a cop?'

'Chief of Police Brian T. Hanrahan. Lieutenant Raymond R. Carletti.'

'Two dead men that don't interest anyone,' Casey said.

'Sergeant Devon "Crick" Critchlow, Patrolman Christopher Calder, Detective David Cullen.' He glanced to the side, his Adam's apple bobbing as if he was hesitating saying more. Then: 'Former Captain Robert B. McTeague.'

Casey got chills up her arms hearing his name with the others. 'What about them?'

'A select few of Landon's clients.' He paused a few seconds, as if letting it settle. 'Some guy called Gates was in the files too – ever heard of him?'

This awful sliding feeling, as if she was about to fall off the edge of the world. 'Clients for what?'

'Whitlock was a dark-money man. He knew how to move it, how to hide it, how to work it, all that stuff. We've dealt with his kind before.' Stringer flicked his finger between himself and Wright. 'You know any reason why the people on that list might've been in need of his services?'

Casey's feet went numb, as if she was standing in an ice bath. 'How do you know all this?'

Stringer tilted his head. 'We're thorough. Once Darcy Whitlock hired us to compromise Landon, we looked at everything, and it didn't take much to figure out what he was into in his professional life. He was cautious, but we got enough to see the outline. I think one of his clients – probably one of the names I just told you – figured out we were looking at him and got nervous; maybe they kept tabs on him as standard and saw us doing the same. Probably assumed we were going after him because he's got links to every dirty cop in this city, not realising it was just a divorce job. Then when he called you to start informing on people, it confirmed their worst fears. So they decided he had to go.'

Casey's head was spinning so fast she almost sat on the ground. 'How ... how did you know he called me?'

'We were on him that morning – we knew where he left his car. After the shootings, we got inside before you guys could get to it, found the phone then. I saw he'd called you the day before and that's when I put two and two together and got five. When you tried to call him again later that day, it felt like you were trying to give yourself some cover – pretend you didn't know he was already dead.' He tipped his head to the side, almost an apology. 'I was wrong. It was only when I saw you weren't out to hurt Maddy Rushton that I realised he picked you because he thought he could trust you. Then it was obvious why he was calling you.'

Wright thrust the bag of donuts towards her again. 'Like I said, peace offering.'

Before Casey could refuse it, she felt the weight of the bag in her hands – it was empty.

'Landon got spooked because he knew we were on him, and he thought the people he worked for had sent us,' Wright said. 'That's what we think, anyway. So he decided it was time to cash in his chips and talk to you. They couldn't let that happen.'

Casey let the bag hang limply by her side. 'But how did they know? That he was calling me?'

Wright shrugged. 'Who did you tell?'

Casey looked at her in disbelief. Dana, Billy – who else? McTeague? In the moment, she couldn't remember, her brain reeling.

Wright turned to leave.

'Wait, what about his car?' Casey's voice sounded detached, as if it was someone else's, the cop in her needing answers even when the questions didn't matter anymore.

'We left it open, Someone must've nicked it,' Stringer said, turning to go. 'This place is crooked as anything. Great for people in our line of work, but I'd be pissed off if I was on the other side of it.' He pointed at the bag in her hand, then walked away.

'Hey, wait...' Casey threw her arms out. 'You can't just lay this on me and walk off.'

But Wright had already made it back to the car to start the engine, and as soon as Stringer was inside, she pulled away.

Casey spun around and threw the empty Krispy Kreme bag across the room.

But as she did, something small spilled from inside and onto the carpet.

Not empty. She went to retrieve it from under the coffee table.

A memory stick. She held it in her hand, staring at it like it'd fallen from space.

She weighed the chances it was a virus or some other kind of scam, but it felt too low-rent for them, and then she realised there was nothing on her battered old laptop worth stealing anyway. She slotted the stick into the USB port and waited, a million files filling the screen when it finally loaded up, the same jumble she felt inside.

She opened one then another, scanning, trying to take it all in at once, her focus shot. It might as well have been in a different language. Money transfers, company documentation, banking records; at first it seemed like they were mocking her, a worthless stack of paperwork designed to make her feel stupid.

But then she started seeing the names.

Hanrahan. Carletti. Calder. Gates.

She skimmed faster, one she was looking for above all the others, not wanting to find it—

But there it was, in black and white. Robbie McTeague.

She pressed her face into the sofa, wishing it away. The suspicions she'd always fought off, lies cloaked in false oaths.

It'd never ended or gone away, just retreated into the darkness where it thrived.

She knew then what she was really looking at: a paper trail that led right to the top.

And she'd just been given matches to burn the whole thing down.

ACKNOWLEDGEMENTS

I'd like to express heartfelt thanks to my publisher, Karen Sullivan, editor, West Camel and all the team at Orenda Books, without whose encouragement, support and dedication this book would not exist. It's a lucky writer who finds people who not only believe in the stories they want to tell, but work tirelessly to help make them the best they can possibly be and get them into readers' hands – and I might be the luckiest.

My sincere thanks to my agent, Maddalena Cavaciuti, whose belief in my writing reignited my passion for telling these stories, and whose input into the manuscript was invaluable.

My thanks, as always, to my family, for pushing me to chase my dream and for all their love and help along the way.

A special thank you to everyone at SGW for making me so welcome and, in particular, to Angela Disher for her friendship, kindness, warmth and empathy in the best and worst of times. For a lifetime dedicated to books and reading: here's your name in print, Mrs D...

Thank you to my friends for all the good times shared and those still to come.

And, most importantly, thank you to all my readers, old and new. It's been nearly ten years since my first book was published, and your continued support means everything. I hope I can keep entertaining you with my stories for many more years to come.

For MAW. My love always.